P

moonblood

TALES OF GOLDSTONE WOOD

Heartless

Veiled Rose

Moonblood

moonblood

TALES OF GOLDSTONE WOOD

ANNE ELISABETH
STENGL

BETHANYHOUSE

a division of Baker Publishing Group
Minneapolis, Minnesota

© 2012 by Anne Elisabeth Stengl

Published by Bethany House Publishers
11400 Hampshire Avenue South
Bloomington, Minnesota 55438
www.bethanyhouse.com

Bethany House Publishers is a division of
Baker Publishing Group, Grand Rapids, Michigan

Printed in the United States of America

Library of Congress Cataloging-in-Publication Data
Stengl, Anne Elisabeth.
    Moonblood / Anne Elisabeth Stengl.
        p.   cm. — (Tales of goldstone wood)
    ISBN 978-0-7642-0781-5 (pbk.)
    I. Title.
PS3619.T47647675M66 2012
813'.6—dc23   2011044546

Book design by Paul Higdon
Cover illustration by William Graf

12 13 14 15 16 17 18   7 6 5 4 3 2 1

To my Erin . . .
and sweet Annie!

PROLOGUE

THE UNICORN STOOD before the gates of Palace Var. It guarded the paths to and from Arpiar, watching them with eyes that burned through all tricks and disguises. The roses climbing the stone walls of Var cast their moonlit shadows upon the unicorn's back in dappled patterns. If a wind swelled, those patterns shifted, but the unicorn never moved.

The Queen of Arpiar could see the unicorn through a window in her chambers, where she lay upon her pillows. She turned her gaze away, closing her eyes.

"My queen," said her headwoman. "The child lives. You have a daughter."

Across the darkened chamber, a newborn made no sound as gentle hands wrapped it in red and gold. When the babe had not cried at its birth, the queen had thought perhaps it was dead.

"A daughter," she whispered. Tears slipped down her cheek. "No."

Before she could dash traces of weeping from her face, her husband entered. Without a glance for his queen, he went to the cradle and looked inside. He smiled, and though his face was more beautiful than tongue could tell, the queen shuddered at the sight.

"A daughter!" Triumph filled the king's voice. He turned to the queen and laughed in her face. "A pretty daughter, my pretty bride. With blood as red as the red, red rose. Her name will be Varvare."

"Please," his wife spoke in a small voice. "Please, my lord."

"Please what, sweet Anahid?" The king laughed again and moved to the queen's bedside. He took her hand and, though she struggled against him, would not release his hold. "You'd think I was disappointed in you. On the contrary, beloved, I could not be better satisfied! You have proven more useful than I dared hope."

He dropped her hand and addressed himself to her headwoman and the other attendants present. "See to it you care well for my darling Varvare. My perfect rose."

With those words he vanished from the chamber, though the shadow of his presence lingered long afterward.

Nevertheless, the moment he was out of sight, Queen Anahid rallied herself. She pushed upright on her cushions, turning once more to that sight out her window. The unicorn stood at its post in the shadow of the roses, and it was hateful to her.

"Bring me clothes and a cloak of midnight." She turned to her attendants, who stared at her. "At once."

They exchanged glances, but no one moved. In all the realm of Arpiar, not a soul could be found who loved the king. But neither was there a heart that did not sink with fear at the mention of his name. Thus the queen's servants remained frozen in place when she spoke. The queen stared at them with her great silver eyes, and they would not meet her gaze.

"Will no one serve her queen?" she asked.

They made no answer.

Straining so that a vein stood out on her forehead, Anahid flung back the soiled blankets of her labor and rose from her bed. Her headwoman gasped, "My queen!"

In that moment, the princess, who had made no more than a whimper since the time of her birth, gave a cry from her cradle. The piteous sound worked a magic of its own on the assembled servants. One leapt to the cradle and gently lifted the child. Another ran to the queen's side, and a third did as the queen had asked and brought her clean garments and a cloak as black as the night.

The queen was weak from her labor, but her strength returned in the face of need. She let her servants clothe her, then took and wrapped the deep cloak about her shoulders. "Give her to me," she said, turning to the youngest of her maids, who stood trembling near to hand, shushing the babe.

"My queen," her headwoman spoke, "are you certain—"

"Do you doubt me?" The queen's eyes flashed. She took the baby, adjusting the scarlet and gold cloth that bound the tiny limbs tight. She tucked the warm bundle inside her cloak, close to her heart.

"Tell no one I have gone," she said, striding to the door. "Any of you who follows me does so at your peril."

The blackness of her cloak shielded Queen Anahid and the princess as she made her way through the corridors of Palace Var, unseen save by the roses, which turned their faces away and said not a word. She slid from shadow to shadow. Woven enchantments whirled in endless, grasping fingers everywhere she turned, but these Anahid had long ago learned to see and to elude.

But all Paths from Arpiar led past the unicorn.

The queen stood in the darkness of the courtyard, breathing in the perfume of roses, gazing at the silvery gate that stood between her and the empty landscape. She felt the tiny beating heart pressed against her own and gnashed her teeth. "Would that he had been devoured on the shores of the Dark Water!" Then, closing her eyes and bowing her head, she cried out in the voice of her heart, a voice unheard in that world but which carried to worlds beyond.

"I swore I would never call upon you again."

An answer came across distances unimaginable and sang close to her ear in a voice of birdsong.

Yet I am always waiting for you, child.

"I ask nothing for myself, only for my daughter. She does not deserve the fate the king has purposed for her."

What would you have me do?

"Show me where I can take her. Show me where she may be safe."

Walk my Path, sang the silver voice.

There in the darkness of Arpiar, a way opened at the queen's feet. The one Path that the unicorn could not follow. Anahid stepped into it, full of both gratitude and shame, for she had vowed never to walk this way again. But she had no other choice. She followed the Path to the gate, pushed the bars aside, and stepped onto the plains beyond.

The unicorn did not see her. She passed beneath its gaze, her heart beating like a war drum against the bundle on her breast. The unicorn was blind to her passage.

Queen Anahid strode from Palace Var without a backward glance, her daughter held tight in her arms. As she went, the silver voice sang in her ear, and she almost found herself responding to the familiar, half-forgotten words:

> *Beyond the Final Water falling,*
> *The Songs of Spheres recalling.*
> *Won't you return to me?*

She followed the song across the hinterlands of Arpiar, speeding along the Path so quickly that she must have covered leagues in a stride. She came to a footbridge, just a few planks spanning from nowhere to nowhere. But when she crossed it, she stepped over the boundaries from her world into the Wood Between.

The unicorn felt the breach on the borders of Arpiar. It raised its head, and the bugle call of its warning shattered the stillness of the night. Anahid, even as she stood beneath the leafy canopy of the Wood, heard that sound across the worlds. She moaned with fear.

Do not be afraid. Follow me.

"It will find me!"

I will guide you. Follow me.

"Only for my daughter!" the queen cried. "Only for my daughter."

Her feet, in dainty slippers, sped along the Path as it wound through the Wood. She could feel the unicorn pursuing, though it could not see her. But the nearness of its presence filled Anahid with such dread, she nearly dropped her burden and fled. But no! Though she had come so far, she was still too close to Arpiar.

"Please," she whispered. The silence of the Wood oppressed her. "Please, show me somewhere safe."

Follow, sang the silver voice, and she raced after that sound. Her feet burned with each step. How long had it been since she'd followed this Path? Not since she was merely Maid Anahid, a lowly creature unworthy of a king's notice. She had not known then and did not know now where it would lead. She only knew the unicorn could not catch her.

It may have been days; it may have been minutes; for all she knew, it may have been centuries. But the Path ended at last, and once more the forest grew up around her. The queen stood with her heart in her throat, straining her senses for any trace of the unicorn's presence. Panting from her exertion, she struggled to draw a deep breath and almost gagged.

"The Near World," she said. "I smell mortality everywhere. How can my daughter be safe here?"

Follow me, sang the silver voice.

"Will you not accept her into your Haven?"

Follow me.

She saw no choice but to obey. The trees thinned and ended not many yards distant, and though the undergrowth was difficult to navigate in the darkness, Anahid broke through the forest at last. The ground was rocky and inclined steeply uphill, but after a few minutes' climb she was able to take stock of her surroundings. She stood at the bottom of a deep gorge filled from one end to the other with forest, twisting on around a bend beyond her sight. A trail that looked as though it had not been traveled in generations led up from the gorge to the high country above. And over her head, in fantastic, impossible beauty, arched a bridge, gleaming white in the moonlight. She recognized its Faerie craftsmanship and wondered that the world of mortal men should boast so beautiful a creation.

The climb up the trail was difficult, and the queen was near the end of her strength when at last she emerged upon the high country. This was not a land she knew, but it was far from Arpiar. She smelled roses, free blossoms unsullied by her husband's hand. And the moon that glowed above was no illusion. By its glow, she could discern the contours of an enormous garden or park. A king's grounds, she thought. A fit home for her daughter.

The unicorn sang from the Wilderlands below.

Anahid screamed at the sound and started to run but tripped on the uneven soil and staggered to her knees. The baby wailed.

"Why have you brought me to this place?" the queen demanded, though she did not speak aloud. "We are unprotected in the Near World. Even my husband's enchantments must fade. It will find her for sure!"

The Fallen One may not enter the Near World. It must remain in the Wood Between.

The unicorn sang again. But it did not call for the queen, so she could not understand the words. Her daughter ceased crying, and when Anahid looked at her, she was surprised to find two wide eyes blinking up at her. "Don't listen," she said, trying to cover the baby's ears.

She cannot hear its voice. Her ears are full of my song.

Anahid breathed in relief and got to her feet. She moved unsteadily across the terrain until she came to a rosebush, not far from the great bridge. Kneeling, the Queen of Arpiar placed her bundle there and stopped a moment to gaze into her child's face, watching it wrinkle and relax and wrinkle again as though uncertain whether or not to be afraid.

Sorrowfully, Anahid watched the change spread across the little face as the enchantments of Arpiar frayed and fell away. She closed her eyes and placed a hand upon her daughter's heart.

"With all the love I have to give," she murmured, "though that is little enough." Then she closed her eyes and raised both her hands toward the moon, cupping them as though to offer or receive a benediction. "I cry your mercy, Lord, and beg your protections upon my child! Shield her within this land from my husband's gaze. So long as she dwells in this high country, let her escape the spells of Arpiar."

A flutter drew her gaze, and she saw a bird with a white speckled breast land in the rosebush above the child. Its wings disturbed the blossoms so that they dropped great red petals upon the baby's face, the most delicate of veils.

Your child is safe in my protection, now and always.

"Do you promise?" said the queen.

I promise. I claim her as one of mine.

"Then I shall return to Arpiar glad."

You may stay, child. You are not bound to that world.

"I will return," she said.

Another voice disturbed the night, an old voice as rough as the earth, rugged with mortality. "Oi! Who's there?"

Anahid leapt to her feet, cast one last look at her daughter, and fled into the night. At the edge of the gorge, she turned, her enormous eyes watching from the darkness. She saw a stocky mortal man, a gardener perhaps, with gray beginning to dominate his beard, step off the Faerie bridge. He went to the rosebush and knelt. Anahid held her breath. She heard the sharp intake of breath; then the man exclaimed, "Well now, ain't you a sight, wee little one! How'd you end up out here on so dark a night?"

I claim her as one of mine, sang the wood thrush to Anahid.

The queen watched the gardener lift her child, then bowed her head, unwilling to see more. The next moment, she vanished down the trail, swallowed up by the Wilderlands below.

The unicorn met her there.

PART ONE

THE PRINCE

1

THE PRINCE OF SOUTHLANDS was bewitched.

It was common knowledge. Rumor of his bewitchment had been spreading like a plague through the kingdom ever since he was sixteen years old: how the prince had returned from a summer in the mountains, bringing with him a demon child and installing her as a servant in his father's house.

Cheap chitchat, to be sure. But fun fare with which to scare the children on a cold winter's night. "Watch out that you put your muddy boots away where they belong, or the prince's demon will come fetch you!"

At first, nobody believed it. Nobody, that is, except the servants of the Eldest's House, who worked with the girl in question.

"She gives me the shivers!" said Mistress Deerfoot to Cook. "With those veils of hers, she looks like a ghost. What do you think she hides behind them?"

"Her devil's horns, of course. And her fangs."

"Go on!" Mistress Deerfoot slapped Cook's shoulder (for she was rather keen on him). "Do be serious!"

Cook shrugged and said no more, for the demon herself passed by just then, carrying a bucket of water. That bucket was large, with an iron handle, and when full probably weighed nearly as much as the girl herself. Her skinny arms did not look as though they could support such a load, yet she moved without apparent strain. Her face was so heavily veiled in linen that not even the gleam of her eyes showed.

She did not pause to look at Cook or Deerfoot but hastened on her way without a word or glance. When she vanished up a servants' stair, Deerfoot let out a breath she had not realized she held. "Coo-ee! Unnatural strength that one has. What can the prince be thinking to keep one like her around here?"

"He's bewitched," muttered Cook. Which was the only natural explanation.

So the demon girl remained at the Eldest's House. And it was she, said the people of Southlands, who called the Dragon down upon them.

Prince Lionheart stood before his mirror glass, gazing into a face he did not recognize. It was not the face of an ensorcelled man, he thought, despite the rumors he knew people whispered behind his back. It was the face of a man who would be king. A man who would be Eldest of Southlands.

It was the face of a man who had breathed deeply of dragon smoke.

The stench of those poisons lingered throughout Southlands, though in the months since the Dragon's departure it had faded to a mere breath. In the Eldest's House it was the most prominent. On dark nights when the moon was new, one smelled it strongest of all.

But life must go on. Five years of imprisonment under that monster had taken its toll on the people of the kingdom, but they must struggle forward somehow. And Prince Lionheart would struggle with them.

He adjusted his collar and selected a fibula shaped like a seated panther to pin to his shoulder. He never allowed his bevy of attendants to help him dress, rarely even permitted them into his chambers. He'd been five years on his own, five years in exile while the Dragon held his kingdom captive. During that time, he'd learned to button his own garments, and he would not have attendants bungling about him now.

Besides, their questioning gazes unnerved him. Every last one of them, when they met his eyes, silently asked the same question:

"Did you fight the Dragon?"

His fingers slipped, and the point of the fibula drove into his thumb. "Iubdan's beard!" he cursed, chewing at the wound to stop the blood. The pin fell to the stone floor at his feet. Still cursing, Lionheart knelt to pick it up. He paused a moment to inspect it, for it was of intricate work and solid gold. The seated panther was the symbol of Southland's heir. When he became Eldest, he would replace it with a rampant panther.

"Did you fight the Dragon?"

He closed his hand around the brooch. "I did what I had to do," he said. "I had no other choice. I did what I thought best."

Of course you did.

This voice in his head might have been his own. But it was colder and deeper, and it was no memory.

Of course you did, my sweet darling. And now, with the Dragon gone, you will have your dream.

"My dream," muttered Lionheart as he gazed into the mirror once more and fixed the fibula in its place.

He must make his way downstairs now to the half-constructed hall where a banquet was to be held that night. The scaffolds were pulled down for the week, and the signs of construction hidden behind streamers and paper lanterns. The Dragon had destroyed the Eldest's Hall before he left Southlands, but rebuilding was well underway. And though the winter wind blew cold through the gaps in the wall and roof, the banquet must, for tradition's sake, be held there, for this was the prince's wedding week.

A shadow passed over the sun.

Lady Daylily sat in her chambers, gazing at her face in a glass that revealed a young woman who was no longer as beautiful as she had once been. Not that her beauty was far faded. But the poison that yet lingered in her lungs pinched her features, sallowed her complexion, and left her once vibrant eyes filmed over as with dull ash. She was still lovely, to be sure. But she would never again be what she had been.

Her attendants bustled about her, laying out her gown, smoothing the long headdress as they pinned it to her hair, selecting furs to drape over her shoulders and protect her in the drafty Eldest's Hall. Daylily must be as elegant as human hands could make her this evening.

After all, the prince's wedding week was hers as well.

"Out."

The woman pinning the headdress into Daylily's curls paused. "My lady?"

"Out. Now." Daylily turned on her seat. Her face was a mask. "All of you. I would be alone for a moment."

"My lady," said Dame Fairlight, her chief attendant, "the banquet—"

"I believe I have made myself clear."

The women exchanged glances, then, one by one, set aside their tasks and slipped from the room, closing the door behind them. Daylily sat like a stone some minutes before moving softly to her window. There she gazed out across the Eldest's grounds.

Like a prisoner gazing on the boundaries of her imprisonment.

Daylily's view extended over the southern part of the Eldest's lands, off into the parks and gardens that sprawled for acres. These, like Daylily, were no longer what they had once been, ravaged by both the winter and the Dragon. Most of the shrubs and bushes had withered into dry sticks and would never bloom again, come either spring or frost. Only the rosebushes remained alive. But these had not flowered for twenty years and more.

From her vantage point, Daylily saw all the way to where the grounds broke suddenly and plunged into a deep gorge. She saw the white gleam of Swan Bridge, which spanned the gorge in a graceful sweep. But she could not see the darkness of the Wilderlands, the thick forest that grew in the depths of the gulf.

For the briefest possible moment, Daylily thought how she should like to throw on a cloak, slip from the House, make that long walk across the grounds to the gorge, and vanish forever into the Wilderlands.

It was a wild fancy, and she shook it away even as it flashed across her imagination. After all, she was Lady Daylily, daughter of the Baron of Middlecrescent, the most beautiful woman in the Eldest's court (despite the Dragon's work), beloved of all Southlands, and bride of Prince Lionheart. Prince Lionheart, who would one day be Eldest, making her queen. It was her father's dearest wish, the purpose of her entire life.

But how bitter was its fulfillment! Daylily clutched her hands in her lap, refusing even a trace of emotion to cross her face, though there was no one to see. If only she had kept her heart in check. If only she had remained the icy and unreachable statue she must be in order to fulfill this role. If only she'd never permitted herself to love—

She shook her head sharply, refusing to admit that thought. No, better not to dwell on such things. Better to focus instead on the cold reality of her dream come true.

The Prince of Southlands would marry her. But he did not love her.

A movement near to hand caught her eye. Daylily dragged her gaze from the bridge and the gorge to a closer plot of ground. A small figure, stooped and thin, walked among the struggling remnants of the garden. A nanny goat followed behind her like a tame dog, nosing the shrubs for any sign of something edible, while the girl gathered what greenery she found into a bundle on her arm.

She wore a white linen veil that covered the whole of her face.

Daylily gnashed her teeth. In that instant, she looked like a dragon herself. "Rose Red," she muttered. "Witch's child. Demon."

She trembled with sudden cold when the shadow passed over the sun and fled swiftly across her face.

The day was cold, especially for Southlands, which was used to balmy weather even in winter. The goat snorted, and streams of white billowed from her nose. But Rose Red, bundled from head to toe in her veils, scarcely noticed the chill. She searched the bushes of the one-time garden for any sign of life. Some shrubs had miraculously escaped the Dragon's fire and, though withered, still managed to produce some green. Rose

Red ran her hands through them, not noticing if the thorns caught at her gloves or pierced her sleeves. She put her nose up to the leaves, and they still smelled sweet.

It was difficult these days to find anything that could bring freshness to the poisoned chambers of the Eldest's House. But Rose Red cut stems as she could, gathering an armload. She would spread these through her master's chambers while he was busy at the banquet tonight. Perhaps it would cheer him to return and find greenery among those gloomy shadows. Or perhaps he would not notice.

"Beana!" She turned suddenly on her goat, who had a large sprig of leaves sticking out of the corner of her mouth. "Don't eat that. You'll be sick."

"Bah!" said the goat, spattering leaves about her hooves. When Rose Red reached out to snatch the mouthful from her, she shook her horns and turned her tail on the girl.

"Beana, I need every bit I can find. There's precious little as it is without you snackin' on it! You don't behave yourself, and I'm puttin' you back in the pen where you belong."

The goat muttered and trotted several paces back up the path, still chewing. Rose Red turned back to her bush, parting the thin stems to better reach a patch of lingering growth.

She paused, taking a startled breath.

Deep within that tangle of brown and dying leaves, almost hidden by thorns, was a blossom. Pure white, as though made of light itself, and fragrant, extravagant even. It was like nothing the girl had ever seen before.

But when she blinked, it was gone.

The goat, standing some distance now from Rose Red, turned suddenly and shivered. "Bah," she said and trotted quickly to the girl's side. "What do you have there?"

Rose Red backed away hastily. "Nothin' you need to see. You'd probably eat it anyway."

She moved on down the row of bushes as her goat stayed put, poking her nose into the tangled branches. Beana's yellow eyes narrowed, and she stamped a hoof. "Rosie!" she bleated. "What did you see?"

"Nothin', Beana," Rose Red repeated without turning to the goat. Her arms were full by now, and she would need to put the stems in water soon if she hoped to keep them alive long enough for her master to see. "You're goin' to have to go back to your pen now."

"I don't want to go back to the pen."

"I'm sorry, but I cain't take you inside with me. Not so long as you insist on bein' . . . you know . . . a goat."

Beana blinked slowly. "And what else would I be, dear girl?"

Rose Red did not answer. Many things had changed for her during those five years with the Dragon, even more in the months following his departure. Everything she had known was gone. The man she called father was dead. Her home was destroyed beyond recall. Hen's teeth, her goat wasn't even a goat!

And dreams came to life and walked in the real world as living, fire-breathing nightmares.

Sometimes Rose Red did not think any of the events in her recent life could possibly have happened. The rest of the time, she simply pretended they had not. Best to focus on the tasks at hand. She must serve her master. And she must stay out of everyone else's sight as much as possible. Because they all believed it was she who brought the Dragon upon Southlands.

In a way, perhaps she had.

Rose Red sighed as she led the goat back to her pen, where other goats raised lazy eyes and bleated disinterested greetings.

"What was that heavy sound for?" Beana demanded.

Rose Red sighed again. "Sometimes I wish . . ."

"Yes?"

"Sometimes I wish we could go back to the way things were. To the mountain. We were lonely, sure. But we were happier then, weren't we? With old Dad to care for, and our cottage to keep, and no one to . . . to . . ."

She could not finish her thought. How could she bear to say it? No one to look at her like she was a monster slavering to eat their children. No one to startle in fright whenever she entered the room. No one to whisper about her when she'd gone.

She tugged at her veil, adjusting it so that it would not slip off, pulling out stray rose thorns and dropping them to the dirt. Beana's gaze was fixed upon her, and she did not like to meet it. She knew exactly what her goat was about to say.

"We can go back, Rosie."

Rose Red shook her head.

"We can," said the goat. "Your master will provide for our journey. He's said so before. He won't keep you here against your will. We can go back to the mountain. It was foolish to have let him talk us into returning in the first place. Have we really done him any good?"

Rose Red did not answer. She plucked thorns from the long stems, rubbing her hand over the smooth bumps left behind.

"He's more distant than ever, hardly the boy you once knew," the goat persisted. "You rarely see him, and when you do, you rarely speak. He's not your responsibility, sweet child. He never was. And it was wrong of him to place such a burden on you, asking you to come back to the lowlands. It's dangerous here."

Beana stopped herself. To continue would be to say too much. There were some dangers it was best to keep the girl unaware of.

To the goat's disappointment, Rose Red said nothing but opened the pen gate and ushered her pet inside. "Rosie?" said Beana as Rose Red closed and fixed the latch.

"I cain't leave him, Beana," said Rose Red. "He needs me. He came back and found me because he needs me. I know it's foolish to say it, even to think it, but . . . but, Beana, I'm the only friend my master has. Though he rules the whole kingdom, he needs me still." She bowed her head, gazing at the bundle of green under her arm. "Even if there's little enough I can do for him."

The goat watched as the girl made her way back through the gardens and on to the Eldest's House. She felt helpless, and for a moment she cursed the shaggy coat and hooves she wore. "It's tearing her up," she muttered as she lost sight of the girl. "This marriage of the prince's. It's tearing her to pieces inside. Light of Lumé above, I wish we'd never met him!"

A shadow passed over the sun.

Beana shivered and looked up, squinting. That was no cloud. Perhaps a bird. But it must have been a large one, an eagle even, to make that shadow.

A moment later, she thought she caught a familiar scent on the wind. A scent of poison and of anger. But it vanished, and she told herself it was nothing more than the remnants of the Dragon's work.

After all, Beana had bigger things to worry about.

Festive music began to play as the guests of the Eldest arrived and filled the new hall to celebrate their prince and his bride to be. Women in gaudy colors danced with men in silken garments, and their smiles flashed as bright as their jewels, so determined were they to rejoice and forget the nightmare in which they had so recently lived.

Prince Lionheart met Lady Daylily at the door and gave her his arm as support when they entered. Each wore a smile that outshone all the paper lanterns, but they did not look at each other. Cheers rose up from the assembly, drowning the music.

A burst of fire lit the Wilderlands for an instant. A few moments later, a solitary figure began to climb the gorge.

2

EVERYONE AT THE BANQUET watched the prince from behind their smiles.

He was not the boy they remembered. A far cry from it. In the five years of his exile, he had grown into a man. His frame had filled out, though he would never be large, and his face was well shaped behind a black beard. As he sat at the right hand of King Hawkeye, it was impossible not to see the resemblance between father and son. Save for the set of his eyes. Those had the deep-set sharpness of his mother, Queen Starflower's, may she rest peacefully with the Mothers of Old. But the expression in his was nothing like that of the dead queen. No, hers was always an expression of strength. Her gaze could pierce the soul of any man in the Eldest's court and wrest his secrets from him in a moment.

Lionheart's, by contrast, was that of a haunted man.

"Did he fight the Dragon?"

Lionheart could almost hear the whispers passing from table to table. Every time a lady of the court leaned close to her neighbor to whisper something behind her fan, he could have sworn he heard the words. He found it nearly impossible to concentrate on the flow of talk going on around him. His bride to be sat on his left, carrying on a lively conversation with her father, the Baron of Middlecrescent, and with Lionheart's cousin, Foxbrush.

At least Daylily's part of the conversation was lively. Her father spoke hardly a word but kept glancing from Lionheart to King Hawkeye and back again, sometimes turning to look at Foxbrush. And Foxbrush answered only in mutters and refused to meet anyone's gaze.

Poor Foxbrush. Lionheart took a moment from his own concerns to spare his cousin a pitying thought. He was so far gone in love with Daylily, Lionheart could feel the jealousy seeping from him.

Not that Foxbrush would ever have had the courage to speak up to her himself. He was much more comfortable buried in his academic pursuits. No, Foxbrush would never have what it took to marry a woman like Daylily. Daylily was a consort fit for a king.

You will be king, sweet prince, spoke the cold voice in Lionheart's head. For an instant, he saw white eyes before his own. *I have promised you your dream, and your dream you will have.*

The vision vanished, and Lionheart found himself eye to eye with Baron Middlecrescent. He quickly dropped his gaze. The baron always reminded him of a cross between a fish and a bulldog, all staring eyes and jaw. Thank the Lights Above, Daylily didn't take after him!

"Did he fight the Dragon?"

Lionheart ground his teeth and pinched the bridge of his nose. The talk in the banquet hall whirled in his head, a hurricane of babble, but all he could discern was that one phrase, again and again. He thought he would suffocate.

"My son." King Hawkeye's voice was as tremulous as a man of eighty's, though he had not yet reached his sixtieth year. The Dragon's poison had aged him far before his time. But he placed a thin-skinned hand on Lionheart's shoulder. "My son, are you unwell?"

Lionheart turned to his father. So many words rushed to his mouth, words he longed to speak. "I did what I could, Father!" he wanted to cry out. "I ensured Southlands' safety! Perhaps I did not fight the Dragon.

Perhaps I did not slay him. But who can face such a monster? Is it cowardly of me that I could not do what no man has done before me? I did all that was within my power, and I made certain he would never return. Don't think it cost me nothing! I gave up that which was most dear to me; I gave him the heart of my love in exchange for safety. Was that an easy price?"

But the words died upon his tongue. Instead he said, "The excitement. It's been a long day."

Hawkeye smiled the ghost of a smile. "You need a dance with your lady to cheer you, lad. What say you, Daylily?"

For the first time during the banquet, Daylily turned her brilliant smile Lionheart's way. Yet it was to the Eldest she addressed herself. "What would you have of me, dear Majesty?"

"A dance."

"With pleasure."

"No, no, not for me! My dancing days have passed. But for this son of mine whom you seem inclined to wed at the week's end. Dance with him for me, will you?"

At last Daylily looked at Lionheart. Her smile never altered, but he saw the veil that fell across her eyes as clearly as Rose Red's linen covering. "I will gladly dance with my prince," she said through that smile.

He rose and bowed over her hand, then led her to the floor. The Eldest gave the signal; the court musicians hastily took up their instruments and struck a tune. Lionheart took Daylily in his arms. She was as soft and supple as granite, but she moved with expert grace, refusing to meet his eyes.

They danced a few measures, Daylily's long skirts shushing softly across the floor, the train of her headdress floating lightly behind her. One of the musicians began to sing:

> *"Oh, Gleamdren Fair, I love thee true,*
> *Be the moon waxed full or new!*
> *In all my world-enscoping view*
> *There shineth none so bright as you."*

Lionheart groaned.

"Something amiss?" asked his lady.

"This song." He stopped dancing, not caring that all the court looked down on them in surprise. "I hate this song."

Her masklike face altered into the most subtle of frowns. "It is a song of Eanrin, Chief Poet of Rudiobus."

"I know," said the prince. "Believe me, I know."

"It is the most renowned of all his ballads." Her voice was as cold as a winter morning before sunrise, contrasting with the brilliance of her smile.

"I won't dance to it," said Lionheart. "It's the worst verse ever written, and that's saying a great deal for Bard Eanrin." He started to go, but her hand suddenly tightened.

"Don't leave me, Lionheart," Daylily hissed. "Don't leave me standing here."

"I won't," said he. "You can return to the table with me until the musicians learn to play something bearable."

"You cannot insult me like this. In front of the whole court." No one watching them could have guessed at her words from the expression on her face. "You cannot."

"It's not an insult if you walk with me."

"I will not."

"There we are, then."

"Dance with me, Lionheart," said Daylily. "Or—"

"Or what? You'll threaten me?" He shook his head and dropped her hand. "I'm not playing your games."

With those words he turned and strode away. The singer faltered, but the musicians kept playing. Lionheart approached the table, meeting first the gaze of his father, then that of Baron Middlecrescent. The baron looked like thunder. Lionheart sank into his seat beside his father and took a deep gulp from his goblet.

"Lover's quarrel?" asked Hawkeye.

"I hate that song," said Lionheart with a shrug, setting his goblet back down. Then he sat upright, gripping the arms of his chair, his mouth dropping open.

For Foxbrush had made his way to the dance floor, taken Daylily in his arms, and whirled her away in time to that music beneath the warm glow of the lanterns. The musician sang:

> *"Sing ye of all the lovers true*
> *Beneath a sky of sapphire hue.*
> *In light o' the love I bear for you*
> *All theirs must fade like morning dew."*

And every one of Southlands' barons saw it.

Lionheart knew what he should do. He should rise up, storm to the dance floor, challenge his cousin to a duel . . . or simply take Daylily from his arms, laughing it all off like a big joke, and dance away to that pathetic tune. Either of which would have satisfied her. Either of which would have satisfied the barons.

Lionheart pushed back his chair, not caring how it scraped and drew the attention of every man and woman in the room, nobility and servant alike. He bowed to his father with as much dignity as he could muster and withdrew from his own wedding banquet.

He hastened along the dim corridor, uncertain whether he was furious or relieved to get away. The passages were mostly deserted here, for everyone, even the servants, was busy back at the hall. He needed a few moments of peace. That was all. A few moments to collect his thoughts and reinforce himself before returning. He needed—

"Lionheart!"

He turned, and Daylily stood before him. The light of a wall sconce cast a glow upon her hair and lit her eyes ablaze in her otherwise still face. "Lionheart, how can you do this to me?"

Lionheart drew a deep breath before answering. It would be best not to shout. Even in these quiet passages, someone might overhear. "Do what, Daylily?"

"Desert me on the floor, in front of everyone. And then huff out of there like a merchant's spoiled brat."

"I told you. I don't like that song."

He could almost feel the pressure of her anger hitting him like a wall as she neared. Yet her face remained quiet as death. "Can you be so foolish, Lionheart?" she asked. Her voice was deep for a woman's, strange coming from that dainty mouth. "Can you not have realized?"

He made no answer but allowed her to draw nearer until she could drop her voice still lower.

"Your life is not about likes or dislikes," said Daylily. "Not anymore."

His eyes narrowed. "What are you saying?"

"You may become Eldest someday, but your power in Southlands hangs by a thread."

Everything went still inside Lionheart. For the moment he had control of himself. He needed to grab hold of that moment now, with all his might, or regret it forever. "You don't know what you're talking about, Daylily."

"Don't I?" She was so close now he could have reached out and given her a good shake if he allowed himself to. "I am the Baron of Middle-crescent's daughter. I know what goes on in your kingdom better than you do, better than you ever have. Remember, you were absent those five years. You escaped."

"It wasn't like that."

"Wasn't it? If not escape, what was it?" Her words, though spoken softly, were harsh in his ears. "How did you manage to elude those years of enslavement, of poison? How did you manage to slip out when everyone else who tried was burned to a crisp? How did you time your little jaunt across the Continent so swimmingly as to return just after the Dragon had ceased to find our poor land interesting? If not escape, Lionheart, what was it?"

"You know why I left," he said, his voice near a whisper. "You were there when I made my decision. You sped me on my way. I went to find the secret to defeating the Dragon. I left in order to help you."

"Is that why you returned so boldly *after* the Dragon had torn apart your father's house? *After* he ravaged your people's lands? *After* he killed your mother?"

"Stop now. Stop."

"No, Lionheart! You need to know what they're saying about you. Friend of demons, that's what they're calling the man to whom I am betrothed. Bewitched."

He snorted. "And you believe this nonsense?"

"How can I know what to believe? The Dragon did not harm you. He let you escape the poisons under which the rest of us suffered. Did you ever watch your dreams burn and die and burn and die again before your very eyes?"

I will give you your dream, whispered the cold voice in his mind. *You will be Eldest of Southlands.*

He grimaced, shaking his head as though to rid himself of that ever-present voice. "What do you want, Daylily?" he demanded. "What will it take to please you? That I fawn over you, that I jig to every nonsensical ballad that strikes your fancy, just for your amusement?"

"Not for my amusement, Lionheart. For my father's."

With an inhuman effort he forced back the words that threatened to spill like fire from his tongue. But she continued.

"It is only by his will that you remain Prince of Southlands. Have you not guessed it? Should the Council of Barons vote to disinherit you, your father will have no choice but to comply with their wishes. Or risk revolt."

Lionheart's mouth was dry. His veins seemed to pulse fire. "The Council has not been called."

"Not yet. But it can and will be called faster than you can imagine should my father say the word. Can you really be so ignorant? Your father knows, though he may not let on. Should the Council be called, they will vote against you, and Hawkeye will appoint a new heir."

Lionheart could not speak the name aloud, but his lips formed it even so. "Foxbrush."

"I will be Queen of Southlands, one way or the other—"

Before she could finish, Lionheart grabbed her shoulders. It took everything in him to keep from shaking the teeth from her skull. Instead, his fingers dug into the furs draped about her elegant frame, and his eyes burned into hers.

"Don't threaten me. Not now. Not after everything I've gone through to come this far. I won't hear it from you, nor from your father. I am the Eldest's only son, and I will sit on my father's throne. There's nothing you, your father, or anyone can do to prevent me from having what has been promised me. So keep your threats, my lady! You waste your breath."

"Oh, Leo!" For a moment, her mask melted away. He saw a flash of true compassion, of sorrow, even fear. "I am not threatening. I am warning you!"

His fingers relaxed in surprise even as Daylily lowered her lashes, shielding her eyes. When next she looked at him, she was herself again, cold and unreadable. "Do you think I want to see your fool of a cousin on the throne?"

Lionheart let go and backed away, turning from Daylily. She put out a hand and almost touched his shoulder but withdrew it at the last. "It need not happen as I have said. You can prevent my father from calling the Council."

"How?" said Lionheart through clenched teeth. "By making a fool of myself before the court with displays of doting affection?"

No one watching could have guessed at Daylily's thoughts had they seen her face. She swallowed slowly and blinked once. "That will not be necessary," she said. "There is a much easier method of winning my father's approval and the approval of all Southlands."

"And that is?"

"Get rid of the demon."

He turned upon her. She stood like a queen of old going into battle, her shoulders set and eyes hard. "You know of whom I speak."

No words would come. His mouth opened and closed.

"Rose Red," said Daylily. "That creature has bewitched you long enough. Have you not heard how she consorted with the Dragon? Have you not heard—"

"Not another word, Daylily," he hissed.

"No, you will hear me!" she declared, and this time it was she who grabbed him, clutching the front of his shirt in a tight fist. "That stoop-shouldered monster has ensorcelled you since you were a boy. Don't you think it strange that none of the rest of us is so enthralled by her? Have you not heard what my father has whispered into the ears of everyone in court? How the creature kidnapped me and dragged me back to the Eldest's House to join the other prisoners. How she sacrificed your mother—"

He took her hand in both of his and wrenched her grasp away. "You lie."

"Maybe," she whispered, once more lowering her eyes. "But I would do much more, Leo, to see you dismiss her."

Lionheart's hands tightened painfully over her fingers, but she would not pull away. "You have always preferred her. She has always been your friend. And what of me? Was I never good enough? Must I be forever inferior to that . . . monster?"

"Rose Red is no monster."

Daylily laughed. "Are you blind as well as a fool?"

"And I am no fool."

He pushed her hand from him as though he would like to banish her from his presence. Daylily backed a step away and clutched her crumpled fingers to her chest. But she did not break Lionheart's gaze.

"I will not dismiss Rose Red," he said. "Nor will I see any harm come to her. She is under my protection as sanctioned by the Eldest himself. Even your father cannot gainsay the Eldest's express order."

"Not yet," said she.

They stood in the shadows, lit by a solitary candle sconce, two specters in a haunted house. Far away, the music of the banquet continued to play as the people of Southlands celebrated the upcoming nuptials of their prince and his lady.

"Will you return to the hall with me?" Daylily asked.

"I will not."

The Baron of Middlecrescent's daughter turned and floated back down the corridor as silent as a shadow, vanishing around a bend. Lionheart watched her go, his mind whirling with too many thoughts to sort through. He turned blindly, continuing up the passage, taking the first turn up a servants' stair.

He found himself face-to-face with Rose Red.

Moonlight fell from a window in the passage and lit upon her veils, making them luminous in the otherwise dark stairway. She was a phantom, a ghost of some troubled past, standing there in the silver light, her face shrouded, two porcelain pots clutched in her arms. Lionheart startled back. Then he growled.

"Did you hear?"

"Y-yes, my prince," she whispered.

He pounded a fist against the stone wall, then leaned his forehead against it, sighing. "Rosie," he said, "I was wrong to ask you to come back. I should have—they don't understand."

"They never have," she replied. "No one ever has. Except you."

He shook his head. "I've been unfair to you. It was wrong of me to have brought you here, to have asked you to leave the mountain."

"But . . ." Her voice was very small, trembling. "But I'm glad you did."

Lionheart shook his head. Imprisonment and despair closed him in on all sides. He must struggle for his dream. He must fight. He'd come too far to back down now. "I think I must send you back, Rosie. For your own sake."

"No!" The agony in her voice startled him, and he took a step back in surprise when she suddenly went down on her knees before him, setting aside her pots and wringing her hands. "No, Leo, don't say that." He smiled a little at her use of his old nickname. She never called him that now that she was his servant. It wasn't right. But somehow, it was natural coming from her, his oldest friend. "Send me away," she said, "if it's for your sake. But I vowed to serve you, and I won't leave unless it's what you want. I'll serve you, however you need me to. If that means goin', I'll go tonight. Only let me help you, my prince!"

"Rose Red," he sighed, taking her by the hands and gently pulling her to her feet. When standing, she was still scarcely more than half his size, though he was no giant himself. "I don't know what I'd do without you. We'll speak of this again after the wedding week is past. I cannot think now. I cannot make a decision. Try to stay out of sight though, as much as possible. I fear some harm will come to you. I don't know if I could forgive myself were that to happen."

"Don't worry about me," she said, her head bowed so that the hem of her veil reached to her belt. The belt was of faded red cloth, frayed with age, though among the frayed ends yet lingered glimmerings of gold. Once it had been a blanket, but years of hard use in the mountains had reduced it to no more than a rag. "Don't worry about me. You have enough worries as it is."

"Iubdan's beard, yes!" Lionheart said. Without another word he stepped past her and continued on his way up the stairs. A cold voice rang in his head, a voice that no one else could hear, and he staggered as he went.

Rose Red watched him go, cursing her ineffectiveness. She looked down at the empty pots she had been on her way to fill with water, intending to arrange more greenery in them. How would withering rose stems lift her master's spirits now?

She fled the passage, leaving the pots where they lay, and slipped unseen through the back corridors of the House. Rose Red had always possessed a gift for going unseen when she wanted to, and she avoided the other servants with ease. She escaped through a door and pelted across the near garden. In the struggling rosebushes, she thought she glimpsed many white blossoms, translucent under the moonlight. But when she drew near, they vanished.

Beana startled awake at the creak of the door. Other goats lazily opened their eyes, but Beana lurched to her feet and bleated, "Lumé, child! What's the matter with you? Did you hear . . . Rosie, tell me, did you hear the Fallen One speak?"

Rose Red sank to her knees beside her goat and, wrapping her arms around Beana's neck, plunged her face, veil and all, into the coarse fur. She began to weep.

Beana blinked. "Oh. Well, maybe it's not that after all." She shook her horns, muttered goatily, and knelt down in the straw. Rose Red shifted so that her face was now buried in her goat's back. Tears soaked through her veil, so she removed it. She sat and sobbed, barefaced, in the darkness.

Beana chewed her cud.

When at last the sobs reduced to sniffs, the goat swallowed and said, "All right, child. If you can manage to talk without hiccups, tell me."

Rose Red sat up and pulled her knees to her chest. Her face was nothing but shadows in the darkness of the shed, but her eyes gleamed like small moons.

"I need you to talk sense to me, Beana."

"Do I ever talk anything else?"

"I need you to tell me," Rose Red said, "that I'm a fool."

"If it makes you happy. You're a fool." Beana gave Rose Red's ear a slobbery kiss. "Now, why don't you toddle off to bed? You'll feel much better after a night's sleep, though you'll have a fierce headache after all this weeping and wailing—"

"I cain't seem to help myself!" Rose Red sucked in a long breath and bowed her head to her knees. "I cain't seem to help lovin' him, and I know that she don't, but she'll marry him, and who's to stop her? And he'll never see!"

"Never see?"

"Never see the difference! Between me and her. He'll never see how I love him . . . because he'll never see me."

A long silence lingered in the goat shed. One of the other goats bleated, and several shifted. Otherwise all was still.

"Oh, Beana," Rose Red whispered at last. "My mind plays such cruel tricks sometimes. I can pretend out a whole story of a prince who loves a girl, not because of her beauty, but because she loves him and serves him. Because she would give up everythin' for his sake. And I can pretend his heart is so moved that he finds it possible to look beyond a face like . . . mine."

Beana said nothing. She nuzzled the girl again, but Rose Red pushed her away.

"It's stupid, I know. No one could ever love someone like me, and sometimes, well, sometimes I could just eat my own hand off!"

"Don't do that. It'll disagree with you."

Rose Red turned and buried her face in her goat's fur once more. Beana felt hot tears seeping into her coat. "Please, Beana," the girl said, "please tell me to . . . to buck up or somethin'! He's gettin' married this week, and I've got to serve him, and I cain't do that with all this dreamin'!"

Beana sighed and began to chew her cud again until the girl had finished her second, less stormy cry. When Rose Red sat up once more, snuffling and wiping tears from her cheeks, the goat said quietly, "The dreaming is dangerous, child. You start letting yourself live in dreams like that, and you'll find yourself open to such evils. I've seen it happen time and again to those I loved. . . ." She shook her head violently, clanking the bell about her neck. Then she put out her long nose and licked tears from Rose Red's face, allowing the girl to stroke her soft ears.

In a gentle voice quite unlike a goat's, she said, "But I'll never tell you to stop loving. You see, I believe in hopeless love. Oh yes. I believe in it with all my heart, though you may discount the heart of an old nanny like me. For real love brings pain. Real love means sacrifices and hurts and all the thousand shocks of life. But it also means beauty, true beauty, such as the likes of that brilliant Lady of Middlecrescent couldn't imagine.

"You say it's impossible for anyone to love one like you? I tell you otherwise. I know deep down in the secret places of my soul that a person can learn to love someone like you. Someone uglier by far! With a deep, lasting love that would . . . that would dare to stare in the face of Death himself and shout threats and shake fists for the sake of the one beloved!" She laughed a little snorting laugh and smiled.

Then she was no longer a goat. Anyone looking in that dark shed would have seen at its far end a woman clad in brown and white—a mirage of the moonlight, perhaps—her hair wrapped in crowning braids atop her head, and her arms around the scrawny shoulders of a gangly, ill-formed creature in servant's garb. An awful sight, yet one touched by a certain holiness. And somewhere, beyond the dankness of the stable, a wood thrush sang. Its song filled the night with vast spaces and clarity. In that song, Rose Red's heart lifted as though releasing a heavy burden, and she breathed in clean air.

"This I know," whispered the woman. "I know the depths of impossibility. They are dreadful depths when plunged. More dreadful than you yet know. Even so, do not forget him. Do not forget your love. Not for a moment."

Rose Red raised her face from where it rested against a warm beating heart. But that vision of a tender face, that dream of warm, encircling arms vanished, and she sat nose to nose with a dusty goat.

3

The night was frigid, filled with songs that no one could hear. Or, if they did hear, no one understood the words, no matter how the songs might call to them. Only the moon seemed inclined to listen, and her great eye was dewy with tears.

The moonlight was more unbearable than the cold. Lionheart drew his curtains against it. Someone—Rose Red, most likely—had built a small fire on the grate in preparation for his evening, but its glow did little to ease the gloom around him. He stood awhile with his back to the blaze, drawing deep breaths. His old drapes had been burned and replaced months ago, and some chambermaid had put fresh cuttings in vases and urns about the room. But he still smelled dragon poison.

"Friend of demons." Daylily's voice rang in his head.

He wanted to break something with his own hands, to crush and destroy, anything to relieve the anger that, even now in the privacy of his chambers, he dared not release. No one would understand. No one *could* understand.

He closed his eyes and rubbed a hand down his face. Day after tomorrow, Lionheart would wed the friend of his youth, at last fulfilling the expectations of his dead mother and his half-dead father. With Daylily by his side, he would rebuild his once fertile kingdom, restoring green growth to the desolate fields, reviving life in the ghostly figures of his subjects. If only he could regain their trust!

"Did he fight the Dragon?"

No wonder they doubted now whether or not he was the right man to serve someday as Southlands' Eldest. How could he have left them for so long! And for no purpose—

"No!" he growled. "No, it was for good purpose."

Lionheart took a seat in his high-backed chair and drew it near the fire. He felt no warmth from the dull brands. Flames burned brightly in his mind instead.

Softly he whispered a name.

"Una."

The night stretched before him, sleepless and frozen.

In the darkness before dawn, Beana knelt in the straw of her pen, her eyes wide and alert. Rose Red lay with her head pillowed on the goat's back, her veil partially falling off her face. Gently, Beana reached out and pulled it back into place. Then she lifted her head again, nostrils quivering, ears twitching.

She listened for those silent songs. Although she could not hear them, she knew they must be near. But the air was chilled into otherworldly stillness. Even the moon had set.

The dawn chorus would not begin for another hour at least, a collision of sounds from all the birds flown to Southlands for the winter. There were fewer than in olden days. No birds had lived in Southlands during the years of the Dragon, and even now the usual migrants, displeased with the unnaturally cold winters in the kingdom, flew on across the mountains out to the sea and the warm islands beyond. The absence of their bright colors and brighter songs was keenly felt in Southlands. Everything had changed with the Dragon.

Suddenly, a lone birdsong filled the predawn air. The silver bell-like voice shattered the silence, startling Beana so that her skin shivered under Rose Red's cheek. But the sweet melody flowed like running water, warming the winter.

Rose Red's head came up. She rubbed her eyes wearily. But sleep swiftly fled before that fluid voice. "My wood thrush," she whispered. "Do you hear him, Beana?"

Beana shook her head. "Rosie . . ."

"Shhh!" Rose Red got to her feet, her head tilted to the music. "Don't you hear that?"

The goat listened again to the birdsong, and she heard what Rose Red must have already discerned. There were words in the thrush's voice.

Won't you follow me?

Beana rose ponderously to her feet, the bell around her neck jangling. "I hear it," she said. "My Lord is calling us."

Rose Red hastened to the pen and unlatched the gate. The other goats bleated, grouchy at being disturbed, but Beana ignored them as she usually did (earning her a reputation for snobbery among her kind) and followed Rose Red out to the stable yard.

Dawn was just beginning to break, but its light brought no warmth. Rather, it illuminated the gloom of those stark grounds and barren rosebushes. Southlands, the evergreen, had never known so harsh a winter. Mist curled up between their feet and frost crunched as goat and girl made their way through the near gardens and on to the park grounds beyond.

The thrush called again. They quickened their steps. They found themselves much farther out on the grounds than either would have expected. Rose Red shivered in her thin servant's garb, and her breath caught and froze in her veil. But they did not hesitate. Not until Beana saw the deep gorge cutting the landscape ahead of them did she pause.

"We can't go that way," she said, planting her hooves.

Rose Red, a few steps ahead, looked back. "But he's callin' us."

Beana shook her head, bleating inarticulately. "We're too close to the Wilderlands as it is."

Rose Red stood still. The sun, just cresting the far mountains, shone blindingly on the frost and the wisps of her breath. And the wood thrush sang once more.

Won't you follow me?

As though coming to a decision, Rose Red turned from the goat and continued pursuing that voice, drawing ever nearer to the gorge. Beana tossed her head. "Why, my Lord?" she demanded, then trotted after her charge, catching up to her just as she approached the drop-off.

Together, they gazed into the dark forest far below. The sunlight, which was filling the plateaus of Southlands, seemed to skirt away from those dark leaves. Mists clung to the Wilderlands like stroking fingers. It was a dizzying drop, and Rose Red put a hand on Beana's back for support. She had never been so near one of the gorges without a bridge.

The thrush sang again.

"Must we go down there?" Rose Red whispered.

"Someone is there," said Beana, shaking her horns. "Someone who needs help."

"Very well."

Rose Red took a step toward the edge of the cliff, but Beana bleated in sudden terror. "No! No, child! You cannot go that way!"

Rose Red paused, her heart hammering in her chest, though she could not say why. Perhaps it was simply that terrible fall. But she had grown up in the mountains, and heights had never affected her nerves before.

The thrush sang. *Follow!*

"Beana," Rose Red said, "if someone needs help, ain't that what we're called to give?"

"I'll help," said the goat.

Rose Red snorted. "And who's goin' to take the help of an old goat?"

Beana bleated again, stamping a hoof until it tore the turf. "Very well," she said at last. "But let me go first. I'll find us a Path. And, Rosie! You must not enter the Wilderlands, you hear me? No matter what happens, you must not approach the forest."

"Whatever you say, Beana."

The goat paced along the top of the gorge. The cliff was sheer and the stones sharp, and at first Beana did not think she would find them a way down. But she knew the secret Paths that mortal eyes did not see, and if there was one to be found, it would not long be hidden from her. In due course, she saw one, a thin, glimmering trail, invisible in this world but nonetheless real, leading down the cliff face. "This way," the goat told the girl. Rose Red, who had been trained as a child to find these fey Paths herself, saw where Beana walked and followed close behind.

The way was difficult but not impossible to navigate. Rose Red's hand shook as she clutched rocks for balance, but she did not miss a step. Beana, sure-footed as a mountain goat, progressed much faster in this terrain, and was soon many paces ahead. Suddenly she stopped and shook her head until her bell made a terrible dissonance in the morning air. "Bah!"

A strange voice spoke, soft but hot as fire in the winter air. "Good morning to you too."

Rose Red startled at the sound. "Oh! There *is* someone!"

She hastened a few steps farther down the path and came face-to-face with a dragon.

Sunrise found Lionheart hollow eyed before his shaving glass. He had slept hardly a wink. Throughout the night, his mind had been full of two different voices. One was as familiar to him as his own: a woman's voice, venomous as darkness itself.

You did what you had to do. There was no other way. Now you will have your dream.

Lionheart had lain on his bed, gazing up at the shadows of his canopy, listening to the cold words going round and round in his head.

Suddenly, as though carrying over great distance and time, he'd heard another voice, very soft and sorrowful:

"He won't even recognize me. Leonard . . . how could you love a monster?"

He knew that voice all too well. And he whispered for a second time that night the name he had vowed to forget: "Una."

Thus, when morning dawned, it was a sorry excuse for a prince that dragged himself from his pillow and faced his own reflection in the glass. His fingers trembled as he trimmed his beard and splashed icy water into his eyes. Then he dressed himself, slowly, in princely apparel of blue and scarlet.

Today he must ride out with Daylily and her father and other members of his father's court, through the main street of the Eldest's City, ending at the mayor's house, where they would stop and present themselves to the people of Southlands, all smiles and love. And masks.

Daylily's cheerless face presented itself in his mind. When she smiled, her eyes did not show it. Not so with Una.

Lionheart closed his eyes, grimacing as he finished buttoning his doublet and placed a silver crown upon his brow.

When Una smiled, it filled her whole face, and when she laughed, there was no trace of artificiality.

"Iubdan's beard!" The Prince of Southlands swore through grinding teeth. "You gave her up, you fool."

You did what you had to do.

"I had my reasons. And I would do it again if need be!" His unfeeling mirror stared back at him, reflecting only his self-loathing. Lionheart turned away, unable to meet his own gaze.

He was Prince of Southlands. His kingdom must always come first. He made his way down from his chambers to where the Eldest's court waited to feast him and his bride.

The dragon was clothed in the form of a young woman, hardly more than a girl, her back pressed against the cliff. Her dress, which might once have been very fine, was in tatters, darkened by dirt so that its color was indeterminable. Honey-brown hair hung long and straggly about her, partially covering her face. But she pulled some of it back to look up at Rose Red.

Fire gleamed in her unblinking eyes.

Rose Red stood like a statue for what seemed a small forever. All the memories of the last few years rushed back into her mind. Memories of a dark Path and a black lake; memories of a ballroom lit with ghostly chandeliers suspended in shadows; memories of dancing to discordant music and of jewels gleaming on rich gowns.

Memories of dragons.

The wood thrush sang across the morning. *Take heart, dear one.*

Rose Red swallowed and stepped up behind her goat. "Beana told me someone needed help down here," she said, hoping her voice did not tremble much. "Shoo, Beana," she added, nudging the goat aside so that she could sidle past her.

"Bah!"

The dragon drew back, pressing herself more firmly against the rock. Despite the fire burning so hot inside her that the air steamed from her skin, she did not seem to possess the energy to rise. "Who are you?" she demanded in a harsh voice. But her face was afraid.

Rose Red put out a hand, speaking as gently as she could, though every instinct warned her to flee. "I am nobody," she said. "Who are you?"

The dragon shook her head and suddenly buried her face in her knees. Her body trembled. Could she possibly be cold?

Don't be such a coward, Rose Red scolded herself. *She ain't even as old as you! And she's more frightened than you are.* She took another step and spoke in a soothing voice. "Have you come from the Wilderlands? Are you trying to climb to the Eldest's City?"

The dragon did not look up but shrugged her shoulders.

If she was trying to make her way to the city, Rose Red would have to stop her. The last thing the people of Southlands needed was another dragon in their midst. Though this one was a far cry from her dark Father, she was a dragon nonetheless. Poor, pitiable thing. Rose Red stepped still closer. "You are weak and worn," she said. Then her voice caught in her throat.

The dragon sat with her arms wrapped around her knees. One of them was gray with ash and soot and had traces of burns.

The other was covered in scales.

Rose Red drew in a sharp breath. Her heart raced as the memories returned again, more powerfully than ever, memories of fire and poison and whirling music. Memories of a throne made of twisted dragon skeletons set high on a black pedestal. She felt overwhelmed with the urge to throw herself upon the strange girl, to drag her up and push her from the Path, crashing down to the rocks below.

A cruel impulse, but it raced through her veins in a flooding rush.

Then the wood thrush sang a single word: *Beloved.*

Rose Red breathed out slowly and felt her hands, which had been clenched into fists, relax. Licking her lips, she whispered, "And I see that you suffer." She touched the scale-covered arm.

The dragon sat upright and yanked herself away from Rose Red. "Leave me alone!" There was no violence in her voice, only terror. And Rose Red thought that her transformation must have been recent. This trembling creature could not long have been a dragon.

"Please, m'lady," Rose Red said as softly as she could. "I am not one to judge you." She swallowed, then slowly began to peel the glove off her right hand. "Will you look?"

She held out her bare hand for the stranger to see: hard as stone, each stubby finger ending in a cruel claw. It was her shame and her birthright.

The dragon stared at it, her mouth dropping open. Then she looked up, squinting as though to see Rose Red's eyes through the slit of her veil. "Are you . . . are you like me?" she asked.

Rose Red shook her head. "No, m'lady. But let me help you even so."

Slowly, the dragon lifted her own horrible hand and placed it in Rose Red's. The scales were hot, hot right through Rose Red's stony hide. But Rose Red had expected this and did not flinch. She helped the girl to her feet and said, "You go to the city?"

The dragon nodded, confirming Rose Red's suspicions. Well, she would get her off of the cliff and out of the cold first, then figure out how to dissuade her. What could a young dragon possibly want in the Eldest's City anyway? It was unlikely that Southlands was her home. Her pale skin and fair hair suggested she came from one of the north countries, as far as Parumvir, even. How she came to be so far south was beyond Rose Red's guess. But she wouldn't worry about that now.

Beana turned and led the way up the Path, muttering to herself and sometimes voicing a vehement "Bah!" Otherwise, she said nothing, though she kept casting wary glances back at both the dragon and the Wilderlands below. No one could have guessed which she feared most.

Their going was slow, and the morning was well progressed by the time they reached the tablelands above. As soon as they were upon level ground, the stranger pulled herself from Rose Red's grasp. She was unsteady on her feet, but her face was determined. "Which way to the city gates?" she demanded.

Rose Red frowned. She did not like to think of a dragon, no matter how small and weak, wandering alone through the Eldest's grounds, trying to find the city. "I can take you there myself," she said hesitantly, her mind furiously working to come up with some way to dissuade the creature. "I serve in the Eldest's House. I know the way."

"Serve in the Eldest's House?" Flames darted in the corners of the dragon's eyes, and Rose Red took a step back at the sight. "Have you seen . . ." The dragon paused and ducked her head, blinking as though to drive back the fire. "That is . . . have you heard tell of . . ."

Trying to swallow her fear, Rose Red said gently, "Yes, m'lady?"

The dragon shook her head and turned her back on Rose Red. "Thank you for your assistance. I will find my own way."

Rose Red felt her heart stop. She realized the dragon was about to run. She dared not lose her. Not now, after she herself had helped the creature to the surface. "Please, m'lady—"

The dragon's thin voice transformed into a roar. "Leave me alone!"

Rose Red fell back, pressing into Beana, who stood just behind her. She could not bring herself to speak or move, overwhelmed as she was at the sight of the fire falling from the girl's lips.

Then the dragon was running. Her speed was unnatural, like a shadow flitting across the Eldest's grounds. Embers trailed in her wake. She vanished into the skeletal foliage of the gardens.

Rose Red tried to draw a breath but couldn't. "What have I done?" She grabbed hold of Beana's fur in a grip that should have caused the goat pain. "Oh, Beana! Beana, what have I done?"

But Beana did not seem to hear or understand her. The goat's gaze was fixed on the Wilderlands with deadly intensity. Suddenly she whirled on the girl. "GO!" she cried. "Chase after her! Stop her if you can. But go! Get away from here. Now!"

Rose Red ran. The tone in her goat's voice was more terrible to her even than her fear of the dragon, and she ran with all the speed she could muster. As though in a dream, she could scarcely make her feet move fast enough. She could not hope to catch the dragon, but she ran anyway, back over the park grounds, bypassing the house, and hastening on toward the Eldest's City.

But Beana remained behind, standing above the gorge and peering into the darkness of the trees below.

For she had heard at last that for which she had been listening those twenty years and more; the song which did not sing to her, so she could understand no words. But the noise of it rang through her head with painful intensity.

"Lights Above shield us!" she whispered. "It has come for her at last."

4

THE CROWDED STREETS of the Eldest's City were strung with colored lanterns even in midday. All the folk of the city, from the mayor's young daughters to the lowliest street urchin, were dressed in their finest. Despite the winter chill, women's arms were bared to show off gleaming bangles. Bright scarves festooned the men's necks, trailing behind them like kite tails as they waved and cheered at the passing parade.

They were desperate to be happy, Lionheart thought as he rode his high-stepping horse down the main street. They were desperate for hope. He wondered, however, how many of those smiles were sincere and how many of them were mere reflections of his own.

Daylily rode beside him. She had yet to meet his eyes once that day, yet her smiles were brightest of all. She radiated happiness so intense as to be dizzying. But her horse put its ears back and swished its tail, now and then rolling its eyes.

They came to the mayor's house, and Lionheart dismounted and turned to assist Daylily, only to find that she had already slid from the saddle herself and settled her skirts. Without a glance his way, she took his arm and allowed him to lead her up the house steps. They bowed and curtsied to the mayor and his lady and his cluster of daughters. Then it was inside for refreshments and small talk while the crowd outside played music and danced in the town square.

Daylily was brilliant, as always. How the people of Southlands adored her! A man would have to be blind not to see it. She never left his side yet somehow managed to make conversation with every person in the household from the most powerful barons to the lowliest baronets. Lionheart, by contrast, could scarcely put two words together. It did not matter. Everyone knew it was the bride that counted at a wedding anyway.

"Come, darling," said Daylily, still without looking at him. She gently directed him by the arm instead. "The people must see you again."

He found himself being led up a flight of stairs and around to a balcony overlooking the city square. The square was so packed with celebrants that one couldn't glimpse the cobbles beneath their dancing feet. When Lionheart appeared above their heads, standing at the railing between two flags, they turned as one body and began to shout. It was a noise like thunder.

"Prince Lionheart! The crown prince!" they shouted.

But Lionheart only heard, "Did he fight the Dragon? Did he?"

He forced himself to smile, even to wave. Then he turned and pulled Daylily up beside him, furious at himself for drawing strength from her presence. But in that moment, he couldn't bear to face his subjects alone. Daylily glowed, her smile brighter than the sun. She was dressed in gorgeous furs that framed her delicate face to perfection. Clutching his hand in one of hers, she gracefully waved with the other. The people redoubled their cheers. How they loved the Lady of Middlecrescent!

And suddenly, all the sounds of the city faded away, save one. A single voice calling from the crowd. *"Leonard!"*

Lionheart, as if coming out of a dream, turned and looked down into the milling throng. His gaze met the wide eyes of a pale girl. The only pale face in the throng of brown-skinned Southlanders.

"Una," he breathed.

Daylily's hand on his shoulder startled him. "Lionheart, you look as though you've seen a ghost," she said. "What's wrong?"

"Nothing!" he said, rather too quickly. Then he took his hand from hers, backing away. "Daylily, I must see to something. Wait for me here, and I'll return momentarily. I swear."

For the first time that day she looked into his eyes. He thought his heart would freeze.

"Don't be long," she said.

He pushed through the cluster of the mayor's guests, past the Baron of Middlecrescent and his own father. He paused for a moment to take a long cloak from a peg in the hall and, on an impulse, took the silver crown from his head and dashed it into a dark corner. Then, hiding his rich clothing, he slipped through a small door into a deserted alley behind the mayor's house. When he entered the crowds of merrymakers, nobody recognized him, and he was hard-pressed to push his way through the square to the place where he thought he had seen her. The young people had taken up dancing again, and he was obliged to duck through swirling skirts and swinging arms, taking an elbow in the ribs for his pains.

Then he saw her, white and alone. The people of the city had unconsciously backed away from her, as if she carried the plague. Her face was still upturned to the balcony above.

"Una!" he cried.

She turned, and Lionheart found himself face-to-face with the girl he had once loved.

"Leonard," she whispered. It chilled his heart somehow to hear her speak the name he had taken while in exile. But he hastened forward until they were beside each other, and still the crowds of onlookers kept a short distance.

"Una," he said in a low voice. He could scarcely hear himself in that din, but she seemed to understand him. How frail she looked! Her clothing was in rags and her face was like death, with great hollows under her eyes. The last he'd seen her, she had been a hearty, laughing princess with a smile that glowed. The face before him looked as though it had never smiled. "What . . . what has happened to . . . What are you—"

There could be no talking there, in the midst of that crowd. And

Lionheart could almost feel Daylily's eyes above, searching him out in the crowd. He wore a hood over his face but nevertheless felt too vulnerable. Without another word, he caught her hand, drew her into the shelter of his cloak, and led her through the crowd.

The streets of the city were packed with revelers, but at last he saw a near-empty side street and hastened down it. Then he took another and another, until they came at last to the outskirts of the city, where there were no gates and no other people, only drainage ditches.

Leading the girl onto one of the footbridges crossing a ditch, Lionheart let her go and threw back his hood.

"Where is your father?" he demanded.

"I do not know," said she.

"You are come alone, then?" It was impossible. And yet, by the looks of things, that must be so. "How did you get here? Why was I not given advance notice of your coming?"

"No one knows."

Lionheart shook his head. "You can't do that. You're a princess. You can't travel all the way from Parumvir to Southlands by yourself!"

"But I did."

The prince stared at her, disbelieving. Anger welled up inside him. How could she come here now? Of all times! He had given her up, the sweet princess of Parumvir, the girl he had adored, from whom he had accepted promises and gifts. He had given her up for the sake of his kingdom, and how dared she come to him now? It was too much.

Get rid of her, whispered the cold voice in his head. *You don't need her. You have your dream. Get rid of her, or she'll take it from you!*

He gazed at her again, taking in her haggard appearance. No one would have known she was or ever had been a princess. And there was more, an almost feral quality behind her haunted gaze. Lionheart found himself swallowing back fear. "What has become of you, Una?"

"I could ask the same," she whispered.

"No, I mean it." He gazed into her hollow eyes. They held more than weariness and heartache. "There is something odd about your face. Something not—"

Una smiled. It was a mere ghost compared to the smiles he'd known back when he was court jester for her father at Oriana Palace. "Again, I could say the same." She stepped closer and reached her hand to his face. "That beard . . . "

He caught her hand and pushed her away. "This is no time for jokes."

She withdrew, wrapping her arms about herself. The winter wind blew sharply; she must be freezing in those rags of hers. "Then it is true," she said. "You have killed him."

"Killed whom?"

"My jester."

Lionheart swallowed. Then he said, "I don't know what you're talking about."

"Oh, Leonard!" She tried to touch him once more, but he backed away and turned from her.

"I'm not Leonard, Princess Una," he said. "I thought I told you that."

The girl said nothing for a long moment. Then, in a quavering voice she asked, "Where did you go?"

"Here, obviously. Back to Southlands."

But the girl shook her head. "You know what I mean."

"I don't!" he growled, clenching his fists. "I don't know what you're talking about, and I'm not sure you do either. You aren't speaking rationally."

"Leonard—"

"That is not my name, and I wish you wouldn't use it!" His head throbbed suddenly at the sound of his own voice. How far had he fallen that he could bring himself to speak so cruelly to Una? Una, who had laughed at his antics. Who had provided him with shelter when he was in need. Who had so innocently, so carelessly, given him her heart. He hated himself.

Get rid of her! whispered the Dark Lady.

"I did exactly what I told you," he said wearily, unable to meet the tattered princess's gaze, "went exactly where I said I would, back . . . How long ago was that? Many months! I left your home and traveled directly down here, just as I had purposed while enjoying your father's hospitality."

"And you fought the Dragon?"

Her voice was like a knife in his gut.

"Killed him, even?"

She was close to him now. For a moment, he no longer saw the dark hollows under her eyes. He saw only the sorrow . . . sorrow, mingled with faint hope. She reached out to him again. "Please tell me, my prince." He backed away and leaned against the bridge railing, drawing long breaths. But she followed him, standing close, with her thin hand resting beside his. "Tell me how it happened."

Lionheart struggled to collect his thoughts. What could he say? He could not tell her how it had truly happened. Of course he had his reasons, and who would judge him if that person ever once stood in his shoes? But these words sounded cheap even in his mind. He could not speak them.

"The Dragon was gone by the time I arrived," he said, which was true enough, "leaving my kingdom in ashes, my people rendered near helpless with fear, my father near crazy with sorrow."

"You never saw the Dragon?"

He could not meet her gaze. "Don't think it's been easy. I maybe didn't fight a monster, but the work I've had to do, the blood, sweat, and tears I've poured into rebuilding my people, and will have to keep pouring out for years to come before we'll ever reach our former—"

"You never saw the Dragon?"

He whirled upon her then, his teeth grinding, his eyes wide. "Aren't you listening to me? It was gone by the time I got here."

"That's not what he said."

Lionheart felt the blood drain from his face. Looking at her, he thought that he gazed into the eyes of the Dragon himself. He shuddered and could scarcely find breath to speak. "What?"

"He said you made an agreement." The girl's voice was low as she spoke. Low and hot. "That he wouldn't kill you and would let you return home if . . . if what? What was your side of the bargain?"

She knew. By the Silent Lady, by everything holy and unholy, she knew already! That's why she'd come.

Your dream, my darling, said the Lady. Her fingers grasped inside his mind.

"Una, your voice . . ." he stammered, inwardly cursing how he trembled as he spoke. "What are you saying? Of whom are you speaking?"

"You know whom I mean."

Both her hands latched hold of his arm. Heat seared through the cloak, through his fine clothing, all the way through his skin down to the bone. He yelped and shook her off.

"You burn!" he cried. It was then he knew beyond doubt what had happened. But he could not admit it even then. He forced the thought away with a sickening wrench and said, "Una, are you ill?"

"Yes," she whispered. It was a snake's hiss. "Yes, I am. What was your side of the bargain, Lionheart? When the Dragon agreed not to kill you?"

"You're babbling nonsense," he growled, pressing into the bridge railing. "I've made no bargains with anyone. I came here, just as I told you. Why don't you listen?"

"No bargains?" She stared at the boards of the bridge. Lionheart silently prayed she would not turn those eyes upon him again. "What about the bargain you made with me?"

His mouth was too dry to speak.

"You asked me to trust you," she said. "You asked me to trust you, Lionheart."

"I shouldn't have said that." His voice rasped in his throat. "I must have forgotten. But I should never have said that or anything of the kind to you." He rubbed a hand down his face, struggling again to breathe. What was that smell? Like the poison of the Dragon seeping up from the foul water in the ditch. "And your ring," he said. "The one you so generously lent me. I'd almost forgotten that as well. I will pay you back for it. I promise."

He could never give it back to her. It was long gone from his keeping. Ever since he had offered it to the Dragon in exchange for his own life.

"You promised you'd return." The air was hot when she spoke.

"If I did, I shouldn't have," he said, still struggling to get the words out. "I should have known my obligations would keep me here."

"And her?"

Lionheart grimaced. Then he forced himself to try to look into the girl's eyes. She turned from him. If only he could tell her what he thought! If only he could explain—

You have your dream, sweet one! said the Lady. *Don't lose hold of it!*

"I am going to marry her, Una," Lionheart said. "I had no right to say any of those things I said to you. I am ashamed of any implications I made. They were foolish, thoughtless—"

"Which gives you a right to unmake them now?"

The sun passed behind a cloud as if even his golden eye could not stand to watch the two upon the bridge. Lionheart shivered inside his cloak.

"You asked me to trust you," said the girl.

"I take it back!" Lionheart flung up his hands. "Things change, Una. People change. Can't you get that into your head? My promises to her are good, unlike any I might have made to you." What a lie! But his whole life was a lie now, so what difference did it make? "I made them after winning back my kingdom, under my true name, not in disguise as a . . . as a Fool. As a lackey cleaning the dirty floors of those who should have been my peers! I am not ashamed of any promises I have made to her."

The girl reeled back as though he'd struck her. "You are ashamed of those you made to me?"

"Una—"

"You are ashamed of me?"

"Don't put words in my mouth!" He allowed anger to take over now. Anything to hide the fear and the horror he felt. "I am ashamed of that whole period of my life, that degrading, despicable—"

"You never fought the Dragon."

"No, I didn't."

There. He had said it. But even then, he dared not face the truth of it. "And there's no shame in that," he growled. "I must do what's best for my kingdom. That includes not being devoured by monsters. Can you understand that? My people need me alive, not roasted."

"You never fought the Dragon."

"I told you, Una, sometimes plans change. I'm sorry, but—"

"It isn't enough."

"I can't help that!"

"You never fought the Dragon."

"No." He set his jaw and squared his shoulders. "And I won't."

She looked at him.

Her lips drew back from her teeth. The gums were red as blood. The teeth were long, sharp fangs.

Before he could make a sound, she was upon him, striking at him with an arm that was covered in scales and tipped in razor claws. He flung himself to one side, knocking her arm away as he went, and she careened forward, staggering, doubled over in great pain. She heaved as though vomiting, and a great billow of flame spilled from her mouth.

Fire engulfed the bridge at her feet. Fire filled Lionheart's vision, surrounding the distorted face of the princess. Then she lost all trace of humanity, and a young dragon stood before him.

Lionheart screamed and fell flat on the bridge as a spurt of fire lanced the air over his head. Then he pushed himself up on his hands and knees, backing away as the dragon that had been Una rose up on its haunches and black wings arched on either side of its awful face. "Una!" he shouted.

"You never fought the Dragon." The monster's voice was harsh and full of fire, yet he still heard traces of Una deep inside. Smoke rolled between the long fangs, full of dank poison. "Will you fight me now? Will you kill *me*?"

He was paralyzed in her shadow as she loomed over him. Perhaps he tried to scream. Perhaps he tried to move. But his muscles constricted and would not do as he bade them. He lay helpless before her.

She lowered her head, the fire in her eyes like two ovens melting his face. "Won't you try, my prince?"

With a last effort of will, he flung his arms over his head, allowing the cloak to take the brunt of the heat. This small relief gave him the strength he needed to crawl, and he scrambled to escape. But she caught him from behind and pressed him down flat. A gleaming claw grazed his cheek, like a dagger of polished obsidian. The bridge groaned beneath their weight.

"You killed him," growled the young dragon, embers spilling between her teeth and searing his face. "You killed my Leonard, Prince Lionheart, killed him cruel as murder. But you won't fight the Dragon. *Coward!*"

Lionheart relaxed. His death was certain, and he could no longer struggle against her. He lay like a limp doll beneath her claw, waiting for the fire to strike.

But instead, he heard—like water striking the flames and bursting in cool relief across his mind—birdsong. And in that instant between life and death, he heard words in the song:

I am coming for you.
Wait for me.

The song struck them both with the sharpness of a sword. The dragon raised her head and roared, bellowing flames and agony to the frozen sky. Then black wings tore the air, lifting the monster from the bridge and carrying her off into cold, iron clouds.

So he would live another day.

Lionheart lay amid the wreckage of the dragon's wake.

He would live his death of a life.

"Leo! Leo, no!"

Hands plucked at his sleeves, his shoulders. Through the numbing haze of the smoke, Lionheart thought he saw a wafting veil. "R-Rosie?"

"Leo, I'm so sorry!" Rose Red cried. She wrapped her arm behind his lolling head and neck, grabbing hold of his shoulders. With a grunt of effort, she hauled him into a sitting position. "I'm so sorry!" she repeated. "I came as fast as I could, but I couldn't find her, and they wouldn't let me through the gates, and I only just came . . . oh! I thought you were goin' to get it!"

Lionheart coughed violently. His stomach heaved and contracted at the stench all around him.

"We've got to get you out of here." Rose Red shook her head as though to clear her own mind. Then she braced herself on her stumpy legs, strained a little, and lifted Lionheart to his feet. He vaguely recalled in his stupor how, from the time they were children, she'd always been able to toss him around like a rag doll. Such amazing strength she had! "Put your arm round my neck. That's right. Now this way."

They moved awkwardly, and Rose Red shielded him as they went from the licking flames. Lionheart wondered distantly how much she had overheard and was grateful that she asked no questions. She half carried him from the bridge and out of the smoke that was rising in a tall column to the sky, a memorial to the young dragon's presence.

"Come on, Leo." Rose Red spoke in a soothing, encouraging voice. "Let's get you back to—"

She broke off, freezing in place.

The dragon's smoke had served as a signal. A large crowd of city folk, their terrified faces contrasting horribly with their merry clothing, approached with makeshift weapons in hand. They too paused, hundreds of frightened eyes taking in the sight of their singed prince in the arms of the veiled chambermaid.

Then someone shouted:

"Demon!"

5

THE CRY WAS TAKEN UP.

"Demon!"

"Friend of dragons!"

"Monster!"

As the shouts rose, the courage of the people rose as well. They swarmed the prince and the girl, dragging them apart. "No!" Rose Red cried, trying to cling to Lionheart. "Help him! He's hurt—"

Lionheart, his head full of smoke and fire, held tight to Rose Red without thinking and shouted at those who struck her. But his strength had left him, and before he had time to react, she was pulled from him. Others stood around him, supporting him and saying, "Are you hurt, Your Highness? Did she harm you?"

He shook himself, staring after the mob into which Rose Red had disappeared. They were flowing toward the city gates. He struggled to pull himself into full consciousness. "What are they doing?"

"They'll hang the little beast at last," someone said. "She's bewitched our land long enough."

It took a moment for the words to fit inside his brain. Then he shouted. Energy surged through him and he burst from the arms of those who would help him and raced after the mob. With speed he did not know he possessed, Lionheart caught up with the tail end of them, bellowing for all he was worth. "Unhand that girl! Do you hear me? Unhand her, I say!"

But the crowd was beyond hearing now. They flowed back into the city and round to the city gates, climbing the stairway to the top of the southern wall. In an older, crueler age, Southlands had hanged its criminals from this wall, a gruesome welcome to all those who would enter the Eldest's City. This practice had been abandoned within the last two generations. But the people had not forgotten.

Lionheart beat at the heads of those in front of him, desperate to force his way through the throng. Some thought to fight back, and he received a punch in the eye and a cut lip before the terrified townsfolk recognized their prince and disappeared as quickly as possible. But he could not break his way through; he could not find Rose Red.

He saw a guardsman standing on the fringes of the mob, surrounded by a cluster of soldiers. They uncertainly held their weapons ready. Lionheart raced to the captain, shouting, "Send your men! Cut down these fools and find the girl!"

"Your Highness," the captain said, his face pale, "they want a hanging, and a hanging they'll get. We don't want more dragons in these parts."

"Dragons?" The prince lunged forward and wrested the sword from the captain's hand. Grabbing the man by the cloth around his neck, Lionheart pushed him against the wall and pressed the blade against his throat. "By all the powers of Death and Life-in-Death, if you won't send your men, I'll cut out your heart and feed it to the dogs!"

The captain gasped an answer, and Lionheart backed away, releasing his hold. He held on to the sword and plunged into the mob. He heard the captain give a shout, and suddenly Lionheart was flanked by soldiers. They pressed through the crowd, and the people, seeing the weapons, parted and let them by. Lionheart thought he would smother in that mass of hatred and blind fear, but he pressed on up the stairs, his sword blade forward to plow a path. The stairs up the wall were narrow, and he feared he would never make it through in time. Fire still blazed in his mind, battling with the cold voice in his head that whispered, *She doesn't matter. Hold on to your dream! She doesn't matter, my darling.*

"She does!" he roared. "Out of my way, you devils!" He knew it was hopeless. How could he gain the top of the wall before they flung Rose Red over the side?

Just when he thought he must give up, another voice spoke, drowning out the mob's din, the fire, and the dark whispers of the Lady. It was a voice he recognized.

Make way, it sang.

The crowd before Lionheart parted. With a last burst of energy, he reached the top and found himself face-to-face with a burly man—a butcher, by the stains on his hands—and a bearded merchant, and several other self-appointed leaders of the mob. One of them was twisting a thick noose. The butcher held Rose Red by the shoulders, driving his fingers into her collarbone.

Just as Lionheart gained the top of the stairs, they tore the veil from her face.

Lionheart stared once more into those hideous, moon-wide eyes set in a craggy, bald head. The skin was pasty as dead fish but harder than granite, the jaw set with jutting teeth. For a moment, Lionheart faltered. He gazed into the awful eyes of his childhood friend and shuddered.

She bowed her head.

Lionheart raised his sword and pointed it directly at the butcher's chest. "Let her go," he said.

"Your Highness," the butcher said without loosening his grip, "the demon must die. She let a dragon into the city. Everyone knows she's a dragon herself, or a witch. We can't have her betraying our land no more!"

The man with the noose stepped forward and started to place it over Rose Red's head. She screamed, her dreadful eyes rolling. Without a thought, Lionheart swung his sword and cut the rope. It fell, frayed, upon the stone walkway. By now the soldiers had broken through to the top, and they stood behind Lionheart, weapons upraised.

"Let her go," Lionheart repeated and stepped closer, resting the edge of his blade just below the butcher's ear. "Am I prince or not?"

"Your Highness!" The butcher's eyes were defiant, his teeth gnashing.

"Your Highness, she's bewitched you! Everyone knows it. Let us hang her and save you—"

"I'll kill you," Lionheart said, fire seething in his lungs. He had yet to slay a man in cold blood but had no doubt that in another few seconds he could and would. "I'll kill you, man."

The butcher stared into his eyes, gulped, and released Rose Red. She fell upon her face, gasping, and crawled to Lionheart, wrapping her arms around his feet. He knelt and touched her back protectively but kept his sword upraised and his gaze fixed on the butcher.

"The people won't stand for it!" the bearded merchant cried, spraying spit in his bluster. "They won't stand for her to live anymore! You're not thinking clearly for her spells, but it's the truth we're telling you!"

Lionheart did not let his sword shift from the butcher, but his gaze turned to the merchant. "There will be no hanging," he said. "Not by you."

"The people won't stand for her to go on working her evil on the land," someone in the crowd cried. "We've seen one dragon already today. How many more will she bring?"

"You escaped those five years, prince!" someone else shouted. "You don't know what it's like."

"Friend of demons," someone muttered, and more evil murmurs rippled through the crowd until the sound was thunderous.

The soldiers behind the prince moved into a protective circle around him. The captain said, "You'll have to give her up, my prince. I don't think I can protect you if they take it into their heads to swarm."

"Traitors!" Lionheart snarled.

"That's what they're calling you," someone behind him said.

Lionheart whirled around, his eyes flashing murder. "Who said that?" he cried. "Who voices such treason?"

He saw long faces and shifting eyes, but no one spoke up. The captain said, "You're on dangerous ground, Your Highness. Walk carefully, now."

Lionheart bared his teeth and gripped his sword until the veins of his hand stood out. Rose Red, clinging to his feet, sobbed, her shoulders heaving. But suddenly she looked up and said, "Leo, please, do what you must."

"There will be no hanging today!" Lionheart declared. He stepped away from Rose Red and out of the circle of soldiers, leaping up onto the balustrade along the edge of the wall and balancing there precariously so that the people below could see him. "There will be no hanging!" he bellowed. "We will bring the accused to the mayor's hall for fair trial and there decide what is to be done with her. In accordance with the law." He raised his sword above his head. "Your prince has commanded!"

With that, he climbed back down, suddenly pale and dizzy. He knelt and took hold of Rose Red's elbow, hauling her to her feet and, with the guardsmen surrounding them, marched her back down the stone steps, through the mob and the streets of the Eldest's City. The crowds were crushing all the way to the mayor's house, but word had spread. By the time they reached the house, King Hawkeye, Daylily, Baron Middlecrescent, Foxbrush, and all the court who had come to celebrate the prince's marriage were gathered in the courtyard. Hawkeye sat in a great wooden chair upon a dais, upraised so that he could be seen above the swarms of gathered citizens.

Ungentle in his fear, Lionheart pulled Rose Red up on to the dais and said sharply, "Kneel!"

She flung herself on her knees before the Eldest, bowing her head so that her face was hidden. No expression crossed the Eldest's face at the sight of her, but he drew his feet back slightly. He turned to his son. "What is this, Lionheart?"

Lionheart breathed heavily, sweat dripping down his face despite the winter air. His clothing stank of dragon smoke. "The people of Southlands bring accusations against this girl, my servant, and wish to see her tried according to our law."

Hawkeye nodded, the deep lines of his face sagging. "Have the people a spokesman?"

Lionheart whirled on the crowd. "Who among you wishes to bring charges against this girl before your Eldest?"

There was some scuffle, but finally the bearded merchant from the wall stepped forward, wiping his face and removing his hat as he made many bows before the king. "Your Majesty," he said, "my name is Sparrowclaw—"

"Make your accusations, fat one!" Lionheart spat. Hawkeye reached out and touched his arm, gently drawing him back. "Hush, my son. Let the man speak."

The merchant wiped his face again with a lace-edged kerchief, but he made his voice loud enough to ring through the courtyard. "Your Majesty, my Eldest, everyone knows this girl—this creature—before you is a demon. For years the people of Southlands have been uneasy knowing that she resided within your House . . . at your great mercy, of course. But how can one look at her and fail to see the goblin she is?"

Rose Red remained bowed in a lump before the Eldest, her forehead pressed into the wooden slats of the dais as the merchant continued to say his piece. "Before the years of our imprisonment, all Southlands was concerned by the favor given this person by the prince. 'Twas said she ensorcelled him, serving in his own private chambers for who knew what ends? Then, as you know, sir, she called the Dragon to our land. Did we not all see the way our Enslaver fawned over the girl? She alone of all our people did not suffer from his poison. She alone could cross the bridges. We may have been captives, Your Majesty, but we were not blind! We may be commoners, but we are not stupid!"

"Ignorant dogs—" Lionheart hissed, but his father spoke more sharply this time. "Silence, boy."

"Five years, Your Majesty!" the merchant cried. "Five years of slavery, of fear, of nightmares!" The crowd rumbled in response, all those merrymakers clad in their festive best for the wedding celebration, their faces scarred with past fears and present hatred. "Five years," the merchant continued, made brave by the support he felt about him, "which Prince Lionheart escaped! He does not understand, Your Majesty. This witch has clouded his mind!"

Lionheart brandished his sword, but Hawkeye rose and took hold of his arm. "Lionheart, I am still king," he said. "Stand down."

"And today," the merchant continued, "she has brought another dragon into our midst. Did we not all see the monster that flew over our heads just now? Were there not those among us who saw the dragon disguised as a foreign girl, leading our prince from the city?"

People in the crowd cried their agreement. Lionheart paled and took a step back, his face a mask of fury.

"Then who do we find," the merchant went on, "carrying our prince back from this encounter? The demon girl!"

He pointed at Rose Red where she crouched, and the crowd took up their former cry. "Demon! Friend of dragons! Monster! Witch!"

Lionheart felt defeat surrounding him. He turned to his father and spoke with dismay. "Will you not hear her defense?"

Hawkeye nodded, taking a seat once more. He seemed suddenly so much older than he was, ancient and frail. And Lionheart knew that no matter what Rose Red might say, his father would have to honor the wishes of the people.

Cursing bitterly, Lionheart knelt and put an arm across his servant's shoulders. "Rosie," he said. "Dear Rosie, can you stand and give a defense?"

She shook her head.

"Is there no one who can speak for you?" Lionheart ground his teeth. "They will not hear me. They've decided I'm bewitched. But is there anyone else you can ask to stand by you?"

Rose Red slowly sat up and raised her eyes to Daylily. Beautiful Daylily, in a golden gown, a crown upon her hair, furs about her shoulders. Daylily who knew better than anyone all that Rose Red had suffered during the Dragon's reign in Southlands. Daylily, who had seen Death's realm.

The Lady of Middlecrescent gazed back at Rose Red a long, silent moment. Did she recall the shadows of that Netherworld? Did she recall the skeletal throne by which she had sat when Rose Red had come to fetch her back? Did she see only the death of her dreams or, worse still, their fulfillment?

It did not matter. Daylily's gaze shifted from Rose Red to Lionheart and back. Then she bowed her head over her clasped hands and refused to look up again.

Rose Red turned to Lionheart. "No one will speak for me," she whispered.

Lionheart closed his eyes. "What can I do for you then, Rosie? What can I do?" But she had no answer.

The prince stood up and faced his father. "Please, Eldest, you cannot order her death. I tell you she is innocent. She did not bring the Dragon here, nor the creature that we saw today. I know this girl; I've known her a long time. She is loyal and truehearted. And she is innocent; I swear upon my hand."

"But, my son," said the Eldest quietly, "does your word count for anything now?"

Lionheart stared. Of all the blows in his life, that one struck the deepest.

The Eldest shook his head and continued to speak in a low voice that only Lionheart and Rose Red could hear. "You have lost their trust. Don't think I have not seen. And where does that leave me, Lionheart? I am not long for this world, and when I die, I must pass on rule of my kingdom to one who will not be able to lead. For who will follow you now? Does any man in all of Southlands trust you, who abandoned them in their suffering, who did not return until the danger was past?"

Tears of rage filled Lionheart's eyes, burning more than dragon fire. "It wasn't like that, Father! You know it wasn't!"

"What I know or don't know matters little," said Hawkeye. "What the people, your subjects, *believe* is what matters now." He shook his head and stood once more, stepping around Rose Red and pacing to the end of the dais. He raised his hands, commanding the attention of all assembled in that yard. "I hereby give to my son, your prince, the duty of passing sentence upon the accused."

Angry mutters filled the yard, and Lionheart, as he looked out upon the crowd, saw the fury on each face. They did not think he would do as they wished. They did not believe he could pass the sentence they required. And what would be his fate if he did not give them their will? The Council of Barons and their cold vote. The loss of his inheritance.

The Lady Life-in-Death stood beside him, an unearthly presence. She whispered in Lionheart's ear. *Your dream, sweet prince. Don't give it up now!*

He turned his gaze from the crowds down to Rose Red. She looked up at him, wretched, pleading, and hopeless. He shivered at the sight of her, and she saw and ducked her face, wrapping her arms over her head. *Do what you must, my darling.*

"What is your decision, Lionheart?" Hawkeye asked.

Lionheart's whole body sagged with weariness. Suddenly he whirled upon the crowd and said in a loud voice, "I sentence the accused to banishment. She shall be sent into the Wilderlands, and should she venture to the high country again, she shall be subject to immediate execution. That is my sentence!"

Rose Red gave an inarticulate moan, and the people raised a great cry. Lionheart firmly took hold of the girl's arm and dragged her to her feet, refusing to look at her. A cart was sent for, and he himself stepped into it and pulled her in after him. Holding his sword at his side and ordering the guards to surround them, they set out through the streets of the Eldest's City to North Gate, which overlooked the deep gorge that created the boundaries of the Eldest's grounds. Garbage and filth flew through the air as they went, most of it striking Rose Red, some smattering across Lionheart's burned garments. He steeled himself against the blows and put an arm around Rose Red as protectively as he could. She trembled in his hold as though she would fall to pieces in a moment.

The cart rolled through the gate, and they came to King's Bridge, vast and incredible and older than the city. Already people lined the edge of its span, as near to the gorge as they dared venture. The driver drove the cart through the crowds and to a halt. Lionheart pulled Rose Red down and escorted her to the gorge.

They gazed down the cliff to the Wilderlands below. The thick-growing trees were like an enormous green serpent snaking its way through the chasm. A small footpath, from centuries gone when the people of Southlands had once dared climb down, was still faintly discernible.

Rose Red continued to tremble, and she clutched suddenly at the prince's arm. "I'll die!" she gasped. "Leo, I'll die!" She wanted to say more, but nothing else would come.

Lionheart rested his hand for a moment on top of hers. "Rosie," he whispered, "what else can I do?"

Then he pushed her from him so that she fell to her knees. "Go!" he cried. "Never return to Southlands." He brandished his sword above his head. The watching crowds fell into a horrible quiet, craning to see what happened.

Rose Red gazed at the prince and his sword, her eyes taking in all of him, that face she had loved, that man she had vowed in her heart to serve unto death. And now she had done so, for in that moment, her heart died. The heart that had loved Prince Lionheart.

She said nothing. She got to her feet, shaking so that she felt she would not be able to make the downward climb. Then she stepped to the edge of the cliff and started down the narrow path. As she disappeared from view, Lionheart and his soldiers, followed by the crush of people behind, stepped closer to the edge to watch her descent. The drop was not so deep here, and though she stumbled, she went quickly, as though fleeing the hounds of hell. The forest below seemed to swell, to creep, grasping, up the rock wall.

"NO!"

A shout like a giant's voice, furious and terrible, rolled across the crowd. Lionheart turned, clutching his sword, and saw the crowds parting as though some monstrous bull tossed them aside in its onslaught. His eyes widened, and he braced himself, sword upraised.

A goat burst through, eyes rolling. She barreled past him and skidded to a stop on the edge of the cliff. Then she bellowed like some enormous beast, her voice echoing through the gorge. And there were words in the animal cry.

"No! Rose Red!"

The girl disappeared into the forest.

The next moment, a sound like the rending of the air itself struck the sky. A sound that could shatter hearts and courage, knocking the people of Southlands from their feet. They sprawled on the ground, pressing their hands to their ears as the sound, which wasn't song but its opposite, seared deep into their brains. And there were words that no one understood. No one, save the goat.

At last!

It was stunning. It was dreadful. It was doom.

Then it was gone.

The goat turned to Lionheart. She lowered her head as though to ram him. Then she stood on her hind legs, and she wasn't a goat at all. A woman wearing a silver breastplate and golden belt from which hung a long knife stood in her place. Her hair was piled in a coiled crown on the top of her head, and her face was fierce. Lionheart gasped in horror.

She took a step toward him, drawing her knife. With a swift motion, she knocked the sword from his hand, and it clattered down into the gorge. She took hold of his throat, and her nails dug into his skin. He could only stare into her eyes.

"Tell me, Leo, are you satisfied now?" Her voice drove into his gut. "Have you any idea what evil you have worked? *Coward!*"

She flung him to the ground and turned to the cliff. Without a care for herself, she hurtled over the edge. Lionheart cried out and crawled forward, looking down. He saw a shaggy goat leaping from rock to rock, until at last she as well vanished into the shadows of the Wood.

The sun set. Darkness descended upon Southlands.

Shivering so hard that he could scarcely draw breath, Lionheart whispered, "What have I done?"

6

D AYLILY SAT ALONE. She was often alone these days, which was a relief. Not a week ago, an expressed desire for solitude would have initiated a rain of protests sometimes too exhausting to ignore. But ever since the wedding week, she had only to whisper a command, and her attendants and ladies-in-waiting scurried from the room with hardly a word. Possibly they felt sorry for her. Possibly they could see from the expression in her eyes that any resistance would cost them dearly. Either way, solitude was no longer so difficult an attainment.

She sat in a parlor on the north side of the Eldest's House. A small fire behind a painted screen cast a glow upon her, yet her skin seemed unable to accept its warmth. She might have been a statue rather than a living person.

Her hands were idle in her lap. There was a time she would have kept them busy with some sort of dainty work appropriate for her status. But these days, she failed to see a point in such things. So her hands remained still, but her mind flew in a stormy rush.

The wedding had been postponed. How could she possibly allow it to continue in the wake of what had happened? How could she stand before all the nobility of Southlands beside a groom who looked as though he'd died though his body kept on living? So she had postponed the service, declaring that they should wait until spring, when new growth and warm air would lift the nation's spirits.

Lionheart had expressed no opinion one way or the other. Since that conversation, they had not seen each other. Five days had passed without any indication of that changing.

Daylily rose and paced away from the fire to the window that overlooked the front courtyard. From this very window she had been the first in the House to see Lionheart return from his five-year exile. Later that same day, he had proposed they wed, and her dream had come true.

Only now, she felt it crumbling once more. Which was more dreadful, she wondered, the life or the death of dreams?

A lone figure stood at the gates. Daylily came out of her dark reverie for a moment, surprised at the interest this unknown person drew from her. There was nothing about him to catch the eye, other than perhaps the unusual manner in which he suddenly appeared in the gate archway. His clothing was fine but unadorned. His face, what she could discern of it from this distance, was neither handsome nor plain. The guards at the gate made no fuss about letting him through. And the way he strode across the courtyard to the doors of the Eldest's House, his shoulders back and his head high, implied lordship. Kingship, even. This man, this simple stranger, was a master of men.

Daylily's heart lurched at that one glimpse. At first, she thought she loved the stranger. Then she believed that, no, she hated him rather. Both emotions were silly. She did not know him. She had never seen him before, would never see him again, most likely.

She saw the doors opened to him and watched as he disappeared inside. The unreasonable hatred she felt for the stranger was much too akin to love to be bearable. Dizziness took her, and Daylily returned to sit by the fire, her head in her hand.

Lionheart stood beside his father's throne in the small assembly room where court was held these days. Construction on the new hall was progressing well, but it would be long before it would be open for regular use. Perhaps by spring . . . in time for the rescheduled wedding.

A shiver ran up Lionheart's spine, and he forced himself to focus on the Baron of Idlewild's man, who had brought a report of Idlewild barony. The Dragon's work had been thorough indeed, and the baron's man begged aid, money to supplement the extra costs of rebuilding—an all too familiar plea.

King Hawkeye deferred to Lionheart on most decisions these days. Popular rumor had it that the Eldest planned to step down from his throne and pass the crown on to his son. Lionheart knew better. He knew his father was simply trying to demonstrate trust in his son, to show by example that Southlands could follow the leadership of its crown prince.

But as Lionheart listened to yet another detailed account of barren fields and poisoned crops, he doubted very much that he could satisfy the needs of his people. No man could. But failure on his part would earn him the name traitor.

After all, he had neither fought the Dragon nor killed the demon.

"Prince Aethelbald of Farthestshore!" the herald at the door announced.

Lionheart looked up from the baron's man, surprised. Sure enough, he saw the tall man in the doorway and knew him at once. The Prince. The man he had met at Oriana Palace, the man who had come courting Princess Una, though she rejected him.

The man who had asked Lionheart to come with him to face the Dragon in Southlands.

The Dark Lady had lain quiet in his mind since that day by the gorge. He always felt her presence lurking behind both conscious and unconscious thought, although her voice was still. But the moment Lionheart clapped eyes on the Prince, it was as though she woke from a deep sleep, raging.

Him! Him!

Her voice was like darts of ice. He winced at the pain.

Hate him! Send him away!

Lionheart's head throbbed as the Prince approached. As though at a distance, he heard his father speaking.

"Greetings, Prince. You have journeyed far, have you not? Farthestshore! I cannot remember the last time I beheld a man from Farthestshore."

The Prince approached the throne and bowed low. "Long life to Your Majesty," he said. "Yes, I have journeyed far."

Hate him! screamed the Lady.

The Prince turned to Lionheart. His face was kind, unbearably so, and the eyes were ancient. The eyes of an immortal, Lionheart realized as they settled on his face. But something more than an immortal. Something altogether without age.

And they saw not only him. Lionheart knew, with a part of his mind that he did not like to acknowledge, that the Prince saw the Lady as well.

"Greetings, Prince Lionheart," said the Prince of Farthestshore.

But no, it could not be! Lionheart shuddered at the shame of anyone knowing how the Lady lurked within him, her voice at once seductive and cold. He shook off the idea and forced his voice to remain calm when he replied. "Strange we had no word of your coming, Prince Aethelbald."

"Not so strange. Few would know the paths I take."

"Do you travel with a large company?"

"I travel alone."

Drive him from your father's house! The Lady's voice filled Lionheart's consciousness. He had never heard her so frantic before. No, that wasn't true. Once before he had heard her speak in this same manic tone, when he first met the Prince in Oriana. When the Prince had asked Lionheart to follow him.

Drive him out! He will destroy you otherwise!

Lionheart stood rock still, determined not to shift under the Prince's steady gaze. He felt exposed, but he held himself together. "Do you seek lodging? Allow us to treat you to the hospitality of Southlands."

"No. I seek a word with you, Prince Lionheart. In private, if I may."

Do not listen to him! Send him away! Kill him!

But, despite the roaring in his head, Lionheart could think of no excuses.

He knew of what the Prince wished to speak, and though he dreaded the conversation, he also knew that there would be no escaping it. "Very well," he said. He bowed to the Eldest. "If you will excuse me, Father?"

Lionheart led the Prince from the assembly room, two attendants trailing behind them. When they reached the door of a smaller audience room, Lionheart bade the attendants wait outside as he and his guest entered. All the while the Lady ranted. But somehow, standing so near the Prince, Lionheart found that her voice receded somewhat. He still heard every word, but they were stifled, distant.

The chamber in which they stood was impressive, with maps on the walls and heavy curtains. Lionheart took a seat in a large chair on the far side of the room but offered no seat to the Prince. "At your pleasure," he said.

The Prince stood in the middle of the floor, his arms crossed, though not in hostility. His steady gaze never shifted from Lionheart. "Have you seen Princess Una?"

Lionheart gulped. This was much more direct than he would have expected. He did not like to answer. He remembered a conversation he had overheard between the Prince and Una in the gardens of Oriana, and knew that the Prince had more than a passing interest in the girl. Did he know, then, about her change? Lionheart did not like to be the one to tell him.

He stalled. "Princess Una of Parumvir?" Foolish! How many princesses named Una could there be?

But the Prince merely responded, "The same."

Lionheart forced himself to meet the Prince's gaze. "What makes you think I would have seen her?"

"You have heard of the situation in Parumvir?"

"Yes," said Lionheart slowly. "Dragon-ridden. And the capital is controlled by the Duke of Shippening now, is that right? A great pity. I liked King Fidel. He was kind to me during my . . . my exile." He was blathering, he knew, and the thought made him angry. He broke off short, then finished, "But that is all far from here, and I have much to occupy my mind in my own kingdom." Why did his every word sound like an excuse?

"Una is missing."

"So I understand."

"She fell in love with you."

A long silence held the room. Light shone through the window, striking the back of Lionheart's chair and falling on the face of the Prince in a golden bath. Otherwise, the room was full of shadows. The voice of the Lady whispered from the various corners, as though she flitted from one shadow to the next, an imprisoned bat struggling for freedom. *Hate him!* she hissed. *Loathe him!*

Lionheart said, "What makes you think that?"

"I guessed."

Lionheart shrugged and tried to keep his voice light. "Well, if it bothers you, I have no intention of—"

"Answer my question," said the Prince. "Have you seen Princess Una?"

Lionheart could no longer hold his gaze. He dropped his head. "Yes, I have. She came here not even a week ago. Alone."

The Prince said nothing.

"At first I wondered how she had come here by herself," Lionheart continued. "But . . . she explained in no uncertain terms."

"She came to you as a woman?"

"Yes. But I saw the change."

The sun moved slowly across the afternoon sky, deepening the shadows in the room. Yet even as it shifted from the Prince's face, his eyes retained the warmth of its glow. Was that pity in his eyes? It made Lionheart sick. He would not be pitied!

"See here," he said, clenching and unclenching his fist. "I am sorry about what became of her. I am. But there isn't a solitary thing I can do about it now, is there?"

Silence. Silence and the cold screams of the Lady.

"A lot of things happened during my exile," he rushed on. "Most of them I wish to forget. She was kind to me when I needed a friend, and . . . and I appreciated her kindness. Perhaps I implied more than I felt, but that is hardly—"

"Did you?"

There was no reproach in the Prince's voice. But in that moment, Lionheart hated him more than anything in the world.

"There was too much!" he cried. "Simply too much to do when I came back. I couldn't very well leave, could I, when my people needed me here? Not all of us are free to go chasing across the countryside after dreams or monsters, Prince Aethelbald. Some of us have responsibilities that must come before our own desires."

"And there was your bargain to consider," the Prince said.

Lionheart gasped. He knew! How could he know? That was a secret too dark and too terrible, but which could not possibly be known to any in this world beyond Lionheart. He found his own mind screaming in a voice just like the Lady's: *Hate him!*

He said, "I don't know what you're talking about."

The Prince shook his head. "But you do, Prince Lionheart. I know that Dragon better than you think. I know the game he plays and the bargains he drives."

"That's none of your concern, Prince Aethelbald."

The Prince turned away. "In that case, let me bid you good day."

Lionheart barked angrily, "And just what do you propose to do now?"

The Prince paused on his way to the door and said, "I journey to the Red Desert."

Lionheart's anger momentarily vanished behind surprise. "Are you mad?" No one ventured to the Red Desert. It was a place of death and desolation, long ago poisoned by the vengeful fires of the dragon known as the Bane of Corrilond. Her poisons, though hundreds of years old, still reeked in those blistering sands. It was a land of dragons, so legend said. It was a land of Death.

Yet the Prince stood there, calm as a clear sky after that wild declaration.

Lionheart shook his head. "You are mad, but I see that you're serious." He sighed heavily. "Do not think that I am unconcerned about all this, Prince Aethelbald. If there is anything I can do to aid you in your quest, please accept my help."

"Come with me."

"What?"

Lionheart knew then that this was what their entire conversation had been about. The Prince of Farthestshore needed no word of Una. He had already known about her change and made his plan to venture into the

Red Desert, the likeliest place for a newly turned dragon to be found. No, he had not come for information.

He had come for Lionheart.

Lionheart recalled a moonlit night, not many months gone, in the gardens of Oriana. He had been merely Leonard the jester then, part-time floor scrubber, without a penny to his name. Nearly five years of exile and hopeless searching for a way to destroy the Dragon had left him with hardly a trace of his own princely heritage.

The Prince of Farthestshore had stood before him in that garden and said, *"Come with me, back to your kingdom. Together we can face the Dragon."*

This memory was worse than all the dragon poison Lionheart had ever breathed—the memory and the regret. What might have happened had he agreed? He would never have taken Una's ring. He would never have groveled before the black King of Dragons and bargained away the heart of his love.

Perhaps he would have fought the Dragon.

"Come with me, Prince Lionheart," said the Prince now, his hand extended. "Come to the Red Desert and help me rescue the princess."

Hate! Kill!

"You . . . you cannot seriously—"

Don't let him lure you from your dream! It is madness what he suggests, and it will destroy you!

Bitterness poured from Lionheart's tongue. "You do realize, don't you, that you cannot enter the Desert and survive? Those who have crossed beyond sight of its borders have never returned. You will die there. I cannot abandon my father and my people now for certain death, as you well know."

The Prince looked sadly at Lionheart. "Then I bid you good day," he said, and turned once more to the door.

A second chance had been offered. And now it was gone.

"Wait," Lionheart said, then paused, uncertain what he was going to say. He felt a desperate need that the Prince not go away thinking ill of him. But what had he to offer now? The words came before he had a chance to think them through. "I will send men with you. I will select them myself—strong men, loyal." He rose, gazing at the back of the Prince's head. "It is all I can give you."

Aethelbald did not look back. "Thank you, Prince Lionheart," he said and left the room.

The attendants in the hall put their heads in, but Lionheart waved them away. "Shut the door," he said. When it closed with a click and he was alone, he slowly took a seat once more.

The Lady's voice returned with all its power. But now the Prince was out of sight, she no longer screamed. She wrapped her cold presence around Lionheart like a comforting mother, crooning.

You did what you had to do.

"I did what I had to do," he whispered.

What other choice could you make?

"What other choice could I make?" He sank his forehead into his hand and shut his eyes tight. "What other choice was there?"

Not two hours after watching the stranger's arrival, Daylily watched his departure from the same window. Twelve horsemen in Southlander uniforms followed behind him, though he remained on foot as before. They passed through the gate and on out of sight, leaving Southlands by ways unknown to mortals.

Daylily stood a long time, gazing at the gateway through which the stranger and the twelve riders had passed. No thoughts formed in her mind at this time, none that she could pin down. Then suddenly she knew, without quite knowing how.

She would never marry Prince Lionheart of Southlands.

7

LIONHEART LABORED DAY IN AND DAY OUT at the desk that had once belonged to his mother. Impossible puzzles were presented to him, swift answers expected. But how was he, magician-like, supposed to conjure wealth that was not to be had? How was he to purify poisoned fields? How was he to force growth in desolate places? Yet the messages poured in, carried by thin couriers from across the land, piling in mountains across his desk. Attendants and assistants did what they could, but he needed to check their work behind them, for mistakes would fall upon his head.

All Southlands watched him, eagle-eyed, waiting for some small misstep from the friend of demons.

Lionheart's eyes glazed over as he skimmed a report from the Baron of Fernrise. The letters shifted about on the page under his tired gaze. They gathered together, forming images in his mind, and he was too tired to shake those images away, too tired even to care. They formed the face of Rose Red.

She was ugly beyond description. But when she passed into the shadows of the Wilderlands, Lionheart thought the last good remnant of Southlands had gone with her.

He startled to himself, shaking. No good in thinking such things! Why go over the past? Overworked, that's what he was. He shook his head and rubbed his eyes with an ungentle hand. If only he could get more sleep at night. Ever since the Prince of Farthestshore left Southlands in company with those twelve handpicked men, sleep had eluded Lionheart. He lay awake for hours each night, wondering where they were. Days had slipped by without a word. But of course, it would be much longer before he could expect news of them. It would take them that long at least to even approach the borders of the Red Desert, should they meet no mishap along the way.

But he wondered even so—had they indeed passed over the Chiara Bay to the mainland and on to the desert? Were they even now within those fiery grounds, searching for the "treasure" Lionheart had sent them to find? Were they even alive?

He took up a new set of messages and slowly broke their seals, determined not to allow the next question to form itself completely. But his hand shook as it wielded the sharp letter opener, and the question came.

Could he have helped had he journeyed with them?

My darling, the voice of the Lady immediately intruded in his mind, alluring and repellant at once. *There was nothing you could have—*

A knock at the door brought Lionheart from his reverie. One of his attendants entered, bowed hastily, and said, "Captain Catspaw has returned!"

"Catspaw?" Lionheart dropped the letter opener. "And the men?"

"All twelve of them."

Then the Prince was not with them. His heart sank, and Lionheart set his shoulders. "Send them to report."

"All of them?"

"All."

Captain Catspaw and the others were admitted a quarter of an hour later, during which time Lionheart had tried to adjust himself into a more princely bearing. He sat by his desk like a king upon a throne, his face grave. The men bowed but cast each other sidelong glances. Some looked guilty; others, willful.

"I'm glad to see you safe, captain," Lionheart said, narrowing his eyes at the lot of them. "What news do you bring? Did you find what you sought in the Red Desert?" But he knew even as he asked the question that they had not.

Catspaw cleared his throat. "Your Highness," he said, "you know we are true men of the Eldest and would serve our king to the utmost of our strength—"

"But?" Lionheart's voice was a low growl. "Would you serve me to the same capacity? Tell me, captain. Did you follow the Prince?"

"Your Highness—"

"Did you?"

Catspaw set his teeth. "That man led us by ways no mortal man should walk. Unnatural Paths! Down into the Wilderlands, and when we came up again at the day's end, we had crossed not only all of Southlands but the Chiara Bay itself without so much as wetting our feet! We were in the hinterlands of Shippening before the sun had set. Shippening!"

Lionheart heard terror in the man's voice as he recounted his tale. He could almost feel sorry for him. He himself had once walked a Faerie Path as a boy. It had not been a pleasant experience.

"Then," the captain continued, "he stood there on the edge of the Red Desert—the heart of dragon country—and he bade us follow him. Right down the Dragon's throat!"

"And?" Lionheart asked coldly.

"Have we not had enough of dragons already, Your Highness? We, all of us, have looked into the Dragon's eyes and seen our deaths. And we were powerless against him! Who of us did not count himself blessed beyond belief when the Dragon left and he found himself still living? Yet this man, not even a Southlander, asked us to follow him back into that poison. That fire. What did you expect us to do?"

"I expected you to obey me. I expect you to obey your prince."

In his anger and fear, Catspaw seemed to have forgotten to whom he spoke, and he shook his head violently. "You did not know those five years of enslavement."

"Cowards!" Lionheart snarled, leaping from his chair, his fists clenched. "What do you know of the Dragon? What do you know of those five years and how I spent them? All of you make me sick!"

Catspaw paled before Lionheart's fury and backed away into the cluster of men. But his voice was belligerent when he said, "Forgive us, Your Highness. We did our best, but we could not—"

"Could not?" Lionheart cried, advancing on them as though he would strike them. They backed all the way to the door. "Would not, you mean. Has the honor of Southlands no claim on your hearts? I promised Prince Aethelbald the help of twelve loyal men, and this is how you serve me?"

"Please, Your Highness—"

"Out of my sight!" the prince roared and all but chased them from the room. "Don't let me see your faces again! Out!"

They scurried away, some muttering, others silent as shadows, and the door shut behind them. A second later it crashed open again as Lionheart himself burst forth and stormed down the hall. Household folk scrambled out of his way at one glimpse of his face, and he, in his rage, saw none of them. He came to his private chambers, slamming doors open and closed.

A chambermaid stood with a handful of cuttings, arranging them in a vase. A plain girl with a snub nose, whose eyes nearly popped from her head at the sight of her enraged prince.

Lionheart stared at her. She stared back, trembling, not knowing what he saw when he looked at her face.

"Out," he said.

She scurried from the room as quick as a mouse.

Lionheart drew the heavy curtains shut, reducing the room to a darkness almost as complete as night with only a small fire to alleviate the gloom. He drew a chair up to it, gazing at the dancing flames as they slowly consumed the kindling and wood.

"Cowards," he growled. Then he leaned forward, his elbows resting on his knees, gazing still more deeply into the fire. How long he sat there he did not know, but the flames were beginning to die, leaving the room as black as pitch.

Shameful, those men. The ever-present Lady wrapped her arms around his consciousness. *You should punish them. Rid yourself of those who will not serve you as they should.*

"I should rid myself of those weasels," Lionheart muttered.

You cannot afford to keep them in your service, my prince. They will only hinder your work.

"I cannot afford to keep men like those in my service."

Rid yourself of them as soon as possible. Just as you did the girl.

Rose Red! Her face returned to his mind, twisted in terror as she crouched on the edge of the gorge. His best, his truest friend. A hindrance. But he had not killed her! He had done his best, hadn't he?

He covered his face with both hands, drew a sharp breath, like a sob. "Get out of my head."

Oh, my sweet prince—

"GET OUT!" He leapt to his feet, tears staining his cheeks. Without a thought, he reached into the dying fire, took up a handful of embers, uncaring how they burned his hands, and flung them into the darkest corners of the room. Anything to chase out that darkness. Anything to chase away that voice. "Get out! Go away from me!"

Silence crept in around him. And that silence spoke in the voice of the Lady.

You are nothing without me.

Lionheart collapsed to his knees, his wounded hands shaking with pain, the fingers curled. Mingled with the silence was another voice, a voice from his memory, full of fire. And from the darkness emerged a figure, black and more real than real, although it was nothing but a memory too.

"Give me her heart, Prince Lionheart, and I will let you live."

How could he have done it? How could he have given it up so easily?

"Leave me in peace!" He pulled at his hair with his burned hands, desperate to escape the memory. But he could not. He saw himself groveling before a great black King. He saw his own hand opening, and a small opal ring dropped from his fingers. His own voice cried, *"It's yours. Take it!"*

The memory faded. Lionheart stood again in the silence of his rooms. The fire had died, leaving the coldness of tombs behind. He blinked back the last of his tears and sank once more into his chair.

The voice of the Lady returned.

You did what you had to do, Lionheart.

"I did what I had to do."

There was no other way.

"No other way."

Now take my hand and walk with me, Prince of Southlands, and I will show you what it means to see your dreams realized.

He looked up into her eyes. They appeared before him in a flash of white, gleaming in the darkness. And her hand, blacker than the shadows in the room, extended to him.

In that moment, the Dragon died.

It was like the shifting of continents, the fall of mountains, the end of worlds. The shock of it rippled throughout the Near World and the Far, and every living thing stopped what it was doing, shivering in terror and awe at they knew not what. Fire burst in their minds, then vanished.

But where Lionheart sat in the darkness of his chambers, the fire did not vanish at once. It grabbed hold of him, plunging him into a dream.

He stands upon an abandoned street in a city he does not recognize. Before him writhes the monstrous form he knows too well, the sinuous limbs and the bat-like wings of the Dragon King. The Dragon lies in the rubble and flames he has made of the city, convulsing in death agonies. Fire rains down upon the world. Lionheart cries out and covers his head, but the flames and ashes fall on him without burning.

All is still for a terrible moment.

Then Lionheart whispers, "I will never fight the Dragon."

"NO!"

The Lady's scream blasts the already ruined city, extinguishing the flames of her counterpart. She stands before Lionheart, between him and the Dragon's dead body. She is as tall as a tree, black as nothingness, save for her streaming white hair, which flows behind her, lashing Lionheart's face like so many knives. He shies away from her, but she takes no notice of him. She strides through the rubble toward the corpse, wringing her hands and screaming.

"NO! You shall not have this victory!"

For a moment, Lionheart thinks she speaks to the dead Dragon. Then he sees, rising from the ashes, another form he knows: the Prince of Farthestshore.

This time it is Lionheart who screams, and he throws himself facedown upon the stones. But he cannot resist looking up again.

The Prince's face is resplendent with an unbearable light that banishes the poison from the air. He speaks to the Lady. "Life-in-Death," says he, "you must let him go."

"No!" The Lady is twice the Prince's height, and her voice is foul with hatred. "You cannot have him!"

Do they speak of the dead Dragon? But no, the Lady turns and in three strides is at Lionheart's side. She plucks him from the stones like a helpless kitten and shakes him. "You cannot have him! He's mine!"

The Prince steps down from the Dragon's carcass and approaches. Lionheart is helpless in the Lady's grasp, yet he can scarcely bear to look at the Prince. He wails and tries to cover his eyes, but his arms hang useless at his sides.

"Let him go," says the Prince.

"I won him. We played our game, my brother and I, and I won him!"

"Let him go."

"He is nothing without me. Nothing! If I release him, he will lose everything he holds dear. His life will be over!"

"Better that than the Life-in-Death you offer," says the Prince. He is unarmed, but the Lady trembles as he strides ever nearer. "Let him go."

With a final shriek, the Lady draws back her arm and flings Lionheart with all her strength. He flies through the darkness, straight toward the carcass of the Dragon he never fought.

Flames leap into his eyes.

Lionheart startled awake when a candle's light shone in his face. He sat up in his chair. The room was stuffy with the curtains drawn, but simultaneously cold without a fire. Daylily stood before him, holding a bronze candleholder with both hands. The flickering flame cast strange shadows on her face, emphasizing the hollows under her eyes.

"Lionheart," she said, "you were moaning in your sleep."

He stood up, straightening his shirt and shaking his head to drive the weariness away. Not that it helped. "What are you doing in here, Daylily?" His voice was thick.

She said nothing at first, merely gazed up at him. Were those tears he saw gleaming in the candlelight? "I've just heard," she said.

"Just heard what?" The memory of his dream remained vivid in his mind. The smoking carcass on the street.

"My father told me." Her hand trembled, and the candle flame flickered. "The Council of Barons has been called."

Her words drove everything else from Lionheart's head. He stood still, gazing into those blue eyes of hers, and for a moment he thought how beautiful she had once been.

"That's it, then," he said.

"I . . . I'm afraid so." She licked her lips. Was she uncertain what to say? Daylily was never uncertain. It was not part of the pattern that made up the Lady of Middlecrescent. Yet there was hesitancy in her eyes as she put out a trembling hand and touched his. "Leo."

He pulled back sharply, stepping out of the glow of her candle, back into the deepest shadows of the room. She took a shuddering breath. When she spoke again, however, her voice was steady. "I cannot marry you now."

The Lady's words returned to him: *He will lose everything he holds dear.*

"Of course not," said Lionheart. He turned his back on Daylily and her candle, his shoulders hunched. "Of course not. I understand."

"Please, Lionheart—"

"Go away now, Daylily." His voice was unnaturally calm. "Go away. Marry Foxbrush. Tell him that I hope he enjoys the task of fixing what cannot be fixed and bearing the blame when it remains broken."

She did not reply. Gliding like a ghost, she made her way to the door, pausing a moment to look back. Then, surprising herself, she said, "You should never have banished Rose Red." Lionheart whirled to face her again, but she could not see his expression in the dark. He could see her, she knew, so she raised her chin, her face set in a calm mask. "You should never have banished Rose Red," she repeated. "If you can, you should find her."

"How can you say this now?" he cried. His voice was piteous rather than angry. It cut her to the heart. "You did not speak for her when she needed you. You left her to the mob's demands, refusing to offer help. You would have let them hang her! You let me . . ."

How could he finish? He dropped his head and let the words die.

Daylily remained as cool as ever. She softly repeated, "You should find her, Leo."

Then she left the room, shutting the door in her wake.

Lionheart, alone in the dark, wrung his burned hands at the door. Curses welled up in his mind, too many to escape his mouth. At last, he cried to the silence, "I did what I had to do! There was no other way!"

But this time, no voice in the silence reassured him.

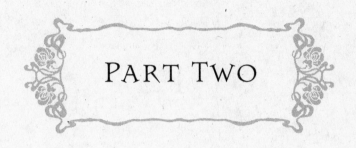

PART TWO

THE OLD BRIDGE

1

IT's tradition," said King Fidel.
"I don't like it," his son replied.

The close confines of the carriage suddenly seemed closer still as the king and his son glowered at each other. They turned away, each looking out a side window. The king's view took in both the distant and not-too-distant towns and villages they passed along the way, and sweeping fields beginning to put forth a show of the harvest to come.

Prince Felix's view was of the sea. Gaheris Road skirted the seaside cliffs, offering travelers a breathtaking vista of tossing waves, of distant sails, and of inescapable bigness. Storm clouds gathered on the horizon.

These were as nothing compared to the storms brewing within Felix's breast.

"It's not a matter of like or dislike," Fidel said. He kept his eyes firmly fixed upon the landscape, careful not to look at the boy. He was afraid he might say something he would regret if he did. In the last two months—ever since Una's wedding—Felix had grown progressively more impossible.

He was inexplicably moody, liable to shout and storm one moment and sink into still more sinister sulks the next.

Rather like now. Fidel drew a long breath, reminding himself that lads of nearly fifteen were often a bit turbulent, and it befit him as king to treat his son with kind but firm resolve. Or at least not to shout.

"It's not a matter of likes or dislikes," he said in what he hoped was a mild tone. "Tradition is what tradition is. Now, of all times, we need to give our people a sense that the security of the past will continue through the present and beyond."

"That doesn't even mean anything," Felix snarled, watching a ship faintly silhouetted on the far horizon. For some reason, he felt an overwhelming desire for the gathering storm to rise up and swallow it whole. Perhaps if he willed destruction hard enough, he could somehow make it happen. His eyes, unseen by his father, narrowed to slits.

"Perhaps, my son," said Fidel through his teeth, "you are refusing to understand the meaning."

"I don't see," Felix said, "how the name of a new palace makes any difference to anyone. It doesn't change anything that happened. It won't make the people feel more secure. And I don't like it."

"The kings of old have always named their palaces after their sisters," Fidel replied. "Amarand, Oriana . . . both of them named for the sisters of the ruling kings of the day. You will be King of Parumvir soon enough. It will please your subjects if you follow the tradition of your forefathers." Here at last, Fidel turned to face his son, who was slumped down so far in the carriage seat that one would never guess the gangly heights to which he had grown in the last few months. He would be a tall man, and handsome too, once he caught up with himself. But Felix's face was almost unrecognizable to his own father.

Unrecognizable but also familiar. Dangerously familiar. With the familiarity of things that should be forgotten yet nevertheless linger and press upon the memory. Something in the gleam of the boy's eyes, something like fire, something like . . .

Fidel shook that thought away, unwilling to dwell on it. The danger was past. Prince Aethelbald had delivered them all from the Dragon's evil fire and smoke. Now was the time to focus on rebuilding, on reestablishing his kingdom. Fidel must not start imagining new enemies.

Especially not in the face of his son.

"Lights Above, boy!" Fidel sighed, hoping his voice sounded kinder than he thought it did. "I don't know why we are even arguing about this."

"You're king," Felix growled. "Name the new palace after *your* sister."

"I have no sister," Fidel replied coolly. "Don't be difficult."

Felix did not respond. He licked his lips, hungrily watching the distant ship. The storm clouds darkened, far away yet so thick and threatening that if he wanted to, he could believe they were smoke, roiling, torrid smoke.

"Are you listening to me, son?"

Harsh eyes snapped to meet the king's. For a moment, Fidel drew back, and his face went deathly white. But the next moment, he shook himself, swallowing back curses. It was only that the events of the past winter were still so near. One must take care not to dwell upon them but to look forward to the future. Even a future including one dreadfully ill-mannered son.

But not a dragon. The Dragon was dead.

Fidel released a breath he had not realized he was holding. "Well?" he demanded.

"What about the Smallman King's palace?" Felix said. "Didn't he live in the House of Lights?"

At this juncture, Fidel hated to concede anything. Yet, after swallowing several hasty retorts, he responded, "True enough. However, according to the Chroniclers, he built onto the House of Lights, and in that new portion he lived and held court. It was called Letania."

Felix's eyes flashed. "Letania wasn't his sister."

"No. She was his wife."

"Why don't we name the new palace for my wife, then?"

"Well, Felix," Fidel said, his voice sinking to a growl despite his best efforts, "if you had a wife, that idea might possibly come under consideration, mightn't it? Unfortunately, as I hope to raise the walls sometime within the next five years, well before you're married, the matter will need to be decided considerably sooner than that!"

And each turned back to his window.

Silence reigned within the carriage. Without, the world was alive with the jangle of harnesses, clop of hooves, and rumble of coach wheels. Fidel traveled with a large entourage on his return journey to what had once been his kingdom's capital city, Sondhold by the Sea. Many months had passed since the king was forced to abandon Sondhold during the Dragon's occupation. Rebuilding of the city itself was already begun, but it would hearten the people of Sondhold to see their king and to know that he would not abandon them in the aftermath of destruction.

Felix sighed but could not relieve the heaviness in his chest. Everything about life these days was aftermath, he thought. Nothing could ever be what he had once believed it to be. Even as prince of this nation, he was helpless. Any existing protections were flimsy, likely to be stripped away in a moment.

Better to be the terror than to be terrorized, he thought. And with that thought, the storm in his breast roared like flame.

Why was he so angry?

Rarely these days did he stop to consider the source of the wrath constantly threatening to erupt from inside him. When the question arose, he could always blame it on someone else. It was the Dragon's fault for destroying the life he knew. It was his sister, Una's, fault for marrying and leaving him behind. It was his father's fault for making him live and pursue his studies in wretched Glencrocus City.

Dragon's teeth, it could even be that cat Monster's fault! The blasted creature hadn't been seen since the day of Una's wedding. And while Felix would have died before admitting it, he missed his sister's furry companion, who had also been his companion and combatant the last many years. Una had gone away, abandoning Felix to a world that was no longer safe. Why did that dragon-eaten cat have to go too?

He ground his teeth, his mind whirling with unfocused blame. Then a thought came seemingly from nowhere but with a flare of furious clarity. *It's Imraldera's fault. She didn't heal me.*

Felix blinked, and his tense jaw relaxed even as his brow wrinkled. Who was Imraldera?

He could picture a face dimly in his mind's eye. Had he invented it? A dark, lovely face; a pair of black eyes; a worried smile . . . and he thought he heard a voice that might have been a memory or might have been a dream.

"If you do not stay and receive the full healing I can give you, the poison will pump through all your veins, and work its way into your heart. And you will die."

A searing pain shot through his consciousness. He gasped and clutched his head.

"What's wrong?" Fidel asked, turning with surprise to his son.

"Nothing!" Felix snarled. His mouth felt hot, as though liquid fire boiled in his brain and dripped down his throat. His stomach churned and heaved, and he grimaced again.

Then everything calmed. The fire reduced, and with it went the image of the dark-eyed woman. Felix breathed deeply, once more turning to the window and the brewing storm out at sea. He wondered if it would drive inland. Remembering suddenly, he searched for the ship he had been watching. It was gone. Perhaps it had sailed to safety. Perhaps he had only imagined its existence.

Everything had changed. Felix had changed. He wondered if he would ever find himself again. Approaching manhood stared him in the face, and the terror of that sight made him writhe with fury—fury so terrifying that he could scarcely breathe.

Felix hunched down in his seat and watched the gathering storm. And the king's entourage drew near to Sondhold and the ruins that marked the top of Goldstone Hill.

Somewhere, not too far away, something smelled both the anger and the fear. It also smelled the sorrow. Sorrow as pungent as the stench of dragon poison, strong though buried deep in the blood of the mortal boy's heart.

It walked in silence in that place between the worlds. Its skin quivered like moonlight glancing off black water. Time was an unknown quantity in its life. The worlds in which it moved and breathed consisted always of Now.

There were moments when, through the heavy veil that always surrounded it, it glimpsed the moon and dimly recalled a Then before Now.

But though it held memories of a thousand centuries, it had never known the breath of Time.

Its ageless voice, the voice of the stars come down from the sky, called. It would not step outside the Wood into the Near World of men. But it sent its voice across the miles, for what are miles to such a being? It sent its voice flying to reach the ears of that boy who sorrowed without knowing of his loss. To a mind full of poison and half broken.

Come to me.

The entourage paused at the high point of Gaheris Road to look down upon Sondhold. Felix opened the carriage door, ignoring his father's protests, and hopped out, running to the crest of the road. From there, he could see the spreading city by the ocean's edge. He could see the docks and the market square, the streets bustling with life.

But it was only an illusion. Sondhold held no life, only ghosts.

Felix trembled, forcing himself to see what was truly before his eyes. The docks, still intact but forlorn without a single anchored ship, stretched like fingers into the ocean. The city itself looked as though a meteor had struck its center and blasted disaster all around. What had once been a thriving market square was black emptiness; all the buildings that remained standing were phantom structures, gutted and lifeless.

"It's a hard sight, son," said King Fidel, coming up beside Felix. "But look!" The king smiled and pointed. "See how far they've already come with the rebuilding."

But Felix could not see what his father saw. He could not see the many laborers hard at work below; he could not see the signs of rebirth. He saw only what the Dragon had done. When he breathed, he did not draw fresh sea air with a promise of coming rain into his lungs. He breathed only dragon smoke.

It was here the Dragon had died. But the poison in Felix's veins roared, *He will never truly die!*

Felix gasped, and his face was ashen. He turned away from the sight.

Fidel, frowning, dared not reach out to him but asked, "Are you unwell? Shall we hasten down to the house prepared for our stay?"

The young prince shook his head. "You go down," he said, his voice more subdued than it had been earlier. His eyes lifted to the near sight of Goldstone Hill, which rose above the city. And beyond the hill was the great, dark expanse of the Wood.

Felix licked his dry lips. "I think I'd like to ride a bit," he said. "Where is my horse?"

Fidel, just as happy to escape his son's unpleasant company for a spell, sent for Felix's mount. As the company from Glencrocus continued on its way, Felix rode his little mare out from among the rest. He waited at the edge of the high road until they had all passed on down. The wind from the approaching storm stirred his fair hair, but otherwise he might have been made of stone.

Come to me.

The voice, whispering without words, called to his poisoned blood.

Grinding his teeth, Felix drove his heels into his mare's soft flanks, driving her down the road toward Goldstone Hill.

2

The gates of Oriana were twisted and broken, melted by dragon fire.

Felix dismounted and left his horse outside as he approached the wreckage. The fire inside him pulsed with the pain of tears, though without their relief. There could be no returning to Oriana, he knew. Not really. The home of his birth was destroyed beyond recall. His father even now made plans to tear down its ruins and to erect a new palace in its place, a symbol of Parumvir's renewed life and health. Felix hated the thought. Hated it especially because he knew it was the right thing to do.

Though the wind was cool upon his face in the deepening gloom, he sweated and was obliged to wipe his brow. Even the memory of the Dragon's fire was too hot. Beyond the gates, the courtyard, torn up by enormous claws, strewn with broken stone, caused Felix to recoil. He let out a shuddering breath and forced himself to continue on his way across the yard, approaching the palace itself.

It was like approaching a giant rotted corpse.

The marble stairs leading to the front entrance were melted. Felix used his hands to climb up them to the doors, which sagged on their hinges, threatening to fall at any moment. He steeled himself and stepped inside.

The hall within was dark. Windows were filmed over with dust and soot, admitting no light. Candle sconces along the walls, those that had not been torn away by looters, hung empty, and shadows gathered everywhere in thick masses. A ghostly wind sighed down the empty corridors like a lost soul.

Not a stick of furniture remained, no rugs and no ornaments other than the few remaining sconces. Felix recalled that his sister's husband had traveled to Oriana after the Dragon's death to collect for Fidel all his treasures and possessions, those that had not been destroyed by fire and smoke. Anything he left behind had since been carried off. Felix wondered what sorts of fools would dare pillage this tomb-like place to steal poisonous objects.

Felix walked through the halls, stepping carefully so as to make no sound, his breath shallow and light. Every so often, he would breathe in the scent of dragon. It was enough to send his heart careening, his veins pulsing with either fear or expectation. A strange sensation, not altogether unpleasant. His limbs shook, and he put out a hand to support himself on the wall.

And suddenly, he found himself wondering, *Where am I?*

His memory was gone. He stood in the great house of his birth, and it was as foreign to him as a stranger's abode. The venom in his blood surged with fright. What was he doing in this ghastly place, alone? Then he shook his head, still more confused. Why would he be anything other than alone? He had no one. He was no one.

His hand rested on something that drew his eye.

Felix turned and saw an old painting, its frame gilded but dirty with ash. It was the only piece that remained on the long gallery wall, but in the murk and gloom, he could not make out the images it depicted.

Curious, Felix took it down and carried it to the nearest chamber. This had once been the family sitting room, where Fidel and his children would retire for an hour or two following supper, just the three of them. When Felix stood in the doorway, he had a flash of recall. He saw himself sitting by the fire, playing a game of sticks and pebbles. He saw his sister watching him from a nearby chair, languorous Monster draped purring across her lap. He saw his father, dozing and pretending not to. He saw many a childhood evening all rolled into one.

Then it was gone. The room was stripped of its furnishings, still more stripped of its memories. Felix stood, his shoulders bowed with a heaviness he could not explain. The room seemed grotesque to him, but for no reason he could understand.

The poison ate at his brain. And the faces of his sister and his father melted away.

Remembering why he had come, Felix took the picture to a window. The curtains were drawn, but he pulled them back in a shower of dust and, because this window was crusted with ashes on the outside, he undid the latch and pushed it open. The dull light of the overcast day poured into the room, revealing the picture in his hands.

Though the canvas was small, it contained five separate figures. Three of them stood on the shores of a great black lake; the other two were on an island in the center of that lake. The three on the shore all shared the same beautiful face. But one wore a crown while the other two were bound together in chains. On the island, one of the figures lay sleeping on an altar of gold, his hands crossed over his breast. Beside him stood a woman who covered her face with her hands, weeping.

Felix put his nose closer to the picture, squinting as he studied it. Then he pulled back with a gasp, for though the figures were badly painted and disproportionate, he recognized one of them as vividly as though he stood in life before him. The figure sleeping on the altar, the one whose face was a skull-like mask.

The Dragon.

He almost dropped the picture, but somehow his fingers clung on. Drawing a deep breath, Felix muttered, "It's only paint." He forced himself to look again.

And it seemed to him, though he knew it could not be so, that one of the figures moved. The beautiful man wearing a crown turned his head (it must have been a trick of that strange light) and looked at Felix.

Come to me.

"Felix?"

The young prince startled and dropped the picture, which crashed at his feet. He spun about, staring into the shadowed room. Something stood in the doorway. Something . . . rather small.

Then a long-haired orange tomcat, his tail held high, padded into the middle of the room. His face—scarred over where eyes had once been—was unmistakable.

"M-Monster?" Felix said. Then he shook himself. The poison thickened in his veins. The memory of his sister's cat came and went, leaving behind a black hole of forgetfulness. Felix knelt and put out a hand, something he would never have done a year before for his sister's cat, whom he loved to hate. "Nice kitty," he said. "Where did you come from?"

"Nice kitty?" The cat put back his ears, and his pink nose twitched. "Lights Above us, boy, you are in a bad way. You positively reek with poison! It's a good thing you got here when you did."

Felix frowned. His brain was on fire, making it difficult to think. He didn't like cats; he remembered that much at least. And he was almost certain that cats were not supposed to talk, which made this one particularly unappealing. He clenched his teeth and stood up, backing to the window.

"Imraldera sent me," the cat continued, his ears cupping forward as he followed the sound of the prince's footsteps. "She said she thought you would come. She hoped so anyway. She wanted me to be here to meet you." The tip of his tail twitched. "I suppose it's foolish of me to ask, but did you miss me? Not that I missed you, of course."

Felix stared, his addled mind trying to form a thought but failing. Part of him wanted very badly to . . . he wasn't sure. Kick the cat. Smash him. Tear him to pieces.

Burn him.

Come to me.

The voice spoke to his rage. It spoke to his brokenness.

Felix turned and looked out the open window, out into the ruins of the palace gardens. Seven tiers down the hillside, with paths crisscrossing, they boasted now only charred stumps and smoldered statues. And where the gardens ended, Goldstone Wood began.

"Well, I suppose you haven't missed me, then," the cat behind him was saying. "Can't say I'm not a little hurt. After all, one likes to think oneself universally adored, doesn't one? But come now. Are you ready to return to the Haven with me? Eh, Felix?"

Felix climbed through the window and jumped to the ground below.

The cat, startled, leapt to the windowsill and called down to him. His sharp ears heard the sound of the boy scrabbling in the dirt, and then the pound of his footsteps as he raced across the garden. The cat's tail lashed again. "This can't be good," he said. "Perhaps the poison has gone deeper than we thought."

Growling, he sprang down into the garden and sped after the long-legged prince.

The garden was both familiar and terribly foreign. Felix felt terror mounting in him as he saw scenes and statues, images that he should know but which, the moment he recognized them, vanished from his memory. He was losing his mind, and there was nothing he could do to catch hold of it again.

Come to me.

The voice rose from the Wood below. Felix chased after it like a lost traveler pursuing the elusive will-o'-the-wisp. He hurtled down the path, through the seven tiers of garden, and stood at last on the edge of the Wood.

In years past, he and Una had run away to play in Goldstone Wood nearly every day. The people of the palace had told many strange and superstitious stories about that forest, and few liked to venture into its depths. None of their servants dared follow them, which had made it all the more attractive to the young brother and sister. Felix's happiest memories were of the games he and Una had invented during their hours deep within the shadows of those trees, down by the Old Bridge.

"Felix! Wait!" came the voice of the cat, faint now, as though calling from another world.

Everything was gone. The memory of his childhood, the image of his sister's face. All gone. Everything was taken from Felix, and only the Wood remained. He stood on the edge of those tree-cast shadows, staring into darkness. There were no memories now to comfort him.

There was nothing but the voice within.

Come.

Felix passed into the trees and made his way down the path to the Old Bridge.

"Dragons eat that boy," the cat snarled, plunging after him.

No one crossed the Old Bridge.

It was one of those unspoken rules that Felix and his sister had always obeyed. Sometimes they'd dared each other to try, to run across and back, bringing some token—a twig, a leaf, a pebble. But though they both declared themselves willing, neither ever did. They would walk halfway and stand as though they'd struck a wall, silently amassing excuses in their heads that neither was willing to speak. Then they would turn around and return to the safe and familiar side farther up the hill.

But when Felix, reaching the end of his headlong flight, stumbled to the edge of the stream and stood upon the first boards of the bridge, he could not remember Una. Nor could he remember any reason he might not cross this way.

And the voice called him from beyond.

Come to me, child of mortals.

The Wood watched him as he stood there, his hands limp at his sides, his face empty as the memories played through his mind and vanished. There was nothing but trees, cool and peaceful, rustling their leaves above his head in sweet whispers.

Come to me.

Felix gazed across the Old Bridge. He thought he glimpsed something, some large being, a darker shadow beneath the shadows of the trees. Unafraid, he stepped onto the bridge, which clunked hollowly beneath his boots. In four strides he was across. One more step, and he would stand in the leaves on the far side.

"*Felix!*"

Felix turned, though he recognized neither the voice nor the name. He saw the orange cat, every hair standing on end, empty sockets where eyes should be, standing on the far side of the bridge.

"Felix!" he yeowled. "Don't cross over!"

Felix bared his teeth. And when he spoke, his voice was scarcely human, and smoke trickled from between his lips. "Don't tell me what to do."

"No, wait!"

The next moment, the cat was flying at him, all claws and fur. For an instant, Felix thought he saw a tall man in scarlet with golden hair, hands reaching out to him. But it was only for an instant, for in his surprise, Felix stumbled that final step.

His foot crunched into the leaves of the forest.

Only there was no forest.

No forest, no hill, no cat.

He stood upon a gray plain, one stretching for miles and miles all around him until it met the horizon. Gray that blended into the iron of the sky so exactly that one could scarcely tell up from down but for the cold, pale sun that shone weakly above.

The unicorn appeared at his side.

Come with me, it said.

Felix screamed.

3

IN THE DEEP SHADOWS of the Wood Between, the Hunter stalked.
He'd walked these Paths before, ages ago, searching then for what
he sought now. Still, he found nothing. But his eyes were bright, shining
with light which they took and hoarded so that he could see in the dark
with ease—a gift of his ancestry. He sniffed for traces of a leading scent,
touched contours of ancient trees with sensitive fingers that ended in
claws. His ears strained for the smallest sound.

He'd been called away from his hunt several times, called to serve his
master elsewhere. But each time he returned with renewed will. For now
he stood to lose much more. Now the prospect of failure was worse than
the prospect of death.

Five hundred years he had hunted in the Wood, each moment a century, each century a moment, for Time does not flow a smooth course
in that place. The Hunter was tired beyond measure. He was also keen.

A prophecy of blood waited at the end of his journey. His own blood,
or that of his prey.

PART THREE

THE WOOD

1

LIONHEART STOOD in the sloping gardens of Hill House, breathing deeply of mountain air. Though down in the low country spring had already given way to the sweltering heat and humidity of summer, up here in the mountains, a crisp wind blew constantly. Sometimes it bit so sharp that one would think it could purify all manner of ailments.

It did nothing for Lionheart. His was a sickness of the heart.

He had made the journey to Hill House alone. This would never have been permitted had he made known his intentions, so he had not waited for permission. The moment the Council made its decision and the Eldest named Foxbrush his heir, Lionheart had packed a bundle of necessities and some gold, left a message with his father's steward, and taken the back way out.

He would not stay behind for the pomp and ceremonies to follow. He would not wait to hear the announcement of Foxbrush and Daylily's betrothal.

In the barony of Blackrock he had stayed awhile and sent messages ahead to the town of Torfoot, which was not three miles from Hill House's door. Plenty of folk there were eager for work, and at Lionheart's request they returned to the old house, opened its doors and windows, lit fires, and prepared for his arrival. Since the coming of the Dragon, Hill House had been abandoned. The people of Torfoot were glad to see it opened up again, smoke curling from its chimneys.

But the sight was not as welcoming as Lionheart had hoped. Not even Hill House, where he had known two summers as a boy and of which he treasured many fond memories, could comfort him now. His humiliation was too great.

He had avoided people as much as possible on his journey, and even now at his journey's end he scarcely spoke to the folk of the house. The night of his arrival, he had nodded to the cook, the housekeeper, the maid, and the footman, said nothing, and gone to his room, shutting the door firmly behind himself. The maid left a plate of food outside in the hall. He rose at dawn, opened his door, and stepped right on it, cracking the plate. The maid found it an hour later, along with the empty bedroom. But there was no sign of the disinherited prince.

"Royalty always has their own ways," said Redbird, the cook, when the maid came back and reported his disappearance.

"But does he really count as royalty now?" asked the maid. "I mean, now that he ain't the crown prince no more?"

"Once a royal, always a royal," said Redbird.

But the maid wasn't sure she believed her.

Lionheart had gone out to the gardens when the sun was just rising. Before leaving the Eldest's House, he had shaved off his beard, leaving his face cold now in the morning. He tramped through the familiar but overgrown grounds, recalling boyhood days many years ago when he had been sent to visit his cousin for the summer and spent hours entertaining himself in these gardens.

Back before he climbed farther up the mountain and met the lonely girl who changed his life.

Lionheart had been to Hill House months ago, when he first returned to Southlands after his exile and came searching for Rose Red. It was then that he had knocked out the front boards of the old shed's door in order to reach inside. No one had repaired those boards since, so when Lionheart came to the old shed, he knew what he would find just within its dark doorway.

He put his hand into the mustiness, brushing away spider webs and crawlies, and took hold of the fell sword, Bloodbiter's Wrath. Which looked startlingly like a beanpole. Perhaps because it was one.

Lionheart pulled the beanpole out of the shed and held it in both hands. It was decorated up and down with messy little carvings, including its name somewhere near where the "hilt" should be. It had been his weapon of choice as a boy and had seen many an epic battle up in the mountain forest where he and Rose Red had played their games. He lifted it up, his knuckles whitening as he squeezed it. With very little effort, he could break it in two. . . .

"There are some things that cannot be repaired once broken."

Lionheart startled at the voice and whirled about, brandishing the beanpole. He had thought himself quite alone in the morning stillness. Even now, as his eyes scanned the lawns and overgrown hedgerows, he saw no one.

"It smells to me," the voice spoke again, surprisingly close but from a different direction, "as though you don't know what it is you hold there. Sad, that. How limited mortal perceptions are."

Spinning in place, Lionheart scanned the whole of the yard. Still he saw no one. "Where are you?" he demanded, his voice firm, though his heart raced. "Who are you?"

"Oh, come now, I'm hurt." The voice was masculine, a smooth tenor. Yet there was a slight huskiness to it as well, and an unnatural timbre. "I thought you would remember me. Not that we spent a great deal of time in each other's company, but I like to think I make a lasting impression."

"Where did we meet?"

"Oriana."

At that name, Lionheart's face broke into a sweat despite the chill morning. His brows lowered and he adjusted his grip on the beanpole. "Come out," he said. "Come out where I can see you."

"Really, my lad, you're blinder than I am."

The next moment, a large orange tomcat appeared at Lionheart's feet. It boasted a thick ruff and a plume of a tail, the tip of which twitched continually as it tilted up its whiskered nose. It was a handsome animal, large for a house cat, glossy and healthy looking.

But it had no eyes.

This strange lack made its face altogether too smug as it smiled up at Lionheart. It was a face that would be hard to forget. It was not a face one would expect to speak.

Lionheart gaped. Then he said, "Monster?"

"Ah! You do remember me, then," said the cat with a trill. "Only, I'd rather you did not refer to me by that name. I allow only friends to address me thus, and you, my lad, are far from being my friend." The voice was bright and cheerful, but there was an edge to it that made Lionheart step back. "You may call me *Sir*. Or *Your Grace*. Even *Your Eminence*. I'm not especially picky."

During the course of Lionheart's travels, he had encountered dragons, emperors, sylphs, oracles, priests, dukes—any number of fantastic peoples, mortal and immortal alike. The memory of Rose Red's goat transforming into a tall woman and shaking him within an inch of his life was burned into his memory. But he had never before heard human speech cross the lips of a house cat.

A house cat who had more than one reason to dislike Lionheart.

"You belonged to Una," Lionheart said.

"Well, *belonged* might be stretching the point," said the cat. "Rather, I was her guardian. And a noble occupation it was while it lasted. But my sweet young mistress has since married and gone to live in her husband's kingdom, far, far away."

Lionheart said nothing for a long moment. Una, married? To whom? It did not take long for his imagination to fill in that missing piece. Who else but the Prince of Farthestshore? It must be he. The Dragon truly was dead, then, and his nightmare of several months back was reality.

He would never fight the Dragon.

The cat seemed to be awaiting a reply. "I . . . I am happy for her," Lionheart said.

The cat's tail lashed back and forth. "Your happiness concerns me not a whit. Una is happy, and that is all I care for at present. You, however, have yet to earn my regard, and I am only here now because I was sent. The Lights Above only know why!"

"Sent? By whom?" He hated to ask but needed to know. "By Una?"

"Iubdan's beard, no. By my Master, the Prince of Farthestshore. Though you may be assured, it was not an assignment for which I asked. I would have preferred that he allowed me to search for lost Prince Felix."

Lionheart frowned. "Something has happened to Felix?" He thought of Una and the dreadful change worked upon her by the Dragon. Had a similar fate befallen her younger brother? For a moment, sorrow filled Lionheart's heart. But it was swiftly replaced by something more sinister— a dreadful hope.

So the Prince had rescued lovely Una but left the brother to suffer? So much for his nobility! Even the Prince of Farthestshore had his limits. Generosity and goodness only ever reach so far.

The cat growled. Then, as though he had read Lionheart's mind, he said, "Think no evil of my Master, jester. Your thoughts discredit no one but yourself."

"Since when do cats acknowledge masters?" Lionheart snapped.

The cat's ears went back and his tail lashed again several times. But when he spoke again, he said only: "He has sent me to you, Lionheart of Southlands, though for what purpose I cannot fathom. I would be much better employed searching after young Felix. But I fear he has been taken beyond my reach."

"What happened to Felix?"

"Why should you care?"

Lionheart had no ready response. He couldn't even say that he did care beyond pure curiosity. But something in the cat's manner prompted him to urge an answer. "I saw what became of . . . of his sister."

"Such was not Felix's fate, if that's what bothers you," said the cat. His whiskers drooped and his eyeless face became sad. "No, something far more mysterious has taken Felix. He has heard the unicorn." Like a performer, the cat gave a dramatic pause.

"Um," said Lionheart.

"You have no idea what I'm talking about, have you?"

"No, sorry."

"Mortals," growled the cat. Then he plunged into his story, told with far more embellishments than Lionheart needed. But there were few born who could stop this cat once he began a tale. And Lionheart, leaning against Bloodbiter's Wrath, found himself moved despite every effort to maintain disinterest as the cat's narrative unfolded. He had not known Felix well during his time at Oriana, but he remembered the bright-eyed, fair-haired boy with the teasing laugh and good humor. The idea of something so dreadful and so strange happening to him was hard to take in.

"That moment at the bridge was the last I saw of Felix," said the cat as he reached the conclusion of his tale.

"So you say this creature—this *unicorn*—stole him?"

The cat sniffed. "That's not what I said at all. I said the unicorn *called* him. Whether or not it stole him is a different story altogether."

"But why?"

"Why what?"

"Why would it want anything to do with Felix?"

The cat gave an impatient twitch of his ears. "Who can say? But the unicorn did not want the boy for its own purposes; that is certain. It and its brethren desire little to do with mortals. It must have been sent, and I have a fair idea by whom."

"Yes?"

But the cat was disinclined to communicate further. He started grooming his paw. When he had finished the first, he moved to the second, and when he finished that, he began chewing a back paw as well, spreading the toes so that sharp claws extended.

Lionheart gave up. "What do you want with me, then? Do you suspect I am involved in the boy's capture?"

"Did I say capture?" said the cat, still chewing.

"Disappearance, then."

"I really couldn't say that I had any ideas concerning you whatsoever," said the cat, finally finishing his primping and sitting upright again. "I am only here because my Master sent me. Rather than pursuing any traces of the unicorn or Felix, I am compelled to your little kingdom, all the way up to your little house on your little hill to help you with your little problems." His ears went back. "So tell me, mortal, what are your little problems?"

"I don't have any problems."

The cat snorted. "Funny, that."

"None that need your help, anyway," Lionheart insisted. He looked at Bloodbiter's Wrath, which he twirled idly in his hands. He knew why he had desired more than anything to escape to Hill House. It was as remote a location as could be found in all Southlands, as far as one could get from the Eldest's Court without leaving the kingdom. It was also the location of his dearest memories—of games on the hillside with his best friend, building stick ships and sailing them on a muddy pond, of stories and imaginary battles, of foes that could always be overcome.

Memories of true companionship.

But even those memories were soiled. He knew this, now that he stood once more with the beanpole in his hands. More dirty in his mind even than memories of Oriana and Princess Una were all those thoughts of childhood camaraderie with Rose Red. Rose Red, who had trusted him. Rose Red, who had risked her life for his sake on more than one occasion. Rose Red, who had given up everything to serve him.

Rose Red, whom he had banished to an unknown fate.

"Why don't you go after her?"

Lionheart glared at the cat, who smiled back. "Can you read my mind?"

"No." The cat sniffed and seemed to smile. "I can smell it. Which is made the easier for the stink your thoughts give off. All this self-pity and moping! *I did what I had to do.* Lick my whiskers, you did. Be a man, and face your actions for what they were!"

"You don't understand," Lionheart said, turning his back on the cat. "No one does."

"While I am a firm believer in the uniqueness of each person," said the cat, "the motivations of the spirit are as predictable as the seasons." He paced around to stand once more before Lionheart.

"Why don't you go?" he said to the cat. "You don't wish to be here, and I've told you I need nothing from you. Go search for Felix as you wish and leave me in peace. If your Master complains, tell him I sent you away myself. He can't argue with that."

The cat's voice was a low growl. "That is out of the question."

"Why?"

"The ways of my Master are mysterious, to say the least. He would not leave my young charge to the unpredictable whims of Faerie. I suspect that my search for Felix is somehow wrapped up with your own search. That by helping you I will, in fact, be helping the boy."

"You're wasting your time. I have no search."

"What of Rose Red?"

Lionheart frowned. "How do you know her name?"

"I have my ways. So what about her, mortal?"

Taking care to consider his words, Lionheart began, "I cannot . . ."

"Cannot what? Cannot attempt to repair the damage you've done? And why is that? Because you cannot bear to admit your mistakes in the first place?" The cat shook his head and once more laid his ears back. "Coward."

For a beautiful moment, Lionheart envisioned bringing the beanpole down with a crack on the cat's skull. But there was something dangerous about this cat; a wildness in his every movement, blind though he was. Lionheart suspected that there was more power contained in that small orange body than he could begin to guess.

With a shudder, he stepped around the cat and began striding across the grounds. The cat trilled and kept pace at his heels. He followed Lionheart all the way to the gate that opened onto the road leading up the mountain. The forests were thick beyond Hill House's grounds. Thick and full of secrets.

"You should find her, Leo," Daylily had said.

"I don't know where to begin," he whispered.

"This forest is as good a place as any," said the cat.

Lionheart lifted the gate latch and stepped through to the road. The cat slipped out of the yard behind him. Tail high, he trotted ahead of him up the way, then turned around to say, "Follow me, mortal. I'll show you the Path."

"What path?" Lionheart asked. "Where do we go?"

The cat replied, "To the Wilderlands."

The creature dashed up the road, then turned suddenly and plunged into the dense growth of the forest, his orange tail flicking out of sight. Adjusting his grip on Bloodbiter's Wrath, Lionheart hastened after him.

He would find Rose Red. He would find her and apologize. Somehow, he would make amends for his betrayal. And if it was already too late, he would find her remains and bury them and raise a marker in her honor. After that . . .

But he could not think so far ahead.

The forest swallowed him up.

2

BEHOLD THE PALACE VAR. It is built of mirrors and reflections. It smells of roses. It is swathed in veils.

King Vahe of Arpiar conceived and constructed this edifice in ages long past. It is a wonder of which heaven might boast. Architects of the Near World could but dream of its design, the sacred geometry of its proportions, and upon waking they built marvels of stone and wood—Barareaksmey Temple in the Far East, the Eldest's House in Southlands, Amaury of Beauclair, and fair Oriana by the sea. But these were pale imitations of Var, and their architects must either forget their dreams or despair.

For centuries, Vahe walked the corridors of Var, breathing the perfume of roses, drinking in the varieties that he himself, by his own power and no other's, fabricated. It was a work of great pride. It was a wonder beyond compare.

For centuries, it had been his prison.

Graceful statues of his forebears filled Vahe's assembly hall. These statues raised their white arms to support the vaulted roof, but their faces were downturned. Stone eyes watched the king seated upon a throne of roses. Just as Var was without peer in the worlds, so was its master. Vahe of Arpiar was more beautiful than all the angels ever worked in paint or marble relief. His face was of such perfect proportion that those of lesser beauty found it difficult to look upon him, and his skin was gold-kissed and smooth. Eyes of purest silver pierced the faces of his subjects, reading their deepest thoughts. All knew there could never be a more dreadful beauty than that of the King of Arpiar.

At his right hand sat the queen, who, though not so gorgeous as her husband, was a worthy consort for any Faerie king. Her face was still, her eyes downcast, and bloodred roses crowned her black hair.

On a low stool before the king and his queen sat their daughter. She wore a veil of fine black lace, but through that lace, one could just discern features so delicate that many wondered if she might rival her father's beauty. All her subjects adored her, though none had seen her face or heard her speak. She was their princess. That was all they need know.

The king waited with the queen and the princess, and all his court waited with him, though for what they did not know. A warm sun gleamed through tall windows, and roses unfurled their sumptuous petals both outside and within. Then the doors of Var opened, and the roses closed up, hiding their faces.

For the unicorn appeared.

At the sight of it, even the statues trembled on their pedestals and tried to draw back. Only their limbs would not move. They wished to close their eyes, but their stone lids would not drop. So they watched as the unicorn stepped through the door, passing through space and time without touching either. And all the courtiers of Var fell to their knees and covered their faces, unable to move for fear of drawing the unicorn's eye. Slowly, they slinked into shadows, escaping the hall like silent specters.

The unicorn paid them no heed. It drove before it a mortal boy whose face was empty. Fear had so overwhelmed his senses that his mind had fled him completely. The unicorn prodded him from behind with its cruel horn until the Boy at last stood before the two thrones and the low stool.

If King Vahe himself shivered in the presence of the unicorn, he did not show it. His voice was steady when he spoke.

"Have you done what I asked?"

It had.

"And this mortal standing with his mouth agape, this is a fit instrument for the work I require?"

It was.

The king nodded. "Step forward, Boy."

The unicorn's gift, his jaw slack, did as he was told. Hollow eyed, he gazed up at the beautiful king, the lovely queen, and thought nothing.

Vahe stood. His robes were made of rose petals cleverly woven together, and they smelled of heaven. He plucked a bloom of delicate pink from his rose-woven throne and approached the Boy. The scent from that single rose was enough to overwhelm the senses, both pleasant and a little sickening in its potency. Vahe fingered the flower as he studied the Boy's face. The king was very tall, and his eyes were like diamonds in his stern face. The Boy trembled.

Then suddenly, King Vahe's face melted into a tender expression of pity. "Dragon poison!" he cried, putting out a hand and gently taking the Boy's chin, turning it this way and that as he studied his face. "It's worked through your veins. You poor lad! No wonder the unicorn brought you to me."

The Boy wondered if he should be concerned. He wasn't entirely certain how to be.

"Tell me," said Vahe, "did no one attempt to heal you of this terrible hurt?"

The Boy's mouth moved several times before words came. "I don't . . . know."

"Have you no friends? No family to whom you could turn for help?"

"I don't know."

The king closed his eyes a moment, and when he opened them again, the Boy saw glistening tears. "Friendless. And so young! Boy, you have my sympathies." Vahe released the boy's chin. "Have no fear," he said, taking a step back. "You are come to Arpiar now. To a realm that opens its arms to the outcasts of this world. The rejected. The wounded. You may make your home here, and the power of my roses will prevent the poison in your blood from conquering you. What do you say to that?"

The Boy tried to think, but nothing happened. He glanced at the unicorn, fairly certain he remembered something frightening standing over there. But the unicorn had hidden itself from his sight, though it stood so near that the Boy could feel the heat of its body. He decided that what he could not see could not hurt him, so he twisted his gaping mouth into something like a smile.

"I'd like to stay," he said.

"If you would," the king said, smiling, "you must accept me as your king and be ever loyal to me. Will you agree?"

"Um. Yes?"

Vahe's smile was something rather terrible. It was a smile that inspired devotion, and the Boy felt weak before it. "Here," said the king, holding out the pink rose. "To seal our agreement. Take it."

The Boy reached for the rose. When his fingers closed around the stem, he gasped as a thorn sank deep into the fleshy part of his hand. He dropped the flower, but Vahe caught it. Three pink petals fluttered to the floor, vanishing before touching.

The Boy started to put his hand to his mouth, but the king said, "Stop! Let me see."

Obediently, the Boy held out his hand, and Vahe turned it to better inspect the wound. "The thorn is still imbedded. Here. Allow me to pluck it out."

The king's fingers were swift. The Boy scarcely had time to yelp before the thorn was extracted. A great drop of blood swelled and spilled from his hand, landing in Vahe's outstretched palm.

The king's fingers closed over it.

Vahe offered the rose once more, and the Boy accepted it more carefully this time. As he sniffed it disinterestedly, the king turned to his queen, who had sat watching the proceedings.

"You see, Anahid," Vahe said, raising his closed fist. "My Lady will see my dreams through, no matter what you try."

The queen said nothing. She lifted her silent gaze to meet that of her husband, and met his smile with a smile of her own. Anyone who looked at her could see in a glance that she would slit Vahe's throat if given the chance.

Vahe offered her his arm, and the queen took it, rising from her throne and moving with him across the assembly hall. The king motioned for the unicorn to follow, and it, on feet so delicate that they would not turn a blade of grass, fell into step behind them.

At the door of the hall, Vahe paused and looked back to where his daughter continued to sit on her stool. "Watch over the Boy, will you, sweet child? See to it that he doesn't become lost."

Then they were gone, king, queen, and beast. The Boy stood gazing up at the stone faces of the statues looking down on him. They were lovely, almost as lovely as the king who had so kindly offered him refuge. He found his heart swelling with love for them, love for King Vahe, love for this wonderful, strange place. The taste of that love was as sweet as the rose he held.

He turned to the princess.

"Hullo," said the Boy.

She nodded without looking up.

"What's your name?"

"They call me Varvare," said she.

The Boy tried the name out, thought it odd, and shrugged. Then he asked, "What is my name?"

"I don't know," said Princess Varvare.

3

LIONHEART HAD LEARNED of the Wilderlands in two ways. The first when he was a small child, scarcely old enough to speak but old enough to hear and to comprehend more than his caretakers ever guessed. His nursemaid, a quiet little woman who, in retrospect, he thought must have been quite young, would hold him gently in her lap and speak in a low voice. Some of her talk was nonsense—nursery stories and rhymes that children grow up knowing without recalling where they first heard them. Like the limerick:

> *There once was a cat with no eyes*
> *Who visited town in disguise.*
> *He sang to the king*
> *And purred for the queen;*
> *He fooled the whole court with his lies.*

In the same soothing voice, a voice that beckoned sleep no matter how a little boy might squirm in protest, his nursemaid told of great histories, of heroes, of ancient days. Upon her knee, Lionheart first heard of Maid Starflower and the Wolf Lord; he listened wide-eyed to the tale of the Dragonwitch and the burning of Bald Mountain; he learned how King Shadow Hand bargained with a Faerie queen to save Southlands from invasion. The histories of his kingdom blended as naturally into legends as cream into tea, swirling in indescribable patterns, heightening the flavor.

Within these stories, Lionheart first learned of the Wilderlands.

"We see them," whispered his nursemaid as the sun sank behind the horizon and evening washed the sky dark, "but they are not of our world. They are the Between. They are the Halflight Realm. Just as dusk and dawn are neither day nor night, so the Wilderlands belong to neither the Near World nor the Far. But within them the two worlds meet."

The child Lionheart had gazed into her eyes, wondering. She spoke in the voice that meant she wanted him to sleep, but simultaneously it was not the same as when she recited those foolish rhymes and nursery tales. Beneath the soothing tone there lay a trembling truth, perhaps unrecognized.

"It is said," she crooned, "that the Wilderlands extend across the Continent, but mortal eyes cannot see them. We see only those bits of the Wood that appear in the gorges, but in reality, it covers all this land and on beyond the Circle of Faces, all the way to Goldstone Wood in the northern countries. Some have told me—though I don't say I believe them—that Goldstone and our Wilderlands are one and the same. Were we to see as the Faeries do, we would know that the Wood never ends. That the Between covers all worlds, all the way to the Final Water. Perhaps even Faeries do not see it. Who can say?"

Thus Lionheart learned of them first. Later, his tutors told him the broader facts. The Wilderlands were the romanticized name given that countryside below the tablelands that was, for all practical purposes, useless. The soil could not be turned, the trees could not be tamed, so the people of Southlands learned long ago to remain in the high country above the gorges and make lives for themselves there. Naturally, over the course of time, fantastic legends sprang into being to explain in mythic terms why the folk of Southlands never ventured into the gorges that cut the country with deep, uncrossable ravines.

But mythic or scientific explanations aside, one thing was certain: Nobody entered the Wilderlands.

Yet as Lionheart followed the cat into the shadows of the mountain forest, he realized he had done exactly that. No sooner did he step from the mountain path into the shelter of the enclosing trees, than he stepped into another world entirely.

He did not scream. He stood a long moment in absolute silence. Part of him wanted to turn around, to look and see if he could still find the mountain path and perhaps the gleam of Hill House's gate behind him. But he knew he would not. He could feel forest extending all around him—and it was not the forest he had known as a boy.

A memory encroached upon his mind. No matter how he tried to force it back, it returned with vehemence. This was not the forest he knew. But it was one in which he had walked once upon a time.

Lionheart clutched the beanpole in both hands, squeezing until his knuckles whitened. He recalled himself as a young boy, up in the higher, treeless parts of the mountain as night began to fall. He recalled stepping into the forest that was not part of the world he knew, following a Path that held him like a captive. There were phantoms in that forest, dangerous phantoms that preyed upon his fear. If not for Rose Red, he would never have escaped.

But Rose Red would not rescue him this time.

"Fool," he growled and forced himself to take another step, then another. He did not need rescuing. He was no longer a child but a man. A man with a purpose that he would fulfill. He had sent Rose Red into the Wilderlands, the worst sentence he could give aside from death, perhaps the worst of all. He would not fail her now.

"Did I not tell you to follow me?"

Lionheart pulled himself from his thoughts to find the cat sitting just before him, prim as a dandy at tea.

"I . . . I did not see where you went."

The cat laughed. Cat laughter is a strange phenomenon. It is a silent charade acted out with the tail, the whiskers, and an almost inaudible sniff. This cat, without saying a word, was inordinately mirthful.

"Did you plan to stumble along pathless and hope to turn up somewhere?" he said.

"I didn't think—"

"I never suggested that you did." The cat licked his whiskers. "Have you any notion, my lad, how dangerous it is to wander the Wood without a Path?"

Lionheart, the memories of his last experience in the Wilderlands still present in his mind's eye, said nothing.

"It will drag you in and twist you about," said the cat, "and take you where it wills. If you have no Path, the Wood will give you one, and it is unlikely to be a Path you will like." The cat turned and took a few steps into the trees. "Don't dawdle. Keep up, or you'll soon wish that you had."

"But where are you taking me?" Lionheart demanded, fear holding his feet rooted.

The cat stopped and twitched his ears back. "I'll lead you by safe ways," he said, "to the Lady of the Haven. In her house, you will meet with others who may help you in your search."

Lionheart's mouth was dry when he tried to swallow. He had heard of the Lady of the Haven before; she was referred to in a number of Southland's tales. But the idea of going to her house was not one his mind could support. It was too strange.

He planted his feet more firmly and said in a harsh voice, "Why should I trust you?"

Here the cat turned around and paced slowly back to Lionheart's feet. His shadow, Lionheart noticed, was much bigger than such a small body should have cast. It looked like the shadow of a panther. Every movement spoke of feral grace and power.

The creature stood before him, his eyeless face unreadable. "You have my word," he said.

The word of a cat. Lionheart drew a long breath, feeling the pressure of wildness, of other worlds, weighing upon him. Within a few steps, he had gone so far from everything he knew. None of his long travels in exile, no matter how far they took him, had left him feeling so cut off. And here this creature, this cat that was not a cat, stood before him, representing everything Lionheart wanted to forget. He saw the cat as he had first seen him, perched in Una's lap, purring while the princess scratched him under the chin. His stomach lurched at the memory, and bitterness filled his mouth.

"'There once was a cat with no eyes,'" he muttered, "'who visited court in disguise.'"

The cat's ears went back. "Really, jester," he said with a trace of a growl in his voice, "I would have thought even a man of your profession would know better rhymes than that."

"'He fooled the whole court with his lies.'" Lionheart adjusted his grip on Bloodbiter's Wrath, as though somehow that thin piece of wood might offer him protection. How he wished he'd had the foresight to bring a sword or at least a hunting knife with him! "Whose court was that, cat? Which king and queen did you deceive?"

A long silence strained the air between them. Then the cat flicked his tail. "What, suddenly I am a figure from an ancient bit of nursery nonsense?" He lifted a forepaw and began chewing his toes, the picture of dismissive indifference. "And the next egg you come across you'll ask, 'Tell me, sir, what *were* you doing up on that wall anyway?'"

"Are you ashamed to answer?"

"I am ashamed of nothing. I am a cat." The cat gracefully placed his paw next to the other, sitting as prim as a perfect statue. "Remember, context makes all the difference. You might think differently of that rhyme if you knew by whom it was written."

But Lionheart shook his head. "Why should I trust you?" he said again. And his heart sank, for he knew there could be no satisfactory answer.

But the cat merely said, "I have taken part in many fools' plays and deceptions upon occasion. When I give my word, however, it is one you may trust. I do not make vows or swear loyalties easily." Then he rose and started once more into the deeper shadows, saying over his shoulder as he went, "Besides, what choice have you, mortal man? You're far from your world now."

So it was that, after a moment's hesitation, Lionheart followed. *For the present,* he told himself. *Just for the present.*

The Wood stood tall and menacing about him. He saw an ancient oak, its gnarled roots grasping the ground as a hawk grasps a hare. A cluster of blue-green firs stood just beyond like three old hags, and when Lionheart blinked, he could have sworn that was just what they were. There was nothing left to remind him of the mountain forest in which he and Rose Red had once played. He realized that he did not even walk on an incline. Wherever he was now, there was no mountain.

All this he observed in an instant, yet he had not begun to feel real fear, beyond that first jolt of his heart, when a movement caught his eye.

It came like smoke through the fir trees, seemed to solidify into the semblance of a young man, then returned to smoke, drifting over the moss-grown ground. Lionheart did not breathe as it drew near him, could not move a muscle. Yet the smoke or youth, whatever it was, became aware of him suddenly and wafted toward him. Hazy tendrils reached out like pleading hands, and Lionheart heard a voice.

"At last, you've heard my cries. Brother!" The accent was thick and ancient, making *brother* sound like *brether*. "Take this, my cord's frayed end." The smoke wrapped about Lionheart's fingers, and he thought he felt something pressed into his grasp. "Take it to the Panther Master's folk and be sure you fasten it to the stake."

As though some wind that Lionheart could not feel had caught it, the cloud was dragged away. But the voice lingered, crying, "Bear word of me to the Starflower! Tell her I will yet slay a beast!"

At the last, Lionheart glimpsed the youth again, a savage lad with a fierce, handsome face, clad in skins and armed with a cruel stone dagger.

Then he was gone.

Lionheart looked to see what he now held in his hand. It was a piece of rough woven cord, broken on one end, tied with two clay beads on the other. The beads were decorated with symbols, the names of those who had given them. On one was painted a black panther; on the other, a delicate white blossom, a starflower.

"You know the custom, don't you?" said the cat, sitting once more at his feet.

Lionheart knew. "The rite of passage into manhood. In bygone days, boys would climb down to the Wilderlands and not return until they'd killed a beast. Most often a bird or a squirrel. But some would bring back creatures more fantastic. Creatures which, they say, turned to stone, then to dust when daylight struck them."

The cat nodded. "They never entered the Wood without first tying a long cord about one wrist, the other end to a stake. The village men remained by the stake as the boy entered the Wood, and they pulled the cord occasionally to remind him of his own time, his own place. Thus he would always have a Path in the Wood. But sometimes, the cord would break."

Lionheart looked again at the bit of broken fiber and the two beads. Then he shoved them deep into his pocket. His face set.

"I must find Rose Red. That is my path."

"That's no Path, my lad. That's a quest. Don't confuse the two."

Perhaps Lionheart was mistaken, but he thought he saw a look of keen sorrow on that eyeless face. An expression he could not understand. He saw the cat's pink nose twitch as he turned his face in the direction the phantom youth had gone. He saw the whiskers droop, though the ears were perked forward and intent. And Lionheart wondered (though he told himself it was foolishness and shrugged it off a moment later) if the cat had known that phantom once upon a time.

"Come on, then, mortal," the cat said and continued on his way.

The final statue in the assembly hall of Palace Var was that of the last Queen of Arpiar. When Vahe originally designed Var, he intended to leave out all depictions of his mother but later reconsidered. The queen had been an important influence on his past and still inspired his future endeavors. It would be a shame to omit her likeness from the statues of his ancestors.

Princess Varvare sat in the shadow of her dead grandmother's statue, quietly whiling away the time with a little handwork. She was not very skilled and worked slowly, her unaccustomed fingers weaving delicate threads. Her lace-veiled face was set with concentration, and she did not notice the statues watching her or the looks they exchanged when King Vahe entered the room. Neither did she notice her father until he was quite near. Then she looked up, her face relaxing into a serene expression, and quietly set aside her work.

"Hullo, Varvare," said the King of Arpiar, smiling down upon her. "And how are we today?"

She blinked behind the lace. Her eyes were large and silver.

"Is the Boy settled in comfortably, then?"

She shrugged.

"I hope you know," the king said, folding his arms and tilting his head to one side, "just how glad I am to have you here, my child. Arpiar is a beautiful realm, but it lacked something essential as long as you were lost to me."

Varvare twiddled her thumbs.

"This is rather a lonely place for you to sit all day," Vahe went on, casting his gaze about the great hall. "Don't you find it drafty?" The statue of his long-dead mother caught his eye, and he looked up at her marble face. Slowly, he licked his lips. "Tell me, Varvare, have you made friends with your grandmother? I'm warning you, don't believe a word she tells you." He laughed a chilly laugh.

The princess looked up at the statue looming above her.

"The old queen was very beautiful, you know," Vahe continued, still studying the image of his mother so that he did not see how his daughter shuddered. "She was the most beautiful creature in all of Arpiar. She hoarded beauty for herself." He turned to Varvare again, and his eyes snapped like diamond fire. "She hoarded it, Varvare, do you hear me? And she let her people suffer for the lack. You don't see your father doing anything of the sort, do you?"

Princess Varvare said nothing.

"Arpiar is a place of beauty such as my mother would never have dreamed." Vahe knelt down before his daughter so that his face was close to her own. Varvare averted her eyes. "She dreamt of no beauty save her own," the king whispered. "But I dream of beauty for all the worlds. Beauty such as I have given you." He put out a hand, touching her soft cheek gently through the veil, like a collector handling a priceless work of art. "Here, you can be what you were born to be. Here, you can fulfill your destiny."

At last, the princess looked her father full in the face. "I weren't born for this," she said. "I don't like it, none of it, and I wish you'd let me go."

Vahe drew his hand back as though from a snake, and his lip curled. He got to his feet, adjusting the folds of his red robe. "Mind that tongue

of yours, Varvare. Your gutter voice would destroy even the enchantments of roses."

With those words he left her, and all the statues laughed silently when
his back was turned, laughed and gestured rudely from their pedestals.
But Princess Varvare paid them no attention. She took up her handwork
again, scowling once more in concentration.

Somewhere far away, a silver voice sang to her: *Call for him, beloved.*
She growled through clenched teeth. "Call for *him*? Not likely!"

4

LIONHEART FOLLOWED HIS GUIDE through the trees, one footstep plodding after another. The landscape never shifted. In fact, there were many times when Lionheart believed that they made no progress at all but passed the same gnarled oak, the same crone-like firs again and again. The light that gleamed here and there in bright speckles among the shadows never shifted. Now and then, Lionheart caught a glimpse of sky through the thick branches, and thought perhaps there was no sun, only empty blue above this Wood Between. There was no passage of time, yet Lionheart felt as though a hundred years had passed. A hundred years since he lost his title and, thereby, himself.

"It very well might be," said the cat.

"I beg your pardon?"

The cat stopped, one paw upraised to step over the same gnarled oak root he had stepped over a dozen times before. "I said it very well might be. A hundred years, that is." One ear twisted back, the other pricked forward. It was like a shrug without shoulders. "You step into the Wood without a Path, helpless as a mewling kitten, and you step out of everything you've ever known. Time may or may not be your friend. Spring may or may not follow winter. Up may have traded places with down. And who are you to know any better?

"It's not your world anymore, mortal. Thus it may have been a hundred years since you left home. Or perhaps you won't leave home until tomorrow and will be hard-pressed to catch up with yourself? No one knows, you least of all."

"Are you smelling my mind again, cat?"

"How can I help it? It's so very aromatic."

The cat progressed on his way, the set of his tail conveying more than words could. The creature maintained an aloof silence as they crossed once more over the same dreary landscape. And this was, somehow, the Path to the legendary Haven of the Wood where dwelt the Lady and her great library of scripts and prophecies? Lionheart shook his head. What a fool he was. Rashly throwing his lot in with this cat, plunging into this awful unknown.

How could he be certain this stranger was his ally? If he could no longer depend on Time itself, why should he trust this creature? What had this eyeless, mat-haired old tom done to earn his confidence? The supposedly blind beast walked this uneven ground with the ease of a dancer on stage, which in itself was unsettling. Lionheart found his hands adjusting their grip almost involuntarily around Bloodbiter's Wrath. Perhaps he should—

The cat spun about, all the fur on his body standing on end, his teeth revealed in a long hiss and a snarl. Lionheart leapt back, startled, and thought the creature looked many times his size, huge and threatening. He raised his beanpole, prepared to defend himself, when he realized there were words in the cat's caterwauling:

"Run, mortal, *run!*"

A sudden, hideous baying filled Lionheart's ears, filled his chest, rumbled and shrieked through his body so that he thought his bones would break. He did not want to, but his body moved for him, turning him about to face whatever was oncoming.

He saw roiling darkness, an entity in itself, sweeping down from above.

A hand caught his arm. A voice he did not quite recognize shouted, "I said, *run!*"

Then he was pulled into motion. The darkness slapped down, but still he ran, blindly pushing through leaves and branches and tearing foliage. A back corner of his mind wondered if he still followed a Path, but this was drowned out in the fear that drove him. He still felt that stranger's hand clutching his, and he stumbled after, his body screaming for more air, unable to think anything save, *Run! Run! Run!*

The baying, deeper than night, surrounded Lionheart. Then something pushed him, throwing him from his feet, and he landed flat on the ground. Branches tore at his face. He wrapped his hands over his head, squeezing his eyes shut as though to somehow squeeze from them that one brief glimpse he had caught—an image of darkness with red eyes howling across the sky, dragging deeper darkness in its wake. Lionheart shut his eyes against it, expecting death, expecting tearing teeth upon his bones, upon his very soul.

But the voice of the darkness rolled over him, then on and away. The echoes, slowly dying, lingered with him perhaps for hours.

When at last Lionheart dared uncurl himself and sit upright, he found Midnight had fallen upon this part of the forest, perhaps never to lift. And he was alone.

The Palace Var was full of wonders.

Every corner he turned led the Boy to something new and beautiful. Like a maze, it wound deeper and deeper into itself, and he could not understand its construction. But what did that matter in the face of so much beauty? He discovered entire wings built of crystal and glass in which vast gardens flourished. Waterfalls fell from upper floors and ran into streams that flowed in channels along the halls. Butterflies flocked in abundance, and everywhere, absolutely everywhere, there were roses.

The scent of roses was rich in the Boy's nostrils as he wandered the various passages. Sometimes he passed people who wore garments of red and magenta and the deep blush of sunset, their heads crowned in rosebuds of the same hue. Their faces were beautiful, but he did not recognize them, so he went on by without a word. His eyes were wide to take in all he could of the palace itself. The crystal wing opened to other corridors, and he left behind the indoor gardens and rivulets and passed into a long gallery of rich red and gold.

There hung fantastic paintings, larger than life, of more handsome people, also clad in all the colors of the rose. The women wore headdresses with trains woven of rose petals. The men, more fierce though no less beautiful, wore crowns set with thorns and bloodred buds.

The Boy went on. Everywhere he went, more roses met him. His senses swam in their sweetness. "What a good, kind man King What's-his-name must be," he mused as he wandered. Only a very good king could rule such a kingdom. Only a very good man could grow such roses.

His roving took him back at last to the assembly hall where he had first been presented to King Vahe, but the Boy did not remember this. When he stepped through the doorway and saw the enormous statues staring down at him, a faint uneasiness passed over him. He walked down the hall between the statues, craning his neck as he looked up at their faces. Roses climbed up their pedestals and draped their white limbs in vibrant necklaces and bracelets. Their faces were solemn but beautiful and, the Boy thought, kindly.

Nevertheless, as he neared the end of the hall, a vague recollection tugged at his mind. An almost-memory of something . . . terrible. Something standing at his shoulder. And the almost-memory was worse than a solid memory could be.

He very nearly turned and fled the room but realized that he was not alone. A princess—and he thought that she must be a princess for she was far too lovely to be anything else—sat in the shadow of the final statue, regarding him with great silver eyes from behind a lace veil. The Boy startled, his eyes widening still more and his pale face breaking out with bright red spots on each cheek. "Hullo," he said.

"Hullo," said the princess.

"I think I know you." The Boy smiled and extended a hand, but she did not take it. "If you don't mind my asking, what's your name?"

"They call me Varvare."

"Ah." He nodded, still grinning. Then he said, "And if it wouldn't be too bold . . . What's . . . my name?"

"I don't know."

"Ah." Again he nodded, but the grin faded away slowly, replaced by a sad frown. "I don't either. Have we had this conversation?"

"Yup."

The Boy took a seat on the marble floor at her feet. Even here, roses wound across the floor, petals clinging to his trousers. He could almost see them growing. "Don't you love all the flowers? I don't remember what they're called, but they're pretty, yes?"

"There ain't no flowers."

The Boy shook his head at her. "You don't speak properly for a princess, do you? It's *aren't any*, not *ain't no*. Did no one ever teach you?"

The princess narrowed her eyes at him. But she only said, "If you say so."

Satisfied, the Boy turned his gaze once more to the faces of the statues. "It's a shame, really."

"What is?"

"They seem so beautiful, like nothing I have ever seen before."

Varvare craned her neck to look up into the face of her dead grandmother. She muttered again, "If you say so," and raised an eyebrow.

"But I wish they weren't covered up."

"Covered up?"

"All those . . . those . . . No, I can't decide. It sometimes seems as though there's a . . . like a mask over their faces. I can almost see it if I don't quite look at them. If I look sort of *behind* them, there's another side to them, one more real. But I can't see it. A shame. As beautiful as these are, they must be much more beautiful uncovered!"

Princess Varvare fixed her gaze on the empty face of the Boy, her lips twitching in a wry smile. "They ain't," she said. Then, "Want to help me with somethin'?"

"Sure," said the Boy, pleased by this request.

The princess reached out and took his hands, raising them up to shoulder height. "Straighten your hands," she ordered. "Thumbs out." She arranged them to a foot apart, palms facing each other. "Good. Now hold them steady."

Then, much to the Boy's bafflement, Varvare pulled something from her pocket and began to wind it around his hands, looping back and forth. Like she was winding yarn . . . except there was nothing there.

"Uh . . ."

"Don't drop your hands! You'll spoil it!"

"What are we doing?"

"None of your business. Just hold your hands still."

"I feel silly."

"Maybe you are. Now shush."

The Boy obediently shut his mouth, watching the princess go about her work. She finished winding nothing, slid nothing off his hands, and carefully folded it, stuffing it into the pocket of her long dress. Then suddenly she sat up, craning her neck toward the door. The Boy looked the same direction and again saw nothing. He was beginning to suspect this girl had also lost her mind. "Look," he said, "I think I need to—"

"He's sending for you," Varvare said.

"Who is?"

"The king."

"Your father?"

At that, her face hardened and she looked away, hunching into herself. "He ain't my father."

Before she had finished speaking, however, the Boy had ceased to listen. A cold dread overcame him, one that he recognized more clearly than anything else in all that glorious palace. His eyes widened, and he ducked behind the princess, crouching down with his back against the statue's pedestal.

The unicorn entered the long hall.

It glided rather than walked between the statues, like moonlight sliding along a polished floor. Its progress was both tremendously fast and achingly slow, but inevitable. Like waves eating away at the shore, devouring whole islands, whole continents in time, so the unicorn moved with relentless grace. The Boy trembled and covered his eyes, unable to look. But Varvare sat as still as the statue looming above her and gazed with quiet eyes at the creature approaching.

It bowed its gleaming horn, so thin that it looked as though a child's hand could snap it in two, so sharp that it might pierce mountains to the heart. It bowed its horn, touching it to the ground at Varvare's feet.

Then it spoke.

The Boy could not understand the words. The sound of its voice roiled terror in his gut, and he bit down on his own finger to keep from screaming. He pressed himself against the princess as though somehow her tiny frame could offer him shelter.

But when the unicorn's voice had passed, Varvare replied, "You know I cain't do that. Why do you keep askin' me?"

The unicorn raised its horn, and the depths of its eyes swirled with thoughts that mortal minds could not comprehend. It did not speak to the princess again but this time turned to the Boy, who by now would have eaten himself if he thought he might escape its gaze.

Come with me.

It spoke without language. The Boy immediately rose to his feet, and his fear was so great that he forgot everything beyond obedience.

The unicorn turned and began to lead him from the long hall. The Boy followed. As he went, however, he felt a hand slip into his own, and when he glanced to the side he found that the princess had joined him. The touch of her hand brought relief; some of his own thoughts rolled back into his mind, including awareness of his own horror. But along with that relief came gratitude to Varvare—though he had already forgotten her name—for not abandoning him to the one-horned beast and whatever fate it had for him.

The Palace Var offered no twisting, maze-like passages to the unicorn. It wouldn't dare. Where the unicorn walked, all the halls arranged themselves conveniently before it, all the stairs were straight and true, all the doors were unlocked. They met no one as they went, for the people of Var felt the unicorn's approach and fled so that the palace was as silent as a ruin. The Boy trembled uncontrollably, but his feet moved without his will. Varvare squeezed his hand, a poor comfort, but a comfort even so.

At last they came to a set of double doors taller than any three men and carved all over with roses. It was the very center of Var; the center of the labyrinth to which no one could come without Vahe's permission.

The unicorn touched the lock with its horn, and as the doors swung open, blinding light poured out, as pure as starlight.

Varvare stopped and, biting her lip, slowly withdrew her hand from the Boy's. She knew she could not enter here. He gave her one desperate look, but only for an instant before he was dragged without apparent force through the doorway behind the unicorn, into the glare of light.

The doors shut.

Varvare stood before them, and she did not see carved roses. Rather, she saw the ghosts of roses, like trapped spirits, crying out for help. She put out a hand and gently touched one of those faces. Then she turned and slowly made her way back through long, dark passages into which no sunlight fell, and in which there was no scent of roses, but only the stench of captivity.

Somewhere, far away, she heard the wood thrush sing.

Call for him, beloved.

"I won't," she said.

5

The Hunter stepped onto the Old Bridge and sniffed. He caught the scent of the cat, which he knew, and that of the Boy, which he thought he recognized, though he could not at the moment place it.

But the scent of the unicorn overwhelmed his nostrils, dispersing all thoughts of the others. He growled and backed off the old boards, which creaked under his immense weight. Then he turned and vanished like a bat into the night, continuing his hunt through the vast expanse of the Wood.

The Wood Between spoke not a word. It did not need to. The ground beat a pulse of hostility. Not a hint of evil, but instead a solemn self-regard that insisted on respect. The eyes of the Wood looked down upon Lionheart and were displeased with this stranger.

He sat in the dark, perhaps for centuries, and wondered if another coming upon him in this place someday would see only a puff of smoke, a haze of memory. Everything in him pleaded to rise, to hasten back the way he had come, to find some exit into the world he knew. But a sensible side insisted that there could be no good in wandering in the dark. Eventually daylight would return and he could take stock of his surroundings.

He should have known that dragon-eaten cat would abandon him. Had the creature not constantly trailed after Una back in Oriana Palace? Her devoted pet, surely he must bear him a grudge. All that talk of being sent was nothing more than a cover, a guise wherewith to lead Lionheart deep into this snare of a Wood. And then to leave him.

These thoughts were unfair, and he knew it. When he looked back upon recent events, everything was a muddle. But he knew the cat had warned him to run . . . after that, Lionheart couldn't say for certain. He vaguely recalled a hand taking hold of him and dragging him along. He might have dreamt that, however. And of the cat, he could not say.

Lionheart shivered, pressing his back against the tree. Every few moments he realized that somehow the tree had retreated behind him, leaving him without support in the darkness. Then he would scoot backward to press against it once more. It trembled softly, perhaps in response to a light breeze above, perhaps in disgust.

A rumbling disturbed the silent ire of the trees, and Lionheart felt the pressure around him recede as the Wood withdrew into itself. The rumbling increased, a cacophonous crashing through underbrush, the screech of rusty wheels, and a low voice singing a tuneless song. The wheels creaked and footsteps stomped in time.

> "The king says he,
> 'I'll find the knight
> And eat his nose in one great bite.'
> O jolly way have we!
>
> "The king says he,
> 'I'll find the fool
> And use his backside for a stool.'
> O jolly way have we!"

Lionheart was on his feet with Bloodbiter's Wrath held ready for action long before he saw the light. But when three lanterns appeared, glowing orange and yellow, he found himself too pleased at the prospect of meeting someone—anyone—in that lonesome forest to attempt escape. Instead, he waited.

> *"The king says he,*
> *'He thinks he's wise,*
> *But I will pluck out both his eyes.'*
> *O jolly way have we!"*

The lanterns illuminated a cart on two big wheels, taller than it was wide. A hunched little man hauled it, dressed in long robes that might have been red or might have been purple; it was difficult to tell. He wore a lantern around his neck that swung back and forth like a cowbell as he walked. Two others were strung on either side of the tall cart. His head was down and he focused on his own footsteps.

> *"The king says he,*
> *'I'll find the cat*
> *And stitch his tail into my hat.'*
> *O jolly way have we!"*

With that verse he came into Lionheart's clearing and stopped. He looked up without surprise and met Lionheart's gaze.

"Well met, mortal."

Lionheart nodded but squinted as he did so. The face before him was . . . strange, at best. At first he thought it very strong and golden, the features of a warrior or a lord. Then, as though a passing wind caught the contours and distorted the shape, the face became fiercely ugly. Rocklike and bloated, with saucer-shaped eyes and a leering mouth.

A face such as Lionheart had seen on only one other person.

"Evening, sir," Lionheart said.

"Evening, is it?" The stranger looked up at the sky and studied it a moment. "Midnight, more like. The Black Dogs have been this way, have they? Have you no Time?"

"No," Lionheart said. "I don't know the time."

"I didn't ask if you knew the time," the stranger said, rolling his eyes. "I asked if you had no Time, but I can see for myself that you haven't. If you had, why would you sit so long in such vicious Midnight? No matter. I can sell you some if you like!"

The next moment, the stranger pulled a cord and the tall cart unfolded itself with many springs and sproings into a vendor's stall. Doors swung open, shelves and countertops fell into place, and wares of all sorts assorted themselves with little whirs into pleasing arrangements. Lionheart gasped, and his eyes widened. The stranger laughed and swept his red cap from his head, making an elaborate bow.

"Allow me to introduce myself. I am Torkom, dealer of magicks and marvels across the worlds. Behold!" He took from one of the displays an orange glass bottle filled with sand. "Fresh sifted, and just the thing for the likes of you, new as you are to the Wood. Time himself filled it with his sands, and see how the many colors are layered so pleasing to the eye? Look!"

The dealer shoved the bottle at Lionheart's nose. But Lionheart, who had heard more than one story as a boy on his nursemaid's knee, put his hands behind his back and did not touch the Faerie wares.

Torkom the dealer narrowed his eyes and clucked shrewdly. "Or perhaps you do not mind walking in the steps of the Black Dogs? Better to follow behind them than to run before them, eh?"

Lionheart said nothing. The golden-skinned man replaced the orange bottle, then folded his arms inside the deep sleeves of his robe and fixed Lionheart with a heavy stare.

"Tell me," he said, "what is a mortal such as yourself doing pathless in Goldstone Wood?"

Not knowing how to answer, Lionheart maintained his silence.

Torkom smiled and revealed two rows of sharp fangs when he did so. But the lanterns flickered, and those fangs became white and even teeth behind well-formed lips. "Perhaps you would take more interest in glimpsing your future? Torkom deals in many things, and he knows the secrets. It is dangerous for a man to walk these lands without a Path . . . you could meet any number of folk who mean you harm! But a little knowledge of what the future holds . . . Ah! That will give you a direction, won't it?" His voice was honey-sweet. "What do you say? Shall I—"

"I need nothing from you, sir, though I thank you for your kind offers," Lionheart spoke hastily.

"It's not polite to interrupt."

"Forgive me," said Lionheart. "But as you have already seen, I haven't any time and must speed on my way."

"There is no speeding through the Wood Between without a Path," Torkom said. "You'll wander lost for generations and be drawn at last to the center, where the Dark Water once lay and where now is only the empty Gold Stone. There, you'll die." His smile broadened at those words.

"I am not without a path," Lionheart said with more conviction than he felt. "I'm on a quest."

"Are you?" The dealer snorted a laugh. "Do tell, brave hero! What is your quest?"

"I seek a maiden named Rose Red." Lionheart paused a moment, considering his words, then plunged on. "She looks something like you, sir, in certain lights. But she's small, hardly would come up as high as your heart. She entered this Wood months ago now . . . or perhaps longer. I don't understand time in this place, but it was some months in my world. She has not been seen since, and I must find her."

"She entered the Wood, eh?" said Torkom. "All of her own accord?"

Lionheart opened his mouth, then closed it again. He shifted his gaze away from the dealer.

"You sent her here, did you?"

Again Lionheart did not answer.

"And now you regret—"

"I regret nothing!" Lionheart's voice cracked like thunder in the darkness, and Torkom's eyes blazed with merriment. "I regret nothing I have done, for I did all for the greater good! But I would . . . I would find the girl even so."

"Of course, of course," Torkom crooned. "Naturally you could not have made a mistake, little human! Your kind never does, does it? No, you are but sadly misunderstood. Torkom understands, though. He understands better than you think!"

Lionheart closed his eyes and ground his teeth, and the dealer's laugh was like claws down his spine.

"Rose Red was her name, you say?"

"Yes." He spoke between his teeth.

Torkom clucked to himself, shaking his head. "There are no roses in the Far World or the Near anymore. Not in many years. Except in Arpiar, of course. That's to where Vahe stole them. They say his garden grows nothing else, and the air is thick with perfume. That's what they say, but I wouldn't know. I haven't visited Arpiar in many a long century now."

Lionheart took in these words slowly, frowning. "I'm not looking for a rose," he said at length. "I am searching for Rose Red. A girl, not a flower."

"It's all one and the same in Faerie, mortal!" Torkom said with another snorting laugh. "Take my word for it, if it's a Rose Red you seek and she resembles me in any way—poor dear—Arpiar is the place for you."

Arpiar. The name was familiar to Lionheart, as was the name Vahe. Arpiar was also called the Land of the Veiled People, and it was the home of goblins. According to stories, Vahe had been a goblin king, hundreds of years ago. But in those stories Lionheart remembered, Vahe had been killed.

Stories were stories, however. In the Wood Between or the Far World, who could say what was true?

"Where can I find Arpiar?" Lionheart asked.

Here Torkom burst into full-fledged laughter. The trees themselves recoiled at the sound, hissing through their leaves. But the dealer went on laughing until his side hurt, then wiped his eyes. "I'll tell you how to find Arpiar, no worries! Torkom will speed you on your way to your ladylove!"

"She's not my—"

"But only for a price. I am a businessman, and I give nothing for free, not even directions."

Lionheart said nothing, but his face clearly showed his indecision. Torkom laughed again, and suddenly the handsome features dropped away completely, and Lionheart stood face-to-face with the most hideous person he had ever seen, more hideous by far even than Rose Red had been, for her expression was never, never so cruel.

"A strand of hair," the dealer said. "That is my price, mortal, or you can stand here in this patch of Midnight until the Final Water sweeps all away. But give me a strand of hair, and I'll show you how to step from the Between into the Far World."

Lionheart knew from the look on the goblin's face that this bargain was unsafe. But how could he hope to escape the Wood otherwise? The face of the savage young man came back to him with alarming clarity, and the thin voice begging, *"Bear word of me to the Starflower! Tell her I will yet slay a beast!"* That poor, pathetic vapor of memory.

"Make a decision," Torkom growled. "Make a decision or rot in this place."

"Very well," Lionheart said quietly. He plucked a hair from his head and dropped it into the goblin's waiting hand. Claw-like fingers closed over it, and Torkom smiled once more.

"See you there yonder birch trees?" he purred, putting an arm around Lionheart's shoulders and turning him to face the direction he wanted. Lionheart tensed but felt the muscle in the goblin's arm and knew he could not hope to fight. "That is your Path, between those trees," Torkom said. "They are one of the Crossings into the Far World. You'd never think it to look at them, would you?"

Lionheart blinked. He could not remember seeing the two white birches before now. They gleamed strangely in that dark Midnight, ghostly and skeletal, and he wondered if the Wood had rearranged itself as it wished.

Torkom dropped his arm and gave Lionheart a nudge. "Go on! Our deal is done. Speed on your way to your ladylove, and may Lumé's light shine on you."

"She's not my ladylove," Lionheart muttered. But he adjusted the pack on his back and strode forward, glad to be rid of Torkom's presence. The two birch trees beckoned him, more lovely than any other trees he had yet seen in the Wood. He approached them with firm steps, though his heart beat with suspicion and fear.

He passed between the trees and stepped into the Far World.

Torkom chuckled quietly, looked down at the hair in his hand, then burst out laughing. He tucked the hair into a deep pocket, packed up his wares, and set off through the Wood. Daylight seeped softly out of his lanterns and colored the world around him so that the Midnight of the Black Dogs finally relinquished that part of the Wood. Still laughing, he tramped on his way, singing:

> "The king says he,
> 'I'll find the poet
> And kick him into lunar orbit.'
> O jolly way have—"

He halted.

An orange tomcat sat in his path, delicate pink nose upraised and tail curled neatly about his paws.

"Greetings, good Torkom," he said, raising a forepaw to give it a single lick. "Pray tell me, what was that delightful little ditty you were just chanting?"

Torkom's mouth opened and closed a few times before sound came. "Sir knight!" he stuttered. "What a surprise. Fancy meeting you here."

"Fancy, indeed." The cat gave his paw one final lick, then turned his eyeless face to the goblin. "Give it to me."

"I cry you mercy, good sir knight! Give you what?"

"You know what."

Torkom licked his lips with a thin gray tongue. Then he reached into his pocket and withdrew the strand of hair. He gave it to the cat, who pinned it beneath his paw and smiled. "Thank you."

"I . . . I'll just be going on my way, then, sir, if it's all the same to you," Torkom said, taking another few steps. But the cat stopped him with a flick of his tail.

"Where did you send him?"

"The mortal? He asked the way to Arpiar."

"I'm sure he did. But where did you *send* him?"

"Was he a friend of yours?"

"Let us say only that I am invested in his interests." The cat's voice hardened. "Where, Torkom?"

"Now, please, sir knight, I didn't mean him any real harm—"

"Yes, you did."

"He was just so full of himself, he was, as arrogant a—"

"Torkom," said the cat, his whiskers quivering, "the words of that song are coming back to me. 'The king says he . . .' What was it he says, Torkom? Do you want to sing it for me?"

Torkom gulped. "I sent the lad to Ragniprava's demesne."

"Ragniprava?" The cat squawked something that might have been a laugh and might have been a curse. "Torkom, you dragon-kissed fiend! You've done a number on the lad I could never have dreamed. My best to you in all your dishonest ways."

With that, the cat picked up the hair delicately with his teeth and whisked away into the Wood. Torkom let out a long breath that he had not realized he'd been holding, then grabbed his cart and fled through the underbrush as fast as his legs could carry him.

6

V AHE TOOK PRIDE in many things.

He was proud of Palace Var, his most elaborate creation, which had, over time, become a byword among worlds for grandeur and opulence. "As grand as Var," the saying went, though no one ever believed it. Nothing could be as grand as Var.

Vahe was proud of his roses. It was no mean feat to host a garden so sumptuous, so aromatic. Faerie lords across the Far World would offer strands of hair to possess just one of Vahe's buds. But Vahe never gave them up. Their beauty radiated across all of Arpiar, and such beauty could not be bought, no matter how generous the offer.

But of all the wonders of Arpiar and the glories of his reign, King Vahe took the most pride in his queen.

Anahid stood silently beside her husband in the secretmost chamber of Var. She was the most beautiful woman in Arpiar, but that was no reason for vanity. Vahe himself dictated beauty in his realm, and he could just as easily have transformed the most humble scullery maid into a queen of rare comeliness. And it wasn't her great love for him that pleased Vahe, for Anahid hated the King of Arpiar more than any living person.

That in and of itself gave Vahe reason for pride. For Anahid, despite her loathing, despite her hate, was still his queen. Of her own choice, she had given herself to him hundreds of years ago. Of her own choice, she remained in Arpiar and ruled by his side. There had been times when the rebel flashed out of her, to be sure, and Vahe had been obliged to punish her severely. When the princess was born, for instance. All his plans might have come to nothing had Anahid succeeded in that night's venture.

But that was past. His daughter was safely returned to him, Anahid stood silent by his side, and the unicorn led the Boy to him in the secret chamber. Everything would come to completion now.

Vahe took his wife's hand as he smiled down upon the Boy. "Anahid, you will accompany me, won't you?" It was a command. Anahid made no reply. Vahe patted her arm in a semblance of affection, then released his hold on her and approached the Boy. The unicorn concealed itself, though it remained standing by his shoulder. The moment it vanished from his sight, the Boy relaxed, then forgot about it. He saw the king approaching, and his hand smarted as it remembered what his mind could not—the stab of a rose thorn and spilled blood.

"Are you enjoying your stay in my home?" Vahe asked, placing a friendly hand on the Boy's shoulder.

"Indeed I am," said the Boy, trying to remember why his knees trembled. But the king was smiling, so he smiled back.

"Have you ever," said Vahe, "seen anywhere so beautiful as Arpiar?"

"Um."

"This is Arpiar. This place you're standing."

"Oh! Well, no. But . . . who are you again?"

Vahe clucked, shaking his head, and patted the Boy's shoulder once more before stepping back. "The outside world is a harsh, ugly place, son of mortals. Beyond my kingdom, they allowed you to suffer the poison that now destroys your mind. Here you find healing. Here you find a place of refuge and beauty. Would that all worlds could be as Arpiar!"

"What's Arpiar?"

Tears gleamed in the king's eyes as emotion threatened to overcome him. "Do you see, Anahid," he said, turning to his queen, "how he suffers? Do you see now the good of my plan?"

Anahid said nothing. She regarded the empty-eyed mortal as one regards mouse droppings in the sugar bowl.

"Mortal son," said Vahe, turning to the Boy again, "would you see beauty and light and the scent of roses cover the sins and cruelties of worlds that rejected the likes of you? That rejected me and my people?" He leaned down, taking the Boy's face between his hands and staring into his eyes. The King of Arpiar's face was so kind, so full of understanding—though the Boy didn't quite know what it was he understood. Whatever it was, he knew it must be good, because a face like that could only be good.

"Just say yes," said the king, still in that smooth voice, tears glistening, though he spoke between his teeth.

"Yes?"

Vahe stepped back. "Did you hear, Anahid? He has agreed."

She raised an eyebrow and smiled her murderous smile. Vahe ignored it. He reached beneath his robe, withdrawing a vial of crystal that hung from a cord about his neck. Its contents were red and thick when the king poured them into the palm of his hand. The Boy smelled his own blood without realizing what he smelled, but for a moment it overwhelmed the scent of roses.

Vahe smeared the blood across his own forehead. Then he gripped the Boy's head again, whispering something in a language the Boy did not know—or did not remember knowing—and pressed his bloody forehead to the Boy's.

The next moment, the king drew back, and his face was gone as slack and empty as the Boy's had been.

Anahid stepped forward, took her husband's hand, and led him to a nearby throne. Gently, she assisted him to sit, and he was lifeless as a doll under her hands.

But the Boy smiled suddenly with a quickness in his eye that had not been present since his arrival at Var. Then he spoke.

"What a fine form! Who could have guessed how it feels to be young again?"

His voice was Vahe's.

The queen turned to him and bowed, still without a word.

"But I don't quite feel myself," the Boy who spoke like Vahe continued. "Let me see . . ." Though the expression did not change, the Boy's face and features melted away, replaced with those of the King of Arpiar. He stood across from himself, his new body bright with life and strength, his other still and silent but otherwise an exact reflection.

"You," said the Boy who was now Vahe, pointing at himself in the chair, "you cannot leave the prison of your kingdom. I, however, may go where I please!"

He darted out a hand and took hold of Anahid. "Come, my sweet. I must test these new trappings of mine and see how they fare across the boundaries." He motioned to the unicorn as he dragged the queen from the chamber. "Guard me well in my absence, good slave. We go to the Village!"

The unicorn bowed its horn, and the king and queen departed. Then it turned and gazed upon the still form of the king. In its eyes there shone a light like distant stars that would have broken a mortal heart. But it was a unicorn, and it could not sorrow. So it stood watch as it was commanded, deep in the heart of the Palace of Roses.

Faerie lords and ladies rule demesnes across the Far World. Some call themselves kings and queens and collect courts about them. Some build grand halls and host magnificent banquets. Some send dignitaries to other lords, sign treaties, and play at politics. Some dance together upon lawns under the moon's slow smile and sing ancient songs that they composed only that morning.

But there are others more solitary.

Lionheart knew none of this as he stepped between the white birch trees and into Faerie. He felt no change around him, no strange sensation of distance, nothing he might have expected (though, in truth, he didn't know what to expect) from traveling across worlds. One moment, he was in the Wood Between. The next moment . . .

He stood in a forest of absolute emerald, so vivid, so vibrant, that it hummed the tune of its own color. His feet were planted on the edge of a precipice that swept down before him to an emerald-green valley through which rushed a river. Opposite him, cascading in wild abandon into the valley, were three waterfalls. If he looked without his eyes, he saw that they were three sisters with laughing faces, and the water was their long hair. With his eyes, they were but waterfalls, higher, wilder than any he had hitherto seen, and their churning foam was like a million gleaming crystals.

"Iubdan's beard!" Lionheart let out a long breath and felt his body weaken. He had just presence of mind enough to stagger backward, away from the precipice, before his knees gave out and he collapsed. The air was steamy hot, and the constant hum of color droned in his ears. After a moment, he thought to glance behind him.

The white birches were gone. Gorgeous flowers bloomed before his eyes, dripping like a lady's jewels from vine-covered branches. But no portal back to the Wood Between.

"You can't go back anyway," Lionheart told himself. He spoke aloud, desperate to interrupt the humming. "You can't go back. You must find Rose Red."

There were no roses anywhere that he looked, which surprised him. From what Torkom had said, he'd expected Arpiar to be resplendent in them. But what would he know about such things? The Far World was nothing but stories to him, even now. How could any of this be real? Laughing waterfalls, humming forests . . . It was nonsense!

Lionheart latched on to the one thing he knew for certain. "You must find Rose Red." If nothing else, here was an absolute. And he would never find her sitting under the trees on the edge of a precipice.

Taking in deep breaths of steamy air, Lionheart pulled himself to his feet and began a search for a way down into the valley. He had a good head for heights; during his five-year exile he had taken long sea voyages and learned to enjoy climbing in the rigging, that dizzying world above the decks. But this unearthly plunge to the river below gave new meaning to heights and depths. Every time he peered down, his head swam with the perspective and he was obliged to back away quickly. Sometimes an unreasonable sensation came over him, a compulsion to cast himself over the side, to cease struggling against so great a fall and succumb to it. But those were the thoughts of a lunatic, and he shook them away as best he could. Once, to steady himself, he reached out and grabbed one of the flowering vines looping down from the trees around him. The vine let out a sudden purring sound, sweet as a kitten, and started to wrap around his wrist in a most endearing manner. But Lionheart, not appreciating the gesture, screamed and dropped his hold. He ignored the sad mewling the vine made as he left it behind, and took care to touch no more of its kind.

He could find no descending pathway into the valley. Everywhere the cliff face was equally sheer. There could be no climbing down; he knew that beyond doubt. But what other option did he have? He paused. The sun moved overhead from midday toward late afternoon. This in itself brought Lionheart surprising comfort, for it was more like his world than was the Wood Between. The sun traced hours in shadows, and evening would follow afternoon just as it did in the Near World.

Only, when he stopped to think about it, the idea of spending the night in this forest was no comfort at all.

Though the heat was so tremendous that he removed his cloak and outer layers of clothing, leaving them behind in the forest, Lionheart began to shiver. "You must find Rose Red," he told himself. "This is no time to fall to pieces. You've been through much worse! You must find Rose Red."

Suddenly, the humming of the forest stopped.

The abrupt silence roared in his ears like a thousand battle drums, and Lionheart felt his heart stop beating for an instant. Every muscle in his body tensed, though he knew not why.

Then he heard breathing. Deep, deep breathing.

He ran.

He did not look behind to see what pursued him; he only knew he was pursued and ran faster than he had ever run in his life. Right along the edge of that terrible drop, without a care for his footing, he fled. And when a tall, slender tree obstructed his way, he did not slacken his pace or turn aside but ran right up the trunk and into the highest branches he could manage. Only then did he realize that his body screamed for air, that his side was ready to split in pain.

He looked down into the blazing eyes of the Tiger.

7

WHERE THE DRAGONS DWELT, all fires were dead.

They crouched in the darkness, their human forms doubled up under the weight of shadows and writhing dreams.

He's gone. Our Father.

They had felt the anguish of his passing, and all had roared in death pains. When the roaring stopped, darkness fell, and none could move to replenish the flames.

The yellow-eyed dragon hid his face in his hands, wondering if this was death. It was worse than he'd imagined. He sat in the interminable darkness, burning inside, alone though surrounded by his kinfolk. His veins pulsed with the tension of expectation for he knew not what; expectation without hope. His mind spun in an endless cycle of memories.

"Take my fire and lose your chains."

In his spirit's eye, he stood once more in shadows he himself had sought. Before him loomed his King, black and enormous, a mountain of hot ash. Those red eyes burned into his soul and smiled.

"Take my fire, and you'll never bow to him again."

"I'll never bow down!" he cried. "Never! I am my own master."

"Your own master, free to choose your own chains. Take my fire."

"Very well. Give it to me."

Then the burning kiss on his forehead. The pain of lava flowing over his body, burning away everything that he loathed in himself, every weakness, every frailty, every kindness that led only to hurt. He screamed in agony, and the scream turned to a roar full of flame.

"I'll choose my own chains!"

"Bow to me."

And he bowed.

But now his Father was gone. He and all his brothers and sisters were alone in the darkness. Worse than death, he lay trapped in chains of his own choosing.

There were many gateways that led to the Village of Dragons. For different people, be they mortal or immortal, that gate appeared differently. Some saw it as a cave shaped like a great wolf's head. For some, it was a dark window in a house that was once a home but was no longer. The gateways to the Village were beyond number, but when a man saw one, he did not doubt what he had seen.

This made little difference to the dragons' privacy. No living person, whether in right mind or otherwise, would willingly pass through the gates and step onto the descending path to the Village of Dragons and the Dark Water. Thus the dragons remained undisturbed. Not one of their kind had been seen since the death of their Father. The Faerie folk could only pray that so it would remain. And they avoided those gateways as children avoid a murderer's grave.

Except for Vahe.

Strong in his new body, he walked with his queen along Faerie Paths out of Arpiar and into the Wood Between. For a moment they stood upon an old plank bridge spanning a small stream. Then Vahe took the queen's hand and led her swiftly uphill. In the Near World, a palace in ruins stood at that hilltop. But in the Between, Goldstone Wood extended over all save the very crest of the hill. Here too there were ruins, not of a palace but of a once-tall tower of black stone.

A doorway remained standing. All around it was forest and the rubble of old stone. But through that doorway was . . . darkness.

"It has been many centuries since I saw Carrun Corgar," said the king with a smile. "What a rundown little heap it is. Nothing like in my day!"

Anahid made no reply. She recognized the stench coming through the door and knew where the gateway led.

"Come, my sweet," said the king and drew her after him, passing over the threshold.

Goldstone Wood disappeared, as did the hill. They stood instead upon a wide, empty desert. This was the form the Pathway of Death took for Vahe and his wife. A landscape as barren as Arpiar was lush. The air was stale and hot.

Tucking Anahid's arm under his own, Vahe strode across the burning sand. Following the Path, they crossed miles upon miles upon miles of blighted land in moments. They traveled with no escort but each other, Vahe glorying in his freedom as, for the first time in centuries, he escaped the prison of his own kingdom.

Anahid's eyes were sharper than her husband's. She glimpsed a gravestone a few yards from where they walked, and on this gravestone gleamed a lantern of purest silver. The queen bowed her head and did not look again at that light. It was not meant for her. She would follow her master to the Village of Dragons without hope.

They came to more ruins. So old were these and so blasted by wind and sun that a mortal eye would not be able to discern what once had been mighty Nadire Tansu, the Queen's City of Corrilond. It was nothing but piles of boulders and rocks, half hidden in sand, colorless save for the Desert's red stain.

Vahe led Anahid into the depths of the rubble. Everywhere lingered the smell of death and burning, though the fires were dormant. Anahid trembled at the scent. It had haunted her nightmares these many ages now. Fire, and two bright yellow eyes staring at her out of the immense darkness of memory. She shuddered now as her husband led her through the narrow passages, away from the sun, and down, down into the caverns below the ruined city. And she wondered . . .

"Magnificent!" Vahe exclaimed. They came suddenly to the mouth of a tunnel and gazed down into the cavern. Below lay the Village of Dragons, silent save for the echo of Vahe's voice. "Behold, my darling," Vahe said, sweeping his arm as though he would grab the whole scene close. "Behold your husband's army!"

Anahid looked and shivered, for in the darkness of the cavern her eyes could see as well as in daylight. A thousand forms lay upon the ground. Some were great beasts, serpentine and heavy, with massive wings and claws and tails that coiled behind them. Some were men, and women too, of all ages.

They were dragons.

They were asleep.

"Come, come," Vahe said and started down the narrow path that led from the tunnel's mouth into the Village. "They'll not wake, sweet one; you needn't fear. But we must inspect them now that we are here, and we must search for the throne." He let go of her hand and leapt on ahead like a child set loose to play. As soon as he reached level ground, he approached the first dragon, a man whose face was half covered in scales and who slept with both hands clenched in fists.

"Look at this one!" Vahe said. "He'll be a captain in my army, wouldn't you agree? I'd love to see him flaming!" He scampered on to another fallen figure—this one a beast of large proportions—exclaiming over the expanse of her wing.

Anahid followed more slowly, looking at the faces as she passed. They all wore the same masks of pain, both the monsters and the men. "Poor fools," she whispered so low that not even the eager echoes could catch her voice. "Poor, sad fools."

"By the Sleeper's waking snort!" Vahe cried from somewhere ahead. "Come, Anahid! See what I have found!"

She did as he bade her, stepping around the crumpled bodies until she found her husband again. He stood before the most enormous dragon of all, a creature as tall as a house, her scales as red as fresh blood. Her face, of all the sleepers', was the most twisted in pain. As though even now she experienced the unending throes of death.

"It's the queen," Vahe said delightedly. "The Bane of Corrilond. What a fire she had back in her day! You remember, don't you, sweetness? It was not long after our blissful wedding day when we saw, even from Arpiar, the glow of flames rising in Corrilond. What a force! Heat carried from the Near World to the Far. There have been few like her in all of history, this most glorious of her Father's children. Like the Dragonwitch reborn, some said."

Anahid shuddered. But the Bane of Corrilond was as stone while she slept.

Vahe sighed, shaking his head. "She'll make a fine general come Moonblood. She'll drive the others to my will as a shepherd drives his flock."

"Or she'll swallow you whole," Anahid said.

"Tut, tut, no wishful thinking, darling of my heart," Vahe said, chucking her under the chin. "There'll be no snacking on this king; our precious daughter will see to that. And speaking of, where is that throne?"

He sped off again through the darkness, darting among the crumpled forms of the sleepers. He stepped on hands and faces without care, for he knew they were too far gone in sleep and despair to stir. He spared no glance for the few feeble huts with their gaping doorways standing here and there. The Dragon's Hoard, a cave stuffed to overflowing with gold and jewels, could not draw his interest. He found an iron cage and paused a moment to sniff it. It smelled of captivity and terror. But it was not what he sought. "Where is it?" he growled and turned back to the main cavern. Then he saw.

It stood in the center.

There, upraised on a block of black marble, was the high seat, the Father's throne, carved like dragon skeletons in black stone, stained all over with ancient blood.

Vahe smiled, and his beautiful face was terrible to behold in that moment. Slowly, almost reverently, he approached the throne. Dragons were piled on top of each other, as though in desperation they had scrambled toward this spot before the sleep fell upon them. Two or three were collapsed against the black marble dais, their hands upraised to touch the stone, their mouths open in silenced screams. Vahe pushed them over, not caring how they fell, then reached up to touch the throne himself.

It was hot, burning the skin of his stolen hand. And the heat carried with it a memory.

He stands in darkness before the throne, which drips with fresh blood. The Dragon sits with a face like a man's but not, pale as death with black eyes. Blood drips from his mouth. Vahe is afraid as he gazes up at him. But he is eager as well.

For the Lady of Dreams Realized is beside him, and she carries a set of dice in her hand.

"I will play for this goblin's life," she says to her brother.

The Dragon grins, displaying all his bloodstained teeth. "Why bother? He will be mine eventually. All of yours must come to me."

"I want him," Life-in-Death repeats. "Play the game with me."

The Dragon shrugs and indicates for her to proceed. Vahe draws in his breath, hardly daring to hope. His dream is so perfect, so grand. He must have a deal with the Lady of Dreams or he can never hope to achieve it. And if he cannot have that, he may as well belong to Death, for what use is his life without his dream?

The dice clatter in her hand. Then they roll across the black marble dais to come to rest at the Dragon's feet. He does not move his head to look at them, so the Lady herself steps forward. Then she smiles.

"The game is done," she says. "I've won."

Vahe screams in triumph and leaps forward, all his fear of the Dragon vanished in that instant. "I know my rights!" he cries, shaking with joy. "My dream fulfilled! My dream!"

Sparks ignite in the depths of the Dragon's eye. "Don't look at me, little king. I'm not the dream fulfiller."

"Dragons!" Vahe cries, wringing his hands eagerly. "Give me dragons! Give me my army! That is what I wish!" He turns from brother to sister and back again, his expression somewhere between a smile and a grimace of pain, so intense is his longing. "Give me dragons, and I will show you what the worlds may be when I clothe them in my veils! There is too much ugliness, too much weakness . . . but I will make them beautiful. And strong. Only give me dragons!"

The Lady of Dreams fixes her white eyes upon her brother's face when she replies, "King Vahe, my darling, I will see your dream realized. But the dragons are not mine to give."

Vahe sees the look exchanged between the Dragon and the Lady, sees the silent argument being waged. But he cannot see who is winning. He shrieks, clutching his head. "You owe me!" His face is very ugly, for he cannot make his veils work upon Death and Life-in-Death. The desperation in his eyes makes them all the more horrible. "You owe me, Dragon! If not for me, you'd yet be bound to that Gold Stone."

"I think you take too much credit, Vahe," says the Dragon, still not breaking gaze with his sister. "It was not you who woke me. It was that pretty little slave of yours, what's-her-name. The Lady of Aiven."

"She'd not have done it but for my persuasion!"

"Your persuasion? Rather secondhand work, I think." The Dragon sneers and at last turns to fix his gaze upon the King of Arpiar. His eyes are ringed in flames. "I hardly feel an obligation."

Vahe screams wordlessly and turns upon Life-in-Death, gnashing his teeth. "My dream! You won the game. I know my rights!"

"You have no rights," hisses the Dragon.

But his sister narrows her eyes and smiles. She croons softly, "I will see your dream realized, Vahe. My brother knows that I will. One way or another."

The Dragon rises from his bloody throne and strides forward as though he would tear the Lady to pieces then and there. But she continues to smile and meet him eye to eye, and it is the Dragon who turns away first. He snarls and spits fire as he speaks.

"Very well, King of Arpiar. Perhaps we can make a deal, you and I?"

As he speaks, moonlight breaks through the darkness above the throne, spilling through a skylight high above and lighting upon the Dragon's face. He snarls again, and the light runs bloodred.

Vahe drew his hand back sharply, hissing at the pain. The memory flashed through his mind in an instant, but in such vivid detail that it might have happened but moments before rather than five hundred years ago. He smiled despite the hurt in his hand.

When he reached out to the throne again he did not touch it, rather letting his hand hover just above the carved stone, feeling the heat from it. The heat told stories, whispered the deaths of hundreds, of thousands. The blood, though old, smelled fresh. Here was a seat of power indeed, though not one on which he would ever sit.

"Anahid," he said, "come see our future."

She did not reply.

Vahe frowned and looked about into the gloom. "Anahid!" he barked.

If she heard him she did not respond, for the queen had been making her own search through the cavern.

She knew she shouldn't. It would only bring pain were she to find him. She rarely felt pain anymore, not after all these years. Perhaps it would be a relief even, were she to set eyes on him once more and feel that sharp sting through her heart, that agony of remorse. Perhaps the suffering would be worth a chance to feel again. But these were foolish thoughts, here in this place of darkness.

Even so, she drifted like a ghost among the fallen ones, studying each face as she went. "You'll not find him," she whispered to herself almost as a comfort, perhaps as a warning. "You'll not find him among these thousands."

One lay with his face in his hands, his knees curled up to his head. Anahid froze, and the world went cold around her. She did not need to see his face to know. The coldness passed, and in its place came that first dart of pain that is so akin to longing. Oh, why? Why did she come here?

"Anahid!"

Her husband's voice rang through the cavern, but she did not care. Nothing mattered now, not Vahe and his little plots, not Varvare and her doom. For the moment, however brief, all that mattered were the dreams of one sad goblin girl, hundreds of years ago. Shattered by guilt, ravaged by time, they presented themselves once more. A tear slid down the queen's cheek, and she put her hand to her face to catch it wonderingly. She'd thought she would never cry again.

The next instant, she was kneeling at his side. His hands were icy cold, but she grasped them and pulled them away from his face. That shard of pain twisted more deeply in her heart at the sight. It was *he*! Of course it was; she'd already known that. But it was *his* face! In that little space of time, as she held his hands in hers and he yet dreamed, it was not the face of a dragon, but *his* face, his dear, dear face.

"Come see our future!" her husband called.

But Anahid could not see the future while gazing at the past. She reached out to touch his cheek, and when she did so, her own tear fell on him.

He woke.

Two bright yellow eyes, dragon eyes, gazed up at her, unseeing. "My Father!" he gasped.

"Diarmid," she whispered.

His gaze focused, the yellow eyes fixing steadily on her. The next moment, he gave a strangled cry and pulled himself to his knees. His arms were around her, and she felt the fire in his chest beneath her cheek as he pressed her close to him. She closed her eyes and allowed one more tear to fall because she could not hear a beating heart. He had none anymore.

"Well, well, well," said King Vahe. "What do we have here?"

8

"WELL, WELL, WELL," said the Tiger. "What do we have here?"

Lionheart scrambled around, trying to find a place to put his left foot and simultaneously pushing aside a bough of leaves. He stared down the long way (how had he managed to climb so far, so fast?) to the forest floor below. "Iubdan's beard!" he breathed. "It talks!"

"Lumé's crown," the Tiger responded in a deep mimic. "It talks."

"Forgive me!" Lionheart hastened to say as the bough escaped his grasp and swung back to strike him in the face. Scratches stung his cheeks. "I don't mean to be rude. But I am a stranger to these parts and am unused to such phenomena . . . my lord," he added.

The Tiger stretched up against the tree. His enormous weight sent the topmost branches rollicking to and fro so that Lionheart thought his stomach might make a leap for freedom. The crown of the tree bent over the precipice, and if the drop had been unbearable before, it was ten times more so when one clung to branches and twigs. Enormous claws sank into the trunk and dragged trenches down to the roots. Then the

Tiger sat back on his haunches. The tree was not strong enough to bear his weight, and he dared not attempt the climb. He gazed up at his captive. "No one enters these lands on purpose, and only a fool by mistake."

Lionheart gulped. "In fact, my lord, I am a Fool, and of no mean scope. I've traveled from Southlands to the great city of Lunthea Maly to the courts of Oriana in the north, entertaining kings and emperors with my foolishness."

"I've never heard of these places of which you speak." The Tiger half closed his enormous gold eyes. "Kings and emperors, you say?"

"Yes!" Lionheart said, his voice very thin as he tried not to look down to the river like a tiny blue ribbon below. "Great masters of kingdoms and empires! Hawkeye, Eldest of Southlands; King Fidel of Parumvir; Emperor Khemkhaeng-Niran Klahan the Eternally Brave and Strong of Noorhitam; Grosveneur of the fair lands of—"

"They cannot be so great if I have never heard of them," the Tiger said, the words nearly lost in a snarl. "Who would these puny mortal kings be to me?"

Lionheart gulped. "Nothing and no one at all, my lord."

The Tiger let out a long growl, and the tree quivered, its leaves shushing like frightened animals. "Heroes," the Tiger said. "You're all alike! Bent on staining your swords with monster blood. Think you might dress the floors of your great halls with my skin, eh, mortal? Is that not why you have come?"

"No, actually," Lionheart said and quickly added, "mighty one," just to be safe. "No, I'm looking for a girl. Rose Red is her name, and she's very small and very ugly. Have you seen her?"

The Tiger, still growling, thought about this. "All the roses," he said at length, "are stolen away to Arpiar. Even mine, though they were once rich in this land, have gone to Vahe's keeping."

"Then this . . . this isn't Arpiar?"

The Tiger roared. The precipice caught and echoed it until it filled the valley. Rocks flung themselves down the cliff in response, and the trees waved their branches in terror. Lionheart's slender tree cast itself about wildly, and he lost one handhold but clung with a death grip to the other, grinding desperate prayers through his teeth to anyone who might be listening. Those prayers must have been heard, for his hold held. But the roar went on, and Lionheart began to hear words in it.

"Arpiar? How could you mistake this place of exquisite beauty, this haven of perfection, for that blighted hole? Have you no eyes to see the splendor? The colors? The jewels? Have you no ears to hear the songs of the trees, the laughter of the waterfalls? Can your nose not smell the incense on the wind? Did your heart not long to die and be buried in this spot of supreme delight? This is not Arpiar! This is the Land of Ragniprava! And who am I? Am I some goblin king who must wear a veil upon his face and cover his kingdom in enchantments? Not so, mortal fool! I am Ragniprava, Bright as Fire, master and god of this realm! I have forbidden any to enter my territory, mortal or Faerie alike, and those who disobey shall know me well and know me very briefly!"

Lionheart wrapped his arms in a bear hug around the trunk, shutting his eyes. The Tiger went on roaring, sometimes slipping into inarticulate rage, sometimes with words, until Lionheart thought he would be deaf long before his strength gave out and he fell to those waiting jaws. But the Tiger stopped abruptly and sniffed.

"Wait a minute," he said. "You have a friend with you."

"What?" Lionheart shook his head. "I have no friend."

"Don't be so down on yourself!"

The voice was high and bright and familiar. The next instant, an orange tomcat without any eyes trotted to the space beneath the tree, right before the Tiger. The cat purred. "Surely someone somewhere must still think well of you?"

"You!" Lionheart cried.

"Did you miss me?" The cat smirked.

The Tiger sniffed again, his huge eyes focused on the little cat. "Who are you?"

"Oh, do forgive me, Ragniprava. Allow me to introduce my—"

Another great roar interrupted him, and Lionheart yelped in surprise as the Tiger suddenly sprang. The cat was just fast enough, however, and a small orange streak outstretched the larger orange streak as the two dashed to the tree not six feet from Lionheart's. Lionheart watched the cat scale to the higher branches with the speed of a squirrel and, if he weren't so frightened of the mighty Ragniprava, he might have laughed at the sight of the cat's tail puffed out as huge as an ostrich plume.

"No one!" roared the Tiger, pacing back and forth between the two trees. "No one calls the Lord Ragniprava by name!"

Lionheart glared across the branches at the cat. "Well done. Looks as though we—" He stopped.

In the tree opposite him sat a man in bright scarlet, tawny hair sticking out from under a jaunty cap. Both his eyes were covered with silken patches.

The Princess of Arpiar did not care for the company of her grandmother. Not that the statue was the old queen herself. But it was filled with the memory of her and was, Varvare thought, a terrible gossip.

Nevertheless, she was the best company to be found in all of Palace Var if only because she actually did speak now and then, even if what she had to say was never worth hearing. All the other inhabitants avoided the princess with such thoroughness that she was lucky if she ever spied one. And if they realized that she saw them, they ducked their heads and fled.

They knew, she thought. They knew that she could see behind their veils.

So she sat in the shadow of the queen, busy with her handwork, half listening to the stony whispers. For the most part they weren't interesting, the vain ramblings of an angry old woman. But sometimes, though she knew she shouldn't, Varvare perked up her ears and listened with more attention.

"He may have murdered me, but he's still a better choice than my other son would have been."

Varvare didn't look up from her work, but her mouth twisted with thought. The news that King Vahe had killed his mother was not new to her. It was the old queen's favorite gripe. But Varvare had not known until now that the old queen had ever had another son. Which meant Varvare had an uncle.

"I told Sosi to kill it."

Well, maybe she'd *had* an uncle.

"Sosi was too squeamish for that kind of work. Anahid was better. But a queen? Faugh! He's made her pretty enough, I'll grant you, but she'll never have the force to rule Arpiar! Vahe likes his ornaments, but he has no idea what it takes to make a queen."

Anahid. Varvare shivered, and her fingers faltered for a moment. Her mother. Her mother who never looked at her.

"Vahe has what it takes, dragons eat his soul. Murdered me before his seventh birthday. That's the kind of mettle it takes to rule Arpiar. Goblins require a ruthless ruler!"

Varvare sighed. As much as the old Queen of Arpiar loathed Vahe, she could go on forever about him. The princess wondered if her grandmother really took such bizarre pride in her murderous offspring, or if Vahe had enchanted the statue to say those things. She focused on her work, ignoring the queen again. Slowly, silver threads spun together into a cord, but the cord was still so thin. She paused and tested it now and then, pulling to see how the fibers held. She had almost used up her last harvest, the tiny tendrils of spells she had pulled from the ghostly roses. She would have to go wandering the halls again soon to gather more.

It wouldn't be difficult, the way the people of Var avoided her. Not even the empty-headed Boy would tag along after her, for he had disappeared since the unicorn led him away. She dared not contemplate his fate too closely; she could only hope he was all right, somewhere in the secretmost places of Var.

"He's made quite a beauty of you, hasn't he?"

Varvare startled. In all the long hours she had sat beneath this statue, it had never directly addressed her.

"You would make an interesting queen."

The princess bolted upright, staring up at the statue. For half a moment, she saw the pure white marble, the image of a goddess, the elegant work of an angel. But she shook that sight away impatiently, tossed aside the veiling enchantments, and looked at the truth that lay underneath.

The statue was crudely carved in black, flaking stone, shaped as though by the fingers of a clumsy child.

"The humility of a chambermaid couched in the body of a princess. An interesting combination indeed."

Varvare got to her feet, swiftly tucking her work out of sight. The statue laughed and twisted on the roughhewn pedestal, feet like claws clutching at a perch.

"Don't worry, little rose-spinner! No one has heard my voice in centuries. I won't be telling your secrets."

"I don't know what you're talkin' about," said the princess, backing away.

"Neither do I."

And the ugly face closed its mouth and was as silent as though it had never spoken. Varvare stood staring up at it, and she couldn't decide if she had invented the whole exchange or not. Perhaps she was losing her mind like the Boy. Or perhaps she'd never had a mind, and everything she had believed about her life was false, and the truth was the harsh, hideous world in which she now found herself. A world ornamented with enchantments, like a gilt sepulcher filled with rotting bones.

When the statue did not speak again, Varvare hesitantly took out her handwork.

Beloved, call for him, said the wood thrush, far away yet ever present.

Varvare growled, her beautiful mouth twisting into a grimace. "Still singin' that song, are we?"

Trust me. Call for him.

She clenched her fists. "If I've told you once, I've told you a thousand times. I will *never* call for Prince Lionheart."

The unicorn in the depths of Var stirred, skin trembling across his body, and he turned his watchful eyes for a moment away from the still form of Vahe to the borders of Arpiar. Palace Var shivered on its foundations, just slightly, so that the courtiers within did not notice.

But an enchantment not of the king's making shot from Var's hall and sped across the blighted plains, breaking through the boundaries into the Wood Between. The silver stream of it, invisible to most eyes, flew past the Hunter's face, and he saw it. With a cry he turned to catch it, but it frayed like old rope as it went, dissolving so that he could not trace it back to its source. Gnashing fangs, he tore after the enchantment, praying that it would not vanish entirely before he discovered where it led.

Vahe, sheltered within the Boy's body, felt the tremble of his kingdom, felt the flying of that stray spell. He let out a moan that rattled throughout the cavernous Village of Dragons, then spread wide his arms and snatched what he needed before he sped back to Arpiar, snarling as he went, dragging his queen and a dragon behind him.

And somewhere in a far demesne, high in a tree, a young man frowned suddenly as something wrapped around his heart and clung there. For a moment he forgot the danger prowling below in an overwhelming sensation of regret and resolve. He almost dropped to the ground to continue his quest then and there, and only a sharp growl from the Tiger prevented him.

All this passed in an instant. Varvare, unknowing, continued her work at a furious rate.

"So don't ask me."

"Who the devil are you?" Lionheart cried, breaking twigs away in an effort to get a better view across to the other tree.

"Who do you think I am?" the stranger snapped.

"How should I know? Where's the cat?"

"Ha! You're blinder than I am."

"I've never seen you before in my life!"

The stranger, ignoring this last comment, put his hand in his pouch. "Here. I retrieved this for you."

He extended his hand, thumb and index finger pressed together, obviously offering something, though Lionheart couldn't hope to reach it. "What is that?" he asked.

"Your hair."

"My *what*?"

"Your hair. The one you so blithely handed off to the goblin dealer! You're lucky you weren't transformed into a toad for your idiocy."

Lionheart's jaw dropped, and he stared at the stranger with the patches over his eyes. "Cat?"

"NO TALKING!" the Tiger roared, and Lionheart and the red-clad man clutched their tree trunks. "No one speaks unless Ragniprava gives permission! I am master here, and I cannot bear idle chatter. Why else do you think I banished all living creatures from these lands?"

Lionheart's gaze traveled from the Tiger, to the stranger, back to the Tiger again. Then, with widening eyes, he shot a last glare the stranger's way and hissed through his teeth, "It *is* you!"

"SILENCE!"

The stranger who was sometimes a cat shoved Lionheart's hair back in his pouch, then made sharp shushing motions with his hands, scowling for all he was worth. The Tiger got his wish as a deep quiet fell over that part of the emerald forest, interrupted only by the panting of Ragniprava himself. Even the waterfalls across the valley had ceased their laughter and watched the goings-on with watery eyes.

Lionheart tried not to move, though his left foot, tucked up under him, was going numb and a branch dug into his side like a dagger. His mind whirled with possibilities, but all of them ended with the snap of enormous jaws, perhaps heralded by a swipe of gargantuan claws. That, or a long fall with an abrupt conclusion.

The cat-man across the way wasn't any help. He moved about in the branches of the other tree, nimble as a squirrel, not making a sound, though his long arms and legs should have been snapping twigs and rustling leaves with each movement he made. The Tiger paced, huffing great breaths between his teeth. The sun passed overhead and began its dip toward the horizon, and Lionheart wondered what it would be like, spending the night in a tree. And whether or not he would topple out when he finally nodded off.

Suddenly, Ragniprava spoke. "I'll not climb up after you. Such does not befit a lord of my stature. You'll have to come down."

"Many thanks for the thought, mighty lord," the cat-man said with a trace of a smile. "But if it's all the same to you, I'd just as soon stay where I am. The view of your realm is quite marvelous. Is that Goldstone River below us, perchance? Nasty character, that River, quite the libertine, they say! I do hope he's not been playing the fool with your lovely waterfalls."

"I grow weary waiting for you to drop."

"Not so weary as I shall grow hanging on!"

The Tiger sank down on his haunches and puffed his whiskers. "If we must wait, you will have to amuse me."

"I should think we're amusing enough, dangling like baubles from these branches." The cat-man swung about like a trapeze artist, still without making a sound. He did not move as a blind man should. Lionheart shifted his numb foot, cursing as blood rushed back in a million pinpricks.

The Tiger eyed them both, shifting his gaze from one tree to the other. At last he said, "I'll make you a deal, trespassers and ill-doers. If you amuse me, I'll let you down and host you in my own home for supper."

"*For* supper or *as* supper?" the cat-man asked.

The Tiger only smiled. "Will you make a deal?"

"I do not doubt," the cat-man said, tilting his head shrewdly, "that I could amuse you, mighty lord. Am I not Eanrin, Chief Poet of Iubdan Rudiobus, Knight of Farthestshore, bard and storyteller, devotee of the fair, the only, the most glorious Lady Gleamdrené Gormlaith, cousin of Iubdan's wife? Perhaps you have heard of me."

"*Eanrin!*" Lionheart nearly dropped from his perch then and there.

But Ragniprava only licked his lips. "Proof is in the doing, little cat," he said. "Sing us a song, and if I am amused, I'll let both you and your mortal friend down. What is more, I'll not eat either but treat you both to my own royal hospitality. You have the word of Ragniprava."

Eanrin grimaced but quickly changed it into a bright smile. "The mighty lord is most generous—"

"*Bard* Eanrin?"

"—how can I do aught but oblige?" With those words, the poet stood up on his branch, supporting himself with only one hand on the trunk, and gave a twirl of his red cape. "For your listening pleasure, Lord Bright as Fire, I give you a sonnet composed in ancient days, before the moon's children fell. 'In Splendor's Vault Thou Art!'"

As Lionheart looked on with sagging jaw and the Tiger gazed through half-lidded eyes, Iubdan's Chief Poet sang:

> *Fair Gleamdrené, in splendor's vault thou art*
> *Shining lone and sweet among the flow'rs of night.*

From all thy sisters thou must stand apart
As Hymlumé outshines the imrals bright.
Like priests of old, in sacred reverence I
Will spread thy fame across the distant shores.
Thy praises ring from depths of sea and sky,
From mountaintops to sweeps of lonely moors.
Ever I, with heart unchangeable,
Deep adoration swelling in my breast,
Will walk far pathways for thy praise to tell,
Wand'ring always in divine unrest.
My one desire to sing till my last breath
Devotion's fire and then to pass in death."

The song ended, and the poet bowed his head and pressed his free hand to his heart. A poignant silence followed.

Ragniprava yawned.

Lionheart had seen one or two bored audiences in his days as a performer, had lost many a crowd to a series of yawns. But not once had a yawn been so full of huge, pink tongue and the light of orange sunset glaring off long, sharp fangs.

In a surge of panic, he pulled himself upright and, deftly swiping the Chief Poet's tune, burst out with:

"O brother mine, it's not my fault thou art
Whining lowly underneath thy bed tonight!
Did I not tell thee if thou threw that dart
The hound would turn and give thy rear a bite?
Sniff and snort, no sympathy have I
For one who interrupts Old Masher's snores.
Thou got'st what's coming, so blubber on and sigh,
Then up and at 'em! Thou canst do my chores.
Thou sayest nay? Don't think thou'lt weasel out!
That is unless thou cares not if I tell
The pretty girlie next door all about
How thou and Masher get along so well.

> *I thought thou'd see my point. Here is my broom.*
> *I'll leave thee now to dust and sweep the room."*

Eanrin turned with open mouth gawping toward Lionheart, his golden hair bristling like a cat's tail. "Of all the—" he began but was interrupted by the Tiger's laugh.

A tiger's laugh is a horrible thing, in many ways more horrible than a tiger's roar, and the emerald forest of Ragniprava trembled and huddled into itself at the sound. But as the Tiger laughed, he stood upright on his hind legs and melted into a tall man with dark skin and wildcat's eyes, clad all in orange and white and black. He wore a turban set with tiger-eye stones, and a huge sword hung from his belt. His fingernails were long and curved, and they glinted when he clapped his hands, exclaiming:

"Magnificent! Magnificent, my boy! The look upon that poet's face when you began to sing is worth more than both your lives! I don't remember the last time I was so well amused. Indeed, good poets both, you must do me the honor of visiting my house. Come, come, Eanrin of Rudiobus, and tell me the name of your mortal friend!"

But the poet, for once in his life, was rendered speechless. Lionheart took a trembling bow. "I'm Leonard the Lightning Tongue," he said.

9

King Vahe swept back into Var, trailing Anahid and a dragon in his wake, and all the folk of Arpiar trembled to see his face. Their master was mighty indeed, for who but the most powerful of kings could wake one of the sleeping dragons? So they drew back from him and said not a word as he passed through the perfumed halls, through the labyrinthine corridors, to the center and his secret chamber.

The unicorn met him at the door.

"I know, I know!" Vahe cried. "I felt it too! But was there any breach?"

The unicorn shook its head slowly, though its eyes spoke warnings. Vahe chose not to see those, however, and continued past his slave to where his own body sat waiting silently on the throne. With a harsh word and an upswept hand, he lunged forward as a fencer attacks. The next moment, the unnamed Boy fell headlong across the floor, his eyes closed in unconsciousness.

Vahe's body on the throne blinked once, twice. Then he raised his head. "Get this creature from my presence and keep him out of sight," he said. "I don't want to see him until I call for him again. Now!"

The queen knelt beside the Boy, who groaned softly where he lay, and helped him to his feet. He staggered and sagged against her, and might have pulled her back to the ground. But the yellow-eyed dragon stepped forward and took him under the arms, lifting his weight from Anahid. When he did so, he saw the Boy's face and gasped suddenly with recognition.

The memory of a dark night, of horsemen pursuing and a chase through the Wood came to him. He'd poisoned the Boy that night. And now his veins ran thick with dragon venom.

The yellow-eyed dragon held the Boy gently and helped Anahid guide him from the chamber. The Boy walked as one heavily drunk and grimaced with pain, though he did not come fully awake.

"Wait," said Vahe before they reached the door. They stopped and looked back. He pointed at the dragon. "Come here."

Anahid turned wide eyes to meet the dragon's gaze. Only an instant passed before he lowered his face and helped her adjust her grip on the Boy. Then he was gone and she passed from the chamber, the door shutting behind her.

The yellow-eyed dragon paced slowly back across the room to Vahe's throne. It was a seat of roses, bloodred and fragrant. The smell was noxious to the dragon, and he grimaced as he neared. Vahe smiled.

"I know you," he said.

The dragon said nothing.

"I never thought I'd see a Knight of Farthestshore within these walls again. Not since my dear brother's last visit."

"I am no knight," the dragon hissed, and a forked tongue flickered between his lips.

Vahe's smile grew. "Look to your left. Tell me what you see."

The dragon turned to where the unicorn stood, its horn lowered. "I see nothing," he said, though in truth his eyes did perceive a faint glimmer, like the glare of sunlight darting briefly off black ice. "Nothing," he repeated as though to convince himself.

"Look again," said the King of Arpiar.

This time, the unicorn revealed itself.

"Father's fire!" the dragon screamed and crumpled onto the floor in shivering terror. Flames licked about his teeth in his panic. "The beast! The one-horned beast!" He covered his eyes, desperate not to see, but the image of the unicorn burned inside his mind.

Vahe rose and stood over the dragon, laughing quietly. "Hymlumé's fallen children are no welcome sight for eyes such as yours or mine. But I tell you truly, son of fire, the unicorn is my slave, given me by the Lady of Dreams herself, and he will do as I command. You, however . . ."

He knelt and took the dragon's head between his hands. His fingers were long and tapering but strong as steel, and he clenched the dragon tightly and forced him to look into his eyes. The dragon's face was lengthening, becoming more reptilian, and fire glowed in the back of his throat, yet Vahe did not flinch.

"Listen to me," he said. "You were not awakened at my bidding, and you are bound not to me but to my wife. But that was true long ere now, was it not? Since before you were filled with fire, and you gave her your heart. Since before I took her from you.

"Listen to me now, erstwhile Knight of Farthestshore. Without the rites of Moonblood, my bindings do not hold you. But you are still in my world. You will obey me. You'll not cross my will, not though Anahid herself compels you. For if you do, I vow to you here and now under the unicorn's eyes that its horn shall be your fate. I'll set the one-horned beast upon your trail, and the Black Dogs themselves could not be more fell hunters. Do you hear me, Dragon's brood?"

The dragon nodded, his eyes rolling both to seek out the unicorn and to look anywhere else. Vahe let him go, and he collapsed into a huddled ball, his arms over his head. The King of Arpiar turned then to the unicorn.

"Go inspect my borders. I do not know where the weakness might be, but someone is searching for my realm and coming much closer than I like. It may be that my brother has not given up even now. Go and see what you can find, then report back to me. Moonblood draws near, and I'll not risk interference with my plans."

The unicorn left on silent feet. Even then, the yellow-eyed dragon could not raise his face for many hours. Vahe, a hard smile on his face, watched him writhe and tremble. But his thoughts were far away with a black, bloodstained throne and a cavern full of sleeping dragons.

Lionheart walked with a tiger and a cat, which, though they now wore the forms of men, were still as much a tiger and a cat as ever. The Faerie lord Ragniprava moved with heavy grace as he escorted Lionheart and Eanrin down a narrow path from the top of the precipice into the valley below. Though Ragniprava was all congeniality, Lionheart found his gaze drawn more often than not to his host's hooked fingernails and noticed the gleam of the remaining sunlight on his teeth when he smiled. He spoke to them as to guests, yet Lionheart felt as captive as he had in the branches of the tree. There was power in this Faerie lord, and though it may be power in check, it could burst forth at any moment.

The cat-man, Eanrin, was aloof, answering any questions put him by Ragniprava with curt words. He refused to acknowledge Lionheart. This didn't surprise Lionheart overmuch. He'd never gotten along well with cats.

Lionheart tumbled through the thick-growing greenery behind the Tiger lord and the Chief Poet of Rudiobus, using Bloodbiter's Wrath for support. What a bit of rotten luck! Of all poets and performers, he was blessed with the once-in-a-lifetime opportunity to meet, to converse with, the most famous bard in all history, the poet who had single-handedly shaped the fortunes of writers and verse-scribblers in all corners of the world; an artist who had witnessed and recorded in lyric stanzas events of history that were so far past as to be rendered myths. A poet so renowned that many doubted the very possibility of his existence!

And Lionheart had to open his big mouth and stick in his big foot.

Nevertheless, another side of him whispered, Ragniprava had preferred his sonnet.

"Behold!" said the Tiger. They had come to the end of the path, deep in the jewel-toned valley. The sun was gone and dusk had settled pink and purple overhead, but the forest still glowed, as though the leaves had gathered and stored the light to last them through the night. "Behold the Palace of Ragniprava!"

There wasn't a great deal to behold.

The remains of what once might have been a temple lay in magnificent ruins, bone-white stone reflecting the forest's green. Toppled pillars lay before the sagging gate, and beyond that the central building seemed to stand only by magic. But Ragniprava swelled with pride as he led them farther into what probably once had been fantastic courtyards and outer chambers. Now the forest was creeping in with slow but indomitable vines and shoots.

"Once," said the Faerie lord, "all this was blocked up. These walls you see lying here were high and closing in on all sides, stifling the sight, the scents, the sounds of my beautiful forest. Unbearable! I tore them down. It is better now, you see? But come, come deeper still."

They passed fountains full of green water, thick with lotus flowers. They crossed pathways grown over with moss, the richest and softest of carpets under their feet. At length Ragniprava brought them to a door carved delicately in panels depicting a story. Lionheart paused a moment, wanting to work out the tale it told. He glimpsed a woman with a crescent moon on her head who raised her arms joyfully in the first panel and later in terror as though warding off some evil. He glimpsed children surrounding her, and in one panel they clutched at her robes as though they were falling, and their faces too were full of terror. And on another panel, he thought he saw a face, a figure he recognized from his darkest, most nightmarish memories.

The Dragon.

All this he had but an instant to take in before Ragniprava opened the doors and, beckoning with his long nails, bade them enter. Lionheart tore his gaze from the carvings, ready to follow, and found the blind poet standing just before him, studying him without eyes.

"What are you gawking at?" Eanrin demanded.

"The woman and children on the door," Lionheart said quietly. "They were . . ."

The poet put out a hand and touched the door, running his fingers lightly over two of the panels. Then he took his hand away sharply, as though burned, and drew a sharp breath. "Orden Hymlumé," he said. "Or informally, *Moonblood.*"

With that, the poet turned to follow the Tiger lord without further explanation. The word meant nothing to Lionheart, and he trailed after the other two, frowning.

The Faerie man had proceeded far ahead of them now, and they could hear him making impatient grunts at their slowness, so they picked up their pace. He led them into the first passage that was still intact, the walls and ceiling where they were meant to be. But even here there was a sense of wildness and exposure, for vines crept along the floor and climbed up the alabaster pillars, blooming with orange flowers. It turned only twice, but after making those turns, Lionheart had the uneasy feeling that he would not be able to find his way back out again. He wanted to look over his shoulder but refused to give in to that desire.

Ragniprava stood at the end of the passage, which opened to an enormous chamber behind him. "Welcome to my banquet," he said with a sweep of a bejeweled hand.

Here was another hall fallen into terrible disrepair. The roof was long since gone, though the walls were yet standing. But vines flowed over these like green waterfalls and poured across the floor so thickly that golden tiles could be glimpsed only at rare intervals. A long banqueting table stretched across the whole of the room, and it was piled high with silver platters on which sat perfectly formed fruit. Golden goblets, shining and set with jewels, held wine like liquid garnet. All gave the impression of having stood there untouched for hundreds of years, and yet not a sign of rot or spoil could be seen.

Seated at the table were a hundred stone princes.

They must be princes, Lionheart knew from the moment he set eyes on them, though they wore no mark of their station. Something about their faces, worked in rough rock though they were, bespoke their heritage. They were as strange as they were noble. One of them had great antlers sprouting from his forehead. Another one's arms were like the wings of a swan. Twins with jewels for eyes sat across from each other, and another had hair that flowed down to his feet.

Every one of them wore an expression of surprise.

"Do you like them?" Ragniprava asked, moving fluidly across the room and smiling at the statues. "I collect princes from all across the worlds. They come here, they and other heroes as well, seeking the Palace of Ragniprava. I do not keep the heroes. But the princes, now, they are fine, do you not think?"

Lionheart stared from them to Eanrin beside him. The poet smiled brightly. Rather too brightly, Lionheart thought. "I have heard of the Lord Bright as Fire's collection ere now but never thought I should stand in its presence. Would that I had eyes to see them! Tell me, mighty one, does Prince Nabhanyu sit in this company?"

"Indeed," purred Ragniprava, moving to touch the head of a prince with a great hooked nose. "He was one of my first."

"And the brothers, Yesterday and Tomorrow?" asked the poet.

Ragniprava nodded to the jewel-eyed twins. "Naturally, Chief Poet of Iubdan."

"Marvelous!" said the poet, flashing another huge smile at Lionheart, who had gone ashy pale. "And Godlumthakathi? Ah, how many sweet ladies did sigh his lack when he vanished long ago! Is he to be found in this great company?"

"Where else?" said the Tiger, nodding to the prince with the antlers. "My collection is the most extensive to be found in all the Far World. Not even the serpent ChuMana can boast so many!"

"Indeed?" said Eanrin. "I have seen ChuMana's collection."

"*Seen* it?" The Tiger gave a mocking laugh.

But the poet nodded, and this time his smile, though smaller than before, had a trace of devilish remembrance behind it. "Yes, Lord Bright as Fire. I saw it with my own two eyes back when I had two eyes with which to see."

A deep growl threatened in Ragniprava's throat, behind his lace-edged cravat. "Then tell me, bard, though you have not *seen* my princes as such, what make you of the comparison?"

For a long moment, Eanrin stood silent. Lionheart felt his heart pulsing. *Lie, dragons eat you!* He wanted to shout it. *Who cares whose collection was superior? The Tiger, that's who, so tell him what he wants to hear!*

Then the poet laughed. "Oh, most noble lord! I cry you mercy. Though I shall never behold these fair statues of yours, I may say with absolute certainty—as one of the few who has been invited to the demesne of both ChuMana and Bright as Fire—that your collection is by far the more beautiful." He added with a shrug, "The serpent's is rather ugly."

Lionheart let out a deep breath he hadn't realized he held. But the Tiger's eyes narrowed as he peered from Eanrin to Lionheart and back again.

"Neither of you happens to be princes, eh?"

"Alas," said Eanrin with a graceful bow, "though hailed as the Prince of Poetry, I am sprung of humble origins and do but serve those of greater blood."

"To be sure," said Ragniprava. In two strides he stood suddenly before Lionheart, nose to nose. "And you, mortal?"

Lionheart gulped. Words clogged in his throat, but he forced them out. "I am no prince, mighty one."

The tiger-eyed man inhaled deeply, his nostrils curling. "I can smell the truth of your heart, Leonard the Lightning Tongue."

"Then you will smell that I am no prince," said Lionheart. He thought of the Council of Barons. He thought of their stony faces when they cast their votes against him. He thought of the triumph gleaming in Baron Middlecrescent's eyes. And he recalled the final words the Eldest had spoken to him:

"Leave my presence . . ."

He closed his eyes, refusing to meet Ragniprava's gaze, not in fear so much as sudden shame.

The Tiger Lord sniffed again but turned away and motioned to both his guests. "Come. Sit. Eat."

So Lionheart found himself taking a place across from Poet Eanrin and between two surprised-looking princes of kingdoms unknown to him. He leaned Bloodbiter's Wrath against the back of his chair. Ragniprava removed his sword and set it to one side of his chair at the end of the table. It was an enormous, double-edged weapon, quite heavy, broadening from hilt to tip. At the hilt was a metal spike, evil as a tiger's fang. It was a sword intended for hacking or cleaving and looked as though it might sever a wild bull's head in a single stroke. The Faerie lord placed it within easy reach of his right hand but otherwise seemed to forget it as he sipped his wine and ate from the bounty before him.

Lionheart, tearing his gaze from the weapon, realized that he was starving, and he didn't quite believe that this was due to some trick on the Faerie's part. Nevertheless, he could not bring himself to reach for the shining fruit. After all, he did not know what exactly had turned these princes into stone.

Eanrin had no such compunction but bit into a juicy nectarine with apparent enjoyment.

"Tell me, mortal," said Ragniprava to Lionheart, "tell me once more what brings you to my demesne. You claim you did not come seeking my skin, which I find difficult to believe."

Lionheart shuddered at the tone in the Faerie's voice. Though he spoke with the tongue of a man, he sounded like a tiger. Lionheart struggled to find his own voice. "I search for a maiden," he said quietly, and his words seemed to sink into the vine-covered walls. "Rose Red."

"And she is a princess," said the Tiger.

"No, no," Lionheart replied hastily. "Certainly not. She was my chambermaid."

Ragniprava nodded knowingly. "And you the master of the house's son, eh? An unlikely romance, and your father banished the girl."

"No!" Lionhearted hated contradicting the Tiger but felt obliged even so. "It was nothing like that."

"Your father did not banish her?"

"No. I did."

"You banished your love?"

"She's not my love."

The vines caught his words and whispered among themselves, like players of a party game, distorting a simple phrase as it travels from mouth to ear so that it comes out wrong at the end. "My love, my love," the vines whispered.

Ragniprava smiled. "Fine professions, mortal."

"Our funny Fool has a talent for professing devotion," said Poet Eanrin between bites of fruit. "Despite his disrespect of high romantic verse."

Lionheart glowered at the poet, who, just as though he could see, smirked back.

Ragniprava leaned back in his chair, the claws of one hand drumming lightly on the tabletop. "Little mortal," he said, "you are in a new world now. Here we follow different rules, rules you must understand. You seek a girl in the realm of Faerie. This means you seek a princess, and you will find her where princesses are to be found. It also necessitates that she is your love, the one desire of your heart. You may not realize it yet, but so it must be. You have passed through the Wood Between. You have stepped over the boundaries into the Far World. Do you think I do not understand these things, the motions and rhythms of the land I have prowled since before the Sleeper awoke?"

Lionheart's jaw worked back and forth. "You don't know the girl. She is a servant. Loyal in service, to be sure, humble and hardworking. But she could never be my love. And she is . . ." He did not want to speak the words that rushed next to his mouth. Bowing his head, he tried to force them back, but they would be said. "She is my best friend."

"Ah. I knew it."

"But she's uglier than an old toad," Lionheart hastened to add.

"You think that makes a difference here?"

A cold silence followed, cold despite the steamy air that wrapped in heavy spices about Lionheart's head. His thoughts muddled, and he found Rose Red's face in all its hideous detail springing to mind: Rocklike skin with deep crevices and crags. White-moon eyes, one half covered by a drooping lid. A snarling mouth, ugly when it frowned, uglier still when smiling. The incarnation of a child's imagined goblin.

He closed his eyes, shaking his head to drive that image away. When he looked again, Ragniprava was beside him, eyes inches from his own.

"The final words," the Faerie growled. "I've smelled them at last. The final words of the Eldest of Southlands, there in your mind. 'Leave my presence . . . *my son!*'"

The next few moments happened in a flash of color and noise. Ragniprava roared, a tiger once more, but before his claw-tipped hand could swipe into Lionheart's face, a scarlet missile flew across the table and barreled into him. The Faerie lord rolled one way, the Chief Poet of Rudiobus another, and Lionheart sprang to his feet and up onto the table, overturning platters of fruit as he did so.

Eanrin leapt up onto the table beside Lionheart. "All right, my lad," he said, drawing a long knife from his belt, "things could get a bit hairy in a moment. Just stay—"

That was when Ragniprava split himself.

Two Tigers, mirror images, sank to the ground in preparation to spring. One set of eyes fixed on the poet, the other on Lionheart.

"Dragon's teeth," Eanrin swore. "There's two of him now, isn't there?"

Both of Ragniprava sprang.

The poet pushed, and Lionheart fell off the other side of the table just before the right-hand Tiger landed on him. His elbow smashed into the knee of a stone prince, but he ignored the shooting pain darting up his arm and crawled under the table, which was too low for the Tiger to fit beneath. From this vantage point, he could see the other Tiger giving chase to Eanrin, who had sprung for the ivy wall and was climbing up it as fast as a monkey. The Tiger leapt and landed on the top of the wall, balancing there to meet the ascending cat-man. Eanrin stopped and dropped back to the floor below, then darted from the banquet hall to the passages beyond, calling over his shoulder as he went, "I'll be back in a trice! Sit tight!"

The Tiger sped after, close on his heels.

10

THE BOY AWOKE gazing up into Princess Varvare's face and, over her shoulder, up at the statue of the old Queen of Arpiar. They could have been twins, he thought, though the one was stone. To his eyes, they were both solemn and beautiful and sad.

"Hullo," the Boy said groggily. "What's your name?"

The princess did not answer but helped him sit up. Only then did he realize he was lying full length on the cold marble floor, and he accepted her help gratefully. "Did I miss something?" he asked, blinking. His head hurt like nothing else, and sitting up sent sharp needles down his neck. He groaned and leaned forward, and Varvare supported him with gentle hands. "I don't remember . . . anything," he whispered. "Where am I?"

"Palace Var," she said. "In King Vahe's assembly hall."

"Oh?" The names meant nothing to him, but the girl was kind, so he leaned against her like a child seeking comfort from his mother. She smelled of roses, and he liked the scent, so he closed his eyes.

The princess sat awkwardly with her arms around the half-conscious youth, and felt the gaze of her grandmother heavy upon her. The other statues laughed and pointed from their pedestals, and she scowled up at them, which only provoked them more. But her ancestors could not touch her from beyond the grave, so she decided to ignore them and concentrated on the Boy. He was groaning and holding his head. Varvare rocked him softly and hummed. Then she sang in a very low voice:

> *"Beyond the Final Water falling*
> *The Songs of Spheres recalling.*
> *When all around you is the emptiness of night,*
> *Won't you return to me?"*

Tears formed in her eyes and fell into the Boy's hair. His groaning ceased, and he slept once more, even as Varvare's voice trailed off into silence.

The unicorn approached.

She looked up and found it pacing silently between the statues, which recoiled from it in terror, writhing on their foundations. But she smiled a little as it drew near, for it was so beautiful.

Princess, it said in that musical language without words. It bowed to her as reverently as it would to its master. ***Princess, the borders of Arpiar are safe. No one will find this realm.***

She shrugged. "All right."

Moonblood is fast approaching.

"So they say. I don't know what any of you mean by it, though."

Princess, will you kill me?

She glared at the unicorn then and unconsciously tightened her hold on the sleeping Boy. "If I've told you once, I've told you a thousand times—I don't kill things! You're old and you're beautiful, and I couldn't kill you if my life depended on it!"

Your life depends upon it.

Varvare shuddered at the unicorn's voice, and she dropped her gaze. "If . . . if that's true, I still couldn't do it."

Then I will know sorrow.

"Well, I'm sorry for you. But that's just how it is sometimes."

Not for Hymlumé's children.

With those words, it left her as silently as it had come. Princess Varvare did not even see it depart; it was simply there no more.

Regret and repentance do not always walk hand in hand.

Queen Anahid wore guilt like weighty chains about her neck, but repentance was far from her. Thus she inflicted upon herself all the torments of love forsaken and the bitterness of slavery under the King of Arpiar. It seemed just punishment for her sins . . . for the lives she had taken as the old queen's slave. For the atrocities she had committed at the bidding of monarchs; first the queen, now King Vahe. She suffered every day, hating each moment of her life, waking or sleeping—for even her sleep was plagued with nightmares.

But it was punishment meted out by herself alone. And in that she found a grain of satisfaction.

Regret, Anahid believed, must be the most intense of all punishments. Regret of chances lost and opportunities forgone. She had made her choice five hundred years ago, however, in turning her back on the love offered her then. For she deserved no such love. Rather, she deserved a life with the king of goblins, bound to his service. She had selected this path with her eyes wide open, and she would make no other choice even now.

But she regretted . . . oh, many, many things!

Anahid sat among the roses in the eastern wing of Var, waiting. The perfume was as poison to her, but over many years she had learned to bear it, even if she never became accustomed to it. She waited, and eventually he came, just as she knew he would.

"Anahid," said the yellow-eyed dragon.

She looked up into the face that had once been Diarmid's. If she felt pain at the sight, he did not see it, for her mask was absolute. "I'm glad you've come," she said.

"Anahid," the dragon said again, as though speaking her name was the sole pleasure he had known in many long generations. He dropped to his knees before her. His hair was long and lank about his face, his skin sallow and his cheeks sunken. Though his features were human, no one could look into those reptilian eyes and fail to see the dragon inside him. The fire that had replaced his heart long ago burned and filled the air with heat.

But for a moment Anahid glimpsed the young man he had once been. "Tell me," she said quietly, "do you love me still?"

The yellow-eyed dragon could not look at her, but he remained kneeling at her feet, his hands outstretched as if he would clasp hers, though he did not touch her. "No," he said. "I can no longer love. I have no heart. It was burned away by Death-in-Life long ago."

The queen nodded at this, and for a moment they sat in silence. Then she said, "Do you remember your love for me?"

"That," he said, "I will never forget."

"Then I will not command you," Anahid said. "Though because I woke you, I could if I chose. But instead, let me ask you. Let me beg, in light of that love you once bore for me."

"I will do anything for you," the yellow-eyed dragon said.

She took his hands in hers. They burned at first, but she did not let go, though he struggled to pull them away. The burning died back, and his fingers lay helpless in her grasp. Only for a moment, however. Then he clutched back, drawing her hands to his breast as if clinging to a lifeline.

Anahid said, "I want you to go from Arpiar. I want you to return to the Prince's Haven. Return to that place where we met so long ago, and where you loved me once. Find the Knights of Farthestshore and warn them of my husband's plan."

The dragon paled, his wan skin turning ashen.

"I have a daughter," Anahid said. "Varvare is her name. You must have guessed what the king intends to do with her."

He nodded. "I saw the . . . the one-horned beast."

She drew his hands up to her lips and kissed them almost fiercely. "Please, my one-time love. Please, the Night of Moonblood will be upon us soon."

"Anahid," said he, "you know what will be my fate if I do as you ask."

Tears glistened in her eyes, but her voice was even when she spoke. "Our lives were both destroyed by Death-in-Life long ago. But my daughter, my sweet Varvare, she may yet live, Diarmid. She may yet know the grace from which we have strayed so far. But only if . . ."

Her words ended in silence as the yellow-eyed dragon raised his face to meet her gaze. Age-old memories passed between them in a moment, along with a knifelike flash of the future to come. And suddenly the dragon took her face in his hands and kissed her forehead, gently, so that his lips would not burn her skin.

Two tears rolled down her cheeks.

Then he was gone, and Anahid remained among the roses, which had turned their faces away, their petals drooping and brown-edged with sorrow.

Fear was not well-known to Sir Eanrin. He generally found it got in the way, so he bypassed the emotion entirely. The last time he could remember being truly afraid, he had lost his eyes, so really, what good had it done him? And after the loss of his eyes, what could anything or anyone take from him that he valued more? His life? What a foolish thing to fear, especially for a cat!

So as he sped through the ruins of Ragniprava's palace, Eanrin was not afraid, though he felt the hot breath of the Tiger on the back of his neck more than once. A touch of concern, perhaps, seeped into his heart; concern for the mortal, though, not for himself.

The twisting passages were easy enough to navigate. For century upon century, Eanrin had explored all the most fantastic palaces and temples and labyrinths of Faerie, and he knew what to expect, even among these ruins. In the darkness that fell as suddenly as the snuffing of a candle, he moved more easily than a man with sight would have, used as he was to blindness.

Lionheart, however, was not so lucky. When all the lights gleaming from the strange plants of Ragniprava's demesne suddenly extinguished, he gasped where he crouched under the table. It was as though ink had been poured into his eyes. He heard the Tiger breathing, snuffling, attempting to get his huge body underneath the low table.

"Come out, little prince," he said. "I don't want to damage you before adding you to my collection, but I will if I must. Come out and it will be easier on you."

Lionheart said nothing. His ears were his only ally, so he scarcely breathed as he strained them to hear every movement the Tiger made. He knew when Ragniprava had drawn up to his right, and he rolled left just in time. He felt the wind of enormous claws swiping into empty air.

"It's no good," Ragniprava said, and Lionheart heard him leap onto the table above. Platters clanged and fruit rolled; then the Tiger came heavily down on the other side. Lionheart rolled right, and again just missed losing an arm. His lungs screamed for air, but still he dared not draw a complete breath. He started, very slowly, to crawl toward the end of the table, between the rows of stone princes' feet.

The Tiger leapt onto the table again, walking just above Lionheart as he moved. "I can hear you, mortal. And I see well in this pitch night. Don't think you can escape the will of Ragniprava!"

But Lionheart crawled on, feeling carefully before him as he went. He thought he must be near the end of the table now, and reached forward, his hand seeking.

The Tiger guessed his plan.

Just as Lionheart's hand touched the hilt of the enormous sword, Ragniprava sprang down, his great bulk knocking aside the chair, shattering it to pieces. The sword, which had been propped against it, clattered down out of Lionheart's reach. The Tiger paced heavily up to it, then instantly was a man again. He picked up the sword, hefting it in both hands. Predatory eyes gleamed in the darkness, fixing upon Lionheart where he crouched beneath the table.

"Come out, come out, mortal man," said Ragniprava. With a heaving cry, he swung the blade. It clove through the stone table, shattering the air as it rang out its strength. Lionheart gasped and crawled back even as the sword came down again. This time a whole chunk of the table fell away. No giant's cleaver could have dealt so deft a blow. "I'll have you out myself if I have to cut away all the stone in my realm!"

Lionheart's hand touched something on the floor. Long and thin but familiar. He took hold of Bloodbiter's Wrath and, dragging the beanpole along, backed out from under the table, opposite Ragniprava. He stood up, bracing himself, the beanpole brandished in both hands.

Ragniprava smiled. "You think to stop my blade with that?"

Lionheart didn't know what he thought. He knew that the table could offer him no more shelter. He knew that he could see nothing in the dark save Ragniprava's gleaming eyes and the light from them glancing off the sword edge. He knew with cold certainty that his final moment had come.

The Tiger leapt over the table, his great sword upraised for the kill. On instinct, Lionheart raised the beanpole to protect himself.

The ring of steel upon steel clanged in his ears, and both he and the Faerie lord cried out in surprise. For Ragniprava's sword had broken into a thousand pieces and lay in shards upon the floor.

Lionheart stood eye to eye with the Faerie. Then he was a tiger once more. Before Lionheart could think to move, the Faerie's bulk came down upon him. Claws drove into Lionheart's shoulder, and his scream was lost in the Tiger's roar. He felt the creature's hot breath on his face, and still he screamed, in rage as much as pain, and waited for powerful jaws to close about his throat.

Then, suddenly, the Tiger's roar ceased. His body fell atop Lionheart, smothering him with its weight. Lionheart gave one last gasp. His eyes rolled wildly and, for a moment, he gazed into the awful face of the Hunter.

Then Lionheart too was silent.

Eanrin, deep in the passages, heard Lionheart's scream and its abrupt end. He cursed and spun around, bracing his feet, his long knife held in both hands. The second Tiger sprang at him, but at the last possible instant, the poet ducked and somersaulted so that the huge cat went over him into the darkness.

Then Eanrin was on his feet and running again, and this time he pursued the Tiger.

Ragniprava turned about in surprise to find the poet lunging at his face with a knife. His bellow filled the whole valley as the blade entered his eye.

Eanrin jumped back, just avoiding a slash of claws to his stomach. He sprang several steps away, crying, "You're yet alive, Lord Bright as Fire. Would you like to retreat, or would you rather I took this life of yours?"

The Tiger crouched to the ground, blood seeping from his mangled eye.

"I'll oblige you either way," Eanrin said, taking a step forward. "What's a single life, after all, to one such as you? But make a decision swiftly, for I must return to the jester."

"You took my eye!" the Tiger snarled. "Death-in-Life devour you!"

"You have another," said the poet. "Not everyone's so fortunate." He took another advancing step. "Would you rather I killed you now?"

The Tiger snarled again, feinting an attack. Then he turned about and disappeared into the darkness of his palace. Eanrin, relieved, let out a huge breath, then whirled and ran back the way he had come.

Lionheart! The dragon-kissed fool! Why had he not done as he was told and stayed put? The Tiger could never have reached him under that table, not if he was careful! The poet cursed to himself again and again as he sped through the corridors. Then he came to the banquet hall where the stone princes and their chairs lay toppled about the shattered table. The Faerie lord's own seat lay in splinters, and . . .

Eanrin took a deep breath and smelled death. But it wasn't a mortal's death.

"Great Lumé's crown!" he cried. "Have I misjudged you, jester? Did you actually slay the beast?"

"No," spoke a voice, terrible though sharp teeth. "I did."

11

LIONHEART STOOD IN STONY DARKNESS, and it was not as bad as it could be, considering. He was pain-free, which was not something he could say for his last few convoluted memories. These were indistinct on all but one point.

Ow!

Among the rest of the jumble that was his mind, that part stood out with crystalline clarity. Better not to try remembering too much, or to try recalling how he came to this place of darkness and silence. He was comfortable, and for the moment, that was all he cared about. So he closed his eyes—or maybe he didn't? It was hard to say in this place—and let out a sigh that did nothing to disturb that enveloping, solid quiet. For the first time in many years, he felt at peace.

That's when he heard a sob.

"By the Flowing Gold, what are you doing here?" Eanrin cried as he stepped into the banquet hall, his hand extended. It was clasped warmly in return, and a voice like falling rocks growled an answer.

"I felt a trembling on the edge of Arpiar," said the Hunter. "Someone calling from within. Only once, and very faint, but I felt it. I could not follow it to its source, but I was able to trace its destination. Here. That mortal, lying yonder underneath Ragniprava's old carcass."

"Is he alive?"

"Not in this body."

"No, the fool, I mean."

"The mortal? Yes, I think so."

"Well, Oeric," said the poet, "I'm glad you turned up when you did, then. Not that I needed you, of course. I had everything perfectly under control. But your ugly bulk may just come in handy." He strolled over to the heap where the Tiger crushed Lionheart, and knelt to feel first the animal's and then the young man's pulse. "A little worse for wear, I should think."

Oeric, massive as a mountain with stone-hard skin and luminous eyes that saw everything in the dark, stepped up beside the poet and, with one great heave, lifted the Tiger off of Lionheart. "We'd best leave this place, Eanrin," he said gravely as his comrade, with sensitive fingers, inspected Lionheart's wounded shoulder. "Ragniprava will not be glad of the loss of this life and will return for our heads soon enough. I'd not like to face him in a rage like that."

"Oh, he'll be a while at least," said Eanrin dismissively. "I took an eye from his second life, and he's off somewhere sulking about it."

"A sulking tiger is no laughing matter." Oeric eyed the carcass beside the fallen Lionheart. The orange and black fur began to gleam faintly in its own light, like fire. The lights of the forest were also slowly returning, illuminating the hall once more, revealing the captive faces of the stone princes. "Who are all these poor devils?"

"No one with whom you should concern yourself," Eanrin said, intent on his work. His smile fell into something of a grimace as he realized the extent of Lionheart's wounds. "They'll remain bound as you see them until Lord Bright as Fire's final life is spent. So unless you want to stay and kill him twice more—"

"And the mortal?"

"He'd be lost while you're at it."

Oeric sighed and knelt to put an arm under Lionheart's shoulders. The dark Southlands' complexion was chalky even in the strange glow of Ragniprava's forest. "Is it safe for me to move him?"

"Safer than leaving him here." The poet backed away as his giant comrade picked up Lionheart as easily as he would lift a child. But Lionheart would not relinquish his hold on his sword.

"A fine piece," Eanrin said, feeling the weapon clutched in Lionheart's fist. "A bit gaudy. He had it with him at Hill House, though it had not yet revealed its true substance to his mortal eye. How little the folk of the Near World trust the power of their own imaginations!"

The hilt was gold, encrusted with jewels, just the sort of weapon that a young boy would dream of wielding. But the steel was true. Magical, even, as evidenced by the broken shards of Ragniprava's weapon lying about them on the stone.

"Let him keep it," Oeric said. "He may be glad of a reminder of this night someday. I saw him. He faced the Tiger as bravely as any mortal might."

Eanrin shrugged but arranged Lionheart's arms so that the sword's blade rested against Oeric's shoulder. "Shall we to the Haven, then?" the poet said. "Imraldera will have an idea what to do."

"Yes," said Oeric. "And you can tell me as we go who this young man is. And why someone within Arpiar would call him, of all people."

They left behind the ruined palace and the lurking presence of Ragniprava, who did not show his mutilated face. Oeric held Lionheart gently and followed his blind guide. Eanrin took them straight through the seemingly impenetrable forest and up the side of the precipice. The waterfalls had ceased their laughter and watched the progress of the two knights. The forest did not hum but waited until these three intruders should depart the wilds of the Tiger's demesne.

Eanrin led them to the two white birches without straying, a feat that even Sir Oeric with night-seeing eyes doubted he could have accomplished. There were reasons why he walked in the blind man's footsteps. Eanrin passed between the birches, and Oeric came behind him, bearing

Lionheart out of the Far World for the time being and back into the Wood Between. The sun was bright as midday overhead, though beneath the trees the shadows were dark green.

"Here is our path," Eanrin said, moving more swiftly now, for he was better acquainted with this terrain. Oeric hastened behind him as around them the world blurred, the shadows and lights blending together as the two knights and their unconscious burden traveled many leagues in a stride.

"You must tell me, Eanrin, who this boy is," Sir Oeric said, the blade of the sword slapping and sliding against his shoulder with each step he took. "How have you fallen in with him, and what has he to do with Arpiar?"

Eanrin sneered a little behind his constant smile. "You wouldn't know him, Oeric, but he was once a prince. He's the Eldest of Southlands' only son."

"Indeed?" Oeric frowned and gazed down at the stony face in his arms. There was something distinctly gray in Lionheart's skin now, beyond mere pallor. The power of Ragniprava was potent, and though Lionheart still breathed, he was slowly turning to stone. He was also getting heavier, though that hardly mattered to one of Oeric's strength. "The lad who gave Princess Una's heart to our Enemy?"

"The same," said Eanrin, and this time his smile vanished, if only for a moment. "And if not for our Prince, my mistress might even now be as heartless and fire-filled as the Bane of Corrilond herself!" His voice became a growl. "I should have left the mortal to the Tiger."

"Why are you with him?"

"The Prince's command. This creature's supposed to help us find the Crossing into Arpiar. Which should interest you, I imagine."

Oeric's eyes widened and he looked again at his burden's hardening face. "He knows a way into Arpiar?"

"Hardly!" Eanrin snorted. "Do you think we'd have ended up in Ragniprava's demesne if he did? No, rather than proving useful, he gave a strand of his hair to old Torkom in exchange for directions to his doom. The fool is useless."

"Our Prince would not have sent you to help him for no purpose," Oeric said quietly. "He always has his reasons."

Eanrin gave a short laugh. "That's good of you to say in light of your hopeless task."

"Our Prince does not give his servants hopeless tasks. They sometimes do not follow an expected path, but they are never hopeless."

"Even five-hundred-year searches for an undiscoverable gate?" Eanrin shook his head. "Your faith does you credit, Oeric. I serve the Prince and will serve him till I die or the Final Waters sweep all this away! But—" And here one hand touched the patches over his empty eye sockets, a swift gesture that Oeric did not notice. The poet dropped his voice and finished softly, "But perhaps I'll always find the paths more difficult to walk than would a man of greater faith."

Then, because he was the Chief Poet of Iubdan Rudiobus, he laughed and filled his face with more smiles. "I'm sorry to say this mortal is a worthless specimen, and I predict even our good Lady of the Haven will want to toss him out on his ear within a day and a night."

"Imraldera never gives up," Oeric said simply. "She didn't give up on me."

"She's an idealist; we'll grant her that."

"Eanrin, tell me now: Does this boy know someone within Arpiar? Someone who would call for him?"

"We believe so, yes." Eanrin turned toward Oeric, and the next moment he was an orange cat standing with tail raised in a plumy question mark. He flicked it twice. "You recall not long ago when the little maid Rose Red, for whom Vahe had been searching, was at last discovered? She was banished into the Wood—the Wilderlands, as the Southlanders call it—outside the circle of protection made for her. Not even her guardian could protect her when Vahe sent the one-horned beast."

Oeric did not answer. He remembered all too well. Rose Red had not been the only one seized by the unicorn that day.

Eanrin twisted his ears and indicated Lionheart with a paw. "It was he who sent her there."

Oeric froze in midstride, gazing down at the face of the young man he carried. He was silent as he studied it. He watched how the slow poison of Ragniprava's spell seeped from the inside out and began to run down his body. Even then, he could not bring himself to speak for a long moment. At last he said in a low, growling voice, "Then he bears the guilt of many sins on his shoulders."

"I told you he was a fool."

The yellow-eyed dragon knew the Crossing to and from Arpiar well enough. He crept there like a shadow, moving as only dragons can so that unfriendly eyes might not see him. The Old Bridge in the forest was a familiar sight, though it was many centuries since he'd last seen it. He crossed over, out of the Far World and into the Wood Between. Vahe showed no signs of stopping him. There were no spells that the dragon could sense on the boundaries of Arpiar to prevent his leaving. But he knew what his doom would be.

He must be swift, very swift, or he would never reach the Haven.

Wraithlike, he fled down Goldstone Hill and into the forest, using Paths he had not trod since days he'd thought forgotten. Every step that took him nearer to the Haven was an agony. The thought of seeing any of his former brethren again was bitter in his heart.

But Anahid had asked. He could not refuse.

The unicorn, on feet too fine to touch the boards beneath, crossed over the Old Bridge and stood a moment in the Wood. It lifted its nose, sniffing the air until it caught the scent it needed. Then it too descended Goldstone Hill, although without haste. It would reach its destination in good time.

PART FOUR

THE PROPHECY

1

T HE LADY OF THE HAVEN sat watch at the bedside of the wounded Lionheart, her hands quiet in her lap. There was little else she could do. He was sinking deeply into the stone of Ragniprava's spell. More than half his body was rock hard now. But worse than that, so was more than half his soul.

Now and then she would sing to him. Her voice was low and almost too rough to be thought pretty. It bore a sound of ancient days, of young people living on a wilder land in a wilder time; a sound of one who lived close to dirt and roots but who also knew how to gaze into the highest vaults of the sky. And the song she sang was old.

> *"Beyond the Final Water falling,*
> *The Songs of Spheres recalling.*
> *Won't you return to me?"*

When she could convince one of her brethren to sit with him, Dame Imraldera would go to her library. There, she searched among her books and scrolls and papers for something that might help. Every time she returned, however, she could only repeat the same song she had sung already a thousand times.

Her fellow knights came and went, ever ready at her call should she need them. Eanrin showed his scornful face, but she glimpsed the concern hiding there. The poet was all talk. She had known him long enough to recognize that. What he truly thought and felt behind those silken eye patches, however, was anyone's guess. Despite all the years they had served together—centuries by the Near World's count—Imraldera still could not fathom the workings of his mind.

Oeric was different. Though his ugly face was like rock, his eyes were as transparent to her as glass. She saw each emotion play through them. She saw the anger, carefully controlled. She saw the desolation and then the faintest hope. Five hundred years he had labored in his quest, a labor of which all others had long since despaired. Yet here, in the form of this fevered young man, lay perhaps the key—the key to entering Arpiar, the key to reaching Var.

She saw how the goblin knight's hand sometimes drifted to touch the knife at his side. She never need speak or move to interfere, but she saw the pain in his eyes and wondered. For this fool who lay unconscious under her care had unknowingly dealt a most painful blow to Sir Oeric. There were some, Imraldera knew, who would not stand in the knight's path to revenge.

Nevertheless, he would turn his sad eyes to her and say only, "Will he recover?"

To that, she could only reply, "He's not gone yet."

So they waited.

If anything could disturb the perfect equilibrium of that quiet, hard place, it was a sob. The sound sent chills up Lionheart's spine, and that peace he had known, if only for a short time, shattered around him.

He waited to hear another.

It was like one stormy night when he was a boy, and his servant put a basin beneath a leak in the ceiling, for even palace roofs sometimes leak. *Drip, drip, drip,* the rain fell in a regular beat, a beat he could fall asleep to. Then suddenly, the dripping was less frequent, the timing thrown off. He heard a last *drip,* then strained his ears for the one that must follow. But it didn't. Wasn't it beating a regular rhythm just moments ago? Would there be—

Drip!

There it was, and he breathed once more.

Then he waited for another.

So it was in that blackness. Lionheart heard a first sob, and it was followed by a second soon thereafter. But Lionheart, though his every muscle tensed with expectation of a third, heard nothing more. He turned in the darkness, casting about for some sign of the sobber, whoever he or she might be. He wondered for half a moment if it was his own voice. But he was altogether too content right now to cry! No, there must be someone else with him in this place, disturbing the stone-silence. He might need to have words with this person when he—

And there it was.

The third sob.

It wrenched his gut, for it was much closer than the others.

Lionheart turned and opened his eyes—if indeed they had been closed, for what difference did it make in this dark?—and saw that he was home.

Home . . . in his father's house, the place of his birth and his childhood years. He knew this room very well, an anteroom used by his father for meetings with his various barons. Maps were nailed to the walls, elegant maps much more useful for decoration than for navigation, and heavy curtains hung in the tall windows. The curtains were new. Lionheart noted that right away with the absolute clarity that comes only to dreamers. The curtains were new, for the old ones had reeked of dragon fumes.

Across from Lionheart was a chair like a small throne, the seat where the Eldest would sit while the visiting baron took a place in a lower chair opposite him. How many times as a boy had Lionheart himself come before his father in this very room? Every time his mother, Queen Starflower, made the threat, *"Just wait until your father hears about this!"* Lionheart had found himself hustled off to this very place.

The comfort of familiarity gave way suddenly to the shame and expectation of impending discipline. But no! This could not be! Lionheart was no longer some baby-faced boy to be lectured for practicing fire-eating in the stables. He was a man, and it was his place to sit in his father's chair. Let the barons sweat, not the son of Southlands' Eldest. So he took the seat and faced the room.

And realized that he sat opposite the Prince of Farthestshore.

Dread dropped heavily in Lionheart's stomach.

"Come with me," said the Prince.

Lionheart gripped the arms of his chair as though he would break them. "See here," he said, "I'm sorry about what became of her. I am. But there isn't a solitary thing I can do about it now, is there?"

"You can come with me," said the Prince.

Lionheart grimaced. "A lot of things happened during my exile. Most of them I wish to forget. She was kind to me when I needed a friend, and . . . and I appreciated her kindness. But I couldn't help what happened next."

"Come with me."

Lionheart tried to look away, anywhere but into those so horribly kind eyes. But he couldn't break that gaze. "There was too much, simply too much when I came back! I couldn't very well leave, could I, when my people needed me?"

"Come with me, Lionheart."

"But I can't go with you! I can't chase after you into a desert full of dragons and get burned to cinders! I cannot abandon my father and my people now for certain death, no more than I could harbor Rose Red when all of Southlands believed her a demon. It would have torn the kingdom apart. Haven't they suffered enough, Prince? I had to think of them, not myself, not Rose Red, not anyone else. Just Southlands. How could I serve my country by facing the Dragon again?"

"Lionheart . . ."

"You know what happened last time! You know what I did as well as I do. I crumpled under his gaze! I could not lift a finger to help myself. I cannot fight the Dragon; I don't pretend that I can! A man has his limits, and who can face that monster and survive? I did the best I could; I ensured Southlands' safety. Is that not enough?"

" . . . come with me."

Here at last, unable to speak, Lionheart wrenched his gaze away from the Prince of Farthestshore.

He saw who it was who sobbed in the dark.

Imraldera watched her patient's face. Though the features did not move, she saw them hardening. She stopped singing over him and sat back with a sigh. Then she turned to the knight beside her.

"The Prince sent you to bring Lionheart to this Haven. Why didn't you lead him here directly?"

"Don't scold so, old girl! It's unbecoming," said Eanrin. He lounged gracefully on a nearby chair, one leg extended and an elbow hooked over the chair's back, the picture of ease. "We were well on our way, I tell you, when we met a couple of old friends of yours."

"Old friends? What are you talking about?"

She saw Eanrin hesitate, noting how his easy pose tensed for a moment. He opened his mouth, closed it, then finally said, "The Black Dogs. We saw the Black Dogs in the Wood."

She narrowed her eyes at him, though the expression was lost upon the blind poet. "Not hunting this mortal, I trust."

"Need you ask?" The poet laughed harshly and shook his head. "Had they hunted the lad, they'd have caught him long ere now, and not a thing could I have done to stop them. I hate dogs."

Imraldera nodded, still watching the poet. His profile was set and intent, as though he were making a study of their patient even without his sight. "You're keeping something from me," she said.

He shrugged.

"Did you meet no one else?"

"I'll tell you no lies, Imraldera," he said, still not turning from the mortal. "But I'll not tell you all truths either. Lumé love us!" He laughed and tossed his golden head. "After all these years, is a man no longer entitled to a secret or two of his own?"

She watched the smile lines about his mouth, the crinkles beneath the patches covering where his eyes had been. She saw them fade as the smile slowly melted from his face again. And she wondered many things but kept her peace. She turned back to her patient, wiping his brow with a cool cloth. "You don't care much for this young man, do you, Eanrin?"

"Can't say that he's a great favorite."

"It's because he doesn't like your poetry, isn't it."

Eanrin glowered. "When have I ever been so petty?"

She made no reply to this but turned once more to Lionheart. He was so young, lying there half succumbed to powerful enchantment. His face had the softness of a boy's despite the thin growth of beard. But the expression was not that of a boy. No child in sleep looked so miserable save in the deepest of nightmares. She wondered what dark paths he walked in his mind. Gently, she put out a hand and brushed the hair across his forehead, which was cold under her fingers.

Eanrin made a rather cattish growl. "Remember, he gave little Una's heart to the Dragon. He didn't fight."

"He's only mortal, Eanrin. Who's to say what any of us would have done in his place?"

"I'd not toss a girl's heart around so blithely!"

"Wouldn't you?"

One of those silences followed which a stranger observing would not have understood. But even a stranger would sense the unspoken tension between two people who did not look at each other and did not speak. Even a stranger would realize that some history existed between these two that he could not guess. And even a stranger would realize that he was intruding on a private moment that could, in a flash, explode into an out-and-out fight or, perhaps, if miracles still happen, dwindle into something like understanding.

But the silence ended instead with the poet rising gracefully from his chair, clearing his throat, and marching across the room to lean against the trunk of a poplar tree. He crossed his arms, the expression on his face something between a sneer and a smile.

"What of Rose Red?" he said.

Imraldera, letting out a long breath between clenched teeth, put a hand to Lionheart's forehead again, though she wasn't entirely aware of him anymore. "Who?"

"The goblin girl who served in his father's house all those years. Are you going to tell me that you would have banished her to certain death when she had done no wrong, just to placate a mob?"

"I'm saying we cannot know what any of us would have done if faced with the same choice," she responded softly.

"Tell that to Oeric. He suffered more than either of us that day."

"Yet he carried the lad here. Even when he knew."

The poet crossed his arms even farther up his chest. He still smiled, though the rest of his face was a distinct scowl. "I did my part."

Imraldera turned to him then, and her voice was urgent. "Do your part now, Eanrin. Help me sing over him. You know your voice is stronger than mine, and together we could call him back."

"I don't fancy singing over the likes of him."

"And what would I have done if you'd said the same of me?" said Oeric.

The lady and the poet turned to the enormous knight entering through the chamber door, which was simultaneously nothing but a thinning place in the branches of a forest grove. He filled the room, towering above both Imraldera and Eanrin as he approached to look upon the ensorcelled Lionheart.

Eanrin snorted. "You wouldn't remember, of course, but I didn't sing over you, Oeric. I let Imraldera deal with that. She's better at that sort of thing, being the nurturing sort."

"We all know that your voice is stronger . . . when you try," Imraldera said.

The poet shrugged.

Oeric did not hear their conversation, for he was studying the face of the boy. He saw something there, something that moved him beyond the anger he felt toward this person who had caused him so much pain. Whatever he saw, he turned suddenly to Imraldera. "I will help you sing him out."

"Will you, Oeric?" Relief filled Imraldera's face. "Despite what he has done?"

Oeric nodded. When he turned back to the stone figure, he whispered, "As one who has been forgiven much, how can I refuse to forgive?"

Aloud, however, he said, "Yes, I'll help you sing. This lad may be our last link to Arpiar. No one in that kingdom could call a statue."

With those words, he opened his mouth and began in a voice as deep as mountain roots:

> *"When eve's shadows fell upon you*
> *And all your heart was overthrown,*
> *When the whispers say no choice to you remains*
> *And teardrops turn into stone . . . "*

Imraldera reached out and took Oeric's huge hand in one of hers and placed her other on Lionheart's cold face. Then she too sang:

> *"Beyond the Final Water falling,*
> *The Songs of Spheres recalling.*
> *When you hear my voice beyond the darkened veil*
> *Won't you return to me?"*

Eanrin stood to one side, his shoulders hunched.

It was Rose Red.

When he turned, Lionheart felt the sudden icy blast of winter and found that he stood on the wall of the Eldest's City. Wind howled, and its voice was the voice of an angry mob, shouting for blood. The faces and figures of a hundred people crowded around him, indistinct as phantoms; but Rose Red, kneeling before him, was clearer than memory. She bent under the painful grasp of the phantom that held her, shielded by a black veil.

Then she raised her head, and he saw that she wore no veil. Instead, black hair fell away from her face, and she looked up at him in surprise.

She was beautiful. She was crying.

Darkness closed in around them. The phantoms vanished; the wall and the angry wind fled. Only he and Rose Red remained. Her eyes were wide and silver, quite unlike the horrible white eyes he remembered see-ing and yet strangely familiar to him. Her sobbing stopped with a choke when she saw him. The coldness of her gaze hurt. He wanted to speak and struggled for words.

"Rosie," he said, "I'm going to find you."

She made no answer.

"I'll make it right."

She closed her eyes and turned away. Her hair veiled her from his gaze.

"Please," he said. "Please, say something."

Only her mouth remained visible behind her hair. He saw her lips move. No sound came, but he knew what she had said.

"You're lost."

Desperation took him, and he reached out to her. But she was miles from him now. How could he make her understand? He wasn't lost! He knew what he had done; he could look back on his own actions with a steady eye. How could he tell her that, given the choice, he would do it all again? His choices had led to suffering, even to sacrifice. But he had made them with good in his heart.

Hadn't he?

She was farther from him now, and his hands would never reach her. No one would sympathize with the pain he had experienced, so caught up as they were with the pain he had caused. Why couldn't they see that he had only wanted the good of his people? Why couldn't they understand?

Why couldn't *she* understand?

"I'll find you!" Lionheart called after her through the haze of dreams. "I'll find you, and I'll explain everything!"

Eanrin listened to Imraldera and Oeric sing, and he heard when Imral-dera's voice faltered suddenly with fear. They were losing the mortal.

Then Imraldera, still singing, turned her gaze upon Eanrin. He felt it, though he could not see it. And he remembered days long ago, back when he'd possessed his sight. Days when those black-as-night eyes of hers could ask him anything, and he would do it. That time was long gone, perhaps, but not forgotten. No, he would never forget.

Only two people in all the worlds could command Bard Eanrin: His Master and . . .

Heaving a great sigh, he stepped up beside them and, after only a moment's hesitation, took Imraldera's hand and felt the pressure of her fingers squeezing his. Then he placed his other hand on Lionheart's head. He sang, joining his voice with the other two:

> *"Beyond the Final Water falling,*
> *The Songs of Spheres recalling.*
> *When all around you is the emptiness of night,*
> *Won't you return to me?"*

Lionheart woke, his eyes flaring wide as he cried out, "I'll explain everything!"

Oeric, his hand still resting on the young man's shoulder, answered quietly, "Don't try."

2

LIONHEART CAME PAINFULLY back to consciousness.

He had drifted in and out of dreamless sleep so many times he'd lost count. Now that the comforting stone around him was gone, waking meant returning to the fiery burn of claw wounds in his shoulder. But each time he woke, the pain was less, and this time when he opened his eyes, stiffness in the muscles bothered him more than anything.

He blinked at the ceiling above him. Then he blinked again when what he had taken for a painted mural of leaves against a blue background stirred in a breeze, the leaves rustling softly. A third blink, and it was a mural once more. Lionheart decided that he wasn't conscious after all and, groaning, closed his eyes and started to turn over.

"You're awake."

The voice that spoke rumbled like falling rock.

"No, I'm not." But Lionheart attempted another look at the world just in case. He still gazed up at a ceiling of leaves that was sometimes real and sometimes a painting. When he turned his head to the side, he found he wasn't alone. Seated beside him in the chamber that both was and was not a forest grove was the most enormous person he had ever seen. He was not awkward in his bulk, however, but reclined gracefully in a low chair, his chin supported on one fist and his legs stretched out before him.

He looked startlingly like Rose Red. Only a whole lot bigger.

Lionheart's head started to throb. He groaned again and decided he might as well go back to sleep, or perhaps just die altogether.

"No, no," said the stranger in that rumbling voice. "Now you are awake, you should drink something."

"I told you, I'm not awake," Lionheart growled.

"I'm afraid you are."

The next moment, a silver cup was held to Lionheart's lips. He realized with some surprise that he was parched and accepted the proffered drink gratefully. Only after he had drained the cup dry did he stop to wonder if this was a good idea. There had been plenty of stories in his nursemaid's repertoire about the dangers of accepting Faerie food from outlandish folk.

Too late now, he thought as the stranger set the empty cup aside on a nearby table, which was simultaneously a holly bush hung thick with berries. Whatever he had drunk started to flow warmly through Lionheart's body, easing the burn and the stiffness in his shoulder. He relaxed muscles he had not realized he was tensing and decided that even if he was now caught in a twisted Faerie spell, it was probably worth it for a drink like that.

The stranger turned huge eyes upon him. "Now," he said, "if you are feeling better, we must talk."

"What if I'm not feeling better?"

"We must talk anyway."

Lionheart pushed himself upright in the down-soft bed. His head spun, and pain darted from his shoulder down his arm, but it wasn't as bad as it might be considering he'd been mauled by a tiger the night before. Or was it a week before? He closed his eyes and tried to shake those thoughts of time away. After all, time didn't count for much in this world—or place between worlds, for he suspected he was in the Wood once more.

"What do we need to talk about?"

"I am told that you seek Arpiar," said the ugly stranger.

Lionheart realized with a start that this person who looked so much like Rose Red must indeed come from the same land as she. Given his prior experience with the unsavory Torkom, he wasn't altogether certain he should trust this person, who was half again taller than the dealer. But he'd already accepted the sweet drink from him, and the stranger was making no signs of suddenly bashing Lionheart over the head with a spiked club or whatever was the usual practice of goblinkind. So Lionheart said, "I am. Where can I find it?"

"If I knew that, I would not be here with you now." The stranger sat forward, bringing his great white eyes much closer to Lionheart's face than was comfortable. "I have been seeking the Land of the Veiled People for the last five centuries."

Lionheart leaned back against the headboard. "Five *centuries*? That's . . . not encouraging."

"Five centuries by your count, little mortal," said the stranger. "Perhaps not so long as the folk of the Far World know it, and scarcely a breath in the Wood Between." He sighed then, a great, gusty sigh. "That isn't to say I have not felt the passing years stretching behind me since Arpiar was lost. But I must seek the realm of my birth, and I shall seek it until it is found . . . or until I perish."

Lionheart gulped, his head still spinning. "Why is it so difficult to find? I mean, I know this world—these worlds—are different from mine. But how can you *lose* an entire kingdom?"

The stranger reclined back in his chair again, relieving Lionheart of some of the intensity of those enormous eyes. "You've heard of islands swept away in massive waves, haven't you?"

Lionheart nodded.

"Arpiar was swept away in a wave of enchantment. Washed beyond discovery. Not destroyed but swallowed whole, five hundred years ago. Soon after Vahe died for the second time."

"Died for the . . . the *second* time?"

"Surely, mortal, you are not wholly unfamiliar with the ways of Faerie? At the least you must know the tale of the Dragonwitch."

Lionheart thought back on the old legend, how the Dragon King's first daughter had been a Faerie queen before her transformation. Heroes had fought her countless times, and twice she had been slain yet come back to flaming life. Only after her third death had she remained in the land of the dead for good.

"But that's just—" Lionheart stopped himself. What good were arguments for reality in this place? The fantastic was all too real here. "Then the King of Arpiar has three lives as well?"

"Had. As do all the lords of Faerie. Ragniprava, whose hospitality you so recently enjoyed, is another such a one. In rescuing you, I took one of his."

"You killed the Tiger?"

"One of him, yes."

"Thanks for that."

The stranger nodded. "Two lives yet remain to Lord Bright as Fire. Perhaps only one; I can't say for sure. All other lords, kings, and queens are gifted the same. Iubdan Rudiobus and his fair Bebo. The Mherking under the sea. Lady Nidawi the Everblooming, the serpent ChuMana, Butannaziba Who Walks Before the Night, and hundreds more. All are blessed—or sometimes cursed—with three lives each. When Vahe took his own mother's third life, that gift passed to him. But he has lost two."

The stranger's eyes no longer saw Lionheart as he recounted a history so long ago as to be unimaginable for Lionheart, yet which to him must have seemed but yesterday. "One life he forfeited not far from here, in a tower that once stood at the crest of Goldstone Hill; the second he lost in the Near World. Since that time, no one has glimpsed Vahe beyond the boundaries of Arpiar. And if anyone has passed into that realm, no one has returned. There are some few who have escaped—Torkom the trader, for instance, though we must wonder if he escaped or was sent by Vahe as a spy.

"Besides him, we know for certain of only one other who has slipped through the barriers of Arpiar into the mortal world, and we know that she left against Vahe's will."

"Rose Red?" Lionheart hazarded.

But the stranger shook his head. "Queen Anahid, Vahe's wife. Some twenty years ago or more by the Near World's count, she escaped her husband's spells, carrying with her a newborn child. She sought to hide the babe from Vahe for reasons we do not know. What we do know is that, in her desperation, she called upon the Prince of Farthestshore for help."

Lionheart went suddenly cold all over. "The Prince of Farthestshore?"

"Do you know my Master, the Prince?"

Lionheart's dream flashed across his mind, and he closed his eyes. "I have met him," he said quietly. "Some time ago."

"Not so long, I think," said the stranger.

Lionheart shuddered and hastily said, "What became of the queen? Vahe's wife, who ran away. Did she escape?"

"No," said the stranger. "Though offered safe haven among us, she returned to Arpiar. But the child remained in the Near World, safe as long as she dwelt inside the circle of protection Anahid called down for her, and guarded always by a Knight of Farthestshore."

His next words, though spoken softly, were as an avalanche in Lionheart's mind: "It was she whom you call Rose Red."

At first no thoughts came, only that rushing crumble of a thousand half thoughts that couldn't take coherent form. The first that resolved into anything he could understand were the words of Ragniprava, smooth as a well-sharpened knife.

"You seek a girl in the realm of Faerie. This means you seek a princess, and you will find her where princesses are to be found."

Lionheart said, "Then Rose Red really is a princess."

"She is Princess Varvare, only child of King Vahe of Arpiar, heir to the throne of the Veiled People," said the stranger.

Lionheart put his hands to his head, rubbing his temples and wrinkling his brow. "And I, by banishing her to the Wilderlands, put her outside the Prince's protection."

"You sent her where Vahe could find her, yes. And he sent the one-horned beast to fetch her back into his realm."

"The one-horned beast?"

"A being you must pray you never meet, little mortal. Not even the knight set to guard Princess Varvare could protect her from such a foe."

Another image, one he had tried many times to forget, came back to

Lionheart: a memory of standing on the edge of the Wilderlands beside a shaggy goat, which turned to him and suddenly was no goat but a fierce woman armed with a long knife. He gulped. "Beana."

"What?"

"Rose Red's pet goat. She was the knight, wasn't she?"

Something like a smile passed over the ugly features of the goblin man. "A goat?" he repeated. "What a form to choose! But, aye, that selfsame goat is a knight in the Prince's service, and a braver one you will never meet." All traces of a smile vanished from the stranger's face. "Now she is gone into Arpiar as well, gone where I cannot follow her, and I do not know if she still lives."

Lionheart was too caught up in his own distress to notice his companion's words or tone. Desperate, he said, "But why all the fuss? If Rose Red is Vahe's heir, surely she cannot be too badly treated in the land of her birth. As his only child, she would enjoy privilege, yes?"

The stranger shook his head. "Why then did her mother risk her life to carry her out of Arpiar?"

"Why?"

"That we don't know for sure. But it isn't hard to make a few guesses. Given Vahe's history of regicide, he may be concerned that his own child will do the same."

"Rose Red wouldn't hurt a fly."

"Vahe does not know that. But then again, if he feared for his own life, why would he labor so long to get her back? In seeking his daughter, Vahe has stolen all the roses of all the realms of mortals and Faeries alike, pulled them into Arpiar never to be seen again . . . no mean feat. But Vahe was always strong."

Lionheart didn't pretend to understand. Instead he asked, "And how are you part of all this? You say you have been seeking Arpiar for the last five centuries, but even by your convoluted Faerie standards of time, Rose Red couldn't have been taken there that long ago!"

"No," said the stranger. "I have been searching for Arpiar since long before the princess was born. For though I am Oeric, renamed and renewed in the Prince's service, I was once nameless, called Outcast even by my friends. I am Vahe's twin brother."

Lionheart stared. "His brother? Then you are Rose Red's—"

"Her uncle, yes."

A small eternity passed before Lionheart spoke again. "You must hate me for what I have done."

"Hate you?" Oeric shook his head, half closing his great eyes. "I cannot hate you, boy. Though you banished a girl who had done you no wrong but served you faithfully all those years, I cannot hate you. Though you placed my love in gravest danger, perhaps caused her death . . . though you betrayed the Prince's Beloved into the very hands of the Dragon, still I could not look on you with hatred. For nothing you have done could equal the evil that I myself have committed against all who loved and trusted me. No regret you ever know will compare to the despair I knew when I recognized what I had done. And no forgiveness you may yet receive will ever outshine the grace that was extended to me, the vilest of all my Master's servants.

"No, Lionheart, I can never hate you, for in truth, you and I are alike, and if our deeds were measured against one another, no one could say yours were the worse. So it is not hatred I feel for you, nor is it judgment I will deal upon your head. Instead, I offer you my help in seeking after what you have lost. For our goals have become one and the same. We both must find the land of Arpiar and rescue Princess Varvare from whatever fate Vahe has for her. Will you have me for your companion?"

The ugly knight offered Lionheart his hand, which was large enough to smash heads with a single blow. Lionheart, pale and wordless, nodded and offered his hand in return. They shook, and then Sir Oeric rose, and if he had seemed huge before, he was a veritable giant now.

"I will leave you to rest, lad. My brother knight Eanrin has proposed to bring you to Rudiobus as soon as you are able, to see what wisdom Queen Bebo might offer concerning you. But you are not yet well enough for the journey. Sleep. We will meet again soon."

Lionheart watched the knight open what was both a door and a branch thick with greenery. Oeric paused and looked back.

"Lionheart, don't try to explain what you have done."

Then he was gone.

The moon never shone in Arpiar. The people of Arpiar did not know this, of course, for Vahe could paint a moon in the sky with as much ease as he could paint their faces beautiful. And his moon was as big and luminous as anyone could wish, and no one knew the difference.

So Varvare alone in all the kingdom knew just how dark the nights were.

She sat outside with the nameless Boy beside her, surrounded by the ghosts of roses. For once, her fingers were not at work but gently fingered the cord in her pocket. It was so thin and delicate that mortal eyes could not see it, but she felt it was strong. Whether strong enough for her purposes, she could not guess. Nor could she know if she would find an opportunity to use it.

The Boy sat beside her, staring emptily up at the sky. He saw the enchantments the princess chose not to see. To him, the sky was full of stars save where the moon was so bright the stars disappeared. He turned to Varvare. "Does the moon have a name?"

"Yes," said the princess. She remembered what a shaggy goat had taught her years ago.

"What is it?"

"Hymlumé."

"What's that mean?"

"Harmony," she said, her voice soft as she recalled the goat's words. "Like when birds sing different songs together and they all blend into one chorus."

"Oh," said the Boy. He gazed up at the black sky. "That's pretty," he decided after a moment. "Do I have a name?"

"I guess so."

"What is it?"

"I don't know."

The Boy sighed. Restless, he got up and wandered through the ghostly roses, which to his eyes bloomed full and sweet. Varvare watched him go, realizing all over again how helpless he was, how sad and lost without his mind. She felt protective of him somehow, though she did not know who he was. He hadn't a friend in the world, not one that he remembered, anyway. And he did not realize the evil that surrounded him.

She set her jaw and vowed to herself, "I'll take him with me when I go. I won't let any harm come to him."

And then her mind was far from the desolate gardens of Var, speeding across distances greater than time and space to a back stairway in a holiday-filled house. She trembled once more in the darkness, clutching an empty urn.

Prince Lionheart stood before her.

"Rose Red," he said, his black eyes burning with the passion of his words. *"I don't know what I'd do without you. I fear some harm will come to you. I don't know if I could forgive myself were that to happen."*

Princess Varvare shook her head, grinding her teeth. "Have you done it now?" she growled. "Have you gone and forgiven yourself? You made such sweet promises, and I trusted you, trusted the friendship we'd had so long. But I was a fool to think you'd remember any of that! Not for a goblin. Not for a demon."

The wood thrush called to her, the voice in her head more real than the silver moonlight that lit up her father's land.

Beloved, call for him.

"I won't! I'll never call for him! I'll never trust him again, no more'n I'll trust you! You call me beloved. You said you'd always protect me. Why then have you left me here? All I did was obey you! I helped the girl up the cliff, and look what happened as a result. I've learned my lesson! You'll make me do what you like, then abandon me as quickly as the prince did. The unicorn says I'm in danger, yet you leave me in this cursed place!"

Varvare bowed her head and suddenly burst into tears, the first she'd cried since that horrible day on the edge of the Wilderlands.

The Boy, when he returned from his wanderings, found her that way. "Princess!" he cried, distressed. "Don't cry!" Though he was a tall boy just on the verge of manhood, he put his arms around her like a tiny child and wept too, because he didn't know who he was, and he didn't know who she was.

The enchanted moon vanished behind a cloud.

3

SLEEP DOES NOT COME EASILY to a mind as frustrated as Lionheart's was following his conversation with Oeric. But when his eyes were so heavy he thought they might fall out if he didn't close them, he gave up and slept.

When he woke next, all his frustrations reared their ugly heads to be solved once more, but his shoulder no longer pained him and he felt better able to cope with the rest. He wondered what kind of magic had gone into the medicine used on his dressings to have worked such wonders against the damage done by tiger claws. And he wondered to whom he owed thanks for his healing.

There was no one else in the room. Its ceiling was now painted in a mural of stars over which clouds sometimes drifted, and the leaves were black silhouettes. He could see the glow of the moon; it had not yet risen far enough for him to spot it above the tree line. A low fire built in what was both an ornamental fireplace and the bole of a tree provided him with enough light. He got up, discovered that he wore only a long nightshirt, and spent the next several moments hunting around for his clothing. There wasn't much to find. He had left his outer layers of garments behind in the steamy forest of Ragniprava, and the thin shirt that remained to him was shredded at the shoulder, though the blood had been washed away.

His trousers, at least, were intact, so he put these on, tucked the nightshirt in, and hoped he wouldn't scandalize any strangers he met by his state of undress.

Lionheart also found a sword.

It was all over gold and jewels, exactly what his boyhood imagination would have pictured heroes of old wielding. He had never seen it before and yet . . . His hand closed around the hilt. He knew the blade immediately: his beanpole, Bloodbiter's Wrath.

He nearly choked on a laugh as a memory almost forgotten came back to him: Standing in Hill House's gardens with Mousehand the gardener, the boy Leo had asked the old man for a weapon to use on his monster hunt, and frowned at what Mousehand had handed him.

"A beanpole?"

"A mighty sword, good sir knight, if you look at it right."

"You mean, use my imagination?"

"I might. Or I might not."

This was no imaginary sword gleaming in the low firelight. The blade was sharp and true, gaudily etched with monsters and vines. Lionheart smiled. He should never have doubted old Mousehand.

He took the sword with him as he sought to exit the room. A doorknob nestled among branches, and when he turned it, he was able to push the branches aside and step out of the clearing, leaving behind his bed and the little fire in the bole of the tree. A corridor of tall trees stretched before him, dark save for a faint glimmer of moonlight.

Suddenly, a flutter like that of a dozen butterflies beat against his face. He waved his hands to chase them off, but there was nothing he could see to chase. The feather-light tapping whirled about his face, rustled his hair, and even pulled at the sword in his hand, and Lionheart yelped and stepped back into the room. Then he steeled himself and strode out of the grove. With a last irritated burst, the invisibles gave a tug at his hair, then left. He drew a deep breath and started walking slowly, pointing his sword forward.

When he closed his left eye, he walked down a forest path with dense moss underfoot. Not a living thing stirred in this place, but the trees themselves whispered soft secrets at him. When he closed the other eye, he stood in a dark-paneled hall with elegant moldings carved in leaf-and-scroll patterns, the walls lined with diamond-paned windows. There were candle sconces between the windows, but none of them were lit.

When he opened both eyes, however, he saw the two scenes at once, the forest and the elegant hall, both thickly carpeted and smelling of woodland dampness and growth. And still no sign of a living creature.

He closed his right eye every couple of paces to better see if he passed other chamber doors. Most of the doors Lionheart saw were shut, and if he tested their handles he found them locked. But he came to a door at last, the largest he had found yet, that was ajar. Closing his left eye, he saw a stand of fir trees spreading their branches like skirts about them, a narrow path leading between. That looked harder to push through, so he closed his right eye instead and walked through the door.

He found himself in an enormous library.

There had been few stories told about the library during Lionheart's boyhood days in Southlands. But he dimly recalled a legend or two in which the handsome hero (his nursemaid's heroes were all handsome and had all borne a distinct resemblance to young Catspaw of the house guard) visited the Lady of the Haven to learn from her vast collection of writings the secret he required in order to rescue his fair damsel in distress (who looked like the nursemaid).

The nursemaid had described it as a mighty room, as tall as the tallest trees, with archways like branches spreading overhead, and ladders stretching up and up so one might reach the topmost volumes. Most of these were said to be written in the lady's own hand, for she took it upon herself long ago to document the history of the Far World and the Near—all the stories and poems and prophecies. He who wrote the Sphere Songs taught her the secret letters and gave her this chamber for the purpose.

And now Lionheart stood, with the moonlight pouring through the topmost branches overhead, gazing in open-mouthed wonder at what he knew must be the library of those nursery tales. It could hardly have surprised him more to discover that the moon truly was made of cheese or that rats really did have an ear for pipe music. His sword hand dropped until the point dragged on the floor as he moved deeper into that moonlit chamber.

The floors were decorated with intricate mosaics swirling in patterns around the tall trees, which were also marble pillars. Lionheart could not see the colors, but he was able to pick out the designs and realized they told stories as detailed as any that could be contained within those thousands of volumes. Most of them he did not recognize. But not five paces into the room he discovered a story he knew quite well: Starflower and the Wolf Lord. He would recognize the face of his homeland's heroine anywhere for, though every artist portrayed her differently, somehow they always caught that same expression on her face, that mixture of fear and trust.

Odd, though. He stopped and looked more closely at the picture. In every depiction of the legend he had ever seen, whether painting or pottery or the enormous Starflower Fountain, the maid was accompanied by a songbird on her shoulder. Here, however, the bird was not present. In its place was a hound, a golden beast with a long, slender face and ancient eyes. It stood by the maid's side, as though to protect her from the monstrous wolf pursuing at her heels.

Despite this difference, the story was unmistakably Starflower's. Lionheart's stomach twisted in a mixture of joy and sorrow. A wave of homesickness swept over him. He continued following the story on the floor farther into the library, curious what else he might find.

Other tales, equally fantastic, that made up the rich embroidery of Southlands' history led him deeper and deeper. He saw the story of the Dragonwitch falling to Bald Mountain, and a depiction of King Shadow Hand, who bargained with a Faerie queen. But all the stories were portrayed with slight variations on the legends he knew so well. These so intrigued him that it was some time before he realized he had not yet looked at the books. This thought brought his head up, and he found himself standing before a great cherrywood desk nearly buried beneath a partially written manuscript, a single burning candle, and a large white quill feather.

Lionheart approached the desk. The enormity of the library shrank into that little glowing world created by the candle as Lionheart's eyes, adjusting to its light, lost the night vision they had gained while walking in the shadows. He propped Bloodbiter's Wrath against the side of the desk and bent to peer at the manuscript lying in the candlelight.

It was written in characters he had never seen before. He frowned, disappointed, and started to step back. But then, the strangest sight of all the strange sights he had seen that night played out under his nose. As he watched, the characters on the page suddenly leapt up and rearranged themselves, not into words he could read, but into images streaming directly into his mind. He saw, rather than read, the story.

What he saw froze his heart.

"It is universally thought impolite to read someone else's private documents."

Lionheart whirled away from the strange writing and found himself face-to-face with a woman whom he had never met. Except . . .

Except that he knew her face.

The Lady of the Haven stood among the trees of her library and gave the impression of being as straight and tall as any of them. In reality, however, she was quite short. She held another candle in one hand, a long white taper, and rather than casting her face into deep crevices of light and shadow, it caused a soft glow on her skin and around her eyes. At one and the same time, she was very young and very old.

"Your attendants told me you were awake and wandering about my home," she said.

"Silent Lady!" Lionheart gasped.

She gave him a funny look, tilting her head a little to one side. "Why do you call me that?"

He could find nothing to say. On impulse, he shoved his hand deep into his trouser pocket and withdrew a leather cord from which dangled two beads, one painted with a panther, the other with a white starflower. He removed the starflower bead and handed it to her. "This belongs to you."

She accepted it in her palm and held it up to her taper light, turning it delicately. Her face was solemn, her expression unreadable.

Lionheart gulped. "We . . . I . . . Eanrin and I met someone in the

Wood. A phantom. He said to tell Starflower that he would yet slay a beast."

"Is that so?" Her face was quiet. She whispered, more to herself than to Lionheart, "Is that, I wonder, what he did not wish to tell me?" Then she shook her head, blinking, and turned her gaze to Lionheart once more. "There are many from Southlands," she said, "who bear the name Starflower."

He nodded. "It was my mother's name."

"Then why do you think this bead belongs to me?"

"It does, though, doesn't it?" He couldn't say how he knew. There wasn't even a songbird on her shoulder to give her away. But her face, while the features were unlike any he had ever seen portrayed, was unmistakable. "You are the Panther Master's daughter, aren't you? Maid Starflower, the Silent Lady?"

She smiled a little then. "I am called Imraldera," she said, "and I am not silent."

But she did not return the bead to Lionheart. It vanished into a pocket of her long green robe.

"You know the saying about eavesdroppers and spies, don't you?" said Imraldera. She indicated the manuscript on the cherrywood desk. "What have you learned about yourself that you wish you could unlearn?"

Lionheart bowed his head. "I already know how that story goes," he said. "I don't need to read any more."

"Have I recorded your part in the tale unjustly?"

"You did but state the facts, my lady."

A soft rustle of fabric, and she stood beside him, her hand on his shoulder. "Call me Imraldera. And I shall call you Lionheart. We two must be friends."

He shook his head and sidestepped away from her and the desk, away from the glow of the two candles. "I know that you despise me."

"How can you know anything I think or feel?"

Lionheart waved a hand indistinctly. "I read what you have written. What you have recorded for all history to know. Someday my name will be part of nursery tales too, won't it? Just like this library. Just like you." His words were bitter, and he shuddered as he spoke.

Imraldera placed her taper in a candleholder beside the other candle. Then she picked up several pages of her work, skimming them briefly. "Yet you said yourself that I recorded only the facts, Lionheart." She glanced at him over the pages, and though he stood beyond the candlelight, he felt her gaze piercing through the shadows to meet his. "Did I pass any judgment?"

"You didn't have to."

She set aside the manuscript and continued to gaze at him. Though he saw no condemnation in her face, it was an unbearable gaze.

"No one here despises you," she said. Then she paused a moment. "Well, Eanrin does. But that's just Eanrin for you. I do not. Oeric does not. Neither does our Master."

Lionheart turned away, cursing between his teeth. "I despise myself."

"The story is not so bad as all that," Imraldera continued softly. "The princess's heart was restored and is even now in safekeeping. The Dragon has been slain."

"But not by me."

"You could not slay the Dragon, Lionheart."

He shook his head. "No. Not anymore. It's too late for that." Once more he cursed and stepped back even farther from the lights. "I meant it all for the best! I only wanted—" But he could not force the words across his tongue. Oeric's voice whispered in his memory, *"Don't try to explain what you have done."* He saw how hollow were his excuses, how pale and sickening when looked at with a cold eye.

"I will find Rose Red," he whispered. "I can do no more. I cannot change the past. But I will find her, this I swear upon the Silent—" He stopped. In Southlands, the most solemn oaths were sworn on Maid Starflower, but somehow this seemed wrong while standing in Imraldera's presence. Licking his lips, he said, "I swear upon my hand."

Imraldera approached him, leaving the circle of candlelight. Her voice was very gentle when she spoke. "Don't think that you can earn absolution."

Her words were like a knife in his gut. For just a moment, Lionheart thought he would sink into despair right there, vanishing into the shadows of that massive library, becoming no more than memory among those tomes of history and legend. But then her hand touched him on the cheek. "Don't think that you can earn absolution, Lionheart," she said. "But forgiveness may yet be found."

He gazed into eyes that shone with the fullness of centuries, and felt her tender hand. The stranglehold of guilt loosened its grip for a moment, allowing the tiniest sliver of hope to slip into place.

"My, my. Isn't this touching?"

Lionheart backed away from Imraldera's hand with all the haste of a boy caught sampling from the honey jar, though he knew blind Eanrin could not have seen the lady's gracious gesture. The Chief Bard stood leaning against a bookshelf, his face full of smiles, but his voice the last word in scorn. "Has she converted you and changed all your wicked ways yet, jester? Our good Dame Imraldera has a talent for such things."

Imraldera gave him a cool gaze. "Scat, cat. We're busy here."

"So I gathered. But I'm afraid the conclusion to this soul-searching moment will have to be postponed. I'm off to Rudiobus with Oeric to seek a word or two from Queen Bebo. I require the mortal."

"Rudiobus?" Lionheart gasped. "Iubdan's beard!"

"Yes, you should get a good look at that while we're there," said the cat-man. "The Flowing Gold too, for that matter, though probably not flowing. And above all, your eyes shall be graced with the blessed sight of that one pure light that shines brighter than all Hymlumé's children, that dream of all dreams, that choicest jewel of all crowns, that bright and spotless—"

"Eanrin," Imraldera snapped, "do have done!"

"—girl I fancy." The poet's smile broadened. "Will you be joining us, Imraldera, old thing? I've written up a new song just for the occasion, and you might want to record it, don't you think?"

Imraldera raised an eyebrow. "The theme of this song?"

"What else? That most glorious of creatures, that paragon of all virtues, that unblemished beacon shining in the—"

"Gleamdren." Imraldera growled and returned to her desk, shuffling papers pointedly. "I've recorded enough poetry dedicated to her to repaper the Giant King's feasting hall. Twice!"

"Then you'll not come?"

"No."

"You might enjoy it."

"No."

"What if I said please?"

"No."

"Pity. I shall give you a personal recitation when I return, then, shall I?"

With that, Eanrin, still smiling, turned his sightless face to Lionheart. "Come, jester. We are off at once. If you're well enough to snoop into private chambers in the middle of the night, you're well enough for a journey. Don't worry. Oeric will be with us to make certain I don't *accidentally* lose you in the Wood between here and there."

Strange how after all the centuries everything felt as familiar as though he'd walked this way but yesterday.

The yellow-eyed dragon had thought never to follow this Path again, had hoped he would never need to. Every step caused him pain in his spirit, pain that he did not like to face. He was grateful, the nearer he came to the Haven, that he no longer had a heart, for it might break and bleed inside him.

Fire lashed from his mouth as he grimaced. What could he say to them? Would they even hear him? How could he keep himself from tearing the flesh from their bones and burning what remained out of pure terror or anger? How he hated them, and every step that took him nearer fanned the flame of his hatred.

But Anahid he could not hate. Though everything in him urged him to burn her to ashes for the hurt she had caused him, the yellow-eyed dragon could not hate her.

So he pursued the Path to the Haven, unaware that the unicorn shadowed his footsteps.

4

"SIT STILL AND TAKE YOUR FINGERS out of your ears!" Lionheart's nursemaid had said long ago, when he was still young enough to enjoy her stories but just old enough to start pretending he didn't. "I'm going to tell you a story of Iubdan."

"Is there a dragon in the story?" asked young Lionheart.

"A dragon? Lumé's light, no! You're much too little a boy to hear stories like that!"

"Foxbrush's nursemaid tells him stories about dragons."

"Well, I'm not one to pass judgment on young Master Foxbrush's nursemaid"—spoken in a tone that was a judgment in itself—"but in this nursery, we shall hear only good and wholesome tales with a moral."

Lionheart made a face that indicated just what he thought of such a plan. His nursemaid continued. "Now, look at that picture there." She indicated the nursery wall. The stones and plaster were painted in garish colors depicting a fantastic scene. In the center, on golden thrones, sat a burly king with a black beard and cherry-red cheeks beside an angular queen with long, long, *long* yellow hair. Before them danced a dozen merry folk, yellow-haired like the queen. Others danced as well: a rabbit and a fox, a squirrel and a ferret, clasping hands and smiling as cheerfully as all the yellow-headed little people, with whom they were equal in size.

It was a silly picture, young Lionheart thought. The fox would eat the rabbit as soon as look at it, and he couldn't remember seeing any dancing squirrels before. What kind of a baby did these mural artists take him for?

To one side stood a singer dressed all in scarlet, with a jaunty cap on his head and a huge smile on his face. Lionheart considered him a right smug-looking person. The artist had painted him gazing with enormous golden eyes at a woman in green, who danced with a badger. Lionheart was no great judge of beauty at that age, but he assumed that the dancing woman was beautiful because of her inordinately large and red lips. She was turned away from the singer; and something about the set of her head implied, even in the childish painting, that she wasn't merely neglecting to see him, but was pointedly Not Looking at him.

The mural was a new addition to the nursery, one of his mother's many "improving projects." Lionheart did not hold it in high favor, but his nursemaid thought it enchanting. "Do you know who those people are?" she asked her young charge.

He squirmed, wrapping his arms and legs into a knot where he sat. "No."

"Sit up straight. That is King Iubdan and his court."

"I know Iubdan," said Lionheart.

"Do you, now?"

"Yes. Master Leanbear says, 'Iubdan's beard!' every time he's angry."

His nursemaid's mouth compressed. "Well," she said through tight lips, "he's a very naughty man for doing so. It's disrespectful, swearing by ancient kings, even if they're only make-believe. If I catch you using a phrase like that, I'll wash your mouth out with soap."

"Did King Iubdan fight a dragon?"

"I told you, no dragons today." His nursemaid leaned back in her rocking chair, relaxing into her story. "Iubdan lives in Rudiobus Mountain," she said, "and it is the loveliest mountain you ever saw, grown over with aspens, and with a snowy peak, not at all like our Bald Mountain. The

Merry Folk have carved out the prettiest caverns and hung them with pine and holly, which is why they call Iubdan's assembly room the Hall of Red and Green."

Lionheart crossed and uncrossed his feet, huffing loudly.

"You'd think they might get cramped in there," his nursemaid went on without taking notice, "all the folk of the kingdom living inside one mountain. But the people of Rudiobus are so small, you see, that the mountain seems as big as the biggest country to them! And it is the dearest sight to watch the tiny folk dancing while the Chief Poet sings and Iubdan and Bebo look on and laugh! See how cheerful Iubdan and his lady are?"

They were altogether too cheerful, Lionheart thought, huffing again.

"There is only one gateway into Rudiobus," said the nursemaid. She was gazing at the mural now with half-closed eyes, recalling the stories she had been told as a little girl. "The Fionnghuala Lynn. And the only way to pass through that gate is on the back of Iubdan's mare. Such a pretty little steed she is! Her mane is scarlet, and her legs are emerald green, and her tail trails behind her in a long crimson plume. But her flanks gleam as gold as your father's crown, and her bridle is covered in gems. She is so small, my prince, that she could stand in the palm of my hand!"

Did anyone actually think multicolored ponies interesting?

"I'm going to fight a dragon someday," Lionheart said, rocking back and forth.

His nursemaid ignored him. "Once Iubdan's mare carries you through the gate, you pass down the long corridors of Rudiobus to the Hall of Red and Green where Iubdan and Bebo sit."

Inspiration struck—an idea for a new face, one Lionheart had never tried before. He slowly crossed his eyes and started to protrude his upper lip.

"Queen Bebo is crowned by her flowing golden hair, more bright and beautiful than any crown Faerie craftsman could make for her. And you'll see the little people dancing, dancing . . ."

Lionheart used his fingers to pull down his eyelids, his thumbs to stick out his ears.

" . . . and the Chief Bard, Eanrin, plays and sings songs he's written for love of the beautiful Lady Gleamdren. Ah! 'Tis such a merry sight—*Iubdan's beard!* What *are* you doing, child?"

"SOAP!" Lionheart leapt to his feet and darted from the nursery, his nursemaid in hot pursuit. "Bring the soap! Nurse said a naughty thing!"

Lionheart had been moved from the nursery to the Prince's Chambers not long thereafter, and as a second child from the Eldest and his queen was not forthcoming, the nursery was left to its lonely self. The mural on the wall faded with time and was for the most part forgotten. But not by Lionheart. Throughout his growing-up years he recalled the childish scene and the silly stories, one of the many threads that wove the fabric of his childhood.

It wasn't supposed to be real.

Anything at all was possible, he realized now, many years later, as he followed the blind poet through the tree-shadowed halls of the Haven, his imagination aching at the thought of being presented before folk of Faerie tales. But he tried to suppress those thoughts in light of a more immediate concern, which was for clothing. He still wore only a night-shirt tucked into his trousers and no shoes to speak of. Eanrin, however, refused to hear whatever protests Lionheart might make on the subject.

"I know it's the middle of the night, I know you want your beauty sleep and all that. But if we're going to make Rudiobus by nightfall tomorrow, we must set out before the sun."

"I'm not saying I need sleep! I'm saying I need shoes!"

Eanrin waved a dismissive hand and continued without another word. It wasn't until they had stepped from the Haven into the Wood beyond—which was very much like stepping from one patch of forest into another patch of forest unless Lionheart closed his right eye—and met Sir Oeric waiting for them that Lionheart got any help.

"He's in his nightshirt, Eanrin," said the huge knight.

"Cozy enough, then, is he?"

"You can't present him before the king like that."

"Why not?"

"Iubdan would not be amused."

"On the contrary. I think my king would be highly diverted."

Oeric said, "What would Lady Gleamdrené think?"

"She—"

"Yes?"

The poet frowned, then shrugged. "Very well, then. Find the mortal some clothes and boots, but hurry it up, will you? The sun could rise any minute now."

Lionheart turned and found Imraldera at the door. Having anticipated his need, she held a green-embroidered long coat, a belt and scabbard, and boots, sturdy but light enough for walking. The coat was very fine indeed, too fine to go with his travel-stained trousers, but Lionheart was not about to complain. He hurried into the garments while the Chief Poet hemmed and hawed and Sir Oeric folded his arms and exchanged looks with Imraldera.

"Is the darling dandied?" Eanrin asked as Lionheart buckled Blood-biter's Wrath to his waist.

"I'm ready."

"Sure you won't join us, Imraldera?"

Imraldera's face was a frosty mask. "Good-bye, Eanrin."

The poet shrugged and suddenly was a fluffy cat disappearing through the forest at a quick trot. Oeric bowed respectfully to Imraldera (who Lionheart guessed outranked the big knight somehow), then motioned Lionheart to follow him on the trail of the cat. Lionheart fell into step behind the enormous man, and soon the Haven was far behind in the moonlight.

"Are we truly going to Rudiobus?" Lionheart asked.

Oeric grunted.

"To see King Iubdan? And Queen Bebo?"

"Yes."

Not even the strangeness of Ragniprava's realm had been as over-whelming as the simple thought of visiting Iubdan in the Hall of Red and Green. What if they looked like the little caricatures painted on his wall? This was a thought too terrifying to contemplate.

"Why will Dame Imraldera not join us?" he asked Oeric at length.

The ugly knight gave him a quick glance, his white moon eyes gleam-ing with their own strange light. Lionheart could not meet their gaze. "Sir Eanrin," said Oeric, "is famous throughout the ages for being the lover of Lady Gleamdrené Gormlaith, Bebo's cousin. You did know that, didn't you?"

"Everyone knows that," said Lionheart.

"Including Dame Imraldera."

"And . . . what? She hates his dreadful verses even more than I do?"

Oeric thought a moment, his jaw shifting as he considered answers. At last he said, "What Dame Imraldera thinks of Eanrin or his poetry is, I believe, Dame Imraldera's affair. And," he quickly added, "if I were you, I should keep my tongue behind my teeth, where it belongs on this subject."

Lionheart shut his mouth again and didn't press for more answers.

They walked for some while in silence other than the crunch of leaves and twigs under Lionheart's boots. Oeric moved without a sound, and the cat was far ahead. "Did we lose Sir Eanrin?" Lionheart asked.

"No," rumbled Oeric. "We follow the same Path."

Lionheart could discern no Path. The night was old now, and the moon had sunk into the tangle of branches. As they went, Lionheart sometimes felt a strange sensation, as though the steps he took were carrying him over much greater distances than one mere stride at a time. His vision was indistinct save straight ahead, so he fixed his gaze on Oeric's broad back and tried not to glance to either side. The Wood was huge, and he could feel its hugeness all around him, as palpable a presence as either Oeric or the poet.

"Where are we?" he asked after a while.

"We follow the Prince's Paths," Oeric replied. "It is unsafe to step into Goldstone Wood without a Path. We Knights of Farthestshore always walk the Paths of our Prince, and we do not become lost."

Lionheart frowned. "Goldstone? So that's not just a wood in northern Parumvir?"

Oeric cast him a glance over his shoulder. "Goldstone Wood extends much farther than it appears to in your world, mortal. Here in the Halflight Realm, it connects all worlds. Your Wilderlands are just as much a part of Goldstone as the little clump of trees that bears the name in Parumvir."

Lionheart shuddered and stopped trying to wrap his mind around concepts too strange to be thought.

Dawn came suddenly, as though they had stepped across some stark dividing line between Night and Day. Lionheart's head hurt. Nothing was certain to him anymore, not the path he followed, not these strange comrades with whom he found himself linked. Not even his own identity.

The story he had read from Imraldera's manuscript haunted the edge of his mind. That man he'd read about shared his name. But could he truly be Lionheart, the Eldest of Southlands' son? All his good intentions and noble ideals faded to nothing in light of Imraldera's simple presentation of the facts. He'd betrayed the girl he loved. He'd banished his loyal servant. He'd failed to rescue Southlands.

"I'm going to fight a dragon someday," young Lionheart had told his nurse.

But he'd never fought the Dragon.

Oeric stopped abruptly, and Lionheart, looking around from behind him, saw the cat sitting in the Path. "Here," the cat said with a flick of his whiskers. Oeric nodded. The next moment, the cat leapt from the Path and vanished behind an old, moss-eaten stump.

"Step across," Oeric said to Lionheart, waving him to follow.

Lionheart looked at the stump. "This is a crossing into the Far World?"

"As long as you're quick enough. Go on!"

It is always good policy to heed someone who stands half again taller than you. Lionheart did as he was told, stepping over the stump; and just like when he had crossed into Ragniprava's demesne, he felt no sudden jolt, no dizzying sensation, nothing for which he could brace himself. He simply stepped out of the Wood Between and into the world beyond as naturally as stepping from the hall into the dining room.

He stood on the shore of a shining silver lake that steamed with frost as the evening came on. The sun setting behind the mountain cast its crags into black silhouette. Snow covered not just the topmost peak but all the forest of aspens in the lower slopes as well. The air was like knives in his lungs, his face so cold it burned, and Lionheart was more grateful than ever to Imraldera for providing him with the green jacket.

Eanrin, a man once more, smiled brightly from the shores of the lake. "I confess, I was not expecting Winter to be paying a call just now. Last time I visited, everything was awash in Summer. Ah well. Where's our ugly friend?"

"Here," said Oeric, appearing at Lionheart's side. Their breath frosted on the air. "Have you hailed the gatekeeper?"

Eanrin nodded. "I hear her even now." And he pointed across the lake.

Like dangling prisms on a chandelier, the edge of the water tinkled with forming ice, but most of it remained open. Across its surface, spreading ice beneath tiny green hooves, came the mare of Iubdan, trailing a scarlet tail. Lionheart did not see her at first, despite her brilliant colors, because she was so small she might fit in the palm of his hand.

The lake froze in a cold path as the little horse crossed over. She stood at last upon the ice but did not step onto land.

"Iubdan's beard," Lionheart breathed.

"Jester, meet Órfhlaith," said Eanrin, sweeping his hand from Lionheart to the mare. "Órfhlaith," he addressed the mare, "this is our jester."

The mare tossed her head and whuffled, so tiny and delicate and yet so horselike. Lionheart could only gape, his mouth open.

Eanrin laughed. "It's rude to stare."

Lionheart's jaw clamped shut, and he hastily averted his gaze. Eanrin laughed again and swept an elaborate bow. "You first, little mortal. Climb aboard!"

"What?" Lionheart's gaze flickered to the mare again, and he shook his head. "You want me to . . . I'd squash her!"

The poet straightened up, that incessant smile still on his face, but his eyebrow quirked. "Perhaps Oeric would like to show you the way?"

"But that's—" Lionheart shut his mouth, remembering where he was. In a world where Time could be sold in a bottle, anything was possible.

Sir Oeric strode forward and straddled the tiny mare's back. Of all the bizarre sights Lionheart had witnessed, this one most stupefied. For the enormous knight mounted Iubdan's mare without either of them apparently growing or shrinking; rather, it was Lionheart's perspective that altered. Oeric strode into the water, and though it was but a few paces, by the time he reached the mare's side, he was of a height to ride her. And yet, though Oeric was so big he could have tossed Lionheart over his shoulder without a thought, Órfhlaith could still have stood comfortably in his palm.

Lionheart shook his suddenly pounding head as it struggled to understand. Bodies need not be bound by size. Not here, in the Far World.

Oeric settled comfortably onto the mare's back, and she, with a toss of her brilliant mane, carried him across the icy lake, leaving Lionheart goggle-eyed on the shore.

One by one, they crossed behind the white mist of the Fionnghuala Lynn, the great waterfall cascading down the frozen mountainside. Lionheart was glad that Oeric had gone first, for a stern company of guards was ready to meet them, and there was nothing jolly about these so-called Merry Folk. They took Bloodbiter's Wrath from him without a word, secreting it away somewhere. Even when Eanrin greeted them with a hearty "What ho!" and called each by name (Lionheart wondered how he did this when he couldn't see them), not one of them cracked a smile. But they led the two knights and Lionheart through the caverns of Rudiobus Mountain.

The Hall of Red and Green looked nothing like Lionheart had ever envisioned, and yet exactly as he had always known it must be. The cavern walls and roughhewn pillars were festooned in holly and pine, lit by a thousand and more candles. Pipe music and wild drums filled his ears, and yellow-headed people dressed in green and white filled the dance floor . . . along with several squirrels, two rabbits, and a silver fox, who danced just as well, albeit with animal variations on the steps. Yet when he blinked, Lionheart saw that they weren't animals at all, but people whose contours revealed an animal shape underneath.

Eanrin leapt forward ahead of Oeric and Lionheart. His red coat flashed like a cardinal's wing, and he could not fail to draw every eye in the room. He darted like a leaf on a breeze as the dancing people scattered to make way for him, and he ended in a flourishing bow before the thrones.

Lionheart saw for the first time the King and Queen of Rudiobus.

Iubdan Tynan, the Dark Man of Rudiobus, alone of those who lived within the mountain boasted hair as black as the night. He claimed it was because Evening herself was his mother and Night his father, but since no one living could remember a time when Iubdan was not King of Rudiobus (except Bebo, who kept her own counsel), no one could vouch for the truth of this.

What was true, Lionheart quickly discovered, was that this king, so ancient that the ancients could not recall his beginning, looked nothing like the painting on the nursery wall.

Neither did Queen Bebo, for that matter. Other than the king's black beard and the queen's golden hair, there was nothing about the faces of these two to suggest their caricatures. Rather than burly, King Iubdan was powerful: red cheeked, yes, but the redness was from much time spent in the sun, and there wasn't a smile to be seen on his face as he gazed down at his Chief Poet. And Queen Bebo, rather than the long-nosed, long-faced woman she'd been painted as, was childlike and delicate in her features, though her eyes were old and solemn. Her hair was not unbound and flowing to her feet but rather coiled and arranged in a great crown about her head, more beautiful than any crown wrought of metal and jewels. It gleamed in the icy cold of Rudiobus like sunlight bursting through an overcast sky.

"Oh, it's you" was Iubdan's kingly greeting of his poet. His black eyebrows drew together in a thick line. "About time you showed up again, wouldn't you say?"

"My lord and king!" Eanrin cried, raising his arms theatrically. "Many years now have I been absent from Ruaine-ann-Rudiobus! How long has it been since I set joyful eyes upon your face?"

"Hmmm. That would be a number of centuries, my eyeless songster," growled the king.

"Or heard the dulcet sounds of my sovereign's voice?"

"Maybe not quite so long."

"Six years by the Near World's count, my Lord Dark Man," said Queen Bebo in a voice as golden as her hair, "since the Prince sent our good Eanrin to guard his Beloved."

"And six long years they have been, my liege," said the poet, his face a mask of tragic long-suffering. "How I have missed your mighty company in the interim."

"Enough of this bosh." The king crossed his arms, clothed in silks and in black gleaming fur. "I'd begun to think I hadn't any Chief Poet at all. Don't suppose I do, even now. You haven't come to amuse me, have you, cheeky cat."

"What other view could I possibly have in seeking out your royal company?"

"Let me think." The king rubbed his beard. "Might there be a certain lady hereabouts for whom you carry a torch?"

All the assembly chuckled so that the Hall of Red and Green bubbled with ill-suppressed laughter. Lionheart looked around for that other famous figure of whom he'd heard so much, that inspiration for all the most wretched poetry a schoolboy had ever been forced to stomach: the fair Lady Gleamdrené Gormlaith. Because all eyes in the room were suddenly turned toward her, she wasn't hard to spot.

She was not what Lionheart had expected.

For one thing, her lips were not inordinately large or red. Neither was she, as far as Lionheart was concerned, especially beautiful. She radiated the pure immortal glow of all Rudiobus's merry people. Other than that, she had one of those faces that, if she smiled, could be pretty, and if she sulked, would be sulky. At the moment, she was sulking for all she was worth.

Eanrin turned to her as though he had eyes to see exactly where she sat and, with another flourishing bow, proclaimed in a voice that rang throughout the Hall of Red and Green, "Sweet flower of my delight, once again I find myself in your gracious presence! Might these longing ears hear the honeyed tones of your voice in gentle greeting?"

Lionheart frowned. He had been a performer himself long enough to know a performance when he heard one. Something in the poet's tone did not ring true. He eyed Eanrin, his dramatic stance, his face full of longing . . . and he saw the lie that it was. Or not a lie, but rather, a mask.

And he thought to himself, *Eanrin is hiding something.* But he could not guess what. After all, what could Eanrin have to hide from the lady who all history knew was the great love of his life?

Perhaps Gleamdren saw that mask as well. And perhaps this explained why she folded her arms, turned up her nose, and refused to look the poet's way.

Iubdan laughed. "Is that stony silence answer enough for you, bard? After a thousand-some years of Not Speaking, my wife's cousin is not about to relent in a mere six!"

Eanrin clapped a tragic hand to his forehead and turned away, his shoulders slumped. But two seconds later, he was all smiles and once more addressing the king and queen. "Actually, my liege, my companions and I have come to beg a boon. See yon mortal?" He waved a hand Lionheart's way. Lionheart stood beside Oeric, still behind the solemn guard of honor. The sovereign rulers of Rudiobus turned their ancient eyes on him, and it was all he could do not to duck behind Oeric's bulk. But Queen Bebo smiled at him.

"He has been given into our keeping by the Prince of Farthestshore," Eanrin continued.

"Why?" asked Iubdan. His expression was not so welcoming as the queen's.

"The worlds wonder," said the poet. "We thought perhaps my queen might shed some light upon the subject."

If Queen Bebo heard the request, she said nothing. Her quiet eyes were fixed on Lionheart, and the smile had not yet left her face. Lionheart wanted to break her gaze but found himself incapable. There was nothing unfriendly in those eyes. They merely looked. But they looked deeply.

"What say you, Bebo, my love?" Iubdan asked, nudging his queen with his elbow in a manner most unkingly. "Have you a prophecy or some such?"

Slowly, Bebo nodded her head. Just once. Then she said, "When the moon has risen, my lord. Then we shall listen and hear what we may."

Iubdan pursed his lips, shrugged at Lionheart, then addressed his poet. "There you go, Eanrin. Will you stay and dine with us until moonrise?"

"Many thanks, my king," the cat-man said.

"And will you sing?"

"Indeed, I shall! A song to the choicest fruit among the harvest, a song to the star that gleams most bright in the jewels of the night, a song of the voice as pure as—"

"No," said Bebo, turning suddenly to Eanrin. Lionheart took a great gasp of air as soon as her gaze left him. He had not realized he was holding his breath. "No," said the queen, softly. "Tonight, you must sing *Ordenel Hymlumé Nive.*"

Though the assembly had been quiet, the hush that followed was as thick as the ice forming on the lake outside. For Queen Bebo had spoken in the old tongue from the ages before the Near World was formed, the language she had learned from the sun and the moon themselves, which even the Faerie folk were loath to speak. And just like the characters written on Imraldera's manuscript in the library, the words, when spoken by Bebo, re-formed themselves in Lionheart's mind, and he heard instead: "You must sing *The Night of Moonblood*."

The candles wavered and dimmed, or perhaps it was simply all those golden faces darkening and shrinking away that made the room seem suddenly so shadow filled. Lionheart shivered, and the words echoed in his mind.

As much to his surprise as anybody's, it was his voice that broke the silence, whispering, "What is Moonblood?"

5

IMRALDERA SAT AT HER DESK but did not write. Her mind was reviewing images she had not witnessed but which she could imagine with the clarity of one who had. Scenes of Lionheart presented before Iubdan and his lady; of Oeric looming so huge above the little folk of Rudiobus; of Eanrin singing his foolish love ditties to the snub-nosed maiden who wanted nothing to do with him.

But no.

She stood up and moved down the long line of bookshelves, searching for a certain volume. It did no good to wonder about that encounter, to speculate on what Queen Bebo might see when she gazed at Lionheart under the Sphere's light. Imraldera had remained behind for her own purposes, and she must pursue them.

Her finger, tracing the spines of ancient texts, stopped suddenly as though of its own accord. She plucked the book from its place, knowing without reading the title that it was the one she sought. Evening was falling again outside, so she lit a candle on her desk before opening the leather cover to read what she had found.

The legend on the first page read: *The Night of Moonblood.*

"The Night of Moonblood."

Eanrin stood in the center of Iubdan's Hall, his head bowed, his voice low. Every eye in that assembly fixed on him, and every heart caught at his words.

"The night Death-in-Life ascended to the heavens and spoke his lies to the children of Hymlumé in a voice they thought more fair than their mother's song."

As the poet spoke, it was as though his words were a truth Lionheart had long known deep in his heart. His mind was filled not with the revelation of something new, but rather with the recollection of something his spirit had known since birth.

"She watched them fall," said the Chief Poet, his voice no greater than a whisper, though it filled all of Rudiobus. "She watched them step out of their heavenly dance, the rhythm of the song she and Lumé had sung since the worlds were first created. Her children heard the voice of Death-in-Life and they thought it beautiful. And Hymlumé watched them as, one by one, they fell like meteors from the sky. Those who had never noticed the Sphere Songs singing in the night heard instead their silencing. And while the thunder of that silence yet rang in their ears, they heard the voice of Hymlumé crying out."

And here Eanrin sang in a voice Lionheart had never heard before, a voice as old as Time or older. As he sang, the icy hand of winter grabbed the passages of Rudiobus, freezing the air, the heart, and all the little folk bowed their heads. At first the words were incomprehensible to Lionheart, though simultaneously familiar. He thought he must have heard them once before, though he could not recall where.

"Els jine aesda-o soran!" Eanrin sang. *"Aaade-o Ilmaan."*

Then, just as Bebo's words had restructured themselves in Lionheart's mind, he found the lines sung by the bard becoming clear in his mind.

"If I but knew my fault!

"I blessed your name, oh you who sit
Enthroned beyond the Highlands.
I blessed your name and sang in answer
To the song you gave.

"Beside the Final Water flowing,
My brow in silver bound,
I raised my arms, I raised my voice
In answer to your gift.

"The words spilled forth in lyric delight,
In song, more than words.
Joy and fear and hope and trembling
Burst forth from all restraint.

"Who could help but sing?"

The song spoke of joy such as Lionheart had never known; but it was a joy made all the more vivid by the pain of its loss. He shuddered, and he felt himself bracing for what he knew must come, for though he had never before heard it, he had known this story all his life.

Eanrin sang:

"Now I cry to you again,
My arms raised once more.
My hands outspread to shield my face
From that which lies before.

"Is the fault in me?"

Imraldera in the Haven ran her finger beneath the lines of her old book and read them with silent lips moving:

The torrents roar, the waves are scarlet
As blood, reflecting flame.

Oh, ravaging flame, burn and burn!
Light my face in fury!

Only spare my children.

I see them running, running, stumbling
Running, as the heavens
Break and yawn, tear beneath their feet,
Devouring, hungry Death!

A beautiful princess sat hunched in the shadows of her ancestors in a place where the moon could not shine. And though she spoke not a word, her heart cried the song through the blackness of her father's palace:

Where is my fault?

Did I misunderstand the song, the gift
You gave? Was I wrong?
I thought you spoke across the boundless.
You sang, and I replied.

I thought you spoke to me, but now
I hear voices below;
Terror, screaming from the pit.
I thought you sang to me!

In the dungeons of Var, a knight sat in utter darkness, bound with iron chains to a cold wall. Her head bowed to her chest, all her weight sagging against the biting shackles, she whispered:

"I sang back to you.

"Children running. Oh, children, hear
My voice, the song I learned
From o'er the water. Hear no more
The voices in the pit.

"Can you hear me?"

Eanrin sang, and no one saw the tear that fell from beneath a silken patch, for all eyes were fixed on a vision of the past. Iubdan and his queen clasped each other's hands as the memory swept over them, and they mouthed the words of the song:

> *"I blessed your name with my first breath,*
> *The song you gave to me.*
> *I sang to you in praise of beauty,*
> *I sang in praise of truth.*
>
> *"Children running, beauty crumbling.*
> *Oh, Truth, where are you?*
> *My song is frozen in my heart.*
> *I can no longer sing."*

Varvare, alone among the veils, whispered:

> *"Will you answer?"*

The lone knight in the dungeons spoke suddenly, though nobody heard. But she raised her face and sent her voice ringing through those empty cells:

> *"Children, children, you cannot escape*
> *The screaming pit.*
> *Only death to your great treasure*
> *Will quell its awful greed."*

And Varvare whispered again:

> *"Will you answer?"*

Eanrin raised his fists to his temples, and in his mind he stood once more before the Dark Water, alone and far from his path. Across his memory flashed the last thing he would ever see with his golden eyes. The dart of cruel knives. Then darkness. And pain.

He sang:

> "I blessed your name with the gift
> You gave. This voice of mine,
> This burning heart, my children's wealth
> I used to bless your name.

> "Will you answer?"

"Will you answer?" asked Varvare.

"Will you answer?" asked the shackled knight.

Lionheart, cringing against the darkness that overshadowed Iubdan's Hall, whispered through clenched teeth: "Will you answer?"

Eanrin allowed that last question to hang in the air, the notes unresolved and tense.

Then, deep as the night but rich and full, Oeric's voice filled the awful silence.

> "I blessed your name in beauty.
> In fear I still must sing.
> I blessed your glorious name in truth,
> I bless it now in doubt."

Suddenly, all the folk of Rudiobus—the king, the queen, Lady Gleamdren, the stern guards, the dancers and revelers—raised their faces and sang with the Chief Poet. The sound rolled over Lionheart like rushing wind and water, stirring him deep inside so that he thought he must break to pieces. He shut his eyes as it swept across him.

> "I need no answer. Do not answer.
> You are true and you
> Are right, and your name is mighty.
> Your name is my life.

> "By your name, I accept my doom."

The song ended. Iubdan's Bard lowered his hands and softly said:

"So Hymlumé was pierced by her children's cruel horns as they turned away from her and fled willingly to their destruction. She heard Death-in-Life laughing over her as she bled across the sky. But behind his laughter, all the children of the Lower Worlds heard her sing the Sphere Songs even as the lifeblood flowed from her.

"So it was that He Who Gave the Song appeared and cast the Dragon from the sky. All the way to the Lower Worlds he fell, flaming, and was bound to the Gold Stone, there to sleep a thousand years for the evil he had caused.

"The Song Giver turned then to Hymlumé and tended her wounds. He set her once more upon her high seat, there to sing in a voice more beautiful than before. For he promised her that night that her children should not all be lost. Since that time, she has never ceased to sing her hope, her trust. Though the people of the Near World have long since become deaf to her voice, and even those of the Far find it too easy to forget.

"But every five hundred years, the moon remembers that dark night and shines red upon the Lower Worlds. And the fallen children of Hymlumé walk among us still."

Lionheart opened his eyes just as Eanrin finished speaking and found Queen Bebo standing before him. Oeric and the Rudiobus guards were now a short way off, and he was alone with the queen.

"Come with me," she said and beckoned him.

He fell into step behind her, and they left the Hall of Red and Green, which was bright once more with candles. She led him to a winding stair, and an icy draft blew howling down, freezing his face. But she began the ascent, and Lionheart followed with all haste behind her, even as the voices of Rudiobus echoed behind him.

> *"We bless the name of he who sits*
> *Enthroned beyond the Highlands.*
> *We bless his name and sing in answer*
> *To the song he gave."*

Imraldera closed her book, and many thoughts spun in her head. The Night of Moonblood would be upon them soon. Why did she think that it somehow related to that poor, lost Prince of Southlands? That his story was in some way bound up in the loss of Hymlumé's children?

"I do not understand," she whispered. Night had fallen outside, and the moon, almost full, gleamed through the windows of her library so bright as to make her candle unnecessary. She pinched the candle out, then left her desk and made three paces to the window to gaze up at the star-filled sky. "I do not understand. Nothing fits together. What about poor Felix? And Oeric's love, captured, perhaps slain by Vahe? Do they play into this sorry tale?"

She leaned against the window frame, weary from her many thoughts. "I cannot work this out on my own."

Far off in the depths of Goldstone Wood, a wood thrush sang its silver notes.

Suddenly, a cloud passed over the face of the moon, snuffing out its light like her candle. Imraldera stood in the darkness of the library she knew so well. Yet in that moment, it felt foreign and unsafe. A shiver of warning from some unknown source ran through her, and she whirled around.

Two yellow eyes blazed like sparks behind her.

"Hello, Imraldera," said the dragon. "I'm back."

6

THEY MET NO ONE on the stair, and none of the candles set in crevices along the wall were lit. Moonlight poured down the long stairwell, making each step a contrast of highlight and shadow.

Lionheart followed the queen, the coldness of winter biting down. His breath trailed from him in visible tendrils, but the queen was barefoot, he noticed, and her robes were airy and soft. Cold was unable to touch her.

The music from Iubdan's hall faded into silence, and the moonlight grew ever brighter. After what seemed like hours, Lionheart saw an open doorway ahead, and through this Bebo led him. He gasped as he stepped from the narrow confines of the long stair. He stood at the summit of Rudiobus Mountain. A silvery world lay below him, including the lake, which was now frozen like glass. The air was sharp in his lungs, and his face felt like it would burn away in that cold. The snow covering the slopes of the mountain, and the woodlands beyond, caught the moonlight and reflected it back until all the night blazed in an icy parody of daylight.

Then, even as he watched, the world fell away.

The night sky itself spread below him, an inky-black landscape unbroken but for a few straggling clouds. Stars bloomed as the brightest flowers around him, and the world, wherever it was, was far from sight. Lionheart stood on the top of Rudiobus Mountain in the Gardens of Hymlumé. And Hymlumé herself was so bright and so near, he thought she would blind him.

Lionheart's stomach jolted, and though he prided himself on his good head for heights, this was much more than any mortal could stand. He backed away, pressing himself against the rock of the doorway, and had to force himself not to flee back down that long stairway.

Bebo stepped to the very edge of the mountain and tilted her face to the moon.

"Can you see her, mortal?" she asked.

Lionheart struggled to find breath. He realized in a distant sort of way that he was no longer cold, though his breath still steamed the air in small clouds. Perhaps he was dead. No, he couldn't be dead if he still breathed. Maybe he was dying? He moved his lips but no words came, so he shook his head in answer to Bebo's question even though she was not looking at him.

She beckoned him to join her, still without turning around. He did not want to. Everything in him told him to hide, to run, anything rather than to obey. But his feet moved, and he came to her side until he stood within an inch of that forever fall. There was a river flowing down below, perhaps just a little one, or perhaps the most enormous river imaginable but so far away as to seem no more than a stream. Lionheart trembled.

Bebo turned her childlike face to him. She was, he noticed, eye level with him. Queen Bebo might be small enough to stand in his hand, yet she could also look him in the eyes; and, he realized with a start, she could also loom far above him, towering like a giant with a majesty of age and wisdom he could never hope to match.

He would not meet her gaze.

"Take my hand," she said softly. He obeyed. Her fingers were small and delicate, and they could crush every bone in his hand without a thought. "Now can you see Hymlumé's face?"

He looked again at the enormous moon, wincing away from her

brightness. This time, though only for a moment, he saw her, the Lady Hymlumé. Beautiful and awful and vision filling, the sun's wife sat crowned in silver light.

In that instant, he heard her song.

Lionheart fell to his knees and might have slipped right over the edge of that precipice had not Queen Bebo held so tightly to his hand. Tears streamed down his cheeks, and he turned away from the moon and Iubdan's queen and covered his face in shame.

Suddenly he realized he was speaking. "I'll make it right!" he was crying. "I'll find her, I swear it! I'll find her and I will make it right! I wish I could explain myself; I wish you all could hear me, but I know you can't, and that's as well. But I'll make it right when I find her, and then I'll find him and tell him that I've done so, and I'll try to make you see that I'm . . . that I'm . . ."

Listening to himself, he flushed and quickly clamped his teeth down. What a fool he was! He wanted to drag his hand from Bebo's grasp, but she would not let him go. All was silent around them save for Lionheart's own breathing.

He wiped his face free of any last traces of tears and stood up once more, his face set and determined. "I will find her," he said, and only then could he turn again to Bebo.

She was looking at him with her old eyes, and he shivered under her gaze.

"You feel guilt, mortal man?" she asked.

Lionheart clenched his teeth, then gave one short nod. "I am guilty. I betrayed her. I betrayed them both, Una and Rose Red. I cannot help Una now. But I will find Rose Red and repair the damage I have done just as I purposed when I left Southlands. I will regain my honor."

Bebo continued to look. Her golden hair looked white under Hymlumé's gaze.

"Guilt is not enough," she said at last.

"I will do whatever it takes," Lionheart replied.

"Will you die?"

The cold rushed back over him, this time from the inside out. He knew when Queen Bebo asked that her question was not a matter of curiosity.

Lionheart stood there on the edge of forever, the river rushing below him. The decision he made now would echo among the gardens of the sky.

"Princess Varvare must die," Bebo said. "That prophecy was spoken long before her birth, and the sons of Hymlumé sang the truth of it. I heard the song. I know. The Princess of Arpiar must die unless one will die for her.

"You vowed by Hymlumé's light to save her, mortal man."

The stars were a million eyes watching him.

"Would you die to honor that vow?" Bebo persisted. "Would you pour out the blood of a lion's heart so that this girl you have wronged may live? Would your guilt carry you so far?"

But Lionheart could give no answer.

Gently, Bebo lifted his hand and pressed it to her lips. Lionheart gasped at this as though branded, and turned to see that tears gleamed in the queen's eyes.

"I promise you, Lionheart of Southlands," she said in the voice of one who had seen worlds created and destroyed, "you will cross the boundaries into Arpiar before the Night of Moonblood has come and gone. You will be given the choice: your life for hers. What you choose is your decision. No one can make it for you. But I swear by Hymlumé's face, the choice you will have."

Then she let go of his hand and stepped away from the edge, back to the doorway and the long, winding stair. Lionheart followed, casting only one last glance backward. Perhaps he saw Hymlumé's face. Perhaps he saw only a gibbous moon. But he turned away from the sight, his shoulders hunched like a slave's and his heart heavy with a question he could not answer.

Imraldera did not make any sound for a long moment as she stared into those burning eyes. Then she whispered, "It's been a long time."

"It certainly has," the yellow-eyed dragon replied. "I can't remember when last I stepped into your library."

"I can."

"You remember many things, Imraldera, things that others would be just as glad to forget. That's why you keep the records."

In her fear, Imraldera could feel the solid walls disappearing. The library was hers, but it dissolved into the night one portion at a time, and the Wood closed in. Her attendants were far from her, probably fled the moment they smelled dragon fumes. She struggled to maintain a steady voice as she spoke. "What are you doing here, Diarmid?"

He snarled as though she had struck him. "That's not my name!"

He was a dragon now; she had to remind herself of this. It was difficult for her to remember, for she had seen very little of him following his transformation, and in her mind he would always be the golden-eyed, golden-haired youth she had known when he first came to the Haven. Not this strange creature with the sallow face and the blackened hair hanging like rags to his shoulders. But he was a dragon. And if Imraldera knew anything about dragons it was that they could flame suddenly and without provocation. She must tread carefully.

"Have you come to see Eanrin?" she asked.

The yellow-eyed dragon snorted. "My one-time uncle? Not likely. I don't smell him hereabouts anyway. Is he off courting his cruel mistress again? In all these years, haven't you yet convinced him to try his luck elsewhere?"

"What do you want?" Imraldera demanded, her voice suddenly cold. In that flash of anger, her fear receded for a moment and with it the Wood. She felt her library about her again, and she clung to that.

"I want nothing from you," said the yellow-eyed dragon. He could feel her strength, and though his kind, for all their faults, was not given to cowardice, he was a little afraid of her. History had granted him a respect for this dame, soft and frail though she may appear. He took a step back. "I want nothing, but rather I come with a message."

"From whom?" Imraldera knew she sounded as snappish as a fish-monger's wife. She was alone and afraid in her own home, and the feeling soured her mood considerably. "Your Father is dead. You are alone in this world. Or have you and your kind found yourselves a new master?"

"Not yet," the dragon hissed. He seemed bigger now in the shadows of the trees, and his eyes brighter. "My kinfolk are asleep. As they sleep, they watch their dreams die again and again. It makes them very angry. Their fires are building, ready to erupt. But they must wait until the proper time, wait until someone strong enough wakes them. That time is coming, Imraldera."

"How are you awake when all your kinfolk sleep?" she demanded, hating herself for allowing her voice to tremble. The Wood sprang in around her, and once more she felt her library slipping away.

"My true mistress woke me," he replied, and his voice was very low. "It is she who has sent me, despite her husband's power."

Imraldera caught her breath, for she knew whom he meant. "Anahid."

"The Queen of Arpiar," the yellow-eyed dragon said, "sends you and your brethren a message, a warning, rather. Vahe has found himself a body, a mortal one with a broken mind that he is using to move beyond the boundaries of Arpiar. A mortal filled with dragon poison. My own poison, I believe."

Prince Felix's young face flashed across Imraldera's memory. Anger took hold of her again, and she clenched her fists, her eyes snapping. "Vahe does have him, then. Cruel, evil arts! I should have known as soon as Eanrin said the unicorn took him, that Vahe would—"

But the yellow-eyed dragon let out a horrible shriek and fell to his knees, and Imraldera leapt back, pressing against a great tree trunk. "Don't!" the dragon gasped. "Don't speak of that one! You'll draw him! You'll draw him even faster!"

Blood drained from Imraldera's face. "What are you saying?"

"I must show you quickly!" The yellow-eyed dragon cast anxious looks over his shoulders at the deep shadows of Goldstone Wood. The moon's face remained covered in clouds, and the only light came from his frightened eyes. He turned on Imraldera, his face fierce with terror, and lunged at her. She cried out as he caught her arms; his touch burned red-hot. He took both her wrists in one of his hands and grabbed her face with the other, searing her cheek.

"Look into my eyes," he hissed, steam streaming between his teeth. Her mouth was open in silent agony as she felt his fingers pressing into her temple and brow. "Look into my eyes, and see what I saw all those centuries ago!"

Fire blazed in his black pupils, and she fell into his memory.

The dragons crouch in the shadows beyond the light of their Father's eyes and watch as he and his sister play for the life of the goblin king. The yellow-eyed dragon trembles with desire to rend Vahe limb from limb, but he dares not step into his Father's gaze. The Dragon King sits still as stone upon his bloodstained throne and watches his sister's newly won prey.

"My dream!" Vahe screams, turning to Life-in-Death. "You won the game. I know my rights!"

"You have no rights," says the Dragon.

But Life-in-Death speaks in the softest tones. "I will see your dream realized, little Vahe." The dragons shudder at the sound of her voice. "My brother knows that I will. One way or another."

Their Father rises from his throne, smoke issuing from his nostrils, and approaches his sister as though to dismember her. But her smile is fixed unwaveringly upon him; it is he who turns away first.

He snarls at Vahe. "Very well, King of Arpiar. Perhaps we can make a deal, you and I?"

Even as he speaks, the blood of the moon spills through the darkness and shines red upon the throne. It flows even into the darkest crevices, a glaring light that reveals all the hiding dragons, who try to flee. But the yellow-eyed dragon looks on and hears the words his Father says under the light of Hymlumé's remembered pain.

"You desire a gift I have given only one other before. The mortal woman Tavé, as the Faeries call her, was willing to pay the price for the sake of controlling dragons. Are you willing to do the same?"

"I can pay any price a mortal woman can!" said the goblin king. "Am I not glorious beyond the dirt of mortality? Tell me what you require, Death-in-Life."

"You have spun your pretty veils to cover all Arpiar," says the Dragon King. "All ugliness of your kingdom thinly covered by your illusions, yet you have created not a single work of true beauty. Here is my bargain: Grow your own rose, Vahe, a rose fairer than any other. When the Night of Moonblood comes again in five hundred years, offer this rose of yours as a sacrifice to me. On my own throne, compel a child of Hymlumé to spill the blood of your child, and for every drop that falls, I will give you a dragon.

"Will you make this bargain?"

The goblin king shrieks, shaking his fists. "Not even the kings of the Far World can control one of Hymlumé's Fallen! What you ask is impossible!"

Life-in-Death places her hands upon his shoulders. "I will give you a unicorn, my sweet king. I shall see your dream realized."

Vahe turns to her and sees the fulfillment of all his desires, and he laughs. Then he turns to the Father of Dragons and says, "You have my word. The blood of my own lovely rose shall be spilled upon your throne, and the dragons will be mine to command."

"So be it. But be forewarned, little king." The Dragon smiles. "Fail to complete your part, and I myself will come and claim you, and my sister will not stop me."

"No," says the Lady with a radiant smile. "No, should he fail, I will give him over to you myself." Then she leans down and plants a kiss on the goblin's ugly face. "But I shall see your dream realized, my darling, for you are mine."

Imraldera gasped as the yellow-eyed dragon released her, and she fell to the ground, burned almost beyond bearing. But she spoke through her pain. "Rose Red!"

"Yes," said the dragon, turning away from her and clenching his hands into fists. Though he hated her, he couldn't bear to look on her suffering.

The Wood trembled. Goldstone was old, older than the Near World or the Far. But it felt within its boundaries a being older still, and fear raced through the treetops in rustling whispers of warning.

"My Father is dead," the yellow-eyed dragon said, turning this way and that, listening to the Wood, "but his bargain lives on. If Vahe spills his daughter's blood one night from now when Hymlumé shines red in remembrance of her own flowing blood, then my kinfolk will wake. And they will serve Vahe to whatever end he drives them, were he to order them to eat themselves alive."

"He cannot do that!" Imraldera struggled to speak through her pain, her words thin. "Even Vahe is not so strong!"

"What my Father has promised will come to pass. The Lady of Dreams Realized will see to that." He whirled upon her then, and seeing how she cringed in fear of his burning touch, fire rose in his throat.

"I care nothing for your world, Imraldera." Flames lashed from between his teeth, and sparks struck her already ravaged face. "I care nothing if Vahe raises his army and burns you and your Haven and all your records beyond recall. I wish the memory of those centuries was destroyed even now, that my own life was ended and gone, that it never was! But . . ." Here his eyes closed, for a moment sparing her from their awful gaze. "But Anahid would have her daughter safe. Anahid still has a heart, soiled and seared though it may be. And she loves the Princess Varvare. I have no heart, Imraldera. None. But what Anahid desires, I desire."

His eyes flared open, but they looked into the forest over her head, and they were enormous with terror. His voice was a guttural snarl. "Save the girl, Knight of Farthestshore! Don't let her blood be spilled."

He took a step back then, and as he did so he lost all semblance of a man and became a dragon. Dread roared from his throat. "Away from me!"

Imraldera felt the presence of the one-horned beast.

It walked where it willed, and the Wood gave way around it. Even the Haven vanished at its approach. Imraldera, cradling her ruined hands, turned and saw it coming. Its pace was solemn but swift as stars turning overhead, and its horn was white and black at once.

The dragon flamed again. He towered over the unicorn, his wings like great storm clouds, his eyes like lightning. Fire billowed from his mouth, and Imraldera flung herself flat on her face as flames raced over her and struck the unicorn. The unicorn came forward, untouched. The yellow-eyed dragon screamed and beat his wings, crouching for a spring into the air.

A flash of white, and the unicorn leapt. The movement was like the doom of kingdoms, powerful and inevitable. The horn pierced the dragon's hide as a needle pierces silk, penetrating deep into the place where the heart would be had the dragon still possessed one.

The yellow-eyed dragon . . . Diarmid . . . the golden-eyed childe who had fought monsters at her side . . . the young man who had loved a girl named Anahid and lost her . . . shrieked and shrieked again until blood poured from his mouth and clogged his throat.

Then he died.

Imraldera screamed, staggering to her feet and shaking her ruined hands at the one-horned beast. It stood over the crumpled form of a dragon that dwindled into the ruins of a human body. She stumbled forward, hardly knowing what she did, angry again and shouting, "How could you? How *could* you?"

The unicorn turned to her. She saw with overwhelming horror that it was beautiful.

Maiden, it said, *you are hurt.*

"How could you?" she yelled once more, tears streaming down her burned face. "He died a dragon! You killed him as a dragon! Don't you know what you've done?"

The unicorn stepped forward. It was so delicate, Imraldera realized, unreal in its grace. Its eyes were as deep as the sky.

Stretch out your hands.

She obeyed, still crying, shaking with anger and terror. The unicorn bowed its horn, so narrow, so fragile that a child might snap it in two. It touched her hands, and they healed. It touched the burns on her face, and they vanished.

Imraldera stared into those deep, deep eyes. She drew a knife from her belt and raised it.

Depraved though it had become, a unicorn never harmed a pure maiden. This was the final remnant of its glory days when it sang the Songs high in the firmament. Thus it did not kill her. Instead it vanished without a word. Imraldera felt the Wood relaxing about her as the unseen beast sped away from the Haven.

She breathed again and dropped the knife. Then with a sob she knelt by the crumpled form of he who once was Diarmid and held him in her arms. His body was light with the absence of spirit and no longer burned inside.

"He died a dragon," she whispered, cradling his head against her shoulder. His blood stained her robes. "Why? Why did you let him?"

But she received no answer.

Gently she laid the dragon upon the grass, crossed his arms over his chest, and closed the lids over eyes that would never burn again. She whispered:

"I blessed your name in beauty. In fear I still must sing."

Goldstone Wood looked on in silence as the lady sang her benediction over the slain. Then it watched as Imraldera gathered herself up, sheathed her knife, and took the Path to Rudiobus, leaving the Haven behind.

7

T HE HALL OF RED AND GREEN was too hot and noisy for Oeric's comfort. He was accustomed to a solitary life, and the vibrancy of the little people was overwhelming at best. So he spoke a few words to the guard, then slipped away from the hall to wait. He made his way to the waterfall, Fionnghuala Lynn, and stood gazing out from behind its misty curtain to the frozen lake and winterbound wood beyond.

But his eyes saw none of these.

He gazed instead into the past, a past both distant and very near to him. Oeric recalled his own first visit to Rudiobus, long centuries ago, and what Bebo had said to him then. Back before the Sleeper woke and rose up from the Gold Stone. Back before the destruction of Carrun Corgar and before Oeric broke faith with the Prince, his Master.

His face was as hard as the stone of Rudiobus Mountain, and none who saw him could have guessed his thoughts.

Lionheart certainly could not when he descended the long stairway and, to his surprise, found he had not ended up back in the feasting hall as he had expected. He must have taken a wrong turn on his way down, he thought, though he didn't recall there being any turns. Yet Queen Bebo was gone, and here he stood at Fionnghuala Lynn, alone save for the stony presence of Sir Oeric. He approached the massive knight, leaned his shoulder against the wall, and also gazed through the mist of the waterfall. Neither spoke. Echoing through the mountain caverns came the voice of Eanrin, singing his eternal devotion to Lady Gleamdren, sometimes followed by the booming laughter of Iubdan and his court. Otherwise all was quiet, and even the waterfall murmured rather than roared.

At length Oeric said, "I saw you climb the long stair."

Lionheart grunted.

"Queen Bebo's words can be difficult to hear."

Another grunt. Another silence. Then Lionheart, bowing his head, said quietly, "I don't think I can do it."

Oeric turned his huge eyes to look at the small man across from him. Lionheart felt the gaze, it was so intense. But he could not bring himself to speak, to tell the knight his thoughts.

To admit that he did not want to die.

He gulped and said instead, "She says that I will cross into Arpiar."

"What?"

The ugly knight's tone was sharp, and Lionheart glanced up at him uneasily. "She says that before the Night of Moonblood has come and gone I shall cross the boundaries and . . . and find Rose Red."

Oeric continued to stare, and though not a feature moved, his expression slowly hardened into something fierce. "Moonblood is tomorrow night."

Lionheart winced. "It is?"

"Five hundred years I have searched for a Crossing." The knight's voice remained steady and low, but his hands formed into fists. "Five hundred years I have sought to find my brother. To find him and to kill him. For the last time."

Lionheart shuddered, aghast. "You seek to kill your own brother?"

"Yes, little mortal. Yes, I do. Because I am the only one who can. I am Vahe's twin, as like to him in spirit as any two beings can be. And I am as despicable as he, as capable of evil. I proved that long ago when in my pride I believed I could take and use my brother's weapons. For good purpose, of course, or so I told myself. In my arrogance, I did not consider that what I considered good might not in fact be right. No, I saw the evil Vahe worked and said that I would not do the same as he. So I disobeyed my Prince, betrayed my fellow knights, and took what I wanted."

His white eyes bored into Lionheart's, and Lionheart found he could not break his gaze no matter how he might wish to. "I did not trust my Prince, so I used Vahe's power for my own ends. I was wrong. I was so wrong, and oh! What evil did I cause!

"You see, Lionheart, I am no better than my brother. I am he and he is I except . . . except for one thing. I, though I am filthy at heart, vile and undeserving, was offered my Prince's forgiveness. Broken before him, I became the recipient of his grace."

Here at last, the knight turned away, resting his fist against the wall and drawing a deep breath. "Therefore, I and I alone must put an end to Vahe's evil. It is the way of Faerie, strange though it may seem to you. If I cannot save Arpiar, no one can. If I do not cut through the veils, they shall remain in place. For it is I who share Vahe's blood. Did not Queen Bebo say as much long centuries ago? Thus I have served my Prince these five hundred years, thus I have hunted for a way into my brother's realm. And in that time, I have not seen my beloved's face, for I vowed to her that I should not see her again until my people were free."

He turned suddenly on Lionheart and for a moment was even bigger and far more terrifying; Lionheart had never before seen that expression on the knight's face, that combination of despair and anger. "And now you, who may have caused my beloved's death . . . who may have stolen my last chance to speak to her what my heart has kept silent these many centuries . . . who without a thought, without a care, sent her to the one-horned beast, into Vahe's hands . . . You will go where I cannot? You will face my enemy and not I? No! It cannot—"

The enormous eyes closed. As quickly as it had come, the flash of fury was replaced with remorse. Lionheart, frozen in fear, watched the ugly knight pass a hand over his face and draw a great breath.

"No," he whispered. "No, I will not walk that path again. I will wait. Forgive me, Lionheart. I am wrong to forget so quickly."

Once more they stood in silence. Even the singing from the feasting hall was stilled. Lionheart, not entirely certain what had just happened, could think of nothing to say in the face of Oeric's distress. As the silence continued, his own thoughts came creeping back.

"Your life for hers."

The winter air was cold around him, but not so cold as the icy hand that gripped his heart. Had he not been given that choice before?

"Your life for her heart," the Dragon had said. *"An easy enough exchange."*

Now, by some fate or fortune Lionheart did not understand, he was brought around to this moment again, as though the Dragon still lived and breathed his poison into the world. Once more he must look Death in the eyes and . . . what?

He must prove himself a man; that's what. He must make things right. The memory of Hymlumé's face, her voice in that ageless song, returned to him with pain. He must do what was right and see this quest through. He must regain his honor and rescue Rose Red at whatever cost.

And yet.

And yet when the time came, how could he hope to fulfill all the vows he made to himself now? He'd failed once already. He was still the same man. Could his own resolve possibly make a difference where it had not before? His love for Una had not sufficed. Could the guilt he felt for betraying his best friend serve where love could not?

"Dragons eat it all," Lionheart swore under his breath, and the murmur of the falls covered his voice. "Dragons eat it all and be sick upon the lot!"

Why not let Oeric have his day? Let *him* find the Crossing into Arpiar! It was his dragon-eaten quest, after all. Let Oeric take the glory, save the princess, do what he as a Knight of Farthestshore was much better suited to do. Lionheart did not belong in this world of ancient kings and still more ancient prophecies. He was a mortal man, a ruined prince, a failure and a . . . and a coward.

His stomach churned along with his churning thoughts, and Lionheart leaned his head back against the wall, which was damp with spray from the waterfall. Droplets fell on his face, like stinging kisses they were so cold. Even the waterfall was freezing now.

A voice spoke behind him.

"Did you hear that?"

Lionheart startled and whirled about to find Eanrin standing very close. Oeric also turned and growled, "Lumé's crown, Eanrin, must you creep about so? Why aren't you in the hall singing to your—"

"Shhh!" The poet made a sharp motion with his hand. "Listen!"

Lionheart strained his ears. He heard nothing but the breathing of his companions and the swiftly freezing waterfall.

But Eanrin swore, "Great hopping giants, it *is* her!" and leapt forward, breaking through the long icicles formed by the falls. They shattered in crystalline clatter, and Lionheart watched the poet run across the glassy top of the lake.

Then he heard a voice calling, "Rudiobus! Hallo, Rudiobus!"

It wasn't very clear, but he could hear the distress.

Oeric straightened from his slouch against the wall. "That sounds like Imraldera," he said in his deep rumble. Then he too was hastening across the frozen lake, though with much less grace than the blind poet. Hardly stopping to think, Lionheart set off after him, slipping and sliding all the way. It was a strange sensation to him, running across solid water, for it was never cold enough in Southlands to freeze. The moon overhead reflected glaringly from snow and ice, and the forest beyond was all black. He could see no one, but he heard the voice again, this time calling, "Eanrin! Oeric!"

Lionheart was several paces behind Sir Oeric and many yards behind the poet when at last he neared the far shore. Ahead he saw Dame Imraldera collapsed on the edge of the frozen lake. Her green robes were stained dark down the front.

Eanrin leapt to the shore and skidded to his knees beside her, reaching out to feel for her in his blindness. She lay exhausted in the snow but conscious, and she put out a hand to him. He clutched it tight and drew her closer to him. "Imraldera!" Lionheart heard him exclaim. "Is that blood I smell on you?"

"Yes," she said. Her voice trembled. She must be freezing, Lionheart thought. Even as he thought it, he saw Eanrin remove his bright red cloak and wrap it around her shoulders. "Yes, but not mine," she continued.

"Oh, well," said Eanrin, drawing back a little as Oeric and Lionheart both gained the shore. "You gave me quite a start then for nothing, my girl. What's with these dramatics?"

Imraldera's voice caught in a sob. "Diarmid," she said. "Diarmid came to the Haven."

"Diarmid?" Oeric knelt in the snow beside her as well. Lionheart felt awkward and kept his distance. But he heard every word Imraldera said as she related what had happened: Vahe's plan, Princess Varvare's fate, and the death of the yellow-eyed dragon. The two knights listened in solemn silence until she spoke of the one-horned beast. Then Oeric drew in a hissing breath and Eanrin smiled around a curse of, "Dragon's teeth! You don't say?"

"He's dead, Eanrin," Imraldera said, shivering so hard that her voice was unsteady. "Diarmid died there. A dragon."

"It's not your fault," the poet said, patting her hand. "You couldn't stop the beast."

"But your nephew—"

"Hush, now!" To Lionheart's surprise, Eanrin took Imraldera's head between his hands and pressed his forehead against hers. Lionheart would not have guessed the poet capable of so tender a gesture. The lady closed her eyes and let out a shuddering sigh. "Hush, my dear," whispered the poet. "We both mourned his loss long ago."

A clatter of hooves, and Lionheart turned from that strange sight to see King Iubdan himself approaching on the back of his golden mare. Behind him marched a company of guards. As they drew nearer to the shore, he saw that these were not tiny but stood as tall as any man.

"I felt a trembling on the edge of my kingdom. What is the news, my poet?" Iubdan demanded.

Eanrin leapt to his feet and swept a bow after his usual flashy manner, all tenderness forgotten. "Good king," he cried. "My fellow knight has just brought us word of Vahe and the doings within Arpiar!"

He continued to smile and speak in a bright and golden voice even as he relayed the dark story Imraldera had carried to them. Perhaps his voice halted a moment when he spoke of the yellow-eyed dragon's death. Perhaps he trembled when he told of the one-horned beast. But for all his hearers could tell, he might have been passing on gossip at a country picnic. Imraldera, still clutching his cloak about her shoulders, rose to her feet with Oeric's aid and stood silently throughout.

Lionheart, who kept himself a little to one side, listened with growing horror as he heard the story a second time. So the choice would have to be made, he realized. Vahe intended to kill his daughter. Her doom was sure and coming soon. Then all the worlds would tremble under the fire of Vahe's newly awakened army. Tomorrow night! Tomorrow, at Moonblood. Unless . . .

How could there be any decision in the matter? He had failed once before. He could not fail again. What was his life worth otherwise?

. "Well," said Iubdan when Eanrin had done, "there's no good in trying to breach Arpiar, we all know that." He said this with a slight nod toward Oeric, who stood beside Imraldera with his eyes downcast. "We must descend to the Village of Dragons, though not by Death's Path. There is a way across the Near World, through the Red Desert. We will go to the Village and stop this nonsense of Vahe's at its catalyst. We know he must take his daughter there if he intends to spill her blood on Death's throne. What say you, my poet?"

Eanrin smiled still, as beaming as sunshine. But he said, "What of the one-horned beast?"

No one spoke. Even the proud guards trembled where they stood, and Iubdan sat with his mouth open, his breath steaming the air. *They're not afraid of dragons,* Lionheart thought, *nor of goblins. But the very mention of this one-horned beast and they cower like puppies on a stormy night.*

"What else can you suggest, Knights of Farthestshore?" the black-bearded king asked at last.

Somewhat to his horror, Lionheart heard his own voice speak next.

"I will go to Arpiar."

All eyes turned to him, and that was a terrible thing, feeling the weight of all those ageless gazes. He gulped but continued. "Queen Bebo said that I shall enter Vahe's realm before the Night of Moonblood. So if someone would just point me in the general direction, I'd be much obliged."

"Well, there's one small problem," said Eanrin with scorn in his voice. "No one knows where Arpiar is."

"Wait," said Oeric. Given his outburst from earlier, Lionheart fully expected him to jump in on Eanrin's side. But to his surprise, the ugly knight said, "We do have one idea."

"And what might that be, pray?" demanded the poet.

"I know," Imraldera said suddenly, the first she'd spoken since Iubdan's approach. "Eanrin, you told me yourself that you lost Prince Felix to the unicorn when he crossed the Old Bridge on Goldstone Hill. We all know that bridge was once a Crossing from Arpiar built by Vahe long ago. If Felix, as we suspect, ended up in Arpiar, is it not possible that the bridge is a Crossing still?"

"It is possible that the world is round and spins through space like a giant top," Eanrin said, still smiling. "Possible, but no less nonsensical. You know as well as I, old girl, no one can enter Arpiar unless called from within. It doesn't matter what the bridge *used* to be. If Vahe does not want uninvited guests, he won't have them. You can cross and recross that bridge all you like and end up in plenty of unpleasant locales of our beautiful Faerie. But you'll not see Arpiar."

"Do you doubt, then, what Queen Bebo has prophesied?" Imraldera snapped.

"I don't know what my queen had to say to our dear jester," the blind knight replied implacably. "I only know what we have all known since Vahe holed himself away. Arpiar cannot be found."

Oeric cleared his throat. When a person of Oeric's proportions clears his throat, those nearby stand up and pay attention. Even Eanrin's smile faltered.

"I will take Lionheart to the bridge," he said. That was all.

Eanrin turned at the sound of Oeric's voice, facing his fellow knight. Though he had no eyes, they studied each other, back and forth, and what the poet perceived with senses deeper than sight was anyone's guess. Then he nodded once.

"Well," said King Iubdan, raising his thick brows, "I'm glad we're decided. The mortal goes on a goose chase with the goblin, and the rest of us will off to the Village."

Eanrin turned to Lionheart and said in a low voice, "Very well, boy. You'll have your second chance. The Prince must see something in you that I in my blindness cannot, if he is sending you in place of Oeric. But remember, second chances come to few, and you cannot hope for a third. Perhaps your mother did not select your name from pure happenstance. If you truly have the heart of a lion, find it soon. Or we're all lost."

As Eanrin spoke, the wind picked up and pulled the snow in soft curtains up and around him, Imraldera, and the people of Rudiobus. Lionheart blinked and struggled to hear the final words, and when the wind died away and the snow settled again, the others were gone. Lionheart stood alone with Oeric on the edge of the frozen lake.

"Come," said the ugly knight. He turned and vanished into the Wood, and Lionheart hastened to catch up.

8

EVERYWHERE AROUND THE BOY was manic bustle, and nobody paid attention to him. He watched beautiful people, men and women, clad in armor of such elegant work that one would sooner expect to see it in a parade than in battle; though an expert eye would soon discover that it was stronger and more carefully wrought than it first appeared. Sometimes the Boy caught hints of conversations, snatches here and there.

"Tomorrow night," someone said.

"But what if he no longer needs *us* when they are awake?" another whispered, trembling.

"We are his servants. He will care for us as he has always done."

"How can we compare to their fire? We're next to useless! If he does not shield us, we'll be unprotected."

"So would you rather turn away?"

"No—"

"Would you rather lose the face he's given you and walk unveiled?"

"I didn't say—"

"Then shut your mouth and do as you're told. We've been preparing for this night for too many centuries to back out now."

This conversation and others like it bubbled throughout Palace Var. And since the Boy had no mind, nobody noticed him, even if he stood directly in front of them while they spoke, his mouth agape and his eyes wide. Eventually they would become irritated and shoo him on his way. He would not have walked five paces before it all slipped from his memory, leaving behind an empty hole of unease. All the beautiful faces around him were afraid, he knew that, but what had they to be afraid of in this sweet-smelling place?

His wanderings took him to the front hall of Var, where the great doors were open and russet sunlight poured through, staining the marble floors with the glow of sunset. King Vahe stood there, though the Boy did not know who he was. He simply thought him the most beautiful person he had ever before seen, so lordly in his rose-red robes, his brow crowned in golden rose leaves. Beside him stood a queen, also beautiful, but whose beauty tended to fade in the presence of her king. She wore black, and her long hair was braided with bloodred roses, and her face was pale without the faintest blush of life.

King and queen stood in the sunset's glow, the queen standing a little in her husband's shadow, and they waited, oblivious to the Boy or any of their servants around them. They were so still that the Boy began to wonder if they were statues. The queen's face was certainly cold enough.

"Ah!" said Vahe, and the Boy startled. "Look, Anahid!" He pointed, and the Boy looked where he indicated even if the queen did not.

The unicorn approached.

The Boy screamed at the sight and flung himself facedown on the marble floor, unable to move. Anahid dared not raise her gaze, and even the King of Arpiar trembled, grimacing. But the unicorn bowed its horn at Vahe's feet.

Blood dripped from its end and pooled bright against the white stone.

"My good slave," said Vahe, who did not step back, though he might have wished to. After all, he was king and master here. "You have done well. No one disobeys Vahe of Arpiar or flees his protections without consequences. Eh, Anahid? What do you say to this?" He motioned to his silent queen.

Slowly, as though fighting against the very pull of the tides, Anahid looked at the bloodstained horn. No tears filled her eyes; after all, her young love had given himself over to Death long ago. But though fear nearly stole her voice, she whispered, "Did he give his message before he died?"

The unicorn turned to her, and what it said was for her ears only. The King of Arpiar barked, "Don't talk to her! You are *my* slave! Answer *me*. Did the dragon speak to anyone before you skewered him?"

The unicorn turned its horrible eyes upon Vahe, who flinched but did not break its gaze. The king snarled at whatever answer it gave. "Did you kill her, then?"

The unicorn replied.

Vahe roared. "Why not? Don't give me that pure maiden rot! She is my enemy, and you are my slave; therefore she is your enemy as well! Your laws are but antiquated traditions, beast, and they count for nothing here. You'd better get over them before Moonblood, or you'll have Life-in-Death to answer to!"

The unicorn closed its eyes and bowed again.

Vahe cursed viciously and turned to his queen. Anahid was smiling. For a moment, his beautiful face melted away into fangs and flashing eyes, and he struck her across the face. Black claws trailed ribbons of blood across her cheek, and she fell to the floor.

"Wipe that smile off your face, my pretty wife!" Vahe cried. "Your hand is played, but the game belongs to me. You've been my slave from the first. Of your own choosing you gave yourself to me, and you are mine still! You knew it from the beginning, didn't you? The first moment you looked into my face, you knew your doom would be bound up in my will. So it is, and so it will always be. Your love for that dragon boy could not help you. Your love for our precious Varvare will also be as nothing! You will stand by my side and watch the worlds burn, and you will burn with them. You'll not live to see me remake the realms after my own design, not after this rebellion."

Anahid remained where she fell, every line of her body subservient.

But the Boy, who lay prostrate on the ground as well, could see her face, and he witnessed the brief flash in her eyes that was immediately covered by deferential eyelids.

Vahe, however, saw only her hunched shoulders and bowed head, and he turned away with a snarl and a smile, cursing her. He said to the unicorn, "Go now to the Crossing and watch it. No one can breach my walls, but I am not a vainglorious man. I am not unwilling to guard against even unreasonable threats. So go to the Crossing, and if you see any Knights of Farthestshore poking around where they shouldn't, make them aware of my displeasure in no uncertain terms."

The unicorn bowed its horn once more and vanished, and in its absence the Boy found himself able to breathe again.

Vahe turned and gave his wife a last contemptuous look, narrowing his eyes at her crumpled form. "You see, Anahid, what good your little warning will accomplish?"

He swept from the doorway then, and the sky plunged into nightfall in his wake. Anahid remained awhile where she lay, and the Boy, sitting up and rubbing his knees, wondered if she had fallen asleep. He crawled over to her and gently touched her hand. "Lady?" he asked. "Are you all right?"

She sat up sharply at his touch, and for a moment he gazed into the hideous face of a goblin. Then she rose, arranging her robes about her, and she was beautiful and cold and terrible once more. She left the Boy shivering on the floor. And he, after a time, wondered what it was he had just forgotten.

Oeric said nothing as he led Lionheart from the Far World back into Goldstone Wood, and Lionheart was grateful. They stepped onto a Path, and once more Lionheart felt the sensation of traveling many leagues with each stride and the kaleidoscope effect on his peripheral vision. But it did not bother him as much as it had. Perhaps he was already growing used to it. He focused on the broad back of the knight in front of him and wondered how far they were from Goldstone Hill.

So strange, he thought, to be traveling that way again. It wasn't so long ago that he had sat beside an old bridge one afternoon, talking with Princess Una about dreams and hopes for the future. Was it that same bridge to which they hastened now? How cyclical his life had become, returning him to places he never thought to see again. But that, he guessed, must be part of the rhythms of Faerie, as Ragniprava had put it.

The air felt unnaturally warm after the winter of Rudiobus. Lionheart could not guess how much time passed. He knew Moonblood was but one night away, but was that true anymore in this place Between?

"We are near now," Oeric said at long last, the first he had spoken since leaving the icy lake. He turned to Lionheart and, much to Lionheart's surprise, held out Bloodbiter's Wrath. "I thought you might want this," he said, offering the gaudy hilt. "I believe you do have courage in your heart. Take this and prove me right."

Lionheart accepted it and slid it into the empty scabbard at his side. Though the knight turned his back on him once more, Lionheart's spirits lifted at Oeric's words. Not everyone thought him a hopeless fool.

Even if that was the truth.

Their way took them uphill now, and Lionheart thought he almost recognized his surroundings. But he had never before seen Goldstone Hill from the Between. It was similar in many respects to what it was in the Near World. But as they climbed, Lionheart saw that there was no ocean to the west, only more and more trees, stretching on forever. Surely the Between must connect to the sea somewhere, he thought. But that somewhere was not here.

"Dindeitra Tower once stood at the top of this rise," Sir Oeric said quietly as they climbed. "Long before Calix built Palace Oriana, Dindeitra watched over the Near World and the Far from this vantage. Until Vahe took it."

Lionheart wondered who Calix was. He wasn't particularly keen on his history of Parumvir, but he could have sworn it was one of the dozens of King Abundiantuses who had ordered the building of Oriana Palace.

"Vahe took this hill early in his reign," Oeric continued, "and grafted it onto Arpiar when he built the Crossing. He renamed the tower *Carrun*

Corgar. But after his first death, he lost his hold here, and Carrun Corgar returned once more to the Wood Between."

Lionheart, uncertain if he was expected to answer, grunted. Oeric ignored him. "I have been to this place many times during the last five hundred years. I have crossed the bridge and been taken to more realms of Faerie than I can count. But it is as Eanrin said—without a call, no one can enter Arpiar."

Lionheart saw the bridge ahead of them as they climbed, a few old boards spanning a trickle of stream. His heart lurched at the sight. He could almost picture Una, with her flyaway hair half pulled back in a braid, laughing as he juggled stones for her amusement.

"Your life for her heart," the Dragon had said.

And he'd chosen his life.

He put his hand on Bloodbiter's Wrath, grinding his teeth as he followed Oeric to the bridge. He'd not make that mistake again. Not this time.

Oeric stood like a statue before the bridge, his arms loose at his sides. He turned and looked at Lionheart without a word.

"So, shall we step over, then?" Lionheart asked.

"Do you hear a call?" said Oeric.

Lionheart frowned. "I don't think so. I'm not sure what it would sound like."

"Neither am I."

The stream laughed at them as it raced down the hillside into the deeper wood. The trees were not so dense here, and Lionheart could look on up to the crest of the hill. There should be a seven-tiered garden here and, at the summit, a grand palace, perhaps ruined now after the Dragon's visit. But there was nothing like that to be seen in the Wood Between. Instead, trees thinned away until the crest of the hill was open to the sky. And Lionheart thought he saw the moss-grown stones of what might once have been a tower.

"Well," he said, "I suppose I should try to cross."

Oeric placed a restraining hand on his shoulder. "Not without a call. I'd lose you somewhere in Faerie."

"But there isn't any call. Not that I can hear. And time is passing! Queen Bebo said I should cross over, so maybe I am the one person who can?"

Oeric shook his head. "Arrogant mortal." He spoke without malice but rather with sorrow. "You are no different from all the others who thought the same. I am Vahe's brother, and there was a time when I could pass through his spells with hardly a thought. But no longer. And you are just a man."

"Then we came out here to stand and do nothing?"

"We must wait."

"Time is passing!"

"And still we must wait."

Lionheart writhed under Oeric's grip until at last he ceased and the knight let him go. He gazed across the bridge that led only farther up the hill and could not imagine how it could possibly lead him to Arpiar and Rose Red. He had stepped into Faerie several times now, and he knew he could believe what Oeric told him, but that did not make it any easier to understand.

Oeric took a seat on a nearby stone and became as part of the hill, he was so still. Lionheart could not sit but paced back and forth, Bloodbiter's Wrath slapping against his leg. The sun did not move overhead, and the shadows never shifted. But somewhere time moved onward, Lionheart knew. What if the Night of Moonblood was already come, and Rose Red even now was meeting her fate on Death's throne?

No, Queen Bebo had promised, there in the Gardens of Hymlumé where even mortals could hear the Songs of Spheres. She had promised he would have the chance to make his choice, and she would not lie to him.

Lionheart swung about suddenly and strode for the bridge. "No!" Oeric barked, but Lionheart's feet were already on the boards, and he was halfway across.

That's when he saw the unicorn.

It stood in a place outside of worlds, not in the Near, the Far, or the Between. Lionheart saw it as all but pure maidens see the one-horned beast, the fallen child of Hymlumé who heeded the Dragon's voice rather than the Sphere Songs.

It was like a bull, enormous and powerful, eight feet tall at the shoulder, but its head was that of a horse, or like a horse save that its mouth was full of fangs. Spines grew down its neck, back, and tail, and its cloven hooves could destroy mountains with a single kick. Yet it walked with grace, not turning a blade of grass under its step. Like a star, its body was ablaze with fire, burning but never consuming, and its eyes were the pitiless blackness of space, without sorrow, fear, or anger. A great, flaming horn grew from its forehead.

Lionheart screamed and jumped back from the bridge. He would have fallen had not Oeric caught him. "What?" the ugly knight cried. "What do you see?"

"The beast! The one-horned beast!"

And then it stepped across the bridge, and Oeric saw it too. The terror in Oeric's yell was almost as horrible as the unicorn itself. The knight grabbed Lionheart's shoulder and dragged him down the hill. "Draw your sword," he cried as they fled. "Draw your sword but do not fight it!"

Lionheart couldn't draw his weapon while running, but at the moment he did not care. His focus was on his feet as they scrabbled down the steep incline, willing them not to slip and fall and allow him to be crushed under the unicorn's flaming hooves.

Suddenly, it was in front of them, not behind. Lionheart slid to a halt so quickly that he fell. Oeric, however, lunged forward, drawing a long knife as he went and shouting wordlessly. He swung his weapon, but the unicorn turned its horn and cut the blade in two. Oeric, his momentum carrying him, continued down the hill, and the unicorn did not turn to follow him but focused its black eyes on Lionheart.

Lionheart pushed himself up and fled again, uphill this time, numb to all but fear. He knew the unicorn pursued him though he heard not a sound behind him. He knew with the certainty of death.

9

ONLY THE GHOSTS OF ROSES lined the halls where Varvare walked. Like forlorn phantoms, they spread their vaporous leaves and petals as though to plead with her for their release. She could do nothing for them. But she had harvested from their enchantments, her fingers deftly taking stems and leaves.

The time was now or never. King Vahe was distracted, amassing his people for some endeavor she could not fathom, and she had scarcely seen him the last two days. She did not know how long this good fortune would last or how long the people of Arpiar would be kept so busy with their mysterious business. It looked as though they prepared for war, and she shuddered at this thought.

No one saw her as she slipped through back corridors and down a deep stairway. As she descended, the shades of roses receded, for even Palace Var did not always wear its veils. In the dungeons, there was no need to disguise its true face.

There were no lights, but Varvare's eyes required none. Like those of her ancestors who had mined in the deepest mountains, her eyes soaked in whatever light was available and hoarded it away for use in the dark. She walked without hesitation through pitch-black shadows, one hand lightly trailing against the stone wall for support on uneven stairs. The cells in the depths of Var were empty; or if occupied, their prisoners were so silent and still that they may as well have ceased to exist. The princess did not stop to look, for she knew the cell she sought; she had been down this way before.

The final cell was large, and when Varvare looked through the bars in the door she lowered her gaze ten feet to the sunken floor below. The air was dank with mold and neglect, and heavy chains curled like pythons at intervals across the floor. Only one set was in use, binding a lone figure to the wall.

Her age was difficult to guess, for she seemed simultaneously very young and very old. When she sat with her eyes downcast, as she did when Varvare gazed through the bars, she seemed scarcely older than the princess herself, with smooth skin and youthful features, her long hair fallen in tangles about her face. But when she caught the sound of Varvare's shallow breathing, she raised her eyes and suddenly aged by hundreds of years. Hers were eyes that had seen many generations come and go.

"Rosie!" she cried and tried to stand, but the chains were heavy on her wrists and ankles. "Rosie girl, is that you?"

"Hullo, Beana," said Princess Varvare. She put her hands to the bars and pressed her face against them.

"I can't see you to save my life, not in this fierce dark. I was afraid you wouldn't come. I hear them moving about up there, all sorts of awful ruckus. I thought they might take you away with them."

"I don't know how you pick up anythin' down here."

"Oh, I hear many things you don't, my girl, just as your wide eyes can see in the dark while mine cannot. I hear the goblins moving, and I hear the palace humming, and I even hear the voice of the unicorn now and then. And I thought I heard . . ."

Her voice trailed off, and Varvare, who could see her sitting in that cell shackled to the wall, watched her face twist into an expression of deep sorrow. But strangely enough, there was also a trace of hope.

"What did you hear, Beana?"

"I thought I heard the voice of someone I knew long ago. I thought I heard him on the edge of Arpiar. I know he's searching, has been searching for ever so long. If only I could call him!"

Varvare closed her eyes, leaning her forehead against the bars. "You could call him," she whispered.

"Not while I'm in chains, dear one," Beana replied, shaking her head. "My voice has no power as long as these hold me."

"Tell me his name, then," said the girl. "I'll call him myself."

"I wish it were so simple," said Beana. "You cannot call someone you do not know. And if you call, you'll not reach someone who is not already searching for you. But you know this already. Remember how, when we lived on the mountain, I told you to call me should you become lost in the forest? Remember how you did the same for young Leo?"

Varvare nodded, bowing her head. And when Leo had become lost one dark night when they were children, he had called her name, and she had heard him and come to him in an instant, for she was always listening for his voice.

But he would not be listening for her. Not far away in Southlands as he was, married to Daylily and ruling his kingdom. No, he would never give a thought for his former chambermaid. Varvare gnashed her teeth in the dark.

"Curse these chains," sighed Beana, hanging her head. "I was a fool. I shouldn't have plunged after you so rashly. I knew the unicorn waited. I knew it would catch me. I should have known I would end up in chains!"

Varvare shivered, not wanting to remember that fateful day. Images of the strange forest surrounding her, of the distant shouts up the gorge . . . of that moment when she knew she had passed from the Near World into the Between.

Then the unicorn had stood before her, beautiful and deadly.

Come with me, it had said.

Why should she not? It was such a glorious creature. And even if it killed her, what would it have mattered?

But just as she took the first step, a shout from behind had frozen her in her tracks. She'd turned about and seen her goat. But not her goat.

Instead, she was the woman whom Rose Red had glimpsed only a handful of times in all her years. A tall, angular woman with blazing eyes and braided hair, a long knife brandished above her head.

"Fallen One!" Beana had shouted. "Let the girl go!"

The unicorn had turned its eyes, so soft and so deep upon the woman. She had shuddered under its gaze.

You could not keep her from me, it had said. *Not for long.*

"She's not yours," the woman had said, advancing, her teeth bared. "Release her. I command you in the name of my Master. I command you in the name of the Prince of Farthestshore!"

For a trembling moment, Varvare had felt a strange lifting of her spirit. She had felt bindings hitherto unnoticed falling away, and she had realized that she did not want to go with the unicorn. With a gasp, she had taken a single step back.

Then the unicorn had screamed.

Varvare pressed her hands to her temples, desperately wishing she could rid her mind of that sound. Even in memory, it was unbearable, enough to tear her heart in two. And Beana, fearless Beana, who had shouted in the face of the Dragon, had collapsed under the sound.

So they had been brought here, to Palace Var. Varvare had been made a princess, just as the Dragon had always told her she would be, from the time he began plaguing her childhood dreams. And Beana had been thrown in the dungeons.

Varvare grimaced, her brows knitting together. She put her hand in her pocket and withdrew something that shimmered with its own light. It was a cord, tightly woven and thin as spider web, rolled into a ball the size of an apple. "I've been workin' on somethin'," the princess said and put her hand through the bars, holding out the glowing ball of thread. "See?"

"I told you, I can't see a thing in here."

Varvare blinked. "It's shinin', Beana."

"What is?"

The princess licked her lips and drew the gleaming ball of thread back through the bars. "I've made a rope. I took the king's enchanted roses and unwove them and spun them again."

Beana blinked unseeing in the blackness. "That's powerful work, indeed! I had no idea you could do things like that."

"Neither does the king." Varvare pocketed the thread. "I'm goin' to get you out of here."

"What?"

"I can see behind the veils, Beana. My mo— The queen can too, I think. And I know that she can sometimes break the enchantments. I believe I can as well. I'm goin' to release you, and we're goin' to escape, you, me, and the Boy—"

The lady knight surged to her feet in a terrible clash of chains. "Don't," she said. "Don't even try it, Rose Red, I beg you. If you can see his enchantments . . . Don't you see that if you break these chains you will die? The moment they drop from my hands, you will perish."

Varvare gasped and drew back from the door. Then she cursed, "Dragon's teeth!"

"Hen's teeth. You know better than to use such language."

The princess struck the door with her fist, then struck it again, fury shaking her body. "We've got to get out, Beana! I think . . . I think King Vahe plans to kill me."

"What? What makes you say that?"

"I don't know. But sometimes the way he looks at me, I get the feeling he's measurin' me for my coffin. And I don't think he's goin' to wait much longer before he does it."

Beana shook her head but was silent a long moment. She'd had plenty of time to think in that blackness, and had come to several conclusions she could not shake no matter how she tried. At last she said, "Rosie, I know what my Master has been telling you. Don't think I don't. Call for Lionheart."

A long silence filled the air between. At last Varvare said, "No."

"Please, dear girl. My Master knows what is—"

"Your Master doesn't give a monkey's eye for me!" Varvare snarled, and her voice was, in that moment, the voice of a goblin. "I loved him. I really did, Beana. But he doesn't see the likes of me, ugly as I am, one of those monsters he has rejected!"

"That's not true, and you know it," said Beana. "Those are Vahe's spells speaking, not you."

But Varvare scarcely heard her. "He only cares about his great and mighty purpose," she cried, "and someone like me can live and die, and it doesn't make a lick of difference! I'd rather die than do what he asks me, to call for someone who forgot me, then betrayed me, and never once saw me as anythin' but a monster. To be used for his own ends! I'd rather die, Beana. Do you hear me?"

She turned away from the cell door, her arms wrapped about herself. "Besides, he ain't listenin' for me. Not the way I listened for him. It was always that way between us. I know that now."

With that, she left the cell, ignoring Beana's voice, though she cried out after her. Varvare's whole body shook with rage and despair, and she sat down in the black stairway leading up from the dungeons, unwilling to face the people of Var scurrying about above. Somewhere, far away, that silver voice still reached out to her.

Beloved.

"I won't do it!"

Beloved, trust me.

"I cain't! Not anymore."

I will always protect you.

"You've done a dragon-eaten job of it lately."

I will always protect you. This doesn't mean that you will not know pain. But I am here with you. Nothing can thwart the plans I have for you.

"I don't care what plans you have for me! You left me here to rot, and I'm rotten to the core now. I am a goblin's child."

You are my child.

Varvare got to her feet, dashing the tears from her face, and hastened up the steps, two at a time.

Call for him.

"I won't. I'll get myself out of here."

She went to find the Boy.

And Beana, alone in the darkness, bowed her head and whispered prayers she could only hope were heard.

The assembly hall of Var boasted windows that reached from floor to ceiling, at least three stories tall. Roses grew all over around the frames, at least as far as the Boy could see. Varvare saw things differently but didn't bother to explain as much as she flung open a casement and let her shimmering cord drop.

The windows of the assembly hall were many stories high, but this was the only place Varvare had found in the whole palace where a daring descent would leave the intrepid beyond the walls of Vahe's stronghold.

The cord she had woven from stolen enchantments was long enough to tie around the base of the old queen's statue in the hall and still reach most of the way to the ground outside. The Boy stood by with his mouth open, watching her work. He could not see the cord, and it looked to him as though the beautiful veiled princess (whatever her name was) had lost her mind. "What are you doing?" he asked at last.

"I don't know your name," she snapped.

"I didn't ask my name. I asked what you're doing." He scratched the top of his head. "Though, while we're on the subject, what is—"

"I'm getting us out of here."

Varvare tested her weight against her knot, and it seemed to hold. The statue of the old queen scowled down upon her, hideous in Varvare's eyes, beautiful in the eyes of the Boy. But it held its peace, watching as the princess returned to the window and looked down. "Come here," Varvare said, beckoning to the Boy.

He stepped to her side and looked down. "That's a long way."

"We're goin' to climb down," Varvare said. She grabbed his hand and pressed her cord into it. "Do you feel that?"

At first he did not, but something about the look in Varvare's beautiful eyes motivated him to try. The thin line of the cord slid through his palm, and he blinked, startled. No matter how he stared he could not see it, yet the Boy knew he held something. Something strong.

"Do you feel it?" the princess demanded again.

He nodded.

"Good. I'm goin' to tie it round your waist and lower you down."

"*What?*"

"Don't argue with me," she growled. "I ain't goin' to leave you in this awful place, or let the king keep usin' you. You're comin' with me. Then once we're safe, I'll find someone to help me, and we'll come back and rescue Beana." Her eyes flashed as the Boy opened his mouth to protest. "That's the way it's goin' to be. Do you hear? Or do you want to stay here with the unicorn?"

The Boy's mind could scarcely recall where he had been five minutes previous. But the one thing that remained clear in his mind with each passing moment was the memory of the one-horned beast. It drove away the soothing sweetness of rose perfume and left him trembling.

"All right," he whispered.

Varvare quickly secured her cord around him, looping it about his waist and over his shoulders. "When you get to the bottom," she said, "you have to untie it and drop the rest of the way. Won't be far, but careful you don't twist an ankle or somethin', because I don't want to carry you. I don't know how much of a start we'll get before they realize we're gone. You listenin' to me?"

He wasn't. He was staring from the window down that long drop to the grass below. At least he could not see what the princess saw, which was stone-hard dirt and jagged rocks. He would never have had the courage to try then. "Are . . . are you sure you won't let me drop?"

"I'm stronger than I look."

"That's not saying a whole lot."

With some coaxing, she got him to sit in the windowsill and dangle his feet out. And still the statue of the old queen watched, her stone eyes narrowing.

"You ready?" the princess asked.

"Um. Why don't we—"

She put her shoulder to his back and pushed.

A bellow of *"Iubdan's beeeeeard!"* rattled her ears, but she held on to the cord, bracing herself against the window. When the cry at last died away, she looked down and saw the terrified face of the Boy staring up at her from where he dangled not three feet down.

"You all right?" she called.

He made a sound like *"Meep!"*

"I'm goin' to start lowerin' you now. Use your feet along the wall and help me out a bit."

Trembling, the Boy managed to turn himself around, and slowly the princess let down the cord. He was heavier than she'd expected, but she was strong. Though her father had clothed her in veils of delicacy and dainty features, she was still a goblin girl underneath. It took some work, but at last she reached the end of the cord, and the Boy dangled no more than ten feet from the ground. She looked out over the window, trying to shout without actually shouting, which was difficult for him to hear.

"All right, Boy, drop."

"Look at me! I'm floating!"

"Hush up and drop!"

"Who are you?"

"Hen's teeth, Boy, I'm goin' to give you such a shakin' when I get down there!"

At last he understood, and she gasped a grateful prayer when relieved of his weight. Clenching her teeth, Varvare climbed onto the windowsill herself and turned around to begin her descent.

And found herself face-to-face with Queen Anahid.

Her heart stopped. For one horrible moment, she gazed into the goblin eyes of her mother. So this was the end. All her efforts were ruined, here and now, just when she thought she might have a chance.

Anahid blinked slowly, like the eclipse of moons. Then she whispered between fangs, "Hurry, child."

That was all. The queen backed away, stepping into the shadows of the old queen's statue, and Varvare once more knelt on the windowsill, her hands clutching her enchanted cord.

"Hey, up there!" the Boy called from below. "Careful, you might fall!"

Grinding her teeth, Varvare slid from the window and started the long climb down.

"Are you going to sound the alarm, Queen of Arpiar?"

Anahid stood in the shadow of the old queen, her former mistress, from whom she had once known great favor. She shuddered as the memory-voice hissed through her mind.

"You know what you must do."

Anahid turned her gaze up at the statue, so carefully beautiful, just as the old queen had once been, long ago when Anahid had been but an attendant in her service, before Vahe was even born.

"Alert Vahe, Anahid. I command you."

Anahid smiled. It was more like a snarl. "You have no power over me anymore."

Then she raised her hand and twisted her fingers sharply. Her husband's veiling enchantments shifted, then dropped away, revealing the true ugliness of the stone queen's face. With another twist, Anahid wrapped those same veils around the statue's open mouth, thus stifling her voice so that she could not give the alarm.

So Princess Varvare grabbed the nameless Boy's hand and, free of Var, dragged him across the empty plain.

10

His heart in his throat, Lionheart ran, and in his fear he hardly noticed that he fled uphill. The ground flew by under his feet, not leagues in a stride, for he followed no enchanted Path now. No, he was pathless in the Wood, a dangerous place to be, Eanrin had said, but Lionheart hardly cared. He would wander as a lost vapor beneath these trees throughout eternity if only he could escape the monster behind him.

Only it wasn't behind him now.

He couldn't guess how he knew, but he realized with a start that he was no longer followed. Yet the unicorn was near. Nearer than ever, perhaps. But where?

He stopped and stood still in the forest on the hill, surrounded by trees, and he couldn't see a thing but branches and leaves. At last he pulled Bloodbiter's Wrath from its sheath. His breath came in pants, and he kept turning and turning, his eyes searching and finding nothing. Slowly, Lionheart let his blade drop a little and began to climb up the hill once more.

And there it stood, gazing down on him, its horn mere inches from his face.

He screamed and fell onto his back, losing hold of his sword. The one-horned beast stood over him, and the flaming horn aimed at his heart. He cried out and closed his eyes.

But the blow did not fall.

He became aware of a silver song, like water, like starlight, flowing through the Wood and surrounding him. A bird's song, Lionheart thought, but unlike a bird as well. Trembling, he opened his eyes and saw the unicorn above him still. It was not looking at him. Its gaze was fixed on something beyond him.

Lionheart craned his neck around and saw that someone stood just behind him. *Oeric?* he wondered. Sunlight piercing through the foliage overhead cast the man's face into shadow, and Lionheart could see no features. But he heard a voice, strong as a river, speak.

"Away now, Hymlumé's child. Your time is not come."

The unicorn screamed.

It was not a scream that could be described by any comparison Lionheart knew, for its voice was not a sound. It was a life complete in and of itself, a life that suddenly saw itself for what it was and despaired at the sight. It was the whole of disappointment and denial and destruction rolled into a tiny point of time.

Then it was gone.

Lionheart lay for he could not guess how long, his head ringing with the echoes the unicorn left behind. Then he felt a hand touch his shoulder.

"Get up, Lionheart."

He obeyed. It was one of those voices one simply obeyed without question. Then he turned to face the speaker and still could not see his face with the brightness of the sun shining behind him.

"I have brought something for you," said the stranger. For it must be a stranger. It could not be Oeric, who never spoke in such a voice. "Something for you to carry with you into Arpiar."

Lionheart found himself staring at the sword offered to him hilt first. It was a sorry weapon. It might once have been fine, but that was long ago. Now it was a ridiculous thing, the hilt melted and warped, the blade blackened and twisted as though in a furnace.

"I . . . I have a sword," he said, casting about briefly for Bloodbiter's Wrath.

"Not such a one as this."

Lionheart licked his lips. "I don't think . . . I don't mean to be rude, but I don't think this will do me any good."

The stranger continued to hold it out. "This sword has slain dragons," he said.

Lionheart gasped, and he realized suddenly to whom he was speaking. In that same moment, the stranger vanished, and Lionheart stood alone with his hands clasped around the hilt of a pathetic, ruined sword.

The statue queen stood with her arms upraised, holding the ceiling of the assembly hall. She could not lower them to tear the enchantments from her mouth, thus she could not call out to King Vahe when he entered the hall. And he saw nothing, of course, her brainless offspring. What was left to see? Anahid had coiled up the enchanted thread and carried it away with her, perhaps had destroyed it. She had even closed the window and adjusted all the roses around it so that no sign remained of Princess Varvare's escape.

No sign, save the absence of the girl herself.

Vahe stood in the old queen's shadow, his shoulders squared, his gaze sliding slowly across the room as he searched for his daughter. She always holed herself away in this place. None of Var's courtiers entered this room unless summoned, for they all feared the gazes of their former sovereigns. Gazes full of vengeance and hatred, which the veiled goblins knew they deserved. But Varvare had nothing to fear from her ancestors save their scorn, which didn't seem to bother her. Thus Vahe had always been certain of finding her hidden away in this room, staring dumbly into space . . . worthless little thing that she was.

But he didn't see her, and the faintest inkling of concern tugged at his mind. Of course, he had nothing to fear, he told himself. The Lady had promised him the fulfillment of his dream, and she must honor her word.

Yet here he stood on the cusp of fulfillment, mere hours away from the appointed time, and the agony of waiting was almost beyond bearing.

He felt the stone gaze of his mother's statue and looked up with a snarl. But his snarl melted into a smile when he saw the enchanted gag in her mouth.

"Well, Mother, this is a fine look for you, I must say! You have never been more beautiful than when silenced."

The old queen stared down at him. She need only hold his gaze long enough for him to think. To think and to realize.

No one in Arpiar had the power to manipulate Vahe's enchantments except . . .

With a cry, he raised his hand, took hold of the spell threads, and yanked the gag from the old queen's mouth. "Anahid did this!" he roared, and for a moment the veil on his face slipped to show the foulness beneath. "Why? Tell me!"

The statue smiled, and no veils could make her beautiful in that moment. *"Your little princess isn't so spineless as she looks, son of my heart. She unwound your roses and made a rope, and by now she's halfway to the borders."*

"Anahid is behind this, isn't she?" the king declared, wringing his hands and gnashing sharp teeth.

"Only in keeping her mouth shut. My granddaughter has my blood in her veins after all. She is stronger than you thought!"

Vahe did not hear these last words. He was already running from the hall, shouting for his slaves.

The farther they got from Palace Var, the more the pain increased, first in the Boy's hand where the rose thorn had pierced him, then slowly spreading through his veins. Fire that had lain dormant reawakened and burned, and there were no enchanted roses to stifle it now.

His footsteps faltered. "I want to lie down," he told the princess, who dragged him firmly along. The grass under his feet was soft and thick, and the sun was warm on his back. More than anything, he wanted to curl up, close his eyes, and perhaps die. But the princess was firm.

"We're gettin' out of here, Boy. Pick up your feet!"

"But it hurts."

"Nonsense!"

Varvare would not stop. Her eyes saw behind the veils covering Arpiar, down to the barren rock and dust of a plain. Sometimes she glimpsed the ghostly roses of the king's spells, and when she saw them she also saw the Faerie Paths that crisscrossed the kingdom, Paths that could carry a person across great distances in moments. But she dared not use these. They were Vahe's.

So they picked their way painfully across the miles. After the first hour, she knew that the Boy was hurting but chose to ignore it. The next hour, it was not something she could ignore, so she fought it, insisting to him and to herself that it was all in his head. But as the third hour rolled around, she was nearly carrying him. She was strong, but he was so tall and gangly that she could scarcely keep him upright.

And as the fourth hour drew near, she knew they were not going to reach the edge of Arpiar. Palace Var had disappeared, yes, but gray plain stretched to the horizon all around, endless and horrible. The sun was setting in a grim red glare to the west, and it seemed to Varvare that it was a flaming eye, watching them as they struggled.

The Boy collapsed. His feet stumbled on each other, and he fell headlong, pulling her down with him. She crawled out from underneath him and took his face between her hands, patting his cheeks. But his skin was pale as death and hot to her touch. There would be no waking him.

She turned her gaze up to the darkening sky, wanting to curse but too overwhelmed to form the words. She should leave him. She would make much better time without him. Unburdened, it might be possible to reach the edge of Arpiar.

"No," she whispered, touching his burning face again. "I won't let any harm come to him!"

"Too late for that, princess."

Varvare blinked, and goblins stepped from Vahe's enchanted Paths, surrounding her. She should have screamed, should have leapt to her feet and run. But instead, she sat unmoving and watched them closing in. She could feel nothing, neither fear nor disappointment.

"He's harmed beyond help now," said the goblin standing in front of her. "You might as well hand him over. And while we're on the subject . . ." He knelt down and grabbed Varvare's hands. His claws were long and black, and he made no effort to retract them. She felt their sharpness cutting even her own stony skin as he bound her wrists with a thick cord.

Varvare stared into the goblin's wide white eyes, and her face was such that even his ugly heart nearly broke at the sight. "Sorry, princess," he growled, tightening the cord.

One last time, the voice called to her across the unending expanse of Arpiar's plain.

Beloved, call for him.

Varvare bowed her head and whispered, "Leo. I need you. Come to me."

His heart beating just as fast as it had when he fled the unicorn, Lionheart turned and found that he stood near the Old Bridge. How had he missed it before? Quickly he approached it and stood looking across to the forest beyond. He hesitated, and his hands holding the twisted sword shook. What if this wasn't right? What if, as Oeric said, he ended up lost somewhere in Faerie, unable to get back? What if—

The call came.

A voice crying out his name across many leagues.

Lionheart felt it tugging at his heart, pulling him almost against his will across the old plank bridge. He staggered forward, closing his eyes, trying not to see the forest but to follow only that faint thread of voice as it pulled and faded and faded some more. Then it was gone.

Lionheart opened his eyes.

Gray stretched around him. No forest, no hill, no bridge, not even a sky, it seemed, for it blended in so perfectly with the gray of the plain on which he stood. Nothing rose to break the monotony, not as far as his eyes could see in any direction save one. Just to his right stood a host of goblins, armed to the teeth.

And in the middle of them knelt Rose Red, her ugly face staring in opened-mouthed wonder right at him.

"Leo!" she cried.

The goblins turned. He looked at them; they looked at him. Then everything exploded in sudden motion. He was running, but everywhere he turned were goblins, their rocky hides blending almost perfectly into the gray of the plain. Leering faces filled his vision, white eyes on craggy, awful faces. One of them grabbed him by the shirt front, knocking away his sword, though he did not release his grip on the hilt. The monster lifted him right off his feet and dragged him up to its foul and stinking face.

"What is this?" the goblin cried, spitting in Lionheart's eye. "A mortal beast has crossed our boundaries!"

"Smash him!"

"Bite his fingers!"

"Break him!"

"Bruise him!"

The goblin shook Lionheart like a terrier shakes a rat, but still he clung to the twisted sword, as though clutching a last anchor in a storm. The goblins took no notice of it. And the one that held him by his shirt roared to the others, "We must take this morsel to our king. Vahe will know just what to do with a little manling such as he!"

The others burst into terrible laughter, and the sight of their faces was enough to make a man ill. Lionheart caught one last glimpse of Rose Red before he was gagged and flung over the shoulder of the largest goblin in the party to be borne like a sack of flour over the bleak landscape of Arpiar.

At least he was in, he thought. And he'd found Rose Red.

Then he stopped trying to think.

PART FIVE

THE SACRIFICE

1

Oᴇʀɪᴄ ᴘᴏᴜɴᴅᴇᴅ ᴛʜʀᴏᴜɢʜ the forest, careful to keep to the Prince's Path. Never in all the generations of his search had he walked pathless in the Wood, and he would not begin now. Especially not with the unicorn somewhere on the hill.

But the Path did not lead him back to the bridge. Instead, it wound first down the hill, then up again, and he could not see where it would take him for the thickness of the trees. When at last he came to clear ground, he found himself at the crest of Goldstone Hill, facing the ruins of Carrun Corgar.

The once high tower had been built in the early days of Vahe's power, and therefore it had been strong, solid, not spun from enchantments. By building it, Vahe had grafted this whole part of the Wood onto Arpiar, making it a part of his demesne. Then he had linked Arpiar to that small portion of the Near World, an invisible parasite clutching that hill.

The destruction of Carrun Corgar had shaken the hillside and the Wood Between, wrenching the Near World free once more. And now its wreck lay here at the top of the hill, where Oeric shuddered at the sight.

Memories of long captivity, his and others', flooded his mind, and he turned away. Yet the Prince's Path clearly indicated that he should walk among those crumbled stones. "Please," he growled, squeezing the hilt of his knife so hard that it almost broke. "Please, don't make me walk that way again. I've left the past behind. I am ready to face my future, Prince, even if it means my death. Show me the way into Arpiar and let me confront Vahe one last time!"

But the Path did not waver.

Slowly, Oeric followed it. The sun vanished from the sky, and the shadows of the ruins spread like night across the hilltop. Oeric walked trembling into that darkness. He closed his eyes as he went, and in his mind the walls of Carrun Corgar rose up about him: the long, windowless stair, the cells empty but waiting for prisoners. Though he stood with his feet firmly upon the Path, in his memory he climbed that stair.

"Please," Oeric whispered again as his memory self at last neared the top and stood once more at the final door. "Please, don't make me walk that way."

Still, the Path remained true.

In his mind, Oeric put out a hand and pushed open the door. On hesitant feet he stepped out onto the parapet from which one could gaze into the Near World or the Far without crossing into either.

The night was cold. He remembered that. Cold and moonless. No light illuminated that dark place save that which shone from Life-in-Death's white eyes.

He saw her again, standing before his beloved, who was crumpled at her feet. His memory self cried out, and Life-in-Death turned to him and laughed.

"You are no better than your brother. Goblin. Outcast. You are Vahe."

"I am Vahe," Oeric whispered.

"Take what you want. I will give it all to you," said the Lady of Dreams.

Oeric's eyes flew open. The memory vanished, and he stood amid the cold ruins. But Life-in-Death remained before him, and she was as real as the trees and stones.

"You always were mine."

He shook his head.

"I'll show you the way in. Follow me, as you should have long ages ago. Do you think I would make you wait five hundred years before seeing your beloved's face again? Do you think I would leave you wandering forever, without rest?"

Oeric raised the knife in his hand.

"Nameless one, you were always mine. Come back to me and see how I will realize your dreams."

"I have a name," the knight said.

He slashed at her heart.

She screamed and vanished in a vapor, and with her went the darkness, dropping like torn rags. In the glare of sudden sunlight, Oeric stood face-to-face with the Prince.

He dropped to his knees. "My Prince!" he cried. "Forgive me. Her temptations are so strong. I . . ."

The Prince placed a hand on his head. "Oeric," he said, "I know your heart. Your faith does me honor."

Then he raised up the knight, and though Oeric towered over the Prince by a good head, he trembled as the Prince's eyes searched his face. "Follow me now, my brother. The time is very near."

The next moment, Oeric stood alone upon the hill, blinking as one waking from a dream. Then he turned and strode back down, making for the Old Bridge with all speed.

All was gray around him: the faces, the land, the voices, the very ringing in his ears was the gray of loathing and distress. Each step the goblin took jolted a rock-hard shoulder into Lionheart's stomach so that he thought he must be sick, and the other goblins swarmed around, leering and awful and gray.

Then the colors changed.

At first he thought he must be passing out, so explosive were the hues that rushed in as he was carried deeper into Arpiar. Vivid green swirled beneath the goblins' feet; turquoise blue shot across the sky. And his nose was overwhelmed with the scent of roses, an unfamiliar scent that went right to his head with potent sweetness.

The faces changed next. The leering and jeering did not stop but became all the more horrible as the hideous features melted away behind fine bones, smooth complexions, dark-lashed eyes. Male and female, they grabbed at his face, snatched at his clothes, poked and prodded him with their elegant, tapering fingers, every malicious laugh flashing perfect white teeth. They were the most beautiful people he had ever seen, more beautiful even than he had imaged Faerie beings could be. He closed his eyes, unable to bear the sight, and so Lionheart passed into Palace Var without seeing its graceful proportions rising up against the dreamlike landscape.

King Vahe waited in his assembly hall with the one-horned beast at his side. It had flown to him with word of his returning daughter and the Boy, and also warning of the captured intruder.

Vahe had paled. "Gargron?" he demanded, his voice catching in fear.

But no, it was just a mortal creature. Once or twice over the last five hundred years, unwary mortals had stumbled too near the boundaries of Arpiar, and the goblins near the edges would call them in to be toyed with and discarded like so many new baubles. This one could be no more impressive than they.

Varvare and the Boy were prodded before the others. The Boy had recovered his natural color as he neared his enslaver, the fire in his veins and the pain in his injured hand dulling into nothing. The goblins were gentler with him, unwilling to damage Vahe's prized host body, and he smiled inanely at them and at Vahe. His gaze caught with fear as it passed over the unicorn, then faded into passive forgetfulness as the unicorn slid behind invisible veils. By the time he reached the king, the Boy was as cheerful as a kitten.

But Varvare refused to wear the veils.

"Your face shames me," Vahe snarled as the princess's captors dragged her before him. "Why do you insist on this ugly mask?"

She fixed him with her moon-like gaze. When she spoke, her fangs flashed. "I'll choose an ugly truth over your pretty lies any day."

Vahe stepped forward and grabbed her face in one large hand. His fingers were white and delicately veined, the nails polished like mirrors. They squeezed against her forehead and temples, the thumb pressing into her chin. She cried out at the pressure, wrenching against his hold but unable to free herself.

"Leave her alone!"

The voice was feeble, yet Vahe turned. He did not release his hold on Varvare's face, but he felt her body stiffen at the sound of the weak voice. "What have you got there, Kud?" he demanded of the goblin carrying the mortal slung over his shoulder.

The goblin, whose features were as finely chiseled as those of a demi-god, tossed Lionheart in a heap at Vahe's feet before all the assembled courtiers of Var. "A manling, my king. He crossed the bridge."

"Did you call him in?"

"By the cat's eyes, my king, I swear we did not. He wandered in all on his own as far as we can guess."

"I think not," Vahe said. "No one breaches my borders." He gave Varvare's face a last cruel twist, and she screamed. Then he let her fall, and when she raised her head again, she was beautiful and despairing. "No one breaches my borders," Vahe repeated, "unless called."

He approached the manling, who still lay in a heap, and prodded him with a foot, grimacing as he did so as though he'd stepped in something disgusting. "Is it dead?"

"Not so much," Lionheart gasped, opening one eye. "If you please, Your Majesty."

"Not yet, at least," Vahe said, drawing back quickly. "Who are you, and what brings you to my realm? Especially just now, when my hour is come so near."

Lionheart pushed himself upright. He still clung to the twisted sword, surprised that no one had taken it from him. Either they did not see it, or they simply thought it too poor and ridiculous an item to be worth confiscating. But he tightened his grip upon the hilt and felt some extra strength as he gazed up into the unbearably beautiful face of the goblin king.

He turned to find Rose Red. She must be near, he knew, for he'd heard her cry of pain. But where, among all these beautiful faces, was his ugly friend?

Then he saw her.

His eyes widened as their gazes met. She knelt on the marble floor where Vahe had dropped her, her arms wrapped around her body, and he knew beyond doubt that it was she, except that he had seen this face of hers before only in a dream. Her skin was golden and smooth, her eyes large and silver with delicate black brows, and her hair was as long and thick as a river of midnight. But it was Rose Red, he knew as surely as he knew his own name. Rose Red, who had befriended a snobby little boy in the mountains. Rose Red, who had rescued him when he got lost in the Wood Between on a moonless night, who had served him when others fled, who had trusted him to care for her as she had always cared for him.

Rose Red, whom he had promised to protect and then betrayed.

She stared without expression, showing neither surprise nor fear, nor hope, nor anger. Then her mouth opened, and she whispered his name.

He glimpsed her for no more than a moment, but in Faerie a moment can be forever, and it seemed an eternity before Lionheart dragged his gaze back to Vahe's scowl looming over him.

"My . . . my name," he stammered, attempting a winning smile, "is Leonard the Lightning Tongue. I am a humble jester."

Someone snorted. Someone else laughed. "A jester indeed," the goblins muttered and mocked. This little beast wearing only his nightshirt—they'd taken the fine green jacket—and a grubby pair of trousers? This somber-eyed mortal who looked as though he hadn't smiled in a century or more? "Sing us a funny song, then!" someone shouted from the crowd, and the heckling boiled up until it filled the assembly room and even the marble statues writhed in mockery on their pedestals.

Vahe did not laugh. As he gazed down on the self-proclaimed clown, he kept trying to see something just beyond the edge of his vision—a danger that he could not quite identify. He wanted, very badly in fact, to cut the mortal's head off then and there and send it rolling down the aisle for his goblins to chase like so many dogs after a ball. But somehow he dared not.

"Well," he said, and when he spoke the crowds immediately hushed. "You hear your audience's request. Will you entertain us, jester?"

Lionheart got to his feet, shaking so hard that he was uncertain he'd be able to stand upright. He knew that behind the lovely faces surrounding him were monsters, and the knowledge that they were there but he was unable to see them made them all the more terrifying. They were laughing at him already, every last one of them. Laughing because he was so pathetic standing there among them with all his flimsy mortality on display.

He looked down at the twisted sword in his hand and almost felt like laughing himself. What did he think he was doing, barging into this goblin kingdom, the land that wasn't supposed to exist beyond his nursemaid's stories, with nothing but a bit of warped steel and a hatful of arrogance? Did he expect to storm the ramparts alone, burst through Vahe's defenses, carry off the princess, and be home in time for tea?

No, that wasn't it at all. He expected to die.

Lionheart raised his gaze and met Rose Red's, and her face was unnaturally still, more still and unreadable than the faces of the marble statues above him.

This must be it, then, he thought. *This must be the moment when I die. When I open my mouth and say something stupid, and the king cuts me open like a holiday pudding. But my death will spare her somehow. Bebo promised.*

So he opened his mouth and said something stupid:

> *"I blessed your name, O you who sit*
> *Enthroned beyond the Highlands.*
> *I blessed your name and sang in answer*
> *To the song you gave.*
>
> *"Beside the Final Water flowing,*
> *My brow in silver bound,*
> *I raised my arms, I raised my voice*
> *In answer to your gift."*

The hall went silent save for his voice rising clear and clean up to the highest domes above. And how strange he looked, that ragged mortal, standing in the center of all unnatural beauty, singing that tremulous melody! The song of Hymlumé washed over the goblins, and Vahe's veils shuddered.

> *"Now I cry to you again,*
> *My arms raised once more,*
> *My hands outspread to shield my face*
> *From that which lies before.*
>
> *"Only spare my children."*

The unicorn, invisible, trembled. And though only Vahe could see it, suddenly the fire that covered it from horn to hoof extinguished, and it stood black as a cold lump of coal, its eyes fixed on the singing mortal.

> *"I see them running, running, stumbling.*
> *Running, as the heavens*
> *Break and yawn, tear beneath their feet,*
> *Devouring, hungry Death!*
>
> *"Where is my fault?"*

Queen Anahid, hidden in shadows, heard the song as one who hears her death pronounced. She gazed at her daughter, whom she had been unable to save, and resolve cemented in her heart as Hymlumé's sorrow washed over her.

> *"Did I misunderstand the song, the gift*
> *You gave? Was I wrong?*
> *I thought you spoke across the boundless.*
> *You sang, and I replied."*

Vahe stood as one transfixed, his mouth agape. The veil over his face slipped, revealing the monster underneath. He snarled and struggled to replace it, all the while not removing his gaze from Lionheart. The jester's song worked like a spell upon him. His feet were rooted to the floor, and no one in that room could see the battle he waged to free them.

Still Lionheart sang:

"Can you hear me?"

Suddenly, Vahe wrenched himself forward. Lionheart turned from Rose Red and gazed into the monster's beautiful eyes, watched as death descended, a knife in the king's right hand. He recoiled, knowing this was the moment.

But the blow did not fall.

Vahe stood with his knife just above Lionheart's temple, frozen in place, his eyes huge with fury.

What Lionheart could not see was the unicorn, which stood with its horn blocking the king's blow. It spoke not a word, but its face was too terrible for Vahe to bear.

With a roar, the king turned away. Lionheart collapsed once more, still clutching the twisted sword, uncertain what had just happened. Had he died without realizing it?

Perfect silence held the assembly hall in its grip.

Then, from deep in the darkness of Palace Var's underbelly, a voice came, so small that it would have been missed had a single person in that room dared to breathe. But all heard, if only as a faint impression on the edge of their minds, the voice of a chained knight singing:

"I blessed your name in beauty.
In fear I still must sing."

Vahe roared, the sound made the more terrible as it burst from his handsome face. He whirled on Lionheart, frothing at the mouth, and bellowed, "I know what you are! But don't think you can stop me now! I've been promised, and I will have my due! These protections on you now will crumble to ash before the fire I shall wield. This is what I was born to, and you and your fellows will kneel before me and die!"

He barked a command, and strong hands grabbed Lionheart by the arms and dragged him from the assembly, his bent sword bouncing and clattering along behind him.

"Bind him! Clap him in irons!" Vahe cried. "See to it that he can call none of his brethren in behind him!"

Then he whirled upon the princess, who crouched in the shadows behind him. He grabbed her by the chin, forcing her to look at him. "I see it in your eyes," he snarled. "I see what you're trying to hide. You called him here, this mortal creature. Is he your true love, then? Have you given your heart to a dust-bound man? But it's no good, my pretty Rose. A beast like that cannot help you now."

Vahe flung her away from him and motioned to his slaves. "Take her away and prepare her for Moonblood. Make certain she eclipses the fairest rose with her beauty, for nothing less will satisfy. We leave at dawn!"

2

THE VILLAGE OF DRAGONS is neither within nor without the boundaries of Faerie. It lies in the Netherworld, on the pathway to Death's kingdom. Nothing grows in the Village. Things die there instead, even those who make their home in its cavernous darkness. Though the dragons' lives stretch on generation after generation, they are forever dying. Theirs is an existence in which all dreams have perished.

Eanrin, Imraldera, and the people of Rudiobus did not walk Death's Path to reach that dark place, however. They crossed into the Near World and the expanse of the Red Desert, where the Netherworld and the world of mortals overlap. Great stones beaten down by time and disaster jut from the Red Desert like ragged teeth, and all traces of carving are blasted away so that they seem no more than strange rock formations and canyons. A twisting trail leads through these and down into darker passages below, where sunlight can rarely find a crack.

This was the Path taken by the knights and Iubdan. Though dark and dreary, it was less terrible than all other Paths to the Village. The blind poet led them, walking confidently though the others followed with more hesitant steps. Iubdan Tynan led a great host, including Glomar, the captain of his personal guard, who had taken the form of a badger. All marched with their weapons at the ready. The knowledge that they walked behind her and that Eanrin strode on before comforted Dame Imraldera as they descended into the darkness.

But when she saw for the first time the cave of the Village, her heart stopped beating for a moment, and she put out a hand to the wall to steady herself.

For though all the dragons lay sleeping, the air they exhaled was filled with the poison of their evil dreams.

"It's all right, old girl," Eanrin said, and she felt him take her hand. It was difficult to see anything but the dragons in that cavern. They shone dully with their inner fires, though those flames were mostly banked at present. Their hundreds upon hundreds of bodies, contoured in red, filled the cavern with an evil light and cast shadows over all else. Imraldera was grateful for Eanrin's hand. "It's all right," he repeated. "As long as we follow our Prince's way, we're safe."

"I know," she said. "It's just . . . there are more of them than I thought."

An image flashed unbidden across her mind—an image of the world Vahe sought to create. A world of dragons and fire and destruction. Imraldera had seen, centuries ago, the destruction worked upon the Near World when the mortal woman known as Tavé had taken dragons as slaves. Should the King of Arpiar follow in her footsteps, decimating with fire and covering the wounds with flimsy veils of beauty, how could they hope to set things right again?

Eanrin gave her fingers a last squeeze before letting go. "We'll stop him, my girl. You'll see."

He started across the cavern, and Imraldera followed, and after her marched Iubdan and his host. They had to split up as they went to avoid treading on the sleeping dragons, some in withered human forms, others enormous but no less withered monsters. The dragons breathed in quick puffs, and their sides heaved as though they were under heavy exertion. Their sleep could not be restful as they watched their dreams blaze and die.

In the center of that cavern stood the Throne of Death. Imraldera wanted to retch at the sight of its bloodstained lines. Even King Iubdan swore, "Lumé's crown!" Then he barked orders to his soldiers, and the fighters of Rudiobus scattered about the cavern, taking cover behind rocks and walls, the half-ruined huts, and even sleeping dragons.

"Vahe will be here soon."

Imraldera looked down at the orange tomcat sitting at her feet. He smiled up at her. "Come. We'd best prepare our ambush."

He led her to the largest of the dragons, the terrible Bane of Corrilond, who of all the sleepers glowed the brightest. "Her dreams are the most vivid," the poet-cat said as he put out a whiskery nose to sniff one of her cruelly curved claws. "She smells ready to explode! She'll eat half these dragons alive if she wakes, and Vahe wouldn't be much more than a mouthful should she feel the urge."

"She'll have to obey him," Imraldera said. "Life-in-Death will compel her to."

The cat shrugged. "It won't come to that."

He sprang up onto the Bane of Corrilond's great hand, then quickly hopped down, for her scales burned. He gave his paws a quick grooming before sliding into the space between the dragon and the wall, bidding Imraldera to join him. She did, hating her proximity to the red monster. All the folk of Rudiobus were similarly hidden, and when she gazed out across the Village, Imraldera could easily have imagined that she and the poet were the only two creatures left awake in that place.

She crouched down, shivering despite the awful heat of the dragon's body. "In fear I still must sing," she whispered, drawing the knife from her belt.

Blind. The darkness of the dungeons was so absolute that Lionheart felt as though he'd been blinded. Somehow it was a relief after all the careful beauty of Arpiar, beauty that he knew must be false. Except . . .

"Rose Red!" he snarled and struggled fruitlessly against the goblins holding his arms. They laughed at his weak flailing and tightened their grips until he thought his arms must break. At least, as they descended deeper, the sweet perfume of roses cleared from Lionheart's head and he could make his thoughts take shape. But no images would come to his mind in those black depths, as though along with his sight the dungeons also took away all memory of sight.

Except for her face.

"Here we are, little mortal," a goblin said in a honeyed voice. Lionheart heard the grating of a cell door opening, protesting as though it had not been budged in centuries. Then he was thrown forward, and he had the horrible sensation of falling in darkness, unable to judge how far the drop would be. It was only a step or two down, but he might as well have been flung from the Gardens of Hymlumé for all his body jerked and tensed, then convulsed on the floor after landing. Someone was screaming. He realized that it was he and forced himself to stop. The goblins stumped down a narrow stairway, still laughing as they bound his wrists and ankles with shackles so heavy he could scarcely lift them. He felt other bindings slip into place along with the clank of iron: bindings on his spirit, as real as any physical chains.

"No worries, manling," a goblin spoke from the emptiness above him. "You'll not die in here. You'll never again set eyes on a living soul, nevermore taste the sweetness of bread or water. But you'll not die so long as Vahe holds you in those manacles. You'll be immortal. Is that not what your kind longs for most?"

The goblins' laughter echoed through the dark, empty cells long after the clang of the cell door closing had ceased. Lionheart shivered where he lay, his ears ringing, squeezing his eyes shut as though he might squeeze the blindness right out of them.

"Rose Red," he whispered.

What of the choice? What of Bebo's promise? Lionheart struggled to pull himself upright, dragging the chains in terrible cacophony across the stones. Immortality faced him. But what about his chance to choose death, to give his life in place of hers?

"Dragon's teeth!" he snarled, struggling against the shackles, tearing at them with his fingers. It was useless, he knew, but what else could he do? "Dragon's teeth and eyes and tail!" He moaned and sank his head into his hands.

Suddenly he realized.

He had only to call. What a thrice-cursed fool he was for not thinking of it before! The sweet-smelling enchantments must have addled his wits. Oeric said that no one could enter Arpiar unless called from within. Well, Lionheart was within Vahe's dungeons, and that certainly had to count. So he raised his head and shouted: "Oeric! Sir Oeric, come to me!"

His voice echoed back to him a hundred times.

Then silence.

He knew he had not been heard. As surely as he would never see the sun again, he knew his voice had not carried beyond the dungeons. He bowed his head, and if Lionheart wept, there was no one to see.

Somewhere in that cavernous blindness, someone spoke. "It's no use while you're chained."

Lionheart sat upright. He was alone in his cell, he was certain. But this voice was near, perhaps only one cell over. He placed his ear to the stone wall. "Who's there?"

A snort, then: "I'm Beana . . . Rose Red's goat."

He could see nothing, not even in his memory, so he could not recall the face of the woman who had stood on the edge of the cliff above the Wilderlands. But he could recall the feel of her fingers about his throat, and he could hear her voice again, speaking low and piercing as a knife. *"Coward!"*

He pulled back from the wall as though stung.

A silence followed. At length the woman who was a goat said, "You came to find her, then. Good lad."

He trembled at her words but was foolishly grateful at the same time. "I couldn't save her," he whispered, not expecting to be heard. Perhaps he wasn't, but the goat-woman answered anyway.

"Don't give up hope, Leo."

"Are you . . . are you Sir Oeric's lady?" Lionheart asked.

She did not answer for a long time. As he waited he heard noises overhead: the sound of trumpets, triumphant and terrible; the shout of many voices, a roar of excitement like crowds gathering for a tournament.

"I knew Oeric," the goat-woman said softly. "Long ago. Before he was named."

The roar continued, then faded away. *They are leaving Var,* Lionheart thought. *They are taking Rose Red to Death's throne, and they'll spill her blood there.*

The horrible thought came and, though he tried to force it back, continued to intrude. Perhaps this was what he wanted. Perhaps this was what he had hoped for all along, to have the choice taken from him. Was it his fault he was clapped in irons, after all? Could he help it if his song provoked Vahe to this end? Of course not. He had his excuses, his noble intentions interrupted by unforeseen circumstances.

Lionheart grimaced and struggled against his chains. No! That wouldn't be the story of his life! He would succeed; he would die; he would gain back his honor and earn atonement! He must!

The chains were unrelenting.

"All is not lost," the goat-woman whispered through the wall. "Wait a little."

In that darkness where time did not pass, waiting was torture. The sounds above were long since gone. Rose Red was far from him. To have come this close only to lose her now!

He felt something beside him suddenly, something he had not realized was there but which must have been there the whole time. Putting out a hand, he touched the twisted blade of a melted sword. Strange the goblins had not taken it from him.

Somewhere beyond that world, a bird sang.

Won't you follow me?

A cold shriek of protesting iron hinges, and the door to Lionheart's cell swung open. He tried to get to his feet, but the shackles restrained him, so he pressed against the wall as he felt rather than heard someone approaching him through the blind dark. A hand touched his face, a hard, rocklike hand tipped with claws.

A voice like winter spoke. "You are the mortal my daughter loves."

Lionheart did not answer. He shivered under that touch.

"I saw it in her eyes when she watched you sing before my husband. She loves you, though she believes now that it is hate she feels."

The hand left his face. Whoever stood before him was so silent that he heard not even a breath. "Who are you?" he whispered.

"Anahid, Queen of Arpiar."

He gulped. "Do you . . . do you wish to see your daughter die?"

"I will die myself first." The voice spoke as though making a vow.

"Then will you set me free? I can save her, good queen! I've been promised as much. I can give my life for hers. I owe her that, for she served me faithfully and I betrayed her. I owe her my life in retribution, and I swear upon this sword that I will pay the price!"

No answer came, not a sound. Then suddenly, Lionheart felt a kiss planted on his cheek, gentle and sweet, though the lips were like stone.

"Give her that for me, little mortal," Anahid said. "Give her that, and tell her how I loved her."

With those words, Lionheart felt his chains drop away.

There was a cry, like the wind howling on an evil night, and a sudden burst of light. Lionheart yelled and covered his face with his arms, pressing against the wall. But it was over in a moment, and he stood free and unchained in the dungeons of Var. Swiftly he knelt and grabbed the twisted sword, clutching it like a lifeline. But while he felt for it in the dark, his hand brushed the face of the queen lying at his feet.

She was dead.

"Hurry!" said Beana in the cell next door. "Hurry, call for Oeric!"

Lionheart swallowed and felt his way to the cell door. "I'll free you first, my lady."

"NO!" his fellow prisoner shouted. "No, don't you understand? Anahid died breaking your chains. You'll die if you attempt to release me, and you won't succeed as she did. No, you must call for Oeric, and you must hurry to Rose Red. Hurry while you still can!"

As fast as he could in the dark, Lionheart groped his way from the cell and along the wall to the dark stairway, calling Oeric's name as he went.

3

THEY CLOTHED HER IN BLACK, the color of death, and in red, the color of blood, and crowned her in bloodred roses. Varvare, however, staring into her mirror, saw none of these things. Instead she saw rags being draped tenderly across her hunched frame, and a crown of thistles and thorns set onto the bald dome of her head. The veils of her father could not work on her eyes. They could not cover the ugly features of her attendants, some of whom laughed as they prepared her, and some of whom gazed at her sorrowfully.

She knew from their faces, their voices, even their laughter, that Vahe intended to kill her. She simply couldn't guess why.

When they had finished with her, the senior attendant took her by the hand and led her from her chambers and down what most perceived as a glowing marble stairway softly carpeted in rose petals, but which Varvare saw as poorly carved stone, sharp and ragged underfoot.

Vahe waited for her in the Boy's body. Though to the rest of Arpiar he covered the Boy's face with his own, Varvare still saw the soft, boyish features as yet unhardened into a man's, the hazel eyes, the messy shock of honey-colored hair. But the expression was all Vahe's. His real body must be hidden deep within the ever-shifting labyrinth of Palace Var's corridors.

He licked his lips at the sight of her. "You are indeed most fair, my daughter. Hymlumé herself was never so radiant."

But it's all a lie, Varvare thought, bowing her head. *Secretly, I'm as foul as you.*

And she wondered how Lionheart had seen her in the assembly hall. Had he seen the illusion? Or as the horror on his face suggested, had he seen her for what she truly was?

Those thoughts were too painful, so she shook them away as her father escorted her to a curtained litter on the shoulders of two powerful goblins. To her eyes, even the curtains were gray rags. The goblins knelt, and she climbed inside. When they stood, it rocked, and she clutched at the curtain poles to steady herself. She felt like one in a poisoned sleep, carried through a nightmare against her will, unable to wake.

The unicorn stood just beyond the doors of Palace Var. It looked at her as the goblin slaves carried her litter out behind Vahe. It alone of everything around her was beautiful, white and delicate. She allowed her eyes to linger on its face, pure as a star, its long horn gleaming with its own light. It was so beautiful that it could not be anything but good, she thought. Yet it was King Vahe's slave.

It spoke to her again in that voice no one but the person to whom it spoke could hear. **Will you kill me, maiden?**

The princess shook her head and broke its gaze, staring down at her hands instead.

"Lead us onward, beast!" Vahe cried from the Boy's mouth. "To the Dragon Village, and quickly. We have only until moonrise."

The unicorn bowed and turned to take the head of the procession. A roar rose up all around, and Varvare, peering out between the wafting rags, saw that all the courtiers of Var were gathered to follow, leering, monstrous creatures, as monstrous as she. She did not see the queen, her mother. But she assumed she stood among the throng somewhere, lost amid all those awful faces. The goblins sang as they went, a terrible sound to which they marched, and they waved sparse twigs and thistles and more moth-eaten rags with all the enthusiasm of people bearing silken banners.

Varvare could not watch them but buried her face in her hands as the goblin slaves lurched forward behind Vahe and the unicorn. The bindings the king had placed upon her were so heavy, she thought she would break.

The wood thrush sang:

Trust me, child.

But she stopped up her ears against him. She'd obeyed, hadn't she? She'd called Lionheart into Arpiar, and lo and behold, he'd come! He'd come and been locked away, useless and pathetic, waving that twisted sword of his. Just the sort of heroics she could expect, especially from him. Dragons eat him! Dragons eat him and choke on his bones!

A tear slid down her craggy cheek, and Varvare hardly cared in that moment that she journeyed across the bleak lands of Arpiar to her death.

Oeric watched them pass over the Old Bridge.

First came the unicorn, terrible to see, all over fire and destruction.

After it came Vahe, but wearing the body of a boy whose face Oeric recognized. He'd seen this boy at Oriana Palace when he traveled there with his Prince a year ago. What a sad end for the lad to meet, his body taken from him and worn like a set of clothes by the King of Arpiar. Oeric shuddered at the sight.

Following the king came a litter carried by two goblin men, and Oeric saw the Princess Varvare for the first time. Ugly and huddled into herself, she did not raise her gaze from her lap as she was carried into the Wood Between. His heart went out to her, but he dared not move from where he hid.

For behind the litter came all the vast host of Arpiar, tramping single file over the plank bridge. Some he recognized from long ago; most he did not. But they were his people, hideous in aspect, pitiable in spirit.

He shared their faces, he shared their sorrows. And he would deliver them from their slavery.

So when at last they had passed over the bridge and on up the hill, on to the ruins of Carrun Corgar, Oeric remained where he lay. He trembled a little, for fear of the unicorn was still upon him. Then he got up and approached the Old Bridge, clutching his long knife in his hand.

There was still no Crossing.

But there would be. The Prince had promised, and today was the day of fulfillment. He knew it despite all the tired longing of his soul. After five hundred years, today he would see the end.

He stood before the bridge and remembered the centuries of his search, from the first night when he bade farewell to his love and turned away from her, on through those interminable moments stretching one after the other. Many had laughed and called him irrational. They had warned him that his errand was a fool's. But the Prince had promised, and here Oeric stood, weapon in hand.

And suddenly he saw, across the bridge, standing in a place outside of worlds, the face of his Master.

"Come now, my brother," the Prince said.

In the same moment, Oeric heard young Lionheart's voice calling across time and space:

"Oeric! Oeric, come quick! Dragon's teeth, I need you *now!*"

The ugly knight crossed the bridge and returned at last to the land of his birth.

No one walks safely in Goldstone Wood without a Path, so Vahe led his folk in the wake of the unicorn, out of Arpiar, through the Between, and on to the ruined tower. There they passed, one by one, through the gateway and onto Death's Path. Many trembled and would have turned back, but they dared not disobey their lord. So they marched through the darkness, and if some glimpsed a silver lantern gleaming on a lone grave, they turned their faces away from it.

As if with one voice, they sang their awful marching song.

"*The king says he,*
'I'll catch the Fool
And wear his teeth like gleaming jewels.'
O jolly way have we!

"*The king says he,*
'When falls the night
I'll claim the fire as my right.'
O jolly way have we!"

Death's Path wears different aspects for those who walk it. But no matter what they saw around them, all kept time and followed in the unicorn's footsteps.

Princess Varvare sat with her eyes squeezed shut, desperately wishing she could stop her ears. She had walked this Path once before, when she'd ventured this way in search of Lady Daylily, but to follow it again in this company was altogether unbearable. She heard the Dark Water lapping somewhere in the blackness, but the way the unicorn led did not draw near it.

And suddenly, she smelled the dragon poison. Only then did Varvare open her eyes and gaze in horror at what she knew she would see: the Village of Dragons.

There lay the Dragon's children. When last she'd seen them, they had been gorgeous in brilliant clothes and jewels, dancing beneath chandeliers set with black candles. Now they lay in heaps on the cavern floor, fast asleep, their faces filled with pain.

"Beautiful, aren't they?" said Vahe, and she looked to find him standing beside her, marveling through the Boy's hazel eyes. "Have you ever seen such an awesome sight?"

She did not answer.

Vahe spoke to the unicorn next. "Onward, slave. You know the way."

The one-horned beast trotted down the steep way that led to the cavern floor, and Vahe and his host followed. They threaded through the sleepers, and down among them the stench was greater. The people of Arpiar had stopped singing, and Varvare could feel their fear. They were,

Varvare thought, even more frightened than she was. After all, they had never before experienced the darkness of the Village.

Then she saw the throne and forgot everything else as panic swept over her.

It was a thing of ultimate evil and ugliness, and she had loathed the sight of it when she had seen it before. But this time, when her gaze fell upon its bloodstained proportions, she knew she looked upon her own death.

She screamed and leapt from the litter, landing sprawling on the dirt. She was up in a flash and running before any of the litter bearers could catch her. But there was nowhere to run. Everywhere her father's people surrounded her, reaching out with their awful hands to bar her way. She whirled about and darted in fear, only to find herself at last falling on her knees before Vahe, who smiled grimly down at her.

"It's too late for that, sweet child," he said. "Hymlumé will rise soon."

Goblins grabbed her arms and dragged her toward the throne. She could feel in their hands that they wanted to go no nearer to it than they must. But their fear of Vahe was great, and their fear of the unicorn greater still. They approached the dais steps, and Varvare's heart pounded in her throat.

A huge bellow filled the room.

It was wordless as far as she could understand, but it bounced and echoed and enlarged as it went, filling the cavern, deafening her ears. The next instant, from every possible crevice, and even from beneath the sleeping dragons themselves, warriors leapt forth. Her mind was hazy, but she saw the flash of golden hair, the gleam of fierce eyes, and heard the ring of several hundred swords in the air.

From behind the dais a black-bearded king emerged, and his sword pierced the rock hide of the goblin that held her right arm. That goblin fell with a crash, but the other dragged her back. The king gave a shout and sprang forward, flanked by a golden-haired warrior on one side, an enormous badger on the other. The second goblin fell, and for a moment Varvare lay free.

But Vahe stood over her. He spoke a harsh command in a language she did not know, and the next instant the unicorn sprang between them and the black-bearded king. She heard horrified shouts, and when she dared look over her shoulder, she saw that the king and his companions fled the unicorn's pursuit.

Battle raged all around her. Yellow-haired soldiers, all in green and red, locked weapons with the goblins of Arpiar. The goblins towered over the golden ones, but that did not seem to bother Iubdan's host. They shouted and raged and refused to back down even when their weapons bounced dented off the rock skins of their enemies.

But when the unicorn turned its eyes upon them, they fled.

Vahe swore and grabbed Varvare, dragging her to her feet. "I should have known," he snarled. "My dear-hearted brother will be behind this, I have no doubt. Come! I have a promise to claim."

He hauled her across the floor and up the dais steps to the seat of the throne itself. There he paused and gazed up to the cavern ceiling, spitting the most vile curses. "Where is she? Shine, dragons devour you!"

Varvare struggled against his hold, but his fingers dug into her head with unnatural strength.

Suddenly, a cat sprang onto the dais. Every hair of his body bristled, and his teeth showed in a snarl. He had no eyes.

"Vahe!" the cat cried. "Let her go!"

The King of Arpiar turned to the cat and laughed out loud. It was a terrible sound. "Well met, Chief Poet." His voice was smooth as velvet. He released Varvare, and she fell back against the throne. It burned her, and she screamed, pulling away. Vahe strode toward the cat, taking two daggers from his belt as he did so. "Have you come to claim these? I've kept them for you so long now. Do you smell the blood on their blades? I've never washed them clean, not when they served me so well all those years ago!"

The cat arched his back and spat. The creature seemed bigger than a house cat, something more ferocious and terrible. Vahe threw a dagger, and the cat leapt aside. The second dagger flew, and it took a tuft of hair, but the cat remained unhurt. Vahe bared his teeth.

"Come on, then!" he cried, opening his arms wide. "Attack me! Shred to pieces this face of mine! Or wait. Is it my face after all?"

A flicker of light passed over him, and Vahe dropped the veils that covered him.

The blind cat froze. His nose twitched, and his ears pricked forward. "Felix?" he said quietly. "Felix, are you here?"

Vahe laughed. "He's here, little beast. Or at least his body is. A convenient husk for me to wear since his mind broke."

The cat backed away, still uncertain about what he could not see. His nose was overwhelmed by two scents coming at once from the same person. He made a pitiable mewling in his throat. "What have you done to the lad?"

"Made use of what was left of him," the King of Arpiar said. "Since you and your fellow knights did not see fit to give him a complete healing, he was as good as dead. Might as well salvage the remains."

"No!" The cat hissed and jumped forward, and for a moment Varvare thought he would send his claws straight into the Boy's wide eyes. But he changed direction at the last instant and landed instead at Vahe's feet, still growling.

The unicorn sprang onto the dais. Its horn was like white fire in Varvare's eyes, and it trained its gaze on the cat. The cat howled, a human sound in his throat, and fled into the fray below, and the unicorn gathered itself in preparation to leap after in pursuit.

"Wait!" Vahe barked. He hauled Varvare up and forced her into the throne. Her hands gripped the arms, which were carved into the likeness of skeletal dragons' heads. Those carved heads turned suddenly and looked at her with empty eye sockets. She screamed as they writhed and twisted around her wrists, securing her in place. They burned right through her rocky hide.

Vahe stood before her, gazing upward. The battle waged on around him, but the unicorn paced back and forth along the dais, and no one dared approach. Screams and death filled the cavern, and still the King of Arpiar stood gazing up at the black ceiling.

A light gleamed. Panting in terror, Varvare looked up as well and saw a break in the cavern above, a round skylight open to the night. It had been impossible to see before, but now the silver glow of moonlight touched its edge. "She rises," Vahe breathed. Then he raised his arms and shouted above the din of battle. "Look, Hymlumé! You are my witness!"

The unicorn approached Varvare then. The moon shone through

the skylight and lit upon its white body, blinding the princess with the beauty of the creature before her. It bowed its horn and gazed at her with its deep black eyes.

Forgive me, maiden.

Somewhere in the depths of the cavern, the Bane of Corrilond stirred.

4

LIONHEART WAS BLIND all the way up the dark dungeon stairs, and when he at last gained the top, he was blinded all over again by the light shining through the bars of the dungeon door. It took some moments for his eyes to recover, and only then did he dare step into the passage beyond.

The smell of roses threatened to overpower him.

They were dreamy sweet, a sweetness that calms and soothes. Lionheart found himself wanting to sit with his back against the wall and doze off right there. Let the world go on around him; let it crash and burn even! Who cared while the roses were in bloom? Nothing could really be wrong.

He ground his teeth and pinched his nose to keep from breathing the smell. "Oeric," he muttered, "dragons eat you, get in here!" On impulse, he stooped, pulled off his boot, removed one of his dirty stockings and, grimacing, held it to his nose.

The scent of roses vanished, and Lionheart saw Palace Var as it truly was. It was a sight that well matched the smell of his sock.

He continued down the corridor, feeling a terrible fool, holding his flimsy, broken sword out before him. Just the sort of scene Leonard the Lightning Tongue would have written for one of his limericks, he thought. "Find Rose Red," he told himself over and over as he went. But where could he even begin to search? He knew Vahe had taken her from the palace; they must have set out for the Village of Dragons by now. But where, by Lumé's blazing crown, was that?

He turned a corner and found himself facing the passage from which he had come. Frowning, he turned around and retraced his steps only to find himself once more in the same place. Var was not one to let its prisoners escape easily.

"Oeric!" he bellowed one last time. His voice echoed through the empty stone halls and seemed to laugh as it vanished. The palace itself mocked him.

Then suddenly, he felt the walls tremble.

Palace Var sensed a presence it had not felt in many centuries; a presence that saw through its disguises without a thought; a presence that walked its corridors with the commanding stride of a master. Like a misbehaving child caught by its parent, Var quivered, tensed, then relaxed all around Lionheart, as though taking a deep, shuddering breath.

The next moment, Sir Oeric appeared at the end of the hall.

"You're here!" Lionheart cried and hurried to him, still holding his smelly sock up to his nose. The knight gave him a look, but Lionheart ignored it. "You made it!"

"You called me."

"Yes, but I didn't think you'd actually come! How did you cross that plain so fast?"

"The Prince's Paths will carry you far when need arises, young Lionheart," the knight said. "And besides, Arpiar recognizes one of its own." He raised the long knife in his hand. It seemed a pitiably small weapon in proportion to his bulk. "We must find Vahe."

"He's gone," Lionheart said. "He and all his court. I heard them leaving, and I know they took Rose Red with them."

"Yes," said Oeric, "I saw the company pass. But we must find Vahe anyway."

"No, I told you, he led the others. We must follow them quickly before the moon rises!"

Oeric shook his head, and his eyes were no longer on Lionheart but looking up and down the hall, studying the formation of the stones, the lay of the bricks. "Vahe is near," he said. "It is here, in the house of our birth, that I must face him."

Lionheart shrugged him off, exasperated and desperate. "Fine. You go ahead and wander around awhile, but I'm going after them! Except . . ." He bit off a curse. "How do I catch them? Can you show me a Path?"

Oeric focused his awful white eyes on Lionheart once more. "You can remain here and help me," he said quietly.

A chill passed over Lionheart's soul. He could remain, yes. Again, such a lovely, noble excuse. The knight himself suggested it, so how could it be wrong?

"No," he whispered. "I'm going to Rose Red."

Oeric nodded. Then he took Lionheart by the shoulder and led him through the halls. Palace Var dared not try to deceive him but opened its portals until they came to the wide gates. There, Oeric pointed across the wide plain.

"That way, young mortal," he said. Lionheart looked where he indicated. There was nothing to see but more gray plain, forever and ever to the skyline. "That is the Path you must take."

"It leads nowhere."

"Walk that way, Lionheart, holding your purpose firm in your heart, and the Path will open before you. But bear this high." He took hold of the bent blade in Lionheart's hand and raised it up. Its metal was so blackened with ruin that Lionheart half expected it to break off in the huge knight's grip. But it didn't. "Bear this high, mortal. And hurry!"

Lionheart nodded, swallowing hard. Then, stretching the sword out before him, he ran the way Oeric had pointed. Futility snatched at him as he pelted across that flat terrain, never gaining on that far horizon, afraid to look back and find that he had put no distance between himself and the palace.

Then he was on the Path.

He didn't know when or how it happened exactly, but Lionheart knew that it was true. As though someone had grabbed the end of his sword and pulled him along, faster than any man could possibly run. The world on his peripheral vision went hazy, and he sped along as if carried by the wind itself, hardly seeing where he went.

Then he saw the gateway.

He knew it at once, for he had seen it several times before. It was a cave, the same cave he had found with Rose Red in the mountains when he was a boy. Shaped like a wolf's head, yawning and black. The sight of it then had been enough to make him shiver.

It was a gateway to Death's realm.

He hesitated only a moment. Then, setting his jaw, he pressed onward, right into that gaping opening. Darkness surrounded him, as sudden as the Midnight dragged behind the howling Black Dogs. The Path led him down, but it led him straight without any twists or turns. Lionheart was far from Arpiar, far from anywhere he had ever known.

Bebo had said he would have the chance to choose.

A lantern glimmered from a solitary gravestone. He saw it but did not slow his pace. He must stop for nothing, or he might yet change his mind.

A red light appeared before him, and he raced for it as hard as he could, pulled by an unseen force. He thought he saw goblins but was not certain. The stench of dragons filled his nostrils. In the tail of his eye, Lionheart thought he glimpsed Iubdan and warriors of Rudiobus, but his gaze was fixed ahead.

Both near and far at once, impossible to reach in time, he saw the throne of Death. He saw Rose Red bound in its seat.

Bebo had said he would have the chance to choose.

His choice was made. Lionheart opened his mouth and roared as he charged.

Oeric watched Lionheart disappear beyond his line of sight. "Lights Above shield him," he whispered, then turned to face Palace Var once more.

The palace shivered under his gaze.

He strode into its passages like a king returning home. He wasn't king here, and Var knew it. But he was born a prince, and Var knew that as well. It wanted to resist him as he navigated its long passages, wanted to bewilder his mind with its beautiful scents, to send him doubling and tripling back on himself until he went mad with confusion.

It didn't dare.

"Tell him I'm coming," Oeric said to the trembling walls. "Tell him I will find him, wherever he has hidden himself."

With those words, he began to fling open each door he came to, scanning the sparse, cold rooms and moving on without a word. Even the ghostly roses hid their faces before him.

The silver moonlight spread throughout the Village, and its light was painfully bright in the eyes of both the goblins and the soldiers of Rudiobus. They lowered their weapons and shielded their eyes, shying away from each other. A terrible hush filled the cavern as all, with hands over their faces, turned their gazes to the skylight.

"Yes," Vahe whispered. "Yes, look down and see, Hymlumé. See and remember what your children may do!"

The moon's silver disk slid over the skylight hole in an exact fit, her white eye filling the space, and she looked down.

"Remember," Vahe hissed.

And suddenly, the light changed.

A stain began to spread over the face of the full moon, a stain like pooling blood. As it spread, the moonlight turned from white to red, the blood red of pain.

Imraldera stood with her knife clutched in her hand, and she felt a sob catch in her throat at the sight. Moonblood! She remembered the night, remembered the fear of the sky filled with suffering, and the falling stars flaming as they struck the earth.

Eanrin covered his face, his mind calling back images more vivid than any other in his memory, of the White Lady sobbing and pressing her hands to the wounds her own children dealt her.

Iubdan, tears streaming into his black beard, collapsed to his knees. All the host of golden-haired soldiers did the same.

Varvare saw the spreading red glow, but she could not tear her eyes away from the unicorn's deep gaze. For as the moon shone red in remembrance, so the unicorn transformed from gleaming white purity to the hue of blood, spreading from the tip of its horn to the ends of its dainty, cloven feet. For the first time, she saw that it was not the beautiful being she had always seen. It was old and it was fallen. Like a meteor shooting through the atmosphere, so the one-horned beast flamed where it stood, and blood stained the end of its horn.

"You," Varvare whispered, staring at him. "You did this? To Lady Hymlumé?"

Maiden, it said, and its voice was terrible in her mind. Terrible because the children of Hymlumé, even those fallen, could not know sorrow; yet Varvare heard sorrow pouring from its heart. *Maiden, will you kill me?*

"I can't," she said. "You know I can't."

Vahe stood above them, and his voice was harsh when he said, "Do what you must, slave. I command you in the name of Life-in-Death."

Forgive me, the unicorn said, lowering its horn. It took a step toward her, and she felt the tip touch her breast just where her heart was wildly beating. Slowly, gently, the sharp horn pierced her skin. A single drop of blood fell down the front of her ragged dress, and the princess gasped.

A scrape of claws on hard stone. The Bane of Corrilond moaned in her sleep. A slit of flaming orange pierced her eyelids.

"More!" Vahe cried. "Spill it all!"

The unicorn braced itself.

And suddenly the still hush in the cavern was shattered by a bawling roar. Vahe whirled about with a curse, the unicorn startled back, and all the goblins and folk of Rudiobus turned to see a figure clad in a dirty nightshirt rushing with inhuman speed across the crowded floor without a care for those whom he crashed into and toppled as he went. Up the dais steps he flew, a bent and broken sword raised above his head. With a last cry he brought the sword crashing down on the unicorn's blood-tipped horn.

The one-horned beast reared up, its hooves dashing the air. Vahe swore and leapt back, his stolen face contorted into that of a monster. Varvare cried out: "Lionheart!"

Lionheart, carried forward from the force of his blow, landed at her feet. Pushing himself upright on his knees, he gazed into her face and saw her as she truly was, beneath all the veils, beneath all the enchantments.

"Rosie!" he said. "I've found—"

His face went rigid before her gaze, his eyes widening. Then a slow trickle of blood slid from the corner of his mouth.

The unicorn's horn pierced him between his shoulder blades, on through his heart and out the other side. Varvare stared at that dripping tip, then watched it withdraw, as silently and neatly as it had penetrated his body.

Lionheart drew a deep, gurgling gasp. Then he fell to one side, and his face was white with death.

Varvare stared at his fallen form, unbelieving. Then she heard her own voice crying and felt her own limbs wrenching against the bonds that held her.

The unicorn, its body shivering with fire, shook its head swiftly, and blood spattered from the tip of its horn. It turned to the princess once more.

5

NOT A SOUL REMAINED in the twisting passages of Palace Var, unless one counted the lost souls of roses hiding in the crevices and shadows. So confident was Vahe in his own enchantments. All the hosts of Var were emptied to follow him to the Village, and Oeric met no one but his own shadow as he walked those unfamiliar passages. The palace itself watched him with unseen, malevolent eyes, but it dared not interfere with his progress.

Vahe was there somewhere, Oeric knew. Of course, most of his spirit now inhabited that poor young prince of Parumvir. To face that prince and kill him would weaken Vahe but not put an end to his third life. No, the parasitic vine must be ripped out at the root.

Palace Var offered no lights in its long passages. The iron sky prevented sunlight from filtering through rough slashes in the rock that served as windows, and all the torches set in their racks along the wall were unlit. But Oeric needed no light to navigate that darkness. He walked with his head low, like a hound sniffing out its quarry, his knife at the ready.

He came to the assembly hall, which he had seen only once before, long ago, when Vahe tried to bargain with him, tried to offer him a place as his officer in the war he planned to wage on the worlds. Oeric, who was then but a nameless outcast, had tried to kill his brother before the eyes of a dozen or more guards and under the gazes of their stone ancestors. A foolish, hot-blooded act.

He'd failed and returned to imprisonment in Carrun Corgar. He'd lived to commit his great sin.

Oeric snarled as he stepped into that hall, and all the statues looked down on him and writhed in sudden panic at the sight of his ugly face. "I am forgiven," he said as he marched down that long, dark aisle. "I am forgiven, and I have a name."

The former kings and queens shivered and tried to draw back from him, though their feet were imprisoned in the blocks of marble and their stone hands bound to the ceiling they held in place above. Rather than beautiful, noble faces, Oeric saw the twisted features of monsters—monsters rendered all the more hideous for the malice in their stone eyes. Only the last one did not try to hide herself when she could not be hidden. Though there was fear in her face, she laughed at the sight of him.

He stopped at her foot, before the empty throne of Arpiar.

"Greetings, Mother," he said.

She shook her head in more silent laughter, her evil eyes squinting down at him.

"Tell me where I may find Vahe."

"He is too strong for you, my outcast child!" The memory of her voice whispered in his mind. *"I chose him over you. I gave him his strength."*

"And I will live forever grateful for that choice," said the ugly knight. "Tell me where he is."

"I should have killed you both. I wanted to. I gave my handmaidens the command."

"Where is Vahe, Mother?"

"But the soothsayer said I must let you live, and I listened to her words. Great destinies were bound up in your lives, she said. Both of your lives, though to one I gave all power, and the other I stripped of everything and cast into darkness."

Oeric turned from her leering face to study the empty assembly hall. He could feel the workings of Var using its last strength to shield its master from his sight.

"One will wake the Sleeper, the soothsayer said, and be gifted with fire."

He saw the tremble in the air around the empty throne. Vahe would have a secret chamber, buried in the heart of Palace Var where no one could reach him. But the heart of Var need not be a physical location. He put out his hand, stretching toward the throne.

"But the other will serve a power greater still," said the memory of the old queen. *"And the power he serves will extinguish the fire of his brother."*

"So it shall be, Mother," Oeric said, taking another step toward the empty throne.

His hand touched an invisible door.

As soon as he felt it, it shed its veils and became visible before him. They were double doors, taller than any three men, and carved all over with roses. But he impatiently waved aside that illusion and saw instead the faces of trapped spirits carved in expressions of sorrow, frustration, and even agony. He tried the latch and found it locked. His mouth set in a grim line, and he drew himself together. Then, with an animal roar, Oeric flung himself at those great doors, heaving his shoulder against them. They shuddered but stood. He flung himself again, and a crack ran between them. A third time, and the bolt on the far side burst, and both doors swung wide.

Inside on a throne sat the King of Arpiar's own body. Here alone did his veils still work, for Oeric saw a beautiful face, smooth golden skin, elegant but strong hands resting on the arms of the throne. A climbing rose twined about it, but the blossoms were dead.

Oeric raised his knife.

"Kill him now," said the memory of his mother, *"while he sits helpless. Then you will be a true King of Arpiar."*

"I will never be king," Oeric said.

In a loud voice, he cried out his brother's name.

Vahe raged.

His shrieking voice filled the cavern and continued to fill it to over-flowing, and the red light of the moon shuddered in response.

"Kill her! Kill her, slave!" he screamed. "Don't stand there staring. You were given to me by Life-in-Death, and I have a promise to claim! Kill the maid now. This fool is nothing."

The unicorn stood as stone, gazing at the princess bound to Death's throne. For her eyes were fixed upon the fallen form of the dead man.

His blood was already beginning to congeal. His face was rigid in death. But the Princess Varvare, her own voice now silenced, looked upon him, and a world of emotions broke across her face.

The unicorn spoke to her.

You love him.

She gave no answer, but it read the response in her eyes.

He hurt you.

She swallowed. Even the pain of her own wound was forgotten in that moment.

He betrayed you, even to death.

Her eyes closed, and two silver lines of tears streamed down her face.

But you love him.

"Leo," she whispered.

Somehow, through the din of Vahe's screams, through the thick curtain of blood-light streaming through the window above, the unicorn heard something it had not heard in many dark ages.

It heard its mother's voice.

> *Beyond the Final Water falling,*
> *My blessed songs recalling*
> *A promise given that my children should be found.*
> *Won't you return to me?*

It turned its fathomless eyes from the maiden to the skylight above. It saw the Lady Hymlumé, and she bled from many wounds just as she had the night her children pierced her with their horns. But she gazed on the one-horned beast with love in her shining eyes.

A silver voice sang:

> *You are still my child.*
> *Won't you return to me?*

"Kill her, slave!" Vahe cried, his voice faint and far behind the music that only the unicorn heard. "Kill her! Your master commands you!"

The one-horned beast turned away. It passed down the black steps of the dais, its ears deaf to the King of Arpiar's voice screaming, "Come back! If you walk away from your chains, you will surely die!"

It passed between the cowering folk of Rudiobus and the quivering goblins of Arpiar. It passed near the blind poet, who turned his ravaged face away. It passed a lady knight, who alone of all who watched saw it for what it was in that moment, fair and shining and white as pure starlight. And she too drew away from it, filled with fear.

It passed between all of these and approached the one at the end of the cavern.

The Bane of Corrilond watched the unicorn's progress through her slitted eye. Dreams still filled her vision, dreams once held dear, now burning and dying and burning and dying again. She saw the beast like a bull with a fanged face and its sword-sharp horn approaching her, and it was like the death of her dreams personified. Though sleep still clouded her mind, she raised herself upright, her massive claws tearing into the rock beneath her, her fire suddenly billowing up in her throat.

The goblins and the soldiers of Rudiobus screamed as one voice and fell over one another as they scrambled away from the rising red mountain of the dragon. But she did not see them. Her burning gaze was fixed on the one-horned beast. She, who had not known fear since accepting her Father's gift, shuddered where she sat, and her massive wings beat the stale, hot air.

Still the unicorn approached, moving with that world-destroying pace of stars.

The Bane of Corrilond flamed.

Throughout her sleep her furnace had built, and now its heat was enough to knock flat all who stood in that room. But the fire was focused on one small place, that place where the unicorn stood. It took her fire, absorbing it, but still more came, straight from that hollow where her broken heart no longer beat. She stood, bracing her powerful forelegs as the fire billowed from her.

The folk of Rudiobus jumped behind sleeping dragons, using the scale-covered hides to protect themselves. The blind poet grabbed the dame's hand and dragged her with him behind a stone, shielding her with his cloak and body, though the heat scalded his skin. The princess on the throne turned away, her face writhing in pain that had nothing to do with the heat. Vahe alone stood firm and watched with eyes that saw the death of his own dream. For his vow could no longer be fulfilled.

The flame stopped. The Bane of Corrilond swallowed the remaining flickers and sparks, and stared down at that place where once the unicorn had stood.

All that remained was a gleaming white horn.

Vahe screamed and tore his hair, cutting the Boy's stolen face with his fingernails. Then he whirled about and retrieved one of the two knives he had thrown at the cat, brandished it, and took a single stride toward his bound daughter.

A voice he knew all too well rang in his head.

Vahe. Brother. Come to me.

His face went ashen. "Gargron!" he spat.

The next moment, he had flown the cavern, fled the Village, his spirit racing back across the spaces of the worlds.

The nameless Boy, blood streaming down his cheeks, stood with a knife in hand, staring a moment into the wide eyes of the princess. Then he moaned and collapsed, and the knife clattered where it fell.

6

THE MIST IS THICK AND WHITE, *like ghostly hair coiling around him.*
*Lionheart walks on the shores of a river, and it is wide and black,
more like an ocean, he thinks. But it flows swiftly with rushing white water,
and he is afraid to try to cross it.*

So this is the Realm Unseen.

*Looking up, he can see the Gardens of Hymlumé, and believes he sees the
faces of her shining children among the fiery blossoms. But it is all far off,
and the roar of the river is much more present. He wonders if he will meet
anyone else along these shores.*

"So it wasn't enough, was it?"

The voice is one he knows too well.

*He turns and sees a tall, spectral figure approaching through the mist that
flows so thickly up from the river's edge. His cloak is black, as black as his
hair, as black as his eyes. But his face is the white of Death.*

*"You!" Lionheart gasps and backs away. River water rushes over his ankles
and threatens to drag him down. He plants his feet. There can be no more
retreating that way. "You are dead!"*

"I am, yes," says the Dragon. His smile is terrible, revealing long black fangs behind his white lips. "As are you."

The tug of the river is powerful, and Lionheart almost falls. "I don't belong to you!"

"Oh, don't you?" The Dragon's smile grows. "It wasn't enough, was it, little Lionheart? All your guilt. All your noble resolve. You gave your life for the girl you betrayed, but you did not succeed in rescuing her."

"I . . . I stopped the beast."

"Only for the moment." He comes nearer, the shadow of his cloak drawing a blackness around them that is deeper than nightfall. "Did you really think, pathetic mortal, that you could earn atonement? Did you really think that your own sacrificed life could begin to repay the evil you have worked?" Fire flickers in the recesses of his eyes.

Lionheart turns and runs into the river.

The current catches him like hands on his legs and drags him under, and the water is cold as it closes over his head. He wants to scream but cannot, for the air is knocked out of him as he is pulled, struggling, down and down. But the Dragon's laugh penetrates even there, filling his head as water fills Lionheart's eyes, his nose, his lungs.

Then, though darkness overwhelms him and water blinds him, he sees a hand. Desperate, he reaches out and takes hold.

The next moment he is on the shore again, gagging and spitting black water. Someone holds him and thumps his back until he has coughed everything from his lungs. He sits for what seems a long while, shivering, gasping. Then he turns.

And meets the Prince's gaze.

"No," Lionheart whispers, crumpling into a heap, his hands clutching the back of his head. The mist is cold. He'd not thought he would feel anything in the Realm Unseen, but he is frozen straight through to his bones. "No, don't look at me."

"Lionheart," says the Prince, "will you come with me now?"

"I'm worthless," Lionheart says. "I couldn't save her. I couldn't redeem my honor."

"You never can," the Prince replies. He takes Lionheart by the shoulders and forces him to sit up, to face him. "But do you think my grace insufficient to forgive you?"

Lionheart cannot bear to meet those eyes, but neither can he look away. Water drips down the stubble on his face and meets in a stream from his chin. The Prince gazes at him with eyes that see to the very truth of his soul, every unacknowledged cowardice, every sin glossed over with excuses. But in the Prince's eyes is no condemnation but rather an offer.

"Come with me now, Lionheart." His voice is firm, but it is a gentle request, not a command. He remains kneeling in the mud of the riverbed, not caring that he dirties his fine clothes, and his hands hold Lionheart by the shoulders.

Still shivering, hunched over with shame, Lionheart nods. "I will come with you," he whispers.

The Prince rises and pulls Lionheart to his feet. He presses something into Lionheart's hand. When he looks, the dead man finds he that he holds once more the bent and burned sword. He frowns and turns again to the Prince, a question in his eyes.

"Follow me," says the Prince. He starts walking back up the river.

"Wait!" Lionheart cries, desperate. "You know what happened last time! You know what I did! I am a worm before that monster. I cannot face him, not again! I cannot fight the Dragon!"

The memory of his failure engulfs him, and it is more horrible to face now than ever before. He thinks he will collapse; the weight of the broken sword is too much to bear.

But the Prince stands beside him and puts an arm across his shoulders. "We'll face him together this time," he says, slowly turning Lionheart to one side.

To look into the Dragon's burning face.

7

VAHE BLINKED HIS OWN EYES and saw his own hands in his lap. He raised his face with a snarl, knowing what he would find.

Oeric stood before him, a knife in his hand.

"Hello, Vahe."

The King of Arpiar was out of the throne of roses and flying at his brother's throat. But Oeric raised an arm and blocked him, grabbing his wrist and twisting it painfully. Vahe flung out his other hand, took hold of the back of Oeric's neck, and rammed his own rock-hard skull into his enemy's nose. This startled the knight more than anything, and he let the king go. Vahe backed away, panting like a wolf on the hunt, his teeth bared.

"Murderer!" he hissed. His face was like an angel's to the stone eyes of his ancestors looking on. "You come at me when I am defenseless!"

Oeric shook his head. "I could have killed you while you sat unknowing and rid the worlds of your evil." Then from his belt he took a knife, a replica of the one in his hand, and tossed it across the room. The King of

Arpiar caught it by the blade and grimaced when it cut his skin. Normal blades could not pierce the hide of a goblin.

"What malice have you worked into this weapon, Gargron?" he demanded. "Will it turn on me if I use it? Will I slit my own throat?"

"I don't play your games, Vahe," Sir Oeric said, bracing himself, his own knife at the ready.

"Oh, don't you? I remember differently."

He leapt forward, his blade slashing at Oeric's eyes.

The Bane of Corrilond licked sparks from her face and stared with hate-filled eyes at the blackened hole where the unicorn had stood. The horn lay shining there, brighter than ever in the heat of her fire. But she turned away from this. Her anger was still hot inside.

Her kinfolk lay all about her on the floor, asleep, their faces twisted with pain that she knew all too well. She tore into the nearest one with her sharp teeth, burning the scales even as she ripped at them. Mindless fury drove her beyond reason. She saw a movement, some ugly gray face filmed over with a veil of beauty, and she hated the very sight of it. Without a second glance, she shot her flames its way and smiled at the screams that filled the air.

There were more, everywhere, the whole cavern crawling with little gnat-like beings. Like the mortals that had swarmed the streets of her beautiful city long ago, those wretched creatures defiling the purity of stones set in place by her father's grandfather. She had purged Nadire Tansu of those parasites who had betrayed her and sucked the life from her veins. She had destroyed the city beyond recall, but it was cleansed.

The flames rose again in her mind even as they rose in her throat. Nadire Tansu, Destan, Aysel, the cities of her forefathers. She had burned them all, just as she would burn the Village of her kinfolk to rid it of these screaming insects.

"To me, to me!" Iubdan cried to his soldiers as they fled the fury of the red dragon. They hastened to their king, and he spread what protection he could around them with the powers of ancient days. But the goblins were not so lucky. Their beautiful faces melted into terror as they fell beneath her flames.

Imraldera and Eanrin stood behind a rock, and the dame shivered with cold fear even as the heat filled the cavern like a great oven. "Tell me what you see," Eanrin demanded. "Tell me!"

"Iubdan shields his folk, but the people of Arpiar are dying!"

"What of Varvare?"

Imraldera searched through the red glare of the bloody moon and the fires of the dragon. Vahe's daughter remained bound to the throne, as yet unnoticed by the Bane of Corrilond, but unable to move.

Felix and the body of Lionheart lay in a heap at her feet.

"We must help her. She's trapped."

"Right." Eanrin straightened his cloak and adjusted the hat on his head, like a cat giving his whiskers a quick licking. "I'll take care of the dragon. You gather our folk."

"Eanrin, no!" She made a grab too late.

The blind poet, once more a cat, crept from hiding and darted across the cavern, using the bodies of still-sleeping dragons to shield himself from the Bane of Corrilond's fire. The goblins fled, screaming, and some were burning as they ran, but the cat snaked between their feet as he made his way closer. Imraldera watched in horror until he was just under the dragon's nose, still without being seen.

Suddenly, he was a man again, shouting up at the monster's face: "Demarress!"

The Bane of Corrilond turned her fire on him, and Imraldera's heart stopped in that instant when she thought the poet had been incinerated. But then she saw him emerge from behind another sleeping dragon a little ways off.

"Demarress!" he cried. "I have a riddle for you! Will you hear it?"

The dragon raised her head and roared as though she would like to snap up the moon's watching red eye itself. Then there were words in the roar, and the dragon's voice boomed in all listening ears.

"That is not my name!"

"Isn't it?" said the poet, scratching his head, his eyebrows rising. "How unfortunate. This riddle is for Demarress, Queen of Corrilond. She was a keen one for riddles."

Small flames shot between her teeth like darts. "That mortal woman died in my fire long ago."

"Unfortunate," the poet repeated, and he shrugged. "I suppose I'll excuse myself, then."

"Wait!" The dragon shifted her bulk, and the ground shook beneath her. But her flames were swallowed for the moment and her gaze focused on Eanrin.

Imraldera set her teeth and darted from her hiding place while the Bane of Corrilond's head was turned. Fallen goblins reached out to her, their awful faces pitiful with pain. But she must reach the princess. She must reach Felix and poor, broken Lionheart.

"Speak your riddle," said the dragon, sparks dripping from her lips.

"If you insist, O Majestic One!" Eanrin bowed and gave a dramatic twirl, then sang in his golden voice:

> *"I am the remnants of hammers,*
> *Of fire and file, firmly confined,*
> *Beloved of kings and princes.*
> *Those who feel my kiss may weep."*

He stopped there, tilting his blind face up to her, a picture of innocence. "Have you a guess?"

The dragon's eyes narrowed into searing slits of heat.

"Lumé's crown!" Iubdan hissed.

His captain, Glomar, growled, "What is the fool thinking? Does he want to get us all killed?"

Imraldera, still half a world away from the dais, came to a frozen halt and stared up at the dragon, for she too guessed the answer.

"Is that all?" the Bane of Corrilond growled.

"There is more if you would hear it," Eanrin replied.

"Tell me."

The poet sang:

> *"Those who feel my kiss may weep.*
> *And she who never touched me*
> *Will gnash her teeth in vain."*

The Bane of Corrilond roared. Memories long suppressed came flooding back—memories of a proud and noble king, her father, who wore at his side a sword with a golden hilt carved like two wildcats, set with rubies. He smiled down at his daughter.

"Shall I wear your sword someday?" the girl asked.

A shadow passed over the king's face, destroying the smile. *"You'll never be strong enough. Ah! Would that I had fathered a son!"*

The rest vanished in fire and smoke belching from the dragon's gut at the place where the poet had stood.

But he was no longer there.

The dragon saw him, bright as a flying spark, dancing across the cavern, diving behind one sleeping dragon only to emerge from behind another. Everything else vanished in her desperate need to destroy him, to devour, to burn the one who reawakened those dormant memories, who recalled the old king's face so vividly to her mind, who recalled the sword of her forefathers, which she was never permitted to carry.

She did not see the fleeing goblins, had no eyes for the soldiers of Rudiobus. Not even the woman in green who ran across the fire-scorched ground to the dais and the throne could catch her gaze. Her eyes were focused on that one scarlet-clad figure, who laughed at her as he ran, and she would kill him.

Imraldera felt tears on her face as she climbed the dais steps, but she did not check them. She mounted the stairs, and Varvare screamed at the sight of her.

"Hush, child!" Imraldera spoke more sharply than she intended. "Do not draw her gaze!" Then she fell to her knees beside the fallen figures, her expert hands running quickly over them. Lionheart was cold with death, but in Felix she felt the warmth of life. She lifted him up, but his head lolled back on her arm. "Felix!" she hissed through her teeth. "Felix, wake up, boy!"

He groaned, and his eyes blinked open blearily. But they were empty.

"He has no mind," the princess said. Imraldera looked up and saw her sitting limp and broken in Death's throne, no longer struggling. Her face was full of pain—a pain beyond the unicorn's wound in her chest or the burn of the throne itself.

"We've got to get you out of there," Imraldera said, laying Felix down and reaching for the princess's bindings. But the arms of the throne were twisted about Varvare's slender limbs and the carved dragon skulls hissed and rattled their teeth at Imraldera, ready to take her fingers off. She struck them with her knife, but her blade could not dent the stone.

Then came a burst of fire so powerful that the very sound of it knocked Imraldera over on top of Lionheart's body. She pushed herself back up and stared across the cavern.

"Eanrin!" she cried.

Her voice carried. The echoes caught it and dragged it across the walls and ceiling, above the roar of flames.

The Bane of Corrilond turned her heavy head, her eyes fixing upon Death's throne, the seat of her Father, and the blasphemous gnats that crawled all over it. Her snarl knifed through the hot air, and she spread her enormous wings about her as she crawled across the fire-strewn floor.

Oeric raised his knife and blocked the blade that Vahe darted at him. The King of Arpiar caught him about the throat, his elegant fingers squeezing. He was strong, stronger than Oeric, the old Queen of Arpiar knew as she watched them from her stone-carved eyes. For had she not given him his strength when she chose him above his twin?

But Oeric grabbed Vahe's arm and pried away his grasp. Then he pounded his fist into that perfectly beautiful face, shattering the last of Vahe's veils. The enchantment broke away, revealing the truth behind it.

They were mirror images of each other, Oeric and the king, though one was dirty in travel-worn clothes and the other clad in red velvet. Their faces reflected each other's foulness.

"You're an ugly one, aren't you, Gargron?" Vahe spat as he picked himself back up. "I can't say I like the feel of your features on my face. It's no wonder your lady rejected you in the end, is it?"

Oeric did not flinch as he strode forward and lunged with his knife. Vahe blocked and immediately slid his own blade down to strike Oeric's arm. He smiled when the blade pierced the stony hide, drawing a long ribbon of blood.

"My lovely wife, she came to me freely. Of her own choice, she returned to my power and gave herself to me, though she hated me the while." He backed away from Oeric, observing how the knight switched the blade from his right to his left hand. "But you . . . you were not so lucky as I, were you? You watched your lady turn her back on you. She could not bear the sight of your face any longer, could she, Gargron?"

They circled each other like posturing cats watching for a weak moment in the other.

"You say you do not play my games," Vahe spoke, his voice smoother than silk. "But you took my own weapon from me. Life-in-Death can drive a hard bargain, and you could not resist her voice any more than I could. We are so much alike, you and I. Images of each other. Except for one thing."

He lunged once more, and this time his blade plunged into Oeric's right shoulder, and he stood face-to-face with his twin, warm blood seeping down over his hand.

"Except for one thing," he hissed again. "I am the King of Arpiar. And you are the Outcast."

Oeric grimaced, his wide eyes shot with pain. His arm came up to grab Vahe's hand, preventing him from pulling back his blade.

"I am outcast no more," he said.

He sank the knife in his left hand deep into Vahe's heart.

Palace Var shuddered.

Vahe stared into his brother's eyes, his own face etched with disbelief. He tried to speak, his craggy lips striving to form words. Oeric let go of him, and he fell backward, and where he fell the floor cracked. The crack ran out from his body in all directions, spreading like webs up the walls, up the pedestals, up the statues of the kings and queens. The old queen screamed a silent stone scream, and her face shattered into fragments. One by one, the statues fell, and with their fall followed the crumbling of the roof.

The walls of Palace Var trembled again, broke into millions of tiny pieces, and fell as rose petals drifting across the blighted plains of Arpiar.

8

THE DRAGON'S SMILE is hot enough to drive out all the cold in Lionheart's bones. Hot enough to singe his face even from a distance.

"There you are, my little morsel," he says. "A merry chase you've given me. Come to me now, boy. Come to my embrace." He holds his arms wide, and his black cloak drapes like wings.

Lionheart for a moment cannot feel the Prince's hands on his shoulders. For a moment, he stands alone beside the Final Water, staring into the face of Death.

Then the Prince's voice whispers in his ear. "Don't be afraid. I am with you this time."

Lionheart adjusts his grip on the bent sword, sets his jaw, and takes a stride forward.

"That's right," says the Dragon, almost purring through his flames. "That's right, come to me."

Then he sees the sword.

"What have you got there?"

Lionheart opens his mouth to answer, but before the words come, the Dragon has grown, twice, three times, ten times bigger. His face is long and black and covered in scales, and fire pours from his eyes, his nose, and mouth. Black wings beat the mist, which scatters like frightened children, and Lionheart can almost hear the screams of dying dreams fleeing along the river's edge and vanishing into darkness. Only the Dragon and his fire are left.

"Where did you get that?" he roars in a voice that must rise to the Gardens of Hymlumé. "Where did you find that sword?"

Lionheart sees now the power looming over him, the fire of a thousand hells blazing in the Dragon's mouth.

And he sees the fear.

"Did you truly think," the Dragon cries, "that you could stand up to me? Did your boyish dreams tell you that you were the hero of your own sorry little story? You pictured yourself the brave warrior, didn't you, striding across the landscape of your kingdom, brandishing a sword as you do now. You saw it all in glorious detail, how you'd cut off my head and save your kingdom, winning the hearts of your people."

Lionheart shudders, and the tip of the sword wavers.

"But that's not how it happened, was it?" The Dragon raises the crest on his head. "You know how it truly was. How can one such as you hope to face me? I am ageless! I am power! I am the Death-in-Life! You watched your dream burn when you handed your love's heart to me and chose your own worthless life instead. And now you have sacrificed yourself in a pathetic attempt to save the girl you betrayed, and what has that done? She will die upon my throne, die with your dead carcass at her feet!"

Lionheart closes his eyes, his head sagging, and the Dragon's laughter surrounds him.

But the Prince whispers, "I am with you."

Setting his jaw, Lionheart raises his head and faces the Dragon again.

"I will devour you!" the Dragon roars, and terror laces his voice. "I will swallow you now as I should have swallowed you when you betrayed your true love into my hands! When you groveled before me, a quivering mass of mortality! When you proved your colors, you false prince! Disinherited, despised—I will devour you!"

His head darts forward like a cobra to strike, and Lionheart wants to *fling himself away. But the Prince holds him by the shoulders and keeps him standing firm. The Dragon's teeth close only inches from the tip of the broken sword. The heat of his breath and the sick stench of his poison are immense.*

Lionheart gazes into the eyes of Death, and this time he does not blink.

"I am with you," the Prince says in his ear.

Lionheart takes another step forward and raises the sword above his head.

The Dragon screams. His voice tears the darkness with its terror as he retreats, drawing himself up onto his haunches. Then he flames. The blast roars like a rushing tide pouring over the edge of the world, a great wall of destruction.

Lionheart holds the twisted sword before him and feels the flames sweep over him.

9

THE FIRST THING he became aware of was the heat.

After that came the smell.

It was a smell he recognized all too well.

His eyes flew open, and he found himself lying upon a black slab of marble, and people were screaming all around him. Flames danced before his eyes.

"Dragon's *teeth*!" he swore, and that's the next thing he saw.

Enormous, gleaming, flame-wreathed teeth bearing down upon him in the face of an enormous red dragon. He yelped and sat up, putting one hand in a pool of blood and the other . . .

The other touched the hilt of a sword.

He grasped and lifted it, scarcely noticing that it was black and twisted and useless, just grateful in that brief moment to have something to hold on to, something to put between him and the onslaught of fire and teeth and mad red eyes. He rose and braced himself, faintly aware that others clustered behind him, vaguely conscious that someone was shouting,

"Felix!" All his uppermost senses were focused on the monster bearing down on him.

And suddenly, in that moment of absolute panic and madness, he felt calm. Distant, somehow. This had to be a dream, after all. None of this could be real. As though his spirit floated somewhere above him, beyond this—

No! No, his spirit was very present, right here in his body, in this moment, with the dragon bearing down, and he wasn't about to give it up, fire and brimstone take him!

The wood thrush sang in his mind:
I am with you.

Then came the fire.

It rushed toward him, a tidal wave of flame spilling from the dragon's mouth even as she hurtled toward him. He squeezed his eyes shut and raised the sword, a useless gesture against that oncoming death.

The sword caught the fire.

He felt the power through his hands, and it frightened him. He opened his eyes and saw the sword drawing the fire to itself in a long, steady stream. The hotter it grew, the straighter the sword became and the brighter it shone, until it was like a flaming star in his hands. A more perfect weapon was never forged by heat and hammer, and it balanced beautifully in his hands.

The dragon swallowed her flame, her huge eyes widening as she stared down at the blazing star in the mortal's hands.

"Halisa!" she roared in a great cloud of poison and fear. "Fireword!"

He stared at her, stared at the sword, then threw it with all the strength in his arm.

The blade plunged through the armor plating of scales, down into the furnace of her soul. She screamed in agony, an agony stored up over centuries, an agony of hurt and betrayal, of love lost and destroyed; an agony of dungeons in the mind and chains dragged in heavy links. She fell upon the stones, crushing the bodies of her sleeping brothers and sisters beneath her.

Thus, the Bane of Corrilond died. Her body dwindled into that of a woman robed in red, and then vanished in a flurry of dust.

The boy stood on the edge of the black stone slab, panting. When he wiped his face, his hand came away wet with sweat and blood, and he realized that his cheeks were cut in thin lines like scratches. They stung, and he scowled. He whirled about, seeing for the first time with whom he shared this strange dais.

He looked into the eyes of a monstrously ugly girl sitting in a monstrously ugly throne carved all over like bones and dragon skulls. "Who are you?" he demanded.

She gaped at him, then swallowed. "I'm Rose Red," she said.

"Oh." His nose itched with sweat, and he rubbed it with the back of his hand. "I'm Felix." His frown deepened. "Have we met before?"

She nodded.

"Have we had this conversation?"

She nodded again.

"What in all the names of all the dragons is going . . . on . . . here . . . ?"

His voice trailed into nothing as he realized that he stood surrounded by hundreds upon hundreds of sleeping dragons, heaped across the floor among the Bane of Corrilond's smoldering flames. His knees shook, and Felix thought for a horribly embarrassing moment that he might faint. But someone caught him, and when he turned to face that someone, he found himself looking into a pair of black eyes that he recognized.

"Dame Imraldera!"

"Lights Above be praised, you're in your right mind," she said. Her eyes shimmered, and from the look of her smoke-smeared face she had been crying.

A thousand questions rushed into Felix's mouth and jammed against each other in their efforts to get out. But they halted in painful silence at the next sight that met his eyes—the sight of the dead man lying cold upon the stone near his feet.

"Is that . . . is that Leonard? The jester?"

Imraldera made certain the boy wasn't about to topple over, then again knelt beside Lionheart's fallen body. She swallowed the tears in her throat, desperately trying to force them back.

"Prrrlt?"

A fluffy body pressed against hers. Distantly, she heard Felix's voice growling, "What is Monster doing here? All right, I'm confused!"

"Eanrin!" She made a dart for the cat's scruff, but he dodged her hand. "Dragons eat you, cat!"

"Not yet, actually. Sorry, old girl." He sat and wrapped his tail primly about his paws. Her tears spilled over in good earnest now, and Imraldera no longer tried to restrain them.

"I thought you were dead."

"Just a bit singed. But I look a fright, I'm afraid!"

He looked like a bag of rags. His fur was burned away in clumps, and his whiskers had sizzled into crisp little curls on either side of his nose.

"You are lovely," Imraldera said, and she meant it.

"Who the blazes are *you*?" Felix cried, and Imraldera turned to see King Iubdan striding up the stairs. He carried the Prince's sword before him, and it still shone brilliantly white even under the red eye of the moon above them. He ignored the boy and presented the blade to Imraldera, who accepted it. She turned at once to Death's throne, where the ugly princess still sat bound and limp. Grinding her teeth, the dame raised the sword high, and the little carved skulls shrieked just before she cut them off and continued shrieking where they fell for some time afterward.

Varvare slumped out of the throne, and Eanrin, once more a man, caught her.

"And *why* is my cat a *man*?" Felix bellowed.

The goblin girl clung to the poet for a moment, gasping and weak, her eyes closed tight. He shushed her gently, patting her bald head and rocking her like a baby. Then she gave a cry and pulled away, falling over herself as she sought to reach Lionheart's side.

"No, no, no!" she whimpered, taking his cold hand in hers. But his eyes were empty, his spirit fled. Her face was more hideous in a grimace of sorrow, and she covered it with one hand, still holding tight to Lionheart with the other. Then with a ragged gasp, she reached out and closed his staring eyes. "Not Leo."

Imraldera knelt beside her and put an arm around her shoulders. "He was a brave lad in the end," she said quietly. "He meant to make amends by you. You know that, don't you?"

"I don't care!" the princess cried, gulping and gasping through her tears. Burns covered her body, and the place where the unicorn had pierced her must have been terribly painful. But she seemed unaware. "I don't care. He's dead! Oh, please, tell me he's not really. Tell me you can bring him back!"

Imraldera shook her head. "He's beyond my skill to help." Her eyes met those of King Iubdan above the princess's head. "He's beyond any of us now."

The sword blazes whole in Lionheart's hands, shining like the sun. It is the beauty of perfect symmetry and balance. Forged anew in the Dragon's blaze, it is the truest, most splendid weapon Lionheart has ever seen.

The Dragon stares down upon him and begins to shake. Then he screams, and his mighty wings beat the air. He leaps aloft and soars away, trailing his black shadow behind him, fleeing the edge of the Final Water back to the place from which he came.

Lionheart stands staring at the sword in his hands. For the first time he can remember, the weight on his heart eases. It is as though a burden he had not realized he was carrying is suddenly lifted, and his paralyzed limbs can not only walk but run.

He whirls about and faces the Prince. "He's gone!"

"And you will never face Death again," the Prince says and smiles. "Well done."

Lionheart bows his head then, pride sapped from him and replaced with dawning humility. "I would have fled."

"But you did not. I am with you now." The Prince places a hand on Lionheart's shoulder. "You understand, don't you, the difference between guilt and repentance?"

Slowly, Lionheart nods.

"You understand that you can never absolve your own sin?"

Again Lionheart nods.

"But you are forgiven. All that is past is past. The man you once were is no more. The man you are now is what matters, and I declare your name in truth: Lionheart. From this moment forth, you will serve me with the courage of roaring lions, and all my foes will tremble at your name, for they will know that you are one of mine."

Lionheart feels his heart swelling at the Prince's words. He raises his face and meets the Prince's gaze, and this time he can smile.

"Walk with me," says the Prince and begins to lead the way along the shores of the Final Water. Lionheart falls into step beside him, and they walk a long while in silence save for the distant songs above them, the Songs of the Spheres, composed before Time.

At last Lionheart asks, "What will happen now, my Prince?"

"I will give you new life."

Lionheart's gaze drifts slowly to the dark waves of the river. "Will we cross the Final Water?" he asks without fear.

Nobody paid any attention to him.

Felix could ask questions until he was blue in the face, and yet they ignored him. Even Imraldera! Lights Above, didn't he deserve some sort of explanation for all this mayhem? Felix flung up exasperated hands, searching the crowd for some face that looked like it might be willing to give a word of enlightenment.

All around him he saw yellow-headed soldiers gathering, their faces young and sweet but their expressions fierce and sad. They looked remarkably like the illustrations of the Little Folk in the book of Faerie tales he'd grown up reading. Except they weren't little. Or were they? He blinked, then groaned, rubbing his eyes, for the strange people around him were somehow both very small and very large all at once.

Just as Monster was simultaneously a cat and a man.

But he'd known that all along, hadn't he? Felix realized with a start that some secret part of himself had always understood that the strange blind cat who came to him and Una out of the Wood six years ago was no mere cat. Then again, he'd never met a feline that considered itself *merely* a cat. They were all lords and ladies in their own eyes. But there was always something different about Monster. Something altogether smug and ancient.

Felix's head ached. He couldn't watch those clustered around the fallen form of Leonard the jester (by all the dragon fire, what was *he* doing here?), and didn't like to look at the miserable face of the ugly Rose Red. He slipped away from the others, down the steps of the dais, taking stock of the burning world around him. It was something out of the worst of his nightmares. The Village, strewn with the bodies of slain and sleeping dragons, was a scene that had been presented to him in poisoned dreams many times over the last few months, dreams which he forgot upon waking but which never quite left his mind.

There were more than dragons too. More ugly people—goblins, he decided, uglier even than the girl by the throne—lay in miserable heaps among the scaly creatures. Some were dead, some wounded, some simply stricken with fear. But they did not move when Felix passed among them, and he felt pity for them.

Something gleaming caught his eye.

He turned to look more closely. It wasn't so bright a gleam as the light still shining from the brilliant sword. It was much smaller, more delicate. It looked like a horn but was slender as a reed and white as polished ivory. Its glow was faint, but it seemed all the brighter as it lay in a patch of charred and smoking stone.

The stone was still hot but not unbearably so. Felix approached the silver object and put out a hesitant hand to touch it. It was perfectly cool, so he picked it up and stood awhile, looking at it. It was heavier than he had expected, and he needed both hands to lift it. When he turned it, he saw iridescent streaks coiling all the way to the tip.

"What have you there?"

He turned and found his cat standing beside him in man form.

"M-Monster?"

"It's Eanrin, actually. Sir Eanrin, Chief Poet of Iubdan Rudiobus." His cat swept him a flourishing bow, but his face was not smiling. "Now tell me, since I lack the proper equipment to see for myself, what do you have there?"

"I don't know."

"Hand it over."

If his cat had still had a tail, Felix would have been tempted to step on it. As it was, there was nothing for him to do but obey. The tawny-haired poet turned it over in his hands, feeling it from base to needle-sharp tip. Then he said, "Come," and without another word led the way back to the dais. Felix followed obediently, cursing the day that he found himself obeying his own pet. But he did not like to give up that white horn so easily, and he wanted to see what Eanrin would do with it.

"Imraldera," the poet said, kneeling beside her and Rose Red and the broken body of Lionheart, "I found this. Will it help?" And he handed the ivory object over.

"I found it," Felix said, but no one paid him attention.

"The unicorn's horn," rumbled the rich voice of Iubdan. "It has the power to heal, so they say. But not since the days before the children of Hymlumé fell from grace."

Holding it, Imraldera recalled how it had touched her hands and face after only moments before she'd watched it destroy what was left of young Diarmid within the dragon's body. Even in the wake of death, it had brought her healing.

"They still remember, King Iubdan," Imraldera said softly. "They still remember the time before their fall. Some of the good yet remains."

But even as she spoke, the light in the horn faded, leaving behind a cold and even ugly object, like a long, twisted knife. Imraldera shuddered at the sight of it. "But I fear its last act will be destruction, not healing."

Then the goblin princess put out her hand.

She took the horn and grasped it tightly, and when she did, a shimmer passed through it. Blues, greens, and purples shot with gold ran from the tip and blended together into a pure, bright whiteness.

Rose Red saw again the depths of the unicorn's eyes as they gazed at her across the length of its horn and it said, *Forgive me.*

"I forgive you," Rose Red whispered to the still face of the young man she had loved and hated. Then she took the horn and pressed its tip into the cold wound in his heart.

The Prince smiles at Lionheart. "Not yet," he says.
Lionheart feels a jolt of pain.

Lionheart felt a jolt of pain in his heart as, with a great thump, it learned to beat once more. The awful smells of smoke and death surrounded him, roiling his stomach. Something sharp pulled out of his chest, like the removal of a splinter but a hundred times more terrible. "Iubdan's beard!" he swore, grinding his teeth. Those assembled on the black dais gasped.

"Leo?" a voice he knew so well whispered.

His eyes flew open. He saw a wide gray face with eyes like great white disks, and pointed teeth, one of which pushed the upper lip into a dreadful leer. His heart, still relearning to beat, bumped painfully in his chest, but he sat up with a glad cry.

"Rosie! I've found you at last!"

It was then the Prince of Farthestshore appeared.

PART SIX

THE QUEEN

1

As soon as Varvare, still holding the unicorn's horn in one hand and Lionheart's hand with the other, saw the Prince, a wave of remorse swept over her. Remorse for those long, painful nights of anger, of stopping her ears to his voice. At the sight of his face, she knew the truth, and his words came back to her as clear and strong as the day he had first spoken them to her heart.

I will always protect you, he had said. *But that does not mean you will not know pain.*

In the darkness of Palace Var, lost in Vahe's sweet-smelling enchantments, she had rejected him. Shame filled her, made all the more painful because he now looked directly into her eyes and said:

"My child, won't you come to me?"

She was on her feet in a heartbeat, running to his outstretched arms. Like a little girl running to her father for comfort, without a thought for her vile face, her dirty rags, her burned body. His arms closed around her, and he held her gently but with strength, and she cursed herself again and again for doubting him.

"I'm sorry," she whispered.

"You were long since forgiven," he replied.

The goblins of Arpiar, weak and ashamed of their faces without the veils of Vahe, stared up at the figure on the dais. Many of them howled in dismay and covered their heads with their arms, slinking away into darkness. But others, though tears filled their awful eyes, crept closer, like dogs afraid of a whipping for disobedience but unable to resist the call of the master. They saw how gently he held their ugly princess, how he did not seem to see the hideousness of her face, and the sight gave them courage.

Iubdan's soldiers saw the goblins approaching, and Captain Glomar plucked at his king's sleeve. But ageless Iubdan shushed them quickly. The two Knights of Farthestshore, Imraldera and Eanrin, took Lionheart by the arms and helped him to his feet. He too could not look away from the Prince's face, and the memory of a shining sword blazed bright in his mind. Recollection of the dark realm by the Final Water's edge was fading in his mind. But he would never forget, not as long as he lived, that he had fought the Dragon and, with the Prince supporting him, had not backed down.

"Aethelbald!"

Felix leapt forward suddenly, his arms flung wide. "Aethelbald, thank the Lights Above you're here! What is going on? Did you bring me to this place? Nobody will tell me a blessed thing, but did you see? Did you see that I killed the dragon? She was a big one too, but I brought her down!"

"I saw," the Prince of Farthestshore said, putting out a hand to tousle the boy's already messy hair. "Well done."

"How is Una?"

"She is well. She sends her love."

"Is she here?"

"No, Felix." At sight of the boy's crestfallen face, he added, "Don't worry, brother. You'll see her again, and soon. But now . . ."

Here the Prince turned, and his eyes swept over all the great cavern of the Village, still red with fire and the light of bleeding Hymlumé. The dragons lay yet in sleeping heaps, their dark dreams undisturbed. But wide-eyed goblins hid among those sleeping forms. They felt the power of the Prince's gaze piercing down to their souls. They cowered onto their knees, and some fled after their already retreated brethren. Most remained, however. "Now I have business with the Veiled People."

"Not so veiled anymore," said King Iubdan quietly, raising a thick eyebrow as he too surveyed the ugly faces surrounding them.

"More so than you think," the Prince replied. He did not take his arm from around shivering Varvare's shoulders as he stepped up to Death's throne. The remaining dragon skulls writhed under his stern gaze. He spoke a word, a strange word in a language that no one present knew. And suddenly the throne broke apart and scattered into shadows that fled with hisses and snarls behind the glow cast by the Bane of Corrilond's flames. The Prince stepped now into the place where the throne had stood and looked out at those assembled.

"Hear me, people of Arpiar," he said. "Your king is dead."

They knew this already, knew it as clearly as they saw one another's ugly faces. But many moaned to hear it spoken.

"You are a people lost, surrounded by faces you do not know. But I offer you the chance to belong. Come to me, and I will receive you as my own. I will see the rule of Arpiar established once again under a benevolent head. You will be my servants, and I will be yours. What do you say, children of veils?"

No one spoke. Then Varvare, still pressed up against the Prince's side, tugged at his arm. He looked down at her. "I'm always and ever will be your servant," she said, "if you please."

He smiled. "Yes, you are, princess."

Then he touched her face and a wonderful thing happened.

It was difficult for Lionheart to put into words later on because it was so strange. But when the Prince of Farthestshore touched Rose Red, he removed a final veil, a veil that had covered her face most of her life, a veil through which few people had seen. It dropped away, and her true face was one that Lionheart recognized as surely as he would recognize his own face in a glass. It was not beautiful like the masks with which Vahe had disguised his loathsome people. There was nothing artificial, nothing unreal in these features. It was a true face, and truth made it lovely.

And that's what she was, Lionheart realized as he should have realized long ago: lovely.

The goblins watching gasped, the soldiers of Rudiobus raised their eyebrows, and Iubdan muttered under his breath, "By my own black beard!" Felix, his jaw dropping, admitted that the ugly girl wasn't half bad looking after all. Not beautiful like Dame Imraldera, but certainly not half bad.

After that, the goblins of Arpiar moved forward, presenting themselves humbly before the Prince. The Prince of Farthestshore spoke to each one, removing the veils of those who asked him. They weren't goblins after all, Lionheart saw, when they wore the faces they were intended to have from the beginning. They swore allegiance at the Prince's feet, and soon the cavern was full of people crying and singing, standing unashamed beside the golden-haired men of Rudiobus.

When at last he had spoken to them all, the Prince turned to Imraldera and held out his hand. She gave him his sword, shining like a star. He then turned to Varvare once more.

"And now," he said, "are you ready for your first task in my service?"

Her silver eyes were round and perhaps a little scared, but she nodded.

"Then kneel here at my feet."

She did as he bade her, the rags of her goblin gown spilling about her knees. The Prince touched her on the shoulders with the sword as though performing a knighting, for there was no crown. But when he spoke, he said:

"I hereby declare you Queen Varvare of Arpiar, Ruler of the Unveiled People, Mistress of the lands between the Karayan Plains and the Sevoug Mountains beyond Goldstone Wood. Under your rule, streams will flow through the barren places, the people will work the ground and make it fruitful, and Lumé and Hymlumé will smile upon Arpiar once again."

Even as he spoke, the moon above changed. The bloodred light filtered away into clean white that shone softly through the skylight and fell upon the Prince, the sword, and the young queen. The Unveiled People sent up a cheer, and Felix, though still uncertain what had just happened, whooped and hollered, "Huzzah!"

Lionheart remained silent between the two Knights of Farthestshore as they took the long knives from their belts and raised them in salute, a motion echoed by all the golden soldiers of Rudiobus and by King Iubdan himself.

Young Varvare covered her face, embarrassed and afraid. She was a goat girl and a chambermaid, after all, not intended for great destinies, for the ruling of kingdoms. But the Prince of Farthestshore caught her eye, and she heard the wood thrush sing once more:

I will always protect you.

In that moment, she found the faith to believe.

Far away in Arpiar, the land was heavy with loss and withered for want of its shattered enchantments.

Except for the rose petals that continued to fall, a blizzard of color in that bleak realm. As they fell, something happened in the sky above, something that had not been seen in many long ages of that world.

The clouds parted, and the sun looked down upon Arpiar.

Oeric walked through the shower of soft petals, clutching his wounded arm and shoulder and breathing hard. He found it difficult to see where he was going, but he staggered on, wanting to call out yet afraid to. So it was that he stumbled upon the one he sought long before he saw her.

She was kneeling beside the broken body of a goblin wearing a crown upon its head. When Oeric almost trod upon her, she raised her surprised eyes and exclaimed, "You're here!" She was crying.

He collapsed on his knees before her and the dead goblin. "What have you here?" he asked, his voice rough as granite. Now that he was here beside her, he could scarcely look at his lady's face. Centuries of separation, and now he could not meet her gaze.

She swallowed. "It's Queen Anahid. She's dead. She died freeing Lionheart."

Oeric nodded and reached out to touch the dead queen's face, which was very like his own, but still more misshapen in painful death. Seeing those awful features made him afraid suddenly. He turned his shoulder, further hiding himself from the woman beside him.

"We cannot know her heart," he said quietly. "We do not know whom she will meet in the Realm Unseen. But she died well in the end."

"Yes. And she loved my Rosie." The lady wiped viciously at her tears, muttering, "Bah! Can't see a thing for these fool flowers!" Then with a loud sniff, she put out a hand to Oeric, gently touching his wounded shoulder. "You're hurt."

"It's nothing."

She rolled her eyes. "Fiddle. Spoken like a man. You'd say that if your head was cut off." Then she withdrew her bloodstained hand. "We should be going now, shouldn't we? I need to find Rosie, and we must tell the others that Vahe is dead, if they've not figured it out for themselves. You know which way they went, don't you?"

Oeric nodded and started to rise. But the lady put out a restraining hand. "Wait."

His head suddenly went light. The labor of centuries overwhelmed him as though every moment of strain and anxiety had reached its apex here, in this instant. Then it was gone, leaving him weak, unable to think, unable to arrange his thoughts in any order as he sat on an empty plain under the sun and the rain of roses. The sun did shine, and he knew that for truth. The air was sweet, and he knew that for truth as well. His shoulder hurt like fire; he knew that for a truth that would come back to haunt him for many painful months to come.

But when his lady took his ugly face between her hands and kissed him, that was a truth by which Oeric knew worlds were created.

2

VAHE WALKS ALONG THE SHORES of the Final Water. "It's not over," he mutters to himself. "My dream realized. I must have my dream!"

The Lady stands before him. She is miles tall, and her cold white eyes, half closed with disgust, gaze down upon his ugly little form.

"Lady!" he cries when he sees her, falling at her feet. "Lady, my dream! Give me my dream!"

"I gave you everything you needed," she says, and her voice is harsh. "You were the stronger brother, and I gave you all that you required. And yet you have failed."

"You promised me!" He feels the pull of the Water but resists it still. "You promised me my dream! I will make the worlds beautiful after my own design!"

But she turns from him as one turning away from a crushed spider, shivering with repugnance. "I give you up."

Then she is gone, and the Dragon stands in her place.

"All my sister's children must come to me in the end," he says and smiles.

Flames pour from his mouth. Vahe screams and plunges into the depths of the Final Water. But he cannot escape the burning, not even there.

Hymlumé turned her white eye away from the world for a moment and looked about her garden. It was good to remember pain, she knew. Pain remembered intensifies joy. But no good can come in dwelling on old wounds, so she closed her eye, forgot the spilled blood, and sought joy in the faces of her shining children.

A Lost One approached through the Paths of the sky.

The moon turned and saw him shining, without that cruel horn with which he pierced her long ago. His eyes were deep and more beautiful than before, because in them shone the sorrow of repentance.

"My child," said Lady Hymlumé, "I was promised you would return to me."

"How can you love me still, when I rejected you?" it asked in a voice like music. "When I wounded you so?"

"You are my child," she said. "I loved you before Time and will love you when Time has ceased."

A new star shone in the heavens above; or rather an old star, returned to its place, gleaming blue and white. And it joined its voice with the voices of its brothers and sisters, with the music of the spheres, singing in praise of the Song-Giver, in praise of rebirth.

3

THE BLEAK LANDSCAPE OF ARPIAR was hardly the ideal location for hosting a coronation feast. But twisted Palace Var had vanished completely from the face of the plain, leaving not even a scar but rather mounds upon mounds of sweet-smelling rose petals. These had lost the poison behind their sweetness and were very beautiful, Queen Varvare thought, as they swept and billowed about the hard gray earth.

It was hard to imagine this land ever becoming full and green. Even now, when the golden people of Rudiobus had set up merry-colored pavilions—for there was not a single standing structure to be found in all of Arpiar suitable for a queen's habitation—and the brilliant green and red fabric flapped like flags under the sunlight, she could not be blind to the desolation that was her kingdom.

Her kingdom!

She shivered at the thought but tried to disguise it. For she was on a high seat, another beautiful piece brought by King Iubdan and Queen Bebo for the feast, where all the eyes of Arpiar and the gathered guests could see her. It was a most uncomfortable feeling for a girl who had spent all her life avoiding being seen.

But Beana—only she wasn't Beana but an ancient and powerful Knight of Farthestshore, dressed in ivory and blue and crowned with ivy—sat beside her. When Varvare turned to her, she smiled a smile that was reminiscent of the looks the old goat had given Rose Red, a look that said, "Now, now, dear girl, what's all this fuss about? Try to think a sensible thought now and then, and you might find the world easier to manage."

Beyond her sat Sir Oeric, who was, Varvare had learned, her uncle. He had been her father's twin, but he looked nothing like Vahe, neither the beautiful creature her father had deceived his people into perceiving him as, nor the monster Varvare had known. Sir Oeric was huge and he was golden and he was powerful. Perhaps not beautiful; taken feature by feature, neither he nor Beana was exactly what one would call good-looking, not by traditional standards. Rather, they were possessed of an inner serenity that made one think them much more beautiful than any other in the room. It was a beauty that started on the inside and grew more and more outward as time went on, or perhaps as the observer's perception grew.

"I will help you, my queen, if you will have me in your service," Sir Oeric had said when he first knelt before her and swore his allegiance along with all the other folk of Arpiar. "I can offer you the wisdom of many years, which perhaps you will find useful at the commencement of your reign."

"Iubdan's beard!" Varvare had exclaimed, then bit her lip and covered her mouth, glancing about to make certain King Iubdan, seated not far off beside Bebo, had not heard her outburst. "I cain't begin to tell you how grateful I would be!" she continued in a whisper. "I ain't got the first notion about the ruling of kingdoms." She blushed unbearably then and wished she could bite her tongue off at this outburst.

Sir Oeric, however, had chuckled and bowed his head. "I am pleased to know that my service is required."

Something about the way he and Beana were never far from each other's company throughout the course of the feast made Varvare pause for some speculation. But not much of a pause, for she scarcely had time to think during the whirlwind of that day.

Her subjects approached her high seat, knelt, and swore allegiance, and her head spun with their names. Not only they, but also kings and queens of a hundred far-off realms stepped from the Wood Between into Arpiar to meet the new queen and to see this land that had been cut off from all others for five long centuries. There was a man with a fiercely handsome face whose skin was the color of the sea and whose hair was white as ocean foam, and he was the Mherking. There was another, the Lord Who Walks Before the Night (she could not remember his actual name), whose skin was no more than a shadow, though he was clad in yellow silks. A serpent, who sometimes took near-human shape but remained just as much a serpent, bowed before her, and she had to force herself not to draw her feet back when it spoke in its strange voice. A child leading a white lion on a leash, a stag the color of emeralds, and even an enormous one-eyed Tiger . . . all of them presented themselves and brought incredible gifts, and Varvare hadn't the first idea how she was meant to respond to them.

Despite her shyness, the Faerie lords and ladies, whispering behind their hands, decided the new queen was quite lovely and so serene, sitting in the wooden throne brought from Rudiobus, a unicorn's horn clutched as a scepter in her hand. It would be a new age indeed for Arpiar.

But though the queen searched the teeming throng and allowed her gaze to wander across the petal-strewn grounds, she could catch no glimpse of Lionheart.

He kept himself out of the way as much as possible. Besides, he was exhausted. Almost dying takes a lot out of a man—or perhaps he had actually died? He couldn't say for certain now. Either way, he'd received a new chance at life, and he meant to live it.

But he did not intend to begin by foisting his presence on the young queen.

So he drifted about the outermost tents, sampling strange foods from strange realms served by still stranger beings. He tried not to think too much about what living a new life was going to mean just yet. Somehow he knew that a task would be given him, and soon.

He met Eanrin partway around a table of unusually spicy dainties.

"Hullo there, jester," the poet said with a bright smile. Lionheart, who had not made himself known, wondered just how the blind poet had known he was there. "I say, it's a bit discomfiting, isn't it? Old Ragniprava prowling about the place, I mean. I've almost bumped into him once or twice. It's the most socially awkward situation. I mean, what do you say? 'Greetings, my lord, sorry about the eye. Shall we let bygones be bygones?' It's not as though I can make him the whole eye-for-an-eye offer, can I?"

"He'd probably settle for your head instead," Lionheart answered.

Eanrin put a hand into his pouch and removed something Lionheart couldn't see. "By the way, this is yours. I've been hanging on to it for some time now and just haven't had a good opportunity for returning it. Go on! Take it."

With that, the poet dropped a single strand of hair into his palm. Lionheart frowned, but Eanrin flashed another beaming smile. "Since you'll likely find yourself wandering these Faerie ways more often than not in the future, you'd do well to remember this bit of advice: Don't go giving bits of yourself to anybody. Oh, they'll tell you it's a fair price, but—" He shuddered, shaking his head. "Do you take my meaning, lad?"

Lionheart pocketed the hair and thanked Eanrin as solemnly as he could.

"And now," said the poet, "I must off and compose a song worthy of this historic occasion. I'll leave you two to chat."

With that, Eanrin whisked away, and Lionheart turned to find the Prince of Farthestshore standing quietly behind him. Dragon's teeth, how *did* the blind man sense his Master's presence when Lionheart hadn't?

The Prince smiled and as though reading his mind said, "Cats, you know, have far better senses of smell and hearing than have men." Then he indicated for Lionheart to walk beside him, and started away from the noise and celebration of the feast. They walked in silence for a while, and it reminded Lionheart of that moment outside of Time, that moment which his memory could not hold but which his heart would always recall—walking on the edge of a swift, dark river in the Realm Unseen. His heart beat fast, for he knew he was about to receive direction. After all, had he not said then on the edge of that water that he would follow the Prince?

"Lionheart," said the Prince, "if you will agree to it, I should like for you to commence training for knighthood."

Lionheart drew in his breath, and his heart thudded painfully. "It . . . it would be my honor, my Prince."

"Will you swear the oath of service to me now?"

"Immediately, if you wish it."

The Prince drew his sword. "Then kneel," he said.

It was a much quieter affair than the declaration of Queen Varvare's rule. There was no audience. Even the sun above seemed not to see, for it was shining all its warmth upon the young queen and the feasters. But the moment was perhaps more solemn for its privacy, and the oath Lionheart made just between himself and his new Master was as binding in his heart as any made before a thousand witnesses. He grasped the shining sword—so different from the bent and twisted thing he had first perceived it as—in both his hands and swore upon its blade. When he rose, he was Childe Lionheart, in training for knighthood in the Order of Farthestshore. Tears gleamed in his eyes, though they did not fall.

"I have a task for you, Childe Lionheart," the Prince said. "Are you ready to accept it?"

"I will do anything you ask of me, my Prince."

"I do not pretend that this will be easy for you. But trust me when I say that it will be right, that you will be glad of it in years to come."

Lionheart trembled. "Command me, and I will go."

"I do not command you," said the Prince, "but rather I ask that you return to Southlands and the House of your father. There I would have you make peace with him and ease his mind in these twilight days of his life."

A shudder ran through Lionheart, fear of seeing his father's face again. Fear of revisiting that place of his shame where all he knew and loved held him in contempt. But he replied, "I will go at once, my Prince. Only . . ."

"Yes?"

"Only, may I take leave of Rose Red?"

Romantic bards would never have approved the meeting between the newly crowned queen and the bashful squire. Indeed, eavesdropping poets would have liked very much to take both participants, give them a good shaking, and rewrite all their lines for them. But the meeting between Queen Varvare and Childe Lionheart, stolen during the few brief moments she could escape from the crowds and hide behind the shelter of one of the big tents, went something like this.

"I have come to make my farewells, Your Majesty."

Varvare hated that, his calling her "Majesty" and kneeling before her. She still felt like a chambermaid standing before her master, and it was miserably uncomfortable to have the roles reversed. So she said only, "Yes."

"I have a long journey before me. And I am told not to seek atonement, only to serve and to trust. It . . . it won't be easy for me."

"Yes."

Lionheart got once more to his feet but could not bear to look in her face. Perhaps if he had, he would not have tried to speak. But the words came out in a rush. "Rosie, how can I ever—"

"Please," she interrupted. "Please, Leo, don't say anythin' more."

There is a moment that comes into every life when the right word, the right look even, could change the shape of the world forever. The wrong one could as well, though the resulting shape would be different. No word at all, however, and the moment slips by, and things remain unsaid that perhaps should have been said, perhaps shouldn't, and no one can ever know for sure.

For Lionheart and the new Queen of Arpiar, that moment came and went with neither speaking and neither looking at the other, and the world's shape did not change.

Then Varvare said, "Do you know where you will go?"

"Back to Southlands first. From there, I don't know. The Prince has promised me a path. I will walk it and discover where it leads."

"That is best."

Lionheart nodded, rubbing the back of his neck and grinning awkwardly. "Will you do something for me when I am gone? Tonight, during the festivities."

"Yes?"

Still grinning, he pressed a paper into her hands. "It's a song I wrote, back in my jester days. To be played to the tune 'Gleamdren Fair, I Love Thee True.' Will you see to it that someone sings it tonight? When Eanrin will hear it, of course."

She licked her lips, trying not to smile. "I think that might be arranged," she said solemnly.

"Good."

He turned then, just as though he intended to leave without a salute, without a good-bye, and any spying poets would have strangled him within an inch of his life.

But Lionheart looked back and said quietly, "Before I go, I have something that belongs to you."

The young queen stood stiff as a statue when Lionheart stepped over to her. He bent, and she felt his warm breath on her face. Then he kissed her cheek and backed away, bashfully looking at his feet.

"That's from your mother," he whispered. "She asked me to give it to you. With her love."

Were the world a just place and given into Poet Eanrin's hands to dictate, he would have written things as they ought to be. Lionheart would not have bowed like some wooden puppet and left without another word. He would have acted like a man, taken the silver-eyed queen into his arms, and kissed her! He would have told her all the things in his heart that he himself did not fully understand yet, because, honestly, who ever understands those things anyway?

But some stories refuse to play themselves out the way poets think they ought.

In the end, one had to admit that perhaps it was just as well. For Lionheart bowed his stiff bow and turned to go; but as he walked away, he looked back over his shoulder at the little queen, and he faltered, just for an instant, before making those long and determined strides away, kicking rose petals up in his wake.

So Childe Lionheart took leave of Queen Varvare and set forth on the first of what would be many quests in the name of his new Master. And Poet Eanrin was himself charged with another mission very soon thereafter, for someone must escort Prince Felix back to his father.

He found the young prince seated beside Dame Imraldera at one of the many feasting tables. "Well, young sir," said the cat-man, bowing, "are you ready to make your merry way home?"

Felix blinked and thought through his answer as he finished chewing a large mouthful. "Is it safe for me to go just yet? I mean, don't I need to return to the Haven? If I wasn't healed before and that's what led to all this mess, I'd like to be certain I'm healthy now."

Imraldera laughed then, and the young prince experienced many silent ecstasies under the sunshine of her smile.

"Fear not, dear Felix," said she. "You who have carried the Prince's sword and with it slain dragons . . . why, you've received more healing than I could ever give you! You may return to your father's house sound in mind as well as body."

Felix grinned a bit uncertainly. "Will I ever come back?"

"Perhaps one day. When you're older."

"You won't be any older, will you?" he asked with much more daring than he felt.

Eanrin's brows lowered behind his silken eye patches.

Imraldera smiled. "I have not aged in a long time. But then, Time is not the same in the Wood Between as it is in the Near World."

Felix took another bite from his plate, chewing and swallowing thoughtfully.

Eanrin growled, "Up and at it, boy. We've a long journey to make, and I would like to start before the next century. Cheery bye, Imraldera, old girl. Mind you, I'll be back within a fortnight, and I've a whole list of songs that require your scribe's hand!" He slapped the boy, perhaps a little roughly, on the shoulder. "Up!"

Felix rose and saluted Dame Imraldera, then cast a last gaze about the company. His eyes lingered a moment on the queen, so small and lonely on her high seat. But the lady sitting beside her took her hand, and Felix thought to himself, *She'll be all right. She'll be a good queen. Just what this land needs.*

He cast about for the Prince of Farthestshore but didn't see him, and the blind man, now a cat again, was growling and lashing his tail with impatience. "All right, Monster," Felix said. "Lead on."

They traveled quickly on the Prince's Paths, out of the gray plain of Arpiar and into the Wood Between. There Felix found himself blinking in great surprise when he recognized the old plank bridge near which he and his sister had once played many games. "I didn't know we were so close!"

"So close?" the cat asked as he led the way across the Old Bridge.

"So close to Faerie all those years! I mean, we always joked about it, Una and I, but . . . Iubdan's beard, it really does put things in perspective for you, doesn't it? We even found you here!"

"I remember," the cat said. "You needn't remind me. Come along, Prince Felix."

"You know something, Monster?" Felix said as he climbed Goldstone Hill behind the cat. His heart was light as he passed through the familiar grounds once more, full of fond memories. "You know, I think Dame Imraldera is very pretty. What do you think?"

"I think you're slower than a slug, prince, that's what I think," said the cat, and he darted on ahead up the hill. "Last one to the top carries the other one back down the other side!"

Felix groaned, rolled his eyes, and puffed on the trail of the Chief Poet of Rudiobus. As he went, his gaze was caught by something lying in the brush a little out of his way. Curious, he pushed through the bracken to investigate and found a sword. It was an ornate weapon with a golden hilt set with jewels, and the blade was etched all over with intricate figures and the name *Bloodbiter's Wrath*. Felix liked the looks of it, so he picked it up and carried it with him as he followed the cat up Goldstone Hill.

EPILOGUE

A H, THERE YOU ARE, FELIX. I'd just been wondering where you'd gotten off to."

Felix, climbing the path in the wake of the cat, stopped and turned to see King Fidel amid the ruins of Oriana's gardens. He'd been stooping over a green bush but straightened up as he addressed his son.

"Father!" Felix cried and loped over to him. He stopped short, not quite daring to embrace the king. Instead he looked at him, openmouthed, and saw his father's eyebrows bunch into a concerned frown.

"Where have you been?" Fidel asked. "Out in the Wood?"

Felix nodded. "How long have I been away?"

"I don't know," Fidel said. "A few hours. I've been down in the city inspecting the work being done there. I wondered if I might find you up here."

Thunder rolled overhead. The storm blowing in from the sea drew near and would soon release its power upon the shore. Felix stared up at the sky and around at the garden, then back to his father. "A few hours?"

"It was rather unprincely of you to run off," the king continued, turning back to the green bush. "The foreman was expecting to meet his future sovereign, and I was obliged to make excuses. But you were in such a foul temper."

"I was?"

"Do you deny it?"

Felix bowed his head. His memories of recent life were a blur. He felt as though he'd passed into a dream—a dream that lasted for weeks, months, even years!—only to find himself right back where and when he'd started. Nothing was certain. Everything was changed. He drew a deep breath and raised his chin once more. He had faced a dragon, and he had won. Suddenly, despite the gathering storm clouds, the world was a brighter place. It was a place he could master and a place he could serve.

At that moment, he saw what his father was inspecting on the bush. Little knobs and buds sprouted all over in the midst of thickening greenery. And in a few places, the buds were already beginning to unfurl their gorgeous secrets.

"Roses!" Felix cried. "Those are roses!"

Fidel, for the first time in many weeks, smiled at his son. "Indeed. After all these years, the roses have at last decided to bloom again. I think perhaps it is an honor paid Parumvir since the marriage of your sister to the Prince of Farthestshore. What do you think?"

"Maybe," Felix said, bending to gaze more closely at the delicate pink blossoms, breathing in their sweetness, richer even than the smell of the sea. He thought of the spells he'd seen broken. He thought of all the goblin people unveiled. And he knew that the roses too had been set free.

Once more, thunder growled. Fidel patted his son's shoulder, a little awkwardly. "Come, my boy," he said. "We'd best take shelter up in the ruins until this passes over. I see you found your sister's cat! Has he been lurking around here all this time?"

They continued up the path, the cat trailing after them, certainly not following, but as eager as they to escape the coming rain. "I killed a dragon today," Felix said as they went.

"What's that?"

"Nothing." Felix smiled to himself. Some stories, he realized, were best left untold.

The first rain began to fall, landing in his hair, on his face. It felt cool and fresh. It was a rain that might wash away the last of the Dragon's smoke. Liberated roses bloomed everywhere. Old marble statues, knocked from their pedestals, were gaudy with blossoms. And up ahead, the poor, broken ruins of Oriana boasted curtains of climbing roses, which drank in the rain and nodded their dainty heads at the approaching king and his son.

Oriana was destroyed. But when the new palace was built, it would be more beautiful by far, and this garden of roses would surpass the old one.

"I've been thinking about the name of the new palace," Felix said as he and his father, swiftly dampening, hastened toward the sheltering ruins. They ducked into a doorway, the cat just behind them, shaking his wet paws and grooming his soggy tail.

"Is that so?" said Fidel, wiping rain from his beard. "Well, I suppose we're going to have to come to an agreement on it sometime. What ideas do you bring to the table, then?"

"I'd like to call it *Imraldera.*"

Fidel gave his son a sidelong glance. "It's an unusual name. What language is that?"

"An old one."

"What does it mean?"

"I don't know," said the prince. "But I think it's pretty."

And the cat looked up from his grooming, growled, and lashed his tail.

ABOUT THE AUTHOR

Anne Elisabeth Stengl makes her home in Raleigh, North Carolina, where she lives with her husband, Rohan, and a passel of cats. When she's not writing, she enjoys Shakespeare, opera, and tea, and studies piano, painting, and fencing. She studied illustration at Grace College and English literature at Campbell University. She is the author of *Heartless, Veiled Rose*, and *Moonblood. Heartless* won a 2011 Christy Award.

COMING FALL 2012

THE NEWEST
TALE OF GOLDSTONE WOOD

Starflower

Timeless fantasy that will keep you spellbound.

More Exciting Fantasy from
Anne Elisabeth Stengl

Learn more about Anne and her books at
anneelisabethstengl.blogspot.com.

As Princess Una comes of age, a foolish decision leaves her heart vulnerable to an enemy she thought was only a myth. What will Una risk to save her kingdom—and the man she's come to love?

Heartless by Anne Elisabeth Stengl
TALES OF GOLDSTONE WOOD

When a terrifying evil lays siege to the land, the unlikely friendship between Leo and Rose Red undergoes a deadly test. And what began as a game will now decide the fate of a kingdom.

Veiled Rose by Anne Elisabeth Stengl
TALES OF GOLDSTONE WOOD

If you enjoyed *Moonblood*, you may also like...

Bad-tempered, undignified, and only seventeen, Ela can't imagine why the Infinite chose her to be his first woman prophet. But will her new role cost a nation its unity—and her life?

Prophet by R. J. Larson
BOOKS OF THE INFINITE